THE DREADFUL DUKE

THE BAD HEIR DAY TALES

BOOK ONE

GRACE BURROWES

GRACE BURROWES PUBLISHING

The Dreadful Duke

Cover image by Cracked Light Studio, LLC

Cover design by Wax Creative, Inc.

DEDICATION

To all the square pegs. Be proud of those corners!

CHAPTER ONE

"Must I resort to profanity? I am *not* your duke." Finlay Cathcart withdrew his hand from the blessed comfort of a hot, damp towel and grabbed a dry flannel from a stack on the mantel. The left hand was the worst, though the right was also growing temperamental.

"Swear as dreadfully as you please," Leopold St. Didier replied. "The new Duke of Huntleigh can start a fashion in vulgar expostulations, though all the cursing in the world won't relieve you of the title, Your Grace."

Finn had consulted his solicitors on that topic. To free himself of the ducal encumbrance, he'd have to die or commit a hanging felony. Both would be bad for business, especially the dying option.

Bad for morale, too, and Finn guarded his morale jealously. "I will be the least aristocratic duke ever to not prance around in his coronation robes." Finn tossed the damp flannel into the wicker basket by the door and took up the iron poker from the hearth stand.

St. Didier, a prudent soul, found it expedient to study the street below from the safety of the window across the study. "What is the gravamen of your objection to your inherited honors? Do you despise all dukes or only the ones in your own family?"

Gravamen. Fancy term for basis, essence, foundation. Finn had never heard the word pronounced before, but now that he had, he could add it to his stash of toplofty blather. He always picked up one or two gems from St. Didier, and the man was nothing if not elegant.

Sketchable, though one didn't render a duchess's professional snoop in marble.

Finn poked air into the fire, tossed on another square of peat, and held his hands out to the flames. "I have no use for the aristocracy, the monarchy, the penny press, or the preachers. Parasites the lot of them, exceeded by only Parliament for uselessness. Give me a block of high-quality Carrara and I'm a happy man. A crumbling stone wall has more of my respect than your rubbishing dukes. That wall held up through ages of hard winters and broiling summers, and fights every season for its dignity. You've said your little piece, St. Didier —*again*—and now you'd best be on your way before the snow starts."

That's what the throbbing joints of the left hand were announcing: heavy weather on the way. Good sculpting weather, when a fellow could stay in his studio for days, unbothered by solicitors, callers, or importunate investigators.

"I don't mind a little snow," St. Didier said. "You should at least meet your family."

Finn fisted his left hand and got a shooting pain up his arm for his stupidity. "Those people make a mockery of the term."

"So you've said, but you've yet to tell me why. If there's some issue to resolve, an apology in order, a sizable sum to be donated to a charity of your choosing...?" St. Didier let those possibilities drift about the study. He was a quiet man, tallish and muscular, but not the sort of brute to be mistaken for a stone mason turned sculptor. Hair not quite as dark as Finn's own sable locks, dark eyes—probably brown in sunlight—and not given to smiling.

Finn respected St. Didier's tenacity and his self-possession every bit as much as he despised the man's employer.

"Go away," Finn said, facing his guest. "I will not oblige your request, and it would take a larger and meaner man than you, St. Didier, to force me to do anything." *Ever again.*

"Excessive force is seldom an optimal strategy," St. Didier replied. "Has a way of haunting those who rely on it. What do you want, Your Grace? What would persuade you to at least meet with the duchess and your late cousin's mother and widow?"

There was force—taking a sledgehammer to a block of stone—and there was force—using a sharp chisel to tap strategically at the same stone, until all manner of possibilities emerged where plain rock had been.

St. Didier was a tapper with infinite patience, but then, so was Finn, usually.

"What I want," Finn said, "is for you to leave and never come back. Now be a good magic fairy and grant my wish, hmm?"

St. Didier approached the fire, though he stopped a good two yards from where Finn stood. "If the thought of tea with the duchess is too intimidating, then meet with your cousin's widow."

"No." The widow would be worse than the old duchess, all weedy and weepy.

"Then let's have tea with the duchess. She's looking forward to it, in fact."

Finn's temper, which had once been formidable, threatened to lumber forth from the cave where it hibernated.

"All the more reason to refuse. If that old woman were begging from the depths of hell for a glass of water, I'd drink it in front of her and congratulate Lucifer on running a fine establishment." He had considered sculpting that very scene and titling the piece *Restitution*.

"You hate Her Grace?"

Finn considered the question because St. Didier seemed genuinely curious. "'Hatred' creates a connection between the loathed object and the person doing the loathing. I hated the man to whom I was originally apprenticed, and he well deserved the sentiment. I refuse to taint my soul in such a manner where the Duchess of Huntleigh is concerned. She is a matter of complete, stultifying indifference to me."

Stultifying was a recent addition to the word hoard. Finn had picked that one up from a novel and tried it out on Pritchard, who could be relied on to ruthlessly correct faulty pronunciation.

"I see."

St. Didier didn't half begin to start to see, but perhaps he'd get the hell gone anyway. Consult his club gossips and take up harassing some other reluctant recruit to the ranks of the peerage. That was apparently what St. Didier did—found long-lost heirs or credible facsimiles thereof.

"Do you know what will happen if you allow the Huntleigh fortune to languish, Your Grace?"

Tap, tap, tap. "I'll sleep more soundly, you will cease pestering me, and the angels of justice will hold me in fondest regard. Care for a drink?" Finn would have preferred tea, but that would mean summoning Pritchard. Pritchard had a way of lingering and lurking that would not do, given present company.

"Brandy would be appreciated." St. Didier wasn't smiling, exactly, but those dark eyes held a hint of humor. Yes, offering the man a drink immediately after telling him to leave wasn't exactly consistent behavior, but for Finn to pour himself a tot and offer none to his guest would have been rude.

Then too, Finn should have offered the duchess's tame wolf a drink first thing and a tray with sandwiches crusts cut off—and fussy cakes, which would have necessitated fifteen minutes of inane chat before anything substantive was said.

Polite society was a tribulation to any person of sense.

"I have Armagnac," Finn said. He kept a larger selection in the studio proper, which was through the door behind the desk. St. Didier had never seen the studio, nor would he.

"Armagnac will do nicely. Did you do these sketches?"

St. Didier was frankly gawking at the pages on the desk and

managed to make his nosiness look like casual curiosity. *The brute can sketch! Who knew?*

"I did." Finn poured two generous portions and remembered to nose his drink—that was the term Pritchard had used—and to wait for his guest to take the first sip.

"Excellent vintage," St. Didier said swirling the glass and sniffing delicately. "May I ask where you came by it?"

"You know perfectly well that this is from Fournier's shop, just as you knew I'd be in today, and you know I have commissions to see to. Wasting my time—again—is badly done, St. Didier."

"So it is. Very well, then, I will tell you what will happen if you continue to ignore the great good fortune most men would leap at."

"Most men are fools."

"No argument there, but our topic is the fate of the Cathcart family should you neglect the duties that have befallen you. First, the talk will start."

"The talk never stops in Mayfair. You'll have to do better than that." Finn sipped his drink, trying for the elegant nonchalance St. Didier exuded so effortlessly.

And failing, of course. A sculptor's hands were callused, powerful, and often aching. The opposite of elegant.

"This talk will be vicious and aimed at innocents. Your cousin William's aging mama, who never did you any harm, will lose her status as a respected hostess. William's widow, while financially secure, will fade from Society entirely, and what does a widow have but her place in Society?"

She had her freedom. Finn had been assured of that fact by the many Mayfair widows eager to take a brute to bed. They would never invite him to dinner and barely acknowledged him on the bridle paths, so he'd categorically declined their other invitations.

Which had made them only more fixed upon their goal, as if he'd become some fashionable bonnet they simply had to try on.

"William's widow," Finn said, "married the ducal heir with every expectation that she'd become the next Duchess of

Huntleigh. Instead, she has financial security and a ducal connection, of which she is doubtless inordinately proud. I will manage a contented existence without ever making her acquaintance, thank you."

St. Didier was dawdling with his drink. That's what the near smile had been about. Finn's attempt at hospitality had been a tactical error.

"Fine," St. Didier said. "You have no sympathy for Wilhelmina Cathcart. You haven't met her, and for her part, she has had enough of sympathy, but what of the girl?"

Despite the roaring fire in the hearth, despite the Armagnac warming Finn's belly, cold prickled over his arms and nape.

"What *girl?*"

St. Didier moved behind the desk again and pointedly examined the sketch on the blotter.

Another tactical error: Finn had not offered his guest a seat. For the duration of this interview, St. Didier had been wandering about the study, pretending to take in the view, to admire the art on the walls, though the whole time, he'd been looking for a weapon.

And he'd found one.

"Your cousin William left behind a daughter. She's five or six. Her name is Emily. Pretty little thing, but she's become withdrawn. She and the old duke were surprisingly close, and her papa doted on her. Now she's doubly bereft."

Finn said one of the stupidest, most blockheaded, ignorant things ever to come out of his mouth. "Children are resilient."

St. Didier sent him an unreadable look. "As you had to be resilient?"

Pain burned up Finn's arm again, and he realized he was clenching his fingers around his glass. He set the drink on the sideboard.

"I'll show you out. Now."

St. Didier put his libation on the sideboard as well. He was polite, for a wolf, but his manners were simply more weapons. Did the man but know it, he and his manners were at risk for a precipitous, head-first defenestration.

Lovely word. Even Pritchard had been impressed with that one.

"Who is she?" St. Didier said. "The girl in this sketch?"

"She's dead. Died a chrisom death. That sketch is pure fancy, and you are not welcome here again, St. Didier. Please bear in mind that if I'm convicted of a felony—say, cold-blooded murder by strangulation of a pestilential representative of the Duchess of Haughtiness—the title and the entailed wealth will disappear from consideration altogether."

St. Didier's brows rose, and to see him react at all was a consolation. He'd clearly not expected Finn to research the legalities, but that had been Finn's first step in dealing with this whole Cathcart-induced megrim.

Well, the second step, after opening a bottle of smuggled Scottish whisky.

"Emily Cathcart is a small child," St. Didier said, pulling a pair of gloves from a pocket and tugging them on. "Powerless, innocent, without blame. She will be an outcast, an object of talk, her whole life blighted by your stubbornness. William's solicitors will fritter away her wealth, and her mother can do little about it when you refuse to acknowledge a connection. If only you would—"

Finn sliced his hand through the air and once again wrestled his temper back into its cave. "I will see you out, St. Didier, and I will not receive you again. Tell the old besom who hired you that you've failed, that your best efforts resulted in defeat. Another attempt on your part to disturb my hard-won peace will result in me moving my studio to Edinburgh, where I've longed to be for years. Away from England, far from London. Back in the land of my sainted mother. America intrigues me, too, in fact. I'm told Canada is lovely, and they have no meddling duchesses there, only bears, wolves, and venomous snakes."

He held the door, and St. Didier strolled from the room. Finn accompanied his guest past boring old imitation Greek and Roman busts—Pritchard insisted that patrons expected a sculptor's home to have busts—thriving ferns, plush carpets, vaulted ceilings, and a spacious foyer.

Bloody lot of wasted space when children slept in church doorways. One didn't say that. According to Pritchard, one didn't even admit the word *bloody* existed.

"You are a Cathcart," St. Didier said as Finn all but tossed his hat at him. "They are Cathcarts. Those women are as stubborn and proud as you are, and that small child has never done you any discourtesy. Emily has known much grief, and you are happy—eager —to add to her suffering. I understand anger, Your Grace, better than you might think, but I do not understand intentional cruelty to a child."

Neither did I. Finn shoved St. Didier's walking stick at him. "Out. Now." He wrestled with his conscience for a moment, and conscience won. "Please."

St. Didier bowed and took his leave, and for all his appearance gave away, his call might have involved nothing more than a pleasant cup of tea and discussion of a commission for some viscounts' conservatory fountain.

Finn closed the door and locked it. On a previous occasion, St. Didier had used the old, I-forgot-my-gloves trick to return when he'd spotted Finn strolling up the garden walkway.

Devious and persistent, damn the man. "Pritchard!"

The butler cum valet cum finishing governess cum universal authority was never far from Finn's ambit. Pritchard was, like Finn, about thirty, dark-haired, and blue eyed, but the resemblance ended there. Pritchard was slender, stood a mere six feet or so, and conveyed the sense that he'd never hoisted anything heavier than a wine bottle.

He was damned quick with his fists, though, and quicker with a scold.

"Sir?" Pritchard emerged from belowstairs. Finn had no idea what went on down there, but meals were hot, sheets were clean, and hearths kept free of ashes. Proof the household was running well and happily, according to Pritchard.

"St. Didier was here on his usual doomed mission. If he returns, I am not home. I am never home. I do not exist."

Pritchard's gaze slid to the mirror over the sideboard, which would give him a view of Finn's wide shoulders and muscular back. And yes, Finn's hair had been needing a trim for the past couple of years or so.

"Very good, sir. Will there be anything else?"

This was Pritchard's public-rooms act. When a chambermaid could come bustling up the steps, Pritchard was all politesse and dignity. Behind a closed door, he became the avenging tutor from purgatory, sent to bedevil Finn into learning about how to use forks and fashionable French phrases without betraying a barbarian upbringing.

"I'll have a bottle of whisky and a few meat pies, please. I'll be in the studio."

Pritchard's features composed themselves into a mask of deference that nonetheless conveyed disapproval.

"Whisky, in the studio. Of course, sir."

"And meat pies. I don't care if Cook warms them up. I'm hungry."

"Again, sir? One marvels at the regularity of your appetite. Will that be all?"

Five years ago, Finn would have made a rude gesture at Pritchard's insubordination. "Please alert the whole staff that St. Didier has worn out his welcome."

"Of course, sir, and should I have four bottles of whisky sent along to spare the footmen the extra trips?"

That was nasty, but then, Pritchard had pointed opinions about fools who ignored ducal titles.

"Make it five." Finn hadn't allowed himself the comfort and folly of inebriation since he'd been an apprentice, but Pritchard deserved twitting. "And one other thing. Find out all you can about my late cousin's daughter. The child's name is Emily, she's five or six, and apparently not... not thriving."

Pritchard bowed. "Of course, sir. I'll have more information for you tomorrow."

Finn returned to the study, rolled up the sketches on the blotter, and ate a few meat pies, but he left the whisky untouched and served himself another tot of Armagnac. He sat staring at the fire for a good long while, whittling, and occasionally cursing in his mother's native Gaelic.

CHAPTER TWO

"Come along, my love." Wilhelmina Cathcart brandished her Mama-means-business smile and held out her hand. Emily took a diffident grasp and quit the nursery with the air of a prisoner to whom one dungeon was the same as any other.

Emily, once a lively, contrary, dear exasperation on two loud feet, had become a stranger to protests or tantrums of any kind. Even Mama-in-Law was having to work to criticize the girl. *Children should be seldom seen and never heard* had become *Why doesn't that girl ever speak?*

William would have enjoyed the irony while ignoring the magnitude of the problem.

Emily did speak. Wilhelmina assured herself of this as she led her daughter to the steps. Emily spoke to her dolls, to herself, and, when absolutely necessary, to the adults in her ambit. She never yelled anymore, and she never laughed. As Wilhelmina accompanied Emily down the main staircase—"One hand in Mama's, the other on the banister, dearest,"—she tried to recall the last time Emily had smiled.

"Off to the park, my lady?" Travers asked as they approached the vaulted foyer.

"Gunter's," Wilhelmina replied. Travers would report to the duchess their destination, how long they'd been out, and whether they returned with any packages. He looked like the genial, graying butler typical of any Mayfair household, but his hearing and his memory were faultless and his self-interest without limit.

"Some fresh air and a hot chocolate appeal," Wilhelmina went on, swinging Emily's hand gently. Getting out of this house with the child, on any pretext, appealed more strongly still.

"Shall I ring for the coach?"

William's enormous, ornate Town coach had been among his many vanities. "Let's not trouble the stable. Lady Helmsby might send for the coach in our absence, and we wouldn't want to inconvenience her. Emily and I will manage on foot." The distance was three streets and half a square, and the day was brilliant as only sunshine on fresh snow could be.

"I'll alert the footmen, then."

Not a question, though it should have been, and the footmen would be expected to report all details of the outing to Travers. Wilhelmina considered telling her butler that his spies were unwelcome on this outing, except that he'd relay that minor rebellion to the duchess too.

"One footman will do," Wilhelmina said. "The youngest. He's new. What's his name?"

His name was Earnest Haines. He hailed from Hawes, up in the North Riding, where four inches of snow would be merely passing weather. Wilhelmina had hired him herself the previous week. She assumed the duchess would soon buy his loyalty, too, but the fellow would be restless. Yesterday's storm had meant a day indoors for everybody, and the boy was barely sixteen.

"Haines? You're sure you wouldn't rather take Dalton?"

Dalton was the handsomest of the lot, six feet of blond English good looks, about which he was endlessly vain. Dalton was also a schemer and a flirt.

"I'll take Haines. He needs to get his feet wet on London's streets, so to speak, and he has the brawn to carry Emily if she grows fretful."

Though Emily hadn't grown fretful for months.

"Haines it shall be, my lady. Give me a quarter hour to lecture the boy about proper decorum on an outing with our Miss Emily." Travers bustled off, and Emily didn't even watch him depart.

"Would you rather go to the park?" Wilhelmina asked. William had taken them to the park on fine days. At first, the exercise had been one of vanity on his part—heirs to the peerage took inordinate pride in establishing their nurseries—but then he'd become smitten with his daughter, and the outings became joyous in their own right.

"No, thank you, Mama."

"Gunter's suits?"

"Yes, Mama."

Wilhelmina considered tickling her daughter, but that tactic had originated with William, and when Wilhelmina had tried it, Emily had flinched away.

Somebody tapped the front door knocker three times. The hour was too early for proper callers, so this had to be the duchess coming to make one of her rare inspection tours.

Wilhelmina opened the door—let Her Grace start the list of infractions with that breach of protocol—and stepped back. "You are not Her Grace."

The fellow was tall and *large* through the shoulders. His top hat gave him more height still. His turnout was exquisite—black lamb's-wool greatcoat with three capes, black gloves, a scarf about his throat of purple merino wool in a subtle plaid weave.

"I am not Her Grace," he replied in a bass-baritone that went exquisitely with all that dark, expensive wool and soft leather. "God be thanked for small mercies. I am rumored to be His Grace of Huntleigh, though you mustn't tell anybody I came to call. I prefer the name bestowed upon me at birth. Finn Cathcart, at your service. I assume you are Mrs. William Cathcart. Is this Miss Emily?"

St. Didier claimed His Grace had perfect manners when he

chose to exhibit them, but presenting himself well before noon, no footmen, no calling card... Introducing himself rather than having St. Didier on hand to see to the courtesies...

Wilhelmina did not know whether to be amused or intimidated. "I am Mrs. Wilhelmina Cathcart. This is my daughter, Emily," she said, putting a slight emphasis on the possessive.

"Good morning, Miss Emily," His Grace rumbled.

Emily peered up at him, her gaze pensive. She soundlessly mouthed, "Good morning, sir."

"Come in," Wilhelmina said, stepping back. No crested coach waited in the street, but then, in cold weather, the coachy was more likely to keep his team walking. A glance at His Grace's tall boots suggested that, no, the man hadn't bothered with a wheeled conveyance.

The duke had to duck to get through the door. He took off his hat and hung it on a peg near the porter's nook. The foyer, fifteen feet square with a twelve-foot ceiling, abruptly took on the spaciousness of a broom closet.

"Emily and I were about to set out for Gunter's," Wilhelmina said. "Your Grace has timed this call quite early."

He pulled off his gloves, stuffed them into a pocket, and unwrapped his scarf. "I feared I'd lose my nerve if I put the matter off. I won't take up much of your time."

Lose his nerve? That sounded ominous. Wilhelmina steeled herself to be courteous but firm. William had left her a life estate in both this house and in his cottage in Kent, with the remainder going to Emily or her offspring if Emily was no longer extant. Wilhelmina had read his will from first line to last, including all of the silly codicils, because the solicitors had offered her only platitudes and generalities.

If this man, about whom St. Didier had warned Wilhelmina, thought to turn her and Emily out so he could avoid biding with the duchess in the family town house, he'd soon learn that even dukes were subject to the jurisdiction of the Chancery Courts.

His Grace unbuttoned his greatcoat and hung that on a peg too. Making himself quite at home.

"I brought you something," His Grace said, hunkering down to Emily's eye level. "They are crude, but I was distracted when I whittled them. I'm Finn. What shall I call you?"

He reached inside his morning coat and took out something about the size of Wilhelmina's watch pin.

"I made you a bear, you see?" he said, holding his palm out, a miniature wooden bear displayed thereon. "Her name is Ursula, like the Latin and the stars."

Emily put out a tentative hand and touched the wood. The bear was anything but crude, the knife having scored minute lines depicting fur on the surface and the bear's face conveying a smiling aspect.

"Ursula Major?" Emily said, brows knitting.

"Of course. This is Ursula Minor," the duke replied, producing another, slightly smaller carving. "They will fit under your pillow when they need to hibernate, but I thought you might assign the ladies guard duty on your nightstand."

Ursa, not Ursula. Wilhelmina did not correct His Grace because he was a duke, and because Emily—who hadn't had a tea party for her dolls in ages—took the two bears from him.

"I can keep them?"

"I made them for you." He withdrew a third small creature carved of wood. "This is Draco. He's their friend."

The dragon was stunning, and the notion that this enormous, presuming peer had created these carvings... Wilhelmina mentally readjusted all that St. Didier had said of the duke. St. Didier was seldom in error—the duke probably *was* shrewd, commercially astute, socially confident, and a gifted artist—but he was also... unpredictable, and that made him dangerous.

Dragons and bears indeed.

"The dragon is their friend?" Emily asked, touching the point of a half-unfurled wing.

"Draco doesn't care for nights spent under pillows," the duke replied. "Dragons are noted for being very set in their ways. He is loyal to his friends, though sometimes he gets wrathy for the fun of it."

"Wrathy?" Emily examined the dragon as it sat on the callused expanse of the duke's palm. "What is wrathy?"

"Testy, irritable, annoyed. Dragons are sensitive creatures, easily offended. Bears are very patient, by contrast, and good-humored, so they make good friends for dragons. Hold out your hand."

Emily did as she was told. The duke made a great business of flying the dragon onto her palm, complete with whirring and whooshing, and by the time the winged creature landed, the barest hint of a smile was curving Emily's lips.

"You made that up," she said, closing her fingers over her prize, "about dragons being disagreeable, didn't you?"

His Grace rose. "I might have been telling a bit of a story. I wasn't lying."

"Make-believe?" Emily said.

"Precisely. Make-believe." He turned to Wilhelmina. "St. Didier would have me play the make-believe duke, madam. I am uncomfortable with the prospect. Perhaps you could spare me a few moments of your time for a brief discussion?"

At any moment, Travers would bustle up from belowstairs, Haines in tow. Every word out of the duke's mouth would be reported to his titled aunt, and that bothered Wilhelmina exceedingly. The duke's call itself bothered her Mama-in-Law and the duchess would both be peeved that he hadn't visited them first—but she was more than a little concerned that he'd expect her and Emily to vacate the town house.

"Mama, may I keep Draco and the Ursulas?" Emily asked.

The duke held his peace. Wise of him.

"They are a gift to you, Emily," Wilhelmina said. "They belong to you now. Of course you may keep them. Perhaps they'd like to join His Grace and me in a cup of tea?"

The duke's posture eased, and only then did Wilhelmina realize he'd meant what he'd said about possibly losing his nerve. This encounter had worried him.

It worried Wilhelmina, too, but one couldn't be rude to a newly fledged duke. "My personal sitting room, then, and bring your menagerie, Emily. Where did you learn to carve, Your Grace?"

He stalked at her side while Emily trotted ahead, her treasures clutched in her little hands.

"I learned to whittle in a very hard school, my lady, when that skill meant the difference between living and dying. I became good at it."

"Will you excel at being the duke?"

He held the parlor door for Wilhelmina, though Emily ducked through first. "I haven't made up my mind about this duke business," he said. "St. Didier told me that Emily will suffer if I neglect my duties, and I had to see for myself that she was thriving."

He joined them in Wilhelmina's sitting room—the place she came when she needed privacy—as Emily settled on the carpet before the hearth and commenced a game that involved Draco teaching the bears to fly.

"Thriving hasn't happened for some while," Wilhelmina said quietly. "But Emily is safe, and I love her, and time will help."

"She's resilient?" Now that he wasn't bent on charming Emily, His Grace was a far more serious fellow.

"I would not say that, but I am resilient, and I hope she can benefit accordingly. Shall we have a seat?" Wilhelmina settled herself into a rocking chair by the hearth.

His Grace looked around the room and chose the reading chair opposite the rocker, the sturdiest option available. "I gather you don't trust me?" he asked, an outlandishly personal question.

"Of course not. I just met you, and we still haven't been introduced."

"Introductions make people trustworthy?"

"They should."

"And yet, you cannot trust the duchess, can you? I don't trust her either, and St. Didier is the devil's handmaiden. Shouldn't you be ringing for tea or something?"

Of a certainty, Wilhelmina did not trust this man, but he'd made Emily almost-smile, and he likely had no idea of the troops massed in opposition to his continued obstinance where the title was concerned.

"When I ring for tea, I provide an excuse for my butler, a pair of footmen, and a presuming parlormaid to linger outside that door. If they aren't listening at the keyhole, they'll be one floor up, pretending to sweep out the hearth in my bedroom where they can eavesdrop by virtue of the flue." Wilhelmina spoke more quietly as Ursula Major noisily took to the skies above the hearthrug. "I am surrounded by Her Grace's spies, and you will be too."

Fair play required that Wilhelmina offer him that much warning, though she expected His Grace to snort derisively at her overture of goodwill. Instead, he fetched the dustbin from beside the escritoire, then took a small, hooked knife from one pocket and a chunk of wood from the other. He sat with the dustbin between his knees and commenced scraping the knife along the wood.

"Go on," he said. "Who spies on you and why?"

The first shavings went into the dustbin. Ursula Minor took a turn aloft, while the dragon perched on the raised hearth. The toys were beautiful, thoughtful, elegant... Wiliam had been all that, at first.

"The duchess wants custody of my daughter. I refuse to let that happen."

"Don't stop there. Her Grace likely wants custody of me as well. I'm listening."

Well, yes, Her Grace did want dominion and control over the new duke. Edwardia would not stop until Finn Cathcart had been whittled into the next Duke of Huntleigh as Her Grace envisioned him.

"Your father was the youngest of three brothers," Wilhelmina began. "Hubert, Helmsby, and Thornton have all gone to their rewards in reverse order of age. The present duchess, Hubert's widow, is barely cordial with Helmsby's widow—my mother-in-law— and they both take an interest in Emily."

Because Finlay Cathcart was listening, and because he seemed prepared to continue listening, Wilhelmina explained the rest as best she could, and she did not ring for tea.

Cousin William had chosen a lovely woman to be his bride, but William himself probably hadn't realized what a beauty he'd married. Maybe Wilhelmina Cathcart was oblivious to her own charms, but Finn knew an exquisitely arched brow when he saw one. Lovely shoulders, too, and sculpting her hands would require significant patience. Those hands were competent, graceful, and—when they touched the child—tender.

William had doubtless been inundated with entire bouquets of blond, blue-eyed English roses, and he'd passed them up for a woman with Titian hair and green eyes. Wilhelmina Cathcart was also notably un-sylph-like. English roses were to waft gently around ballrooms, but a future duchess was apparently allowed to be sturdy.

The lady came up almost to Finn's chin—tall for a woman, though she was doubtless in heeled slippers or boots—and she had the courage to wear fashion that flattered her. This morning, she wore a walking dress of amethyst velvet, a color suitable for half mourning.

On her, the hue evoked anything but sorrow.

Whoever had designed the dress had an eye for subtlety. The cut was looser than most women preferred, even for a walking dress, and the embellishments—lace at the wrists, green and purple embroidery at the cuffs—were subtle.

"Don't underestimate the duchess," Mrs. Cathcart said as the child explained the rules of an airborne race to her toy bears. "Her Grace is formidable, whether she's deciding on a goddaughter's dancing partners or having a word with the Regent. Mayfair is her jungle, and she is its queen."

"And if I choose not to dwell in that jungle?"

The bears took their marks.

"You can certainly scurry off to Dublin or Paris for a few years, but Her Grace won't live forever. Her priority will be seeing you wed to the party of her choosing, and your duchess with child. Boys preferred, of course."

Finn felt an urge to go flying with the bears, though his flight would take him straight over the Scottish border. *The party of her choosing* indeed.

"I have no objection to marriage in the general case for those so inclined, Mrs. Cathcart, but that old woman has no business meddling in my affairs."

For Finn to think of his hostess as Mrs. Cathcart was awkward. His own dear mama had been Mrs. Cathcart. She'd also been Lady Thornton, though she and Papa had referred to their courtesy titles only when being ironic.

"Say, 'One, two, three, go,' Mama."

"Very well. One... Two... Three... GO!"

The child launched herself from the carpet, a flying bear in each little mitt. Several orbits of the parlor were undertaken, including near crashes by the sideboard, a precipitous dive around the escritoire, and loud midair taunting between the competitors.

She hadn't inherited that lively imagination from her strutting papa.

"It's a tie!" Emily cried when both bears had skidded to a landing on the hearthrug. "They both win!"

Wilhelmina applauded at length. "His Grace must shake the paws of the contestants to congratulate them on their spectacular flying."

Finn obliged. "Will you schedule a rematch when your Ursulas have rested?"

"Yes. And Draco will be the race steward. He says they're both silly, but he doesn't want to hurt their feelings."

"A prince among dragons."

The child kited away, bears in hand.

"I am not to underestimate the duchess," Finn said, knowing another interruption was less than two minutes away.

"Her Grace is shrewd, patient, ruthless, and counts kings and princesses among her allies."

"And you among her enemies?"

Wilhelmina considered the child, whose focus had switched to the dragon. "No, not yet. Soon. I suspect Edwardia is keeping her powder dry until a few more years have passed."

Meaning, until the child was older and more easily plucked from her mother's side. "Why such a fuss over one little girl?"

A soft scratching on the door had mother and child looking up, then at each other. The transformation in the child was the most obvious. She darted to a sewing basket tucked under the sideboard and jammed her toys into its depths. She then took up the place beside her mother's chair, no more expression on her features than the Coldstream Guards wore when standing at attention.

Wilhelmina also became similarly composed before calling out, "Come in."

A roundish, graying, sniffy sort of fellow in a dark suit presented himself. "Madam, we heard the child's upset. I hope all is well. Young Haines is prepared for your excursion, but shall I let the kitchen know you have a caller?"

Since when did the English language admit of a butler's *we*. Not even Pritchard affected that vanity. And if Wilhelmina Cathcart wanted to summon her staff, she was perfectly capable of using the bell-pull in the corner. Moreover, any fool could have heard that Emily was *playing* rather than *upset*.

Finn rose. "No need to bother the kitchen. Mrs. Cathcart, Miss Emily, and I will be visiting Gunter's together. That will be all."

Emily stared at him, and her mother stood without assistance.

"Thank you, Travers. My apologies to Haines, but if tomorrow is fair, he can look forward to escorting us to the park."

Travers bowed. "Very good, madam." After a slight hesitation, "Sir."

He left the damned door open when he departed, so Finn closed it. The corridor was chilly, the parlor at least tolerable. Wasting coal was an offense against God and human decency.

"I've been sighted behind enemy lines. Bound to happen. Shall we escape to Gunter's, or will you send me packing?"

The lady gave him a less-than-friendly perusal. "I should send you packing. I should also loudly decry your rudeness and presumption."

Finn's rudeness, as near as he could make out, had amounted to the merest hint of a possibility of a suggestion of a rebuke to a presuming toad of a butler.

"Are you concerned the duchess and your mother-in-law will find you guilty of abetting the enemy?"

Emily slipped her hand into her mother's, and Finn was acutely aware that children understood far too much at even Emily's young age.

"My life is complicated enough," Wilhelmina replied. "The duchess is not my enemy. I wish you the best, but I will always think of my own responsibilities first."

Meaning the duchess was not *yet* her enemy? The titled branch of the Cathcart family was apparently worse than a studio full of ambitious apprentices. Nobody trusting anybody, nobody even liking anybody.

What else had Finn expected?

Though—so far—he liked Emily and her mama well enough. "Are you advising me to disappear to Paris? My French is rusty." His French regularly sent Pritchard into paroxysms of hilarity, though Finn had managed well enough when he'd spent a year as an assistant in a Belgian studio. Italian had come fairly easily after that, and Spanish was comprehensible to him when spoken slowly.

"You must do as you see fit," Wilhelmina said. "Making an enemy of Travers was not well advised. He has been with this household since William and I returned from our wedding journey."

If Travers took offense that easily, he was an idiot, and probably a tyrant belowstairs too. "I would like to escort you and Miss Emily to Gunter's. I can fetch you in my coach an hour from now, if you'd rather not be seen strolling at my side."

"Mama..." A wheedling note entered the child's voice. "Please?"

Wilhelmina smiled at her daughter, but to Finn, who'd studied the human countenance in depth, the expression wanted for true joy.

"Very well," Wilhelmina said. "By coach. In an hour. You should have called on the duchess first, though, and then upon my mother-in-law."

"I'm just a simple sculptor," Finn said. "All this protocol confuses me. I will make the appropriate apologies for any lapse of manners, but if that interfering old besom thinks to matchmake on my behalf, she'll soon become acquainted with whatever passes for the Huntleigh dower house. Her Grace is the last person I will permit any meddling privileges."

May she burn in hell, et cetera and so forth.

"You already sound like a duke." Wilhelmina was not offering a compliment. "I'll see you out."

When she accompanied Finn to the foyer, Travers was on hand, as was a blond, sullen footman who apparently suffered a passionate affection for his curling tongs.

"Thank you for receiving me at such an unusual hour," Finn said, bowing to Wilhelmina. To Emily, he extended a hand. "Miss Emily, a pleasure."

The child shook far too solemnly. One probably didn't shake hands with children, or with girl children, but as Finn loped down the steps and set off for home, he wasn't concerned about that blunder.

He was instead wrestling with the realization that both Wilhelmina Cathcart and her small daughter were frightened.

Perhaps of the duchess, or of the mother-in-law, or of Society at large. In any case, their situation limited Finn's options, alas for Edinburgh.

He would cheerfully tell the duchess to go to perdition and stay there—brimstone was doubtless her preferred fragrance—but he could not turn his back on a mother and child dwelling in fear. He could ignore crowns, wreaths, titles, wealth, and tiaras, but not a mother and child in need of an ally.

CHAPTER THREE

Years ago, Leopold St. Didier had found the identification and location of obscure heirs a fine and lucrative challenge. His clients were aristocratic families facing ruin, a prospect he had viewed first-hand, and his work had been interesting.

He'd embarked on his calling three earls, four viscounts, a marquess's grandson, and one baron ago. The baron had been particularly vexatious, requiring St. Didier to travel to Boston in winter, but his lordship had come along peacefully when put in possession of the family particulars.

St. Didier no longer enjoyed his job.

The difficulty did not lie in the person of his first duke. Finlay Cathcart was a reasonable man and had accumulated both wealth and standing without benefit of a title. He'd manage well enough once he found his bearings, and St. Didier wished His Present Grace the best in all endeavors.

The work itself proved no difficulty. Thwarting the crown's avarice toward families facing escheat was a meaningful and complicated undertaking. St. Didier preferred chasing down old documents and refreshing dim memories, but retrieving the missing peer bodily was seldom any real hardship, Boston in winter notwithstanding.

The party responsible for St. Didier's malaise sat opposite him, her silver tea service gleaming before her, her aging spaniel panting at her feet. Edwardia, Her Grace of Huntleigh, was of a piece with the Aubusson carpet, azure silk-hung walls, and mother-of-pearl inlaid tea tray. The carpet featured the unicorn rampant from the Cathcart family crest, amid a profusion of pink pineapples, clamshells, roses, and other peculiarities. The parlor, despite twelve-foot ceilings, was warm thanks to the fires blazing in the eight-foot-wide fireplaces at either end of the room.

The parlor was the antithesis of Finlay Cathcart's study, with its heavy, comfortable furniture, slightly worn rugs, plain oak wainscoting, and peaty scent.

"Gunter's." Her Grace silently stirred her tea and set the spoon to the side of the cup. "He's taking mother and child to Gunter's?"

"They are likely enjoying ices as we speak." St. Didier preferred the cinnamon ice, not that Her Grace would give a used tea leaf for that information.

"Ices in winter. Is my nephew daft?"

"He's quite sane, Your Grace." Also very talented and nobody's fool. "I believe Mrs. Cathcart had planned the outing before His Grace intruded, and the duke offered himself as an escort."

The duchess's looks hadn't changed in the ten years St. Didier had known her. She'd been a fixture in Society for twice that long. Elegant, slender, white-haired, and regal. She was of medium height, but her bearing was so majestic as to give an impression of height. Her spine never touched the back of her chair. Even her dog— Charles—never put a paw wrong.

She was, nonetheless, no blood relation whatsoever to Finlay Cathcart.

"Is His Grace intentionally slighting me?" she asked.

St. Didier considered what he knew of the duke. "I'm more inclined to believe he's being tactical. Gathering intelligence first from those least likely to bear him ill will." And assuring himself that the child, Emily, wanted for nothing. The sketch of the dead girl had given the game away, did His Grace but know it.

The duchess's faded blue eyes narrowed. "He hasn't called upon Lady Helmsby?"

William's mama, Wilhelmina's mama-in-law, and Her Grace's rival of old. "He has not."

"You are sure?"

Well, no. With Finn Cathcart, St. Didier did not permit himself the luxury of confidence. The outing to Wilhelmina's home and subsequent jaunt to Gunter's would have gone unreported, except that the man St. Didier paid to watch His Grace's establishment had strolled around to the alley to take a piss.

The new duke had been seen leaving through his own garden gate and, by a series of alleys, wynds, ginnels, and snickets, had arrived at Mrs. Cathcart's door. No peer should have that sort of familiarity with London's lesser-trod paths, but then, Finlay Cathcart's road to the title had been nearly as unorthodox as his London perambulations.

"My sense of the man," St. Didier said, "is that he will disdain all honors attendant to his title, but he will mind his responsibilities. A widow with a small child falls into the latter category."

"William left his wife well provided for, more's the pity. The dukedom could use the coin Wilhelmina stashes in the cent-per-cents. You will inform His Grace that I will receive him tomorrow at two of the clock."

St. Didier was mannerly and considerate by nature, but the duchess had long since earned plain speaking from him. She never issued a request when handing down an order would suffice, even in the presence of royalty.

He rose. "I'm sure any number of footmen would be happy to deliver your summons, but the purpose of my call is to conclude our contractual dealings."

The duchess remained enthroned upon her upholstered Queen Anne seat. "Don't be vulgar."

"I am being polite, Your Grace." St. Didier withdrew a single, folded sheet of paper from his breast pocket and laid it on the tea tray. "That is an exact copy of the bill I've sent your solicitors. I provide you with your own record out of courtesy." A vulgar man, even one feeling slightly rude, would have elaborated on the reasons for the duplicate invoices. "I will expect payment in full within thirty days, per the agreement signed by your own hand."

Her Grace stood with the ease of a woman one-third her age. "Young people today. No sense of decorum. You of all men should know better, sir, than to discuss business with me. Blood will tell."

"If that is meant to be an insult..." St. Didier began.

"That is a compliment. I knew your mother and corresponded with her until her death. She would expect better of you."

That correspondence was news to St. Didier. "Then I thank you for your loyalty to my mother, but by the letter of my agreement with you, I have fulfilled my part of the bargain. His Grace of Huntleigh has been located and made aware of his situation. His particulars have been documented with a sufficiency the College of Arms cannot dispute. Of his own volition, he has made contact with his ducal relations. You know where to find him, and he knows where to find you. My role is complete."

"Your role is complete when I say it's complete."

The spaniel got up on all fours, his expression worried.

"I am not a spy, Your Grace, nor am I indentured to your schemes. My final word of advice to you, which you will doubtless ignore, is to take seriously the ill will Finlay Cathcart bears this family and you in particular. He has been alone in the world since the age of eight and has had a long time to nurse his grudges and vendettas. You cannot impress him with manners, wealth, or social connections. You might well succeed in annoying him further if you attempt those tactics."

St. Didier half hoped Her Grace would summon the footmen to

remove him from the premises. She instead gestured to the dog, who slipped his head under her hand.

"Manners, wealth, and social connections are all I have, St. Didier. If I'm not to wield those to good effect, how will I convince the boy to vote his seat, marry suitably, and take his dukedom in hand?"

St. Didier said a silent prayer that heaven would imbue the new duke with quarry-loads of patience, more patience, even, than was needed to coax delicate beauty from cold, hard stone.

"If you even once refer to him as a 'boy' in his hearing, your aspirations are doomed. I mean this kindly: *Finn Cathcart does not need you.* He will never need you. He does not need the title and will bitterly resent that becoming the duke will cost him his calling as a respected artist. He prefers working in stone to acknowledging his connection to your branch of the family."

That was overstating the matter, slightly. St. Didier had seen Cathcart's hands. Had seen the man wince when making a fist. The number of commissions those hands could fulfill was limited, by time and the realities of advancing rheumatism, if not by ability.

"The problem," said the duchess, "is that you are too much like him. Both of you arrogant to a fault and insufficiently mindful of the appearances. You probably hate him for disdaining what your family would give anything to have back."

She did this. Lobbed Greek fire over the walls of a man's dignity just to see if she could provoke a scream. St. Didier had spent years learning to dodge such volleys from meaner foes than Her Grace.

"I will bid Your Grace good day. If I am not paid in full, to the penny, on time, I will take the matter up with His Grace."

She made an odd sound, one that had the dog again looking anxious. "See yourself out, St. Didier, with my sincere and heartfelt thanks for services rendered. You have indeed done well."

St. Didier was at his club and nursing a brandy before it occurred to him that he might be the only man extant to have heard Her Grace of Huntleigh laugh. He silently toasted Finn Cathcart's chances of besting the duchess and signaled the waiter for another round.

Wilhelmina had thought herself prepared for an eventual introduction to the new duke.

St. Didier had assured her His Grace would come 'round—polite terminology for admitting that Edwardia excelled at getting her way. In this case, the duchess's way would be Finn Cathcart voting his seat as Edwardia advised him to, meekly enduring the carriage parade beside the belles of Edwardia's choosing, and standing up with the diamonds Edwardia favored at Almack's.

Mina's mistake had been casting the new duke too much in William's mold. William had been good at getting his way, too, but he'd also chosen long ago not to thwart or unduly vex the duchess. Hence his marriage to Mina.

This new duke...

He sat on the backward-facing seat of a cozy and capacious Town coach, top hat beside him. As the carriage rolled along, he sketched. Every educated gentleman was expected to be able to render a competent likeness, but Finn Cathcart was not educated, not in the aristocratic sense.

"Child, if you don't hold still, I will end up drawing your nose where your ears should be."

Emily, who'd been swinging a heel against the upholstered bench, ceased fidgeting.

"We don't get out as much as we should," Mina said. "We were in mourning for an eternity, and then the weather turned disobliging."

"This isn't weather," His Grace replied, pencil scratching over his paper. "This is a passing chill. Scotland's the place to go for weather."

"You've been?"

He nodded, frowned, took up an eraser, then resumed sketching.

"My mother was Scottish. Her family builds ships. I get some of my height from them."

What he did not say was that his mother had been from a wealthy *Catholic* family of shipbuilders. His Grace was not a Papist that St. Didier could discern, but the new duke had spent years in Italy, and he wasn't particularly Church of England either.

"Tell me, Miss Emily, what is your favorite flavor of ice?" he asked, turning over a new page in his sketchbook.

"Mama, what is my favorite flavor?"

"You like to see what's on offer before making up your mind."

"Prudent," the duke said, pencil moving rapidly. "I'm for vanilla, myself. Rich and smooth. What about you, Mrs. Cathcart?"

"Mama likes vanilla too. Grandmama says vanilla isn't so-pissed-stick-ated. She means it's not grown-up."

His Grace scowled at his drawing. "So-*fist*-stick-ated. Good word. Vanilla is expensive. I wonder if that's half its appeal. What of Draco —what's his favorite?"

The conversation pattered on, and Mina tried to parse what it was about His Grace that most disconcerted her. William had been tallish, but not the grand specimen his cousin was. Finn Cathcart— she must think of him as Huntleigh, mustn't she?—had more masculine vigor in his arms and shoulders than William, who'd considered himself a Corinthian—had had in his whole body.

And yet, His Grace was comfortable in his own skin in a way William hadn't been. His Grace's dimensions, while impressive, didn't bother Mina. One reason she'd honored her betrothal to William was the Cathcart tendency to height. Mina hadn't towered over her husband.

She was positively dainty next to the duke, and that was... different. He was well spoken, and his turnout was far above reproach, though the purple scarf was a bit odd. She'd seen odder.

And yet, something about the man himself put her on her guard.

When His Grace had assisted Emily into the carriage, he'd all but tossed her up after her mother, like a sack of cotton wool. He spoke to the child directly, when William's efforts had been limited to hearty discourse of the sort dotty aunties turned on nieces and nephews they couldn't keep straight.

And how is Miss Emily today?

Are you being a good girl for Norwich?

Can you greet your Papa in French, my girl?

William had loved Emily, but as one loved a favorite toy.

Finn Cathcart talked to Emily, touched her, and listened to her. Treated her as a person, which was admittedly easier to do as a child gained a few years.

"Are you Draco's papa?" Emily asked. Said Draco had been chosen to join the excursion. He reposed in Mina's reticule, carefully swaddled in a monogrammed handkerchief.

"I am not," His Grace replied, considering his drawing. "Draco was hibernating, I guess you might say, in a chunk of linden. I came along and woke him up with my whittling knife. Maybe that makes me his valet?"

Emily resumed gently thumping a foot against the bench. "You woke him up?"

Mina let the lapse in manners pass, because it had been too long since Emily had behaved as a normal child, fidgety with anticipation on a pleasant outing.

"I used my knife on the wood and peeled away his blankets and pillows and whatnot, and there he was. If you'd like to learn to whittle, I can show you, assuming your mama doesn't object."

The offer, like his willingness to chat with a bored child, also bothered Mina. "Do girls whittle?"

"My mother did," His Grace replied, tucking his pencil behind his ear. "Shipbuilders tend to come from seafaring stock, and whittling on long voyages is both a necessary skill and a pastime. Mama liked birds especially, and when my little hands were capable, she started me in the tradition."

"Did you ever cut yourself?" Emily asked as the coach turned onto Berkeley Square.

"Many times, and my mama would scold me to be more careful, clean me up, and give me a kiss. I'd try to be more careful, but when being uncareful earned me kisses and hugs, I occasionally erred. Tell me what you think."

He passed over the small rectangle of paper he'd been working on.

Emily's brow puckered. "That's me. I look like Mama."

"Somewhat, around the eyes. Your brows are similar, and they are lovely. Almost symmetrical, which is unusual. I assume your jaw and nose come from your papa."

A stillness came over Emily as she stared at the image on the page. The likeness was good, catching the solemnity Emily had acquired in recent months, but also the innocence and sweetness any child her age should possess.

"My papa died," Emily said. "He's in heaven."

The coach came to a halt, as did Mina's maternal monitoring system. Emily hadn't spoken of her father's actual death for months. At the time, she'd asked endless questions.

Where is heaven?

When will he come back?

Is heaven like the attic?

To a small child, heaven was a useless abstraction, and death more of same.

"My papa's in heaven too," His Grace said. "Not an arrangement I care for. How can he possibly be having a grand time with his harp and halo when his darling boy is not there with him? He called me that—I was his darling boy, if you can believe such a thing. My mama has decamped for the same preposterous location. I dislike the situation. What sort of half-competent God takes a loving parent away from a child?"

Neither the Catholic Church nor the Church of England would appreciate that blasphemy, and Emily appeared puzzled.

"Are you mad?" she asked. "I get mad sometimes."

"Angry," Mina said quietly. "You get angry, not mad." Mina did, too, though she hadn't put that name to the emotions. Vexed, frustrated, irked. The accurate word was *angry*.

Very, very angry.

"I was angry a lot right after they died," His Grace said. "Mama went first. Papa followed shortly thereafter. Eventually, I was just sad. I missed them, and I did not understand why they left me."

"Papa went to heaven to be with the angels."

The duke rapped on the roof with the head of his walking stick— a carved dragon, of course. "Not a very satisfactory state of affairs, is it? Papa waltzing with the angels, you and your mama stuck here with me and Draco and the Ursulas. We shall have to make the best of what consolations we can find. I'm for a vanilla ice. What will you ladies have?"

"Vanilla for me too," Emily said, apparently agreeable to a change in subject. "Mama?"

Oh, this would not do, this budding warmth Emily exhibited toward the new duke. Edwardia, Mama-in-Law, the staff... Somebody would note the connection, and connections were vulnerabilities.

"Barberry," Mina said, though vanilla was her favorite. "Emily, shall we walk the square while His Grace places our order?"

"Yes, Mama."

They sorted out mittens and scarves, and His Grace handed Mina down decorously enough. When it was Emily's turn, he simply lifted her onto the walkway.

"Duncan," His Grace said, gesturing to a footman, "you'll see to our ices, please. Mrs. Cathcart and I will take the air. Fetch a few biscuits for yourself and John Coachman and sweets for Miss Emily and Mrs. Cathcart. Your next task will be to show Miss Emily how to make the perfect snowball and to polish her aim on these stately maples. Take her to the shop and let her choose her sweet first."

"Aye, sir." Duncan, a young, red-haired behemoth in fine winter tailoring, grinned and loped off in the direction of Gunter's, Emily's hand in his.

"Duncan hails from the Cairngorms. Knows his way around a snowball. What has turned you up peevish, Mrs. Cathcart?"

"I'm not peevish." Mina was, of course. His Grace had more or less upended her maternal agenda for the outing, and in front of Emily. She was accustomed to that from Mama-in-Law, Her Grace, Travers—half the world was inclined to gainsay her maternal edicts. Of all of them, only His Grace, as head of the Cathcart family, had the right to do so.

Drat the man.

"You are testy," he said. "Annoyed, overwhelmed. When my parents died, I was utterly flummoxed. Eight years old and nobody explained to me how I was to cope. I knew the part about I had to eat and stay warm—we were poor, and I'm not a complete gudgeon—but how was I to *go on?* I became a very angry boy."

"Are you still angry?"

He offered his arm, and Mina took it rather than insult him. "I made sense of the situation when I grew older and saw that anger was pointless. You don't get angry at a mongrel cur for pissing on your rosebushes. He can't help himself, and if somebody's fine mastiff hadn't anointed the same bushes first, the cur wouldn't have done likewise."

The analogy, both apt and appalling, gave Mina a clue as to the origins of her upset—one of the origins. "You cannot use such language around Her Grace."

"St. Didier claimed I could start entire new fashions in profanity if I choose to. I don't choose to, by the way. Do you always patrol the wilds of Berkeley Square at a forced march?"

Berkeley Square, with its stately maples, geometric walkways, and light blanket of snow, was the epitome of urban elegance.

"You shouldn't have to dawdle just because my legs are shorter." Mina wanted to drop his arm, retrieve Emily from the footman, and stomp all the way home.

Why?

"I like dawdling. I get some of my best ideas when I'm dawdling and whittling. An idle mind has room for fancies. My latest commission wants some thought. Garden statues for the Earl of Westhaven's conservatory. He has a place in Surrey not far from Town, and he prefers the shires to London. Westhaven appears to be a complicated man—all big words, literary references, and vast reams of complex, cross-referenced ledgers—but he's a fairly simple fellow at heart. Adores his family and most especially his new countess, likes to work hard, and values his honor. What sort of statues would a man like that love to see every time he walks into his garden?"

Mina had met Westhaven and his countess. Pleasant people, despite the fact that Westhaven was a ducal heir. He and William had had that much in common, but little else.

"Your Grace will have to pass the conundrum of the earl's conservatory to some other sculptor," Mina said, "and Westhaven will understand. I'm surprised he hasn't withdrawn the commission. Word of your good fortune is doubtless making the rounds in the clubs as I speak, and the earl tends to be very well informed."

"His mama's spies put the earl's to shame. Why would Westhaven withdraw the commission?"

For a man who understood grieving children and knew how to make tiny dragons, the question was nearly ludicrous.

"You are a *duke*. Dukes do not take money for whacking away at hunks of stone."

He stopped on the walkway and stood very tall. "Do you consider motherhood to be the business of whacking away at Emily's childish limitations?"

What sort of question...? Mina realized she had offended His Grace, which was just too jolly bad. Perhaps the day was suited to peevishness all around.

"You *cannot* accept commissions. You are a lofty *peer* now, a *gentleman*, a *duke*. To work with your hands for coin, even as an artist, is not *done*."

He grinned, a piratical, impish display of deviltry. "Is delivering

said peer a verbal birching beneath the maples *done?* You can doubtless be heard halfway to Chelsea."

And even raising her voice—double-drat the man—Mina hadn't
got through to him. "Your sculpting and whatnot must become a
hobby, Your Grace." She tugged discreetly on his arm, but he
remained unmoving, a human tree of masculine intransigence.

"Will Her Grace take a dim view of my sculpting?"

"Very. You might be allowed to resume dabbling, as an eccentric
and genteel pastime, after you've made the right impressions in the
spring. A duchess and some children will increase the latitude you're
permitted, provided you vote appropriately, socialize appropriately,
and indulge moderately in only the usual vices."

His Grace tipped his hat to a passing elderly couple who—to
Mina's unending shock—smiled and nodded to him in return.

"Another commission?" she muttered.

"Two years ago. Their family crypt needed some touching up.
Mrs. Griffiths claims my skill with putti is unparalleled. She's invited
me for dinner twice since then."

"And now the likes of Westhaven and his countess will be
expected to invite you for dinner. You see the difficulty?"

The footman emerged from the shop across the street. He held a
tray with his right hand and Emily's mittened hand with his left.

"I see no difficulty," His Grace said, resuming their progress in
the direction of the coach. "If my sculpting will annoy Her Grace of
Huntleigh, I will continue to accept every commission that comes my
way. I will lower my prices, in fact, and encourage the cits and
bankers to hire me."

"Are you mad?"

"Angry, you mean? Yes, and if you expect that I will give up the
art that saved my life and my soul, the art I love and am damned good
at, merely to appease the vanity of some desiccated martinet of a
duchess, you are much mistaken. As far as I am concerned, the
current Duchess of Huntleigh all but murdered my mother and

sister. She can't murder my art unless she thinks to murder me as well, and that is the one crime she will not commit."

He made that shocking declaration, then returned Mina to the coach, ate his ice, and politely inquired after Mina's treat.

The barberry ice was bitter, but Mina barely tasted it. She realized that though she was vexed and bothered and annoyed and even a bit angry, she was also worried.

Finn Cathcart and Edwardia, Duchess of Huntleigh, were engaged in a war of wills destined to have two losers and no victors. Mina, Emily, and any number of other innocents were bound to get caught up in the affray, and that worried Mina very, very much.

And as for the accusation that Her Grace had all but murdered the duke's mother and sister, Mina had no idea what he was referring to, nor did she wish to be disabused of her ignorance. She finished her ice, thanked the duke for his hospitality, and made small talk for the entire journey home.

CHAPTER FOUR

"Spooked," Finn said. "Wilhelmina Cathcart is spooked to the soles of her elegant boots." Very low heels on those boots too. Not worn, simply low—ridiculous woman.

"She's a widow," Pritchard replied, eyeing his queen's bishop as the library clock ticked gently on the mantel. "Widows can become socially uncertain. William Cathcart was a man in his prime, a lofty title all but his. One bad fall from his horse, and his wife's situation changed overnight. Your move."

Finn didn't particularly care for chess—the same sixty-four squares, the same rigid moves by the same pieces, mirroring the same class distinctions that had bedeviled humanity for ages—but chess was one way to lure Pritchard beyond his self-imposed strictures of decorum. The man could no more pass by a chessboard than Finn could ignore an Antonio Verrio ceiling mural.

Finn shifted a pawn one space forward, leaving the piece *en prise* by design. Pritchard despised sacrificing pawns. The tactic drove him nigh barmy, a rare weakness in his strategy.

"Mrs. Cathcart is equal to the challenges of widowhood," Finn said. "Her darling William has been gone for some time, and—if you put that bishop where you're thinking to put him, I'll have you in five moves."

"If I don't move him, I'll be defeated in three." Pritchard knocked over his king with a single finger.

"Finally spotted my rook, did you?"

"And your queen. From what I've gathered, William's marriage wasn't a grand passion, but he and his wife were cordial. She conceived within the requisite year of the marriage, but Emily is—alas for all—a girl."

"Alas for me, especially. Was the match arranged?"

Pritchard began reorganizing the board, returning every piece to its starting square. "Of course. Wilhelmina Lindstrom Cathcart claims an earl for an uncle, and her brother is in line to inherit that title. She could become, by courtesy, Lady Wilhelmina someday soon, assuming she doesn't remarry a peer or courtesy lord, assuming the proper petitions are filed, and assuming her brother doesn't suffer an untimely death. She went to all the best schools, family solidly entrenched in Wiltshire, vast acreage, and was enough of an heiress to catch the matchmakers' eyes. Play again?"

The library was cozy on a chilly night, and Pritchard would win the rematch and be in a better humor for it. Nonetheless, Pritchard *had* lost. That seldom happened, and never without a pitched and lengthy battle.

"I'll gloat over my victory, thank you. What else have you learned about my ducal relations?"

Pritchard finished tidying up the board and sat back. "*You* are the ducal relative now. They are the dependent family. You hold vast acreage, too, you know."

Finn rose from the reading table and went to the sideboard. "You'll join me in a brandy?"

"Only to be polite."

Finn poured two generous portions. "You disdain to drink with me. Such a snob, Pritchard, when you only permit the finest vintages in my cellar. I don't give a lump of cold clay for the acres. You have assured me they are well managed. What of the duchess? Has she any dirty secrets I can use? Maybe we claim an obscure island in the Outer Hebrides to which I can consign her. The inmost circle of hell is said to be frigid rather than hot."

"Your father was the family dirty secret for a time. A wayward, wanton wastrel."

Finn set Pritchard's brandy before him. "You needn't alliterate. It might surprise you to know that Papa was a devoted husband and a good father, also a man of honor, once Mama sorted him out. That the duchess has propagated gossip to the contrary is another mark against her. I realize she was merely his sister-by-marriage, but speaking ill of the dead is nasty, even for her."

Pritchard sipped his brandy. He had the most elegant, graceful hands. A fine, patrician nose too. Finn would have asked him to model those hands, but the request would have mortified Pritchard's delicate sensibilities.

"Perhaps the duchess did not speak ill of the dead. Society seldom needs prompting when it comes to mean-spirited talk. If you're interested in the family's recent history, I haven't much more to offer. The solicitors are an old and venerable firm, serving a few very well-placed families since the days of Good King Athelstan. I'll have a hard time scaling those walls, but the effort has been initiated."

"Don't scale the walls, then." Finn resumed his seat behind the white army. "Tunnel into the cellars. A clerk somewhere in the middle ranks can be persuaded to chat over a pint, and the charwoman will have a few things to say."

"Charwoman. Good point. I hadn't thought of her."

"You forgot the charwoman, you all but handed me a victory, and you haven't swiped a finger over a single spotless surface since you walked through the library door an hour ago. What's bothering you?"

Pritchard scowled at his drink, sipped again, then set the glass aside. "You are."

"You've never hesitated to scold me in the past. What have I done now?"

"This grudge you bear the duchess won't serve. She's an old woman, no real relation to you, and she hasn't long to live. Treating her with cavalier disdain is beneath the dignity of your station."

Finn rose again rather than suffer under Pritchard's brooding gaze. The man should have been a headmaster overseeing a legion of unruly boys. He'd have turned them into proper little automatons in no time.

"She's an old woman," Finn said. "I concede that fact. My sister was a newborn, and the duchess was most cavalier toward her— mortally cavalier—and equally cavalier toward my mother, who'd endured considerable travail in childbed. Papa did not spare me any details, and I refuse to spare the duchess the smallest courtesy."

Pritchard prowled to the hearth. "You must, though. Not for her sake, for yours. You will be judged based on how you deal with her. Pouting and sulking on your part will only let her play the martyr. She'll outflank you with a few wan glances and a sniffy silence or two. She has the ear of the Regent, Your Grace."

"Don't call me that, and I'm not pouting and sulking. A baby—an innocent, helpless baby—meant nothing to the duchess, and I meant less than nothing. Is such a hard-hearted creature even human?"

Pritchard jabbed at the fire, tossed on another square of peat, and pokered it into the precise position most likely to catch and burn.

"A sculptor, albeit a talented fellow," he said, "inherits one of the loftiest titles in the land, along with thousands of well-situated acres, a half-dozen sumptuous dwellings, and a seat in the Lords. His first action in his ducal capacity is to snub the relict of the former duke, an aging paragon of social rectitude. That's what Society will notice, not your long-dead parents' self-imposed hardships, or the death of yet another child who simply failed to thrive."

The rest of the syllogism was plain enough to Finn, loath though he was to admit it: If he was weighed in the societal scales and found wanting—scales tilted against him to begin with—the unkind talk, the speculation, the whispers would land on Wilhelmina Cathcart and little Emily.

Not as hard as they'd land on him, but the head of a household's conduct reflected on the whole family. Wilhelmina was bearing up under enough vexation already, and Emily was not coping well at all.

"You're saying I must negotiate a truce with the duchess."

"Or you must appear to." Pritchard began sweeping the spotless hearthstones. "And take heed: Her Grace and Vanessa Cathcart, Lady Helmsby, were once upon a time rivals for the hand of the old duke. He married neither of them on the first go-round, though Vanessa bagged the ducal spare and the honor of his courtesy title."

"Edwardia had the last laugh, nevertheless, consoling the duke when his duchess of choice went to her reward." Finn's true aunt, and she'd been gone before he'd been born. Might be interesting to see a portrait of her.

"Or Lady Helmsby had the last laugh," Pritchard said, returning the hearth broom to its stand, "because her son was in line to save the title."

"Lady Helmsby hasn't laughed in quite some time, I'll bet." A gratifying thought, considering that the woman was little use to Wilhelmina. "What a stupid lot of games, and I want no part of them. Mrs. Cathcart was good enough to inform me that I must cease sculpting. The lady has some odd notions."

Pritchard picked up his drink from the reading table. "I had hoped St. Didier explained that part to you."

Maybe the thought of Finn without his studio had troubled Pritchard. It certainly troubled Finn.

"The part about how my man of business must return all commissions pending and politely explain that unforeseen circumstances have arisen, et cetera and so forth? Not a chance."

"Society will not—"

"Society can go to blazes. I know that bit about attending a royal levee and making my obeisance before the luminaries in the Lords, but that can all wait until my own affairs are sorted. What aren't you telling me, Pritchard?"

Pritchard finished his drink and returned the glass to the sideboard. He withdrew a folded and sealed epistle from an inner pocket.

"You have been summoned."

Finn took the letter, slit the seal, and scanned the brief, elegantly penned contents. "I'm invited to tea tomorrow at two of the clock, by Edwardia, Her Grace of Huntleigh. Tea. Wormwood and gall would be too good for that woman."

"Are you afraid of her?" Only Pritchard would have the balls—and the insight—to pose such a question.

"Any sane man should be, but unlike my mother and sister, unlike my eight-year-old self, I have no need of her. She can't hurt me."

Pritchard pinched the bridge of his nose. "Your commissions will disappear overnight if she so much as sighs in the right company."

"My commissions are apparently doomed regardless of Her Grace's sighs and glances." Though Finn would complete them anyway. One didn't abandon a project simply because a duchess put on a pathetic show of mortification. "I'll leave the final works in Hyde Park for all to see, and they will be excellent art too."

Pritchard put a fist on his hip, a posture that on any other man would have looked ridiculous. "You cannot fight like an artist, Your Grace. You cannot fight like an apprentice, scrapping with his fellows for the master's notice. You cannot fight like the brawler you once were. You must learn to fight like a duke."

Pritchard's most annoying quality was that he was usually right. "And from whom do I acquire that knowledge?"

"The Earl of Westhaven might have a few ideas. He's something of a prig, but shrewd and pragmatic. Will you accept the duchess's invitation?"

Finn wanted to tear up the paper and return it to Her Grace in little, bitty, wrinkled pieces bearing the aroma of cat pee. He was about to admit as much when he recalled Wilhelmina Cathcart, retreating behind small talk for the duration of a coach ride and parading about in low heels when she ought to be towering above lesser mortals.

"I will accept the invitation, but I'd also like a message delivered to Wilhelmina Cathcart's household tonight."

"It's nearly midnight."

"Shall I take the letter myself?"

Pritchard manufactured a glower worthy of a spinster whose tabby has made a toy of her reading spectacles. "Don't you dare. I'll send Duncan up to your room to retrieve this message."

Finn began blowing out candles, sconce by sconce. "I'll be in the studio."

"Leave the candles for me, please. You intend to go to work now?"

"Like all self-respecting mages, I do my best conjuring by dark of night. Be off with you and stop fretting. For the duration of two cups of tea, I can be civil."

"I am vastly reassured to know such skill has finally befallen you. Good night, Your Grace." Pritchard stalked out, and Finn was left with a puzzle: Pritchard was the majordomo of the House of Proper Conduct. He bent a few rules on a few occasions, out of necessity or practicality, but he'd forgotten to bow upon withdrawing.

Trouble was afoot, and not simply the trouble of a ducal title, a conniving old duchess, and commissions Finn wasn't about to part with.

Real trouble, and the only place to productively ponder real trouble was the studio. Finn retreated to that sanctuary, jotted a note to Wilhelmina Cathcart, and got to work on sketches for the Earl of Westhaven.

Wilhelmina stared at the note beside her plate of eggs and toast. *Wear the highest heels you have.*

What sort of postscript was that? What sort of note was it? Half plea, half challenge… As if tea with Edwardia was some sort of heroic ordeal. At least His Grace had good penmanship. A little flourishy with the initial capitals, and the signature was all wrong—not *Finn Cathcart*, for pity's sake.

Huntleigh. He was Huntleigh now. The sooner the man resigned himself to that—

"Madam, I am sorry to intrude…" Travers looked gleeful rather than contrite. "But you have a caller."

Travers placed a silver salver at Wilhelmina's elbow. A calling card lay thereon—purple ink, of all the affectations.

Finlay Cathcart, a reasonably fashionable address, and a little image in the corner of a winged cherub. At least Mama-in-Law wasn't storming the gates. A siege over breakfast would have been entirely like her.

"*His Grace* will join me, Travers, and I dearly hope you didn't leave him kicking his heels in the second parlor."

Travers withdrew without comment, meaning that the new duke had probably been consigned to admiring the molding in the very sitting room where solicitors, bankers, and—yes—artisans were received. Travers did so enjoy his little villainies.

"Your Grace." Wilhelmina rose before Travers could announce her guest, who predictably shrank the dimensions of the breakfast parlor simply by stepping into it. "Do join me. Travers, please have the kitchen send along a fresh pot."

Travers bowed and withdrew, while the footman who lurked at the sideboard busied himself laying a place at Wilhelmina's right.

"Mrs. Cathcart." His Grace bowed, his smile genial. "Gracious of you to receive me. I trust you are well?"

"Thriving, thank you, and you appear to be doing likewise. Dalton, I forgot to ask Travers to send along more eggs and toast. Will you please remedy my oversight?"

"Of course, madam. Your Grace." Dalton bowed exquisitely, which caused his blond curls to flop over his forehead.

The duke half closed the door behind the departing footman. "Will you come with me this afternoon?"

"I haven't been invited. The duchess well knows to whom she has and hasn't sent an invitation."

"I'm inviting you. If you are on hand, I'm less likely to lapse into profanity, or worse."

"I am not your governess, sir."

He strolled around to the head of the table, where Wilhelmina had been sitting, and patted the back of the chair. "My manners are refined enough. My thinking is that Her Grace will be better behaved with you on hand."

Wilhelmina considered that theory and found it worthy. She allowed the duke to seat her, which he did with appropriate courtesy and correct timing.

"You are right that Edwardia will likely do the pretty, or her version of it, if I'm on hand," Wilhelmina said, replacing her table napkin on her lap. "She will avoid shaming you before another, though in private, she can be scathing. There's plenty of tea in the pot, and I'm guessing you can serve yourself. If you have anything to say that you don't want overheard, you have about two minutes to say it."

The duke poured himself a cup of tea. "How is Emily?"

Not where Wilhelmina had expected him to start. "She enjoyed yesterday's outing to Gunter's. She slept with two bears hibernating under her pillow and a dragon guarding her from the bedside table."

"But this morning, she's back to being peaked and wan?" He added honey and cream to his tea, skimping on neither.

"She's subdued."

"More tea?"

"Please. What prompted this morning's call, Your Grace?" And did the duke look a bit peaked himself? Wan was likely beyond him, but subtle lines fanned out from his forget-me-not blue eyes, and his mouth was bracketed by grooves.

"I came to beg, in the event you were leaving me to brave the duchess in solo combat."

"Have you ever begged for anything in your life?"

He stirred his tea, and somebody had apparently instructed him how to do so silently, and to refrain from tapping his spoon against the tea cup.

"I certainly tried. I wasn't very good at it. My parents were poor, but Mama was frugal and resourceful. I was fed well enough, most of the time, and compared to my competition among the more experienced beggars, I hadn't the knack of looking pathetic. I was big for my age, and that didn't help either."

Wilhelmina was abruptly ashamed of herself. "I'm sorry. I meant the question... flippantly. I didn't mean... You were left *to beg?*"

"Eight years old—too big to be a climbing boy, thank God—but as much in need of sustenance as any other child. Thanks to Mama, I could read and write, which did me no good for a very long time. My father had the sense to die in the spring. I believe he endured the wretched coal smoke of one final winter for my sake, and thus my debut on the streets of London was during milder weather."

Wilhelmina speared a forkful of eggs, then put the food aside. "*Eight years old?* Nobody brought you to your uncle?"

"My father was disowned by his parents, Mrs. Cathcart. Why would anybody expect my aunt and uncle to take pity on a disgraced brother's offspring? Besides, I bolted from the churchyard before Papa was even laid to rest. To my mind, the mines would have been preferable to accepting charity from my titled relations. I was as stubborn as the next child, and also terrified. Papa had despised those people. If you don't intend to eat those eggs, I will."

"They are cold."

He plucked her plate away. "I might have starved," he said, taking up his fork, "but an old sea captain saw me lurking in the park one day, whittling away on a piece of linden left over from some half-rotten tree that had been cut down."

"You had a knife?"

"I always have a knife, and that knife had been my mother's whit-tling knife. The creditors got nearly everything but that and the clothes on my back. Papa left me his watch, and I was allowed to keep that because it no longer worked."

The eggs disappeared with polite dispatch, while Wilhelmina rearranged what she knew—or thought she knew—of Finlay Cathcart.

"So you used your knife to whittle, when you might have used it to steal?"

Of all things, he took out the whittling blade he'd used the day before. The blade was short and hooked, the handle thick and rounded. "The sharp edge is too small to inflict much damage if I used it to stab somebody. A lucky slash across the throat might have results, but an eight-year-old doesn't think in those terms. He thinks, 'This was Mama's knife, and I must never lose it.'"

"What happened?"

"The sea captain knew a wood-carver in need of an apprentice, and though the wood-carver was a mean drunk, he was also tremen-dously gifted. The appropriate introductions were made—after I'd been given a decent meal and had a wash—and I had a roof over my head, until the wood-carver died two years on."

The duke would have been ten years old and not even halfway through his articles. Wilhelmina put the toast rack beside his plate, because the eggs were all but gone.

"And then what happened?"

"The wood-carver's widow arranged for me to apprentice to a potter, who made the wood- carver look like a saint by comparison, but by then I was quick at creating shapes in a solid medium. I sold my whittling on the side, or again, I might have starved. When the potter went to his reward in some drunken melee, I was taken up by his cousin, a mason turned sculptor. I would have been about thir-teen, and I was already as tall as most men. The mason put the muscles on me, and at fifteen, I was sent to a sculptor to learn the rough work aspect of the stone carver's art."

"That was half a lifetime ago," Wilhelmina observed. From one perspective—Society's, perhaps—Finn Cathcart had been a very lucky lad, bouncing from the tutelage of one expert to that of another. Viewed from a mother's perspective, however...

"I knocked around the Continent for a time, starting off with a studio in Belgium when I was eighteen. I had not one word of French or Frisian, though I still recalled my mother's Gaelic. The head assistant was Irish, so we had some words in common, and much of what had to be communicated was visual rather than verbal anyway."

He drizzled honey in a perfect spiral on his toast. "I drifted around the Continent from there, dodging armies on occasion and taking in some of Greece when winters got the better of me. My French was good enough to get me mistaken for a Walloon or a Scot. I apparently speak French with a hint of a Scottish accent and Italian with a French accent. My majordomo is forever correcting my pronunciation no matter what language I attempt."

Dalton returned with a supply of eggs and toast and a fresh pot of tea. He set both on the table and took up the listening post by the sideboard.

"You may be excused," His Grace said, spooning more eggs onto his plate. "And on such a chilly day, please do close the door as you leave. We have only the one hearth in here, after all, and one must not waste coal."

Dalton looked to Wilhelmina, not out of deference, but possibly in hopes that she would overrule the duke's presumption.

"Coal is dear," she said, feeling both naughty and pleased with herself.

"Very good, madam, sir." Dalton flounced out and closed the door with an audible snick of the latch.

"Peat is cheaper," the duke said, tucking into the fresh eggs. "Burns more slowly, too, and smells better, if you ask me. Now that you've heard all about my wicked past, tell me what the duchess wants with me, as best you can divine her objectives. Then we must pay a call on the nursery. I want to see how my friends are settling in. Dragons in particular can be fussy about their surroundings."

Wilhelmina topped up their tea cups and considered her choices. She'd been prepared to leave Finn Cathcart to his fate where Edwardia and Society were concerned, but life had been leaving His Grace to his fate since childhood. To referee this initial skirmish between Edwardia and her nephew would be a small imposition, and might spare both parties some unfortunate posturing.

"What the duchess wants, at least for today, is simply to show Society that you and she are civil."

"I am to put on a farce for the gossips?" He wrinkled his nose and went back to demolishing his eggs.

"You are to disappoint the gossips," Wilhelmina said. "No raised voices, no untoward departures, no porcelain hurled against the chimneypieces."

"I would not disrespect the crockery with such a display. As long as Her Grace behaves, I will refrain from throwing the first punch."

Wilhelmina set down her tea cup. "You were a pugilist too?"

"I have been, also a diker, a bartender, a life model, a drover—ye gods, what a difference a good pair of boots makes—a stevedore, and a guard on the Royal Mail, plus a few other occupations. I thought my back would never recover from all the coach travel in the elements, and that job only lasted a few months."

And wouldn't the gossips just love to get hold of that litany? "We will leave your youthful peccadilloes in the past. The penny press will doubtless dredge them up eventually, but for now, you have an opportunity. If you make a good first impression on the right parties, all of that droving and roving will be forgiven." The life model part, though... He'd be celebrated in the clubs for that foolishness, and the matchmakers would claim to be scandalized while, in fact, being fascinated.

He patted his lips with his table napkin. "You are goading me. Implying that working for a living is a sin Society might graciously forgive if I'm sufficiently charming and humble. See how calmly I ignore your baiting. There is hope for me, yes? Shall we to the nursery?"

"You're sure you wouldn't like more toast?"

"I had already had breakfast before I called upon you, but did not want to refuse your hospitality when a good snack was in order. A walk in the winter air puts an appetite on me." He rose and courteously assisted Wilhelmina from her chair.

An interesting scent wafted around him. Bracing and brisk, rather than sweet or fussy. Rosemary and balsam, perhaps. "You walked here?"

"I live a quarter hour away, perhaps twenty minutes, if you avoid the shortcuts, and I was awake most of the night working. Fresh air always works wonders for the mind, don't you think?"

Wilhelmina did not know what to think. The winter air in London hardly qualified as fresh, and by decree of fashionable Society, a duke was to roll about Town in the lugubrious splendor of his Town coach.

When they reached the staircase, His Grace offered his arm, and Wilhelmina took it. All the way up to the nursery, while they discussed the weather and how far off spring was and might more snow be in the offing, Wilhelmina pondered her guest.

If Edwardia didn't give him a permanent disgust of Mayfair Society, he'd be like no duke ever to make his bow before the sovereign. Whittling for his bread, herding livestock... working, always working, and working hard.

Society would have no earthly idea what to make of him, and when in doubt, the gossips usually turned up catty and unkind. Wilhelmina knew the tedium of running that gauntlet. For the first time, she considered that Finn Cathcart could use a friend, and so—perhaps—could she.

CHAPTER FIVE

"He called upon Wilhelmina?" Lady Helmsby asked. "Escorted her and Emily to Gunter's? You're sure, Dalton?"

Why did the Quality never listen? "I'm certain, your ladyship. His Grace called upon Mrs. Cathcart well before noon, and then an hour later, here comes his Town coach—matching blacks in the traces —and away they go. Miss Emily had a vanilla ice, if I can believe the nurserymaid."

Which Dalton could, because Isaacs was sweet on him. He offered Norwich, the governess, good manners and charm, but any fool could see that Norwich was dedicated to her charge and far above the flirtations of a mere footman.

Isaacs, however, was an easy mark. Sixteen years old and as dimwitted as she was pretty, poor thing.

Lady Helmsby sipped her steaming-hot tea, while Dalton remained at attention, hands behind his back. The kitchen would spare him a cup if he asked—the two households were cordial below-stairs—but that wasn't the point.

The point was that Lady Helmsby, mother to the late William Cathcart, widow of the late Lord Helmsby Cathcart, could keep a mere footman loitering about her sewing room. Her parlor had windows on the street, and thus she did her interrogating from this curtained lair at the back of the house.

"What else can you tell me?" she asked.

Dalton could tell her that she should pay him more for this sort of inconvenience. Nobody had thought to lay, much less light, the sewing room fire. "His Grace was back again at breakfast today. He appears to be an early riser."

Lady Helmsby set down her tea cup. "His sleeping habits are of no interest to me, Dalton. How was he dressed? Was his hair styled *au courant*? Did he drop his aitches or slurp his tea?"

What her ladyship was truly asking was a simpler question: Would the new duke be an embarrassment to the family that could no longer ignore his existence?

Dalton had been in service as a Mayfair footman for ten years. At the age of six-and-twenty, he considered himself an expert on the topic of Town life. Clearly, the duke knew what he was about. He might not know the royal succession all the way back to the Conqueror, but he was educated enough, smart enough, and formidable enough.

"He'll do, my lady, with some polishing. Somebody has kitted him out appropriately, though he did wear a purple scarf. He prefers an old-fashioned queue to coiffures a la mode, and his speech is educated but not sophisticated." By that, Dalton meant that His Grace didn't make mean jokes or quote a lot of blathering Latin.

To malign the man at all made Dalton slightly uncomfortable. Word belowstairs was that himself had been tossed onto the streets as a lad and had managed on native wit and hard work. The poor sod was too big to be a footman, cursed with dark hair—Society preferred blonds, as all the world knew—and not exactly handsome.

His face was weathered, as if he'd worked under many a hot sun or sailed many a tropical sea.

"A purple scarf, you say?"

"Merino wool, ma'am. Excellent quality. Darkish and woven in some sort of hunting plaid, I'd guess."

Lady Helmsby appeared to consider this detail as if it were the key to the whole man. "Unusual, but not outlandish. This might bode well, but what on earth is the significance of calling on Wilhelmina first?"

She wasn't asking Dalton for his opinion, though he had one having to do with scouting neutral terrain before engaging an enemy in battle.

Her ladyship sat back, her gaze fixed on her embroidery. The pattern was all shiny green leaves and prancing lions, as if anybody needed such folderol on a handkerchief. But then, the Quality set great store by pretty folderol.

In repose, Lady Helmsby was pretty, too, as some people considered dried flowers pretty. She was old enough to be Dalton's mama, but looked a good ten years younger than that. She'd been a pale blonde, and time could be kinder to blondes than brunettes. According to Travers, her ladyship had been a very young and well-dowered bride, and she'd presented her husband with a son almost nine months to the moment after speaking her vows.

Her life, since that blessed day, had been directed toward the time when William would become the duke, and then he'd had the stupidity to fall from a galloping horse.

Typical nob foolishness.

"This is not much of a report, Dalton," her ladyship said, pouring herself more hot tea. "Are you sure you're telling me everything?"

"I wasn't quite finished, your ladyship. The duchess has invited His Grace to tea today, and Mrs. Cathcart has agreed to accompany him."

"The duchess sent the new duke *an invitation to tea*, and he accepted?"

"Apparently so." Mrs. Cathcart's lady's maid, a Puritanical soul by the name of Martin, had been in the laundry pressing one of her employer's most staid afternoon dresses. That meant a call upon an august personage, and the duchess was one of few of those spending the winter in Town.

"I cannot begrudge Edwardia the opening salvo, and she had to *invite* him, after all. Point to His Grace. I am gaining a cautiously favorable impression of our duke." Lady Helmsby stirred cream and sugar into her tea and dunked a butter biscuit into the cup. "Wilhelmina will mediate. She's good at that. I suppose I'd best send a similar invitation, though I'm merely the late heir's grieving mother."

She was also a late heir's grieving spouse. Two chances at the tiara, and both had come to nothing. That would vex a woman like Lady Helmsby, though now she was auntie to a duke, which had to be some consolation.

"How is my granddaughter?" she asked, munching her biscuit.

Her ladyship always got around to this display of grandmotherly concern. "Miss Emily enjoyed the outing to Gunter's and is none the worse for having braved the elements."

"What was Wilhelmina thinking, allowing the child out of the house in this bitter weather?"

The weather was merely cold, and the outing had occurred in the toasty confines of a coach nearly as large as a housekeeper's sitting room. The child had for once come home with roses in her cheeks.

"I'm sure I don't know, your ladyship." What child wanted to be shut up indoors week after week, no playmates, no fresh air, no laughter, not a skinned knee or a scraped palm, ever? Even a footman was allowed his half day and darts night.

Lady Helmsby helped herself to another biscuit, though the gaze she turned on Dalton suggested she'd caught the hint of irony in his voice.

"I love my granddaughter, Dalton. My concern for her is without limit. Wilhelmina tries to do a good job, I know, but she's a widow, her family is little more than gentry, and Emily is not a well child."

Mrs. Cathcart's *gentry* family included an earl, and the girl was far from sickly. "Of course, my lady."

"You may go. I will expect you back on Friday, and do remain alert. A new duke throws all into confusion, and he could so easily bungle without even realizing his errors."

Dalton bowed and withdrew, relieved to have the twice-weekly ordeal complete. Travers was also in Lady Helmsby's pay, and she compared their reports for accuracy. Not a woman to cross, despite her gracious airs and pretty needlework.

Dalton offered a slightly less-edited report belowstairs, accepted two cups of China black, and took himself out into the chilly late morning sun.

He did not envy the new duke. The old duchess was nobody's fool, and Lady Helmsby hadn't ceased scheming just because her son had expired. Both of them disliked Mrs. Cathcart, who was determined—in vain—to remain above the affray. Toss in Miss Emily's chronic moping, and His Grace was faced with a small, miserable clutch of females where his family should have been.

When the matchmakers got hold of him, he'd wish he'd never heard the word *duke*.

Finn had edited the curriculum vitae he'd recited at breakfast for Mrs. Cathcart.

He'd left out the part about a shipwreck in the Cyclades, a brief encounter with an Italian jail (he'd sketched his way out of that one), a stint as artist-in-residence at the chateau of an elderly Italian *contessa*, more nights spent out in the elements than the usual shepherd claimed, and more *freedom* than John Bull, much less His Grace of Bull, could possibly imagine.

Finn missed that freedom more with each turn of the carriage wheels. "Any last-minute advice?" he asked as the coach lumbered along slushy streets.

Mrs. Cathcart, looking elegantly stodgy in a gray wool ensemble that did nothing for her coloring, looked him up and down. She occupied the forward-facing bench as a queen occupied her throne, while Finn—back to the horses—felt slightly queasy.

"Tea with the duchess is not a skirmish," Mrs. Cathcart said. "You are merely to offer Her Grace a diplomatic greeting. Your objective is to avoid giving offense."

Finn's objective was reconnaissance. He was scouting enemy territory, testing the strength of the duchess's forces, and gaining insight into her available strategies.

"As long as Edwardia has the same goal where I am concerned, we'll manage."

Mrs. Cathcart twitched at her skirts. "She can open doors for you, Your Grace. She can smooth the way or ensure your path is rocky."

"I neither need nor want to walk through the doors only she can open, and your idea of a rocky path and mine likely diverge considerably."

"You might be surprised." All but muttered as the coach slowed, then took a corner.

Finn had spent the night building an armature for the clay model of Lord Westhaven's first statue. The work was soothing and allowed his mind to wander on two planes. The first plane had been occupied by wire and form and scale and shapes. The second plane had been focused on Wilhelmina Cathcart.

She accentuated neither her good looks nor her handsome height, and she anticipated battle with the duchess over Emily's future. Nonetheless, Wilhelmina was not yet the grim widow she apparently intended to become.

She was stubborn—her heels gave her barely an inch of extra height, which both pleased and amused Finn—and she'd ordered a barberry ice just to be contrary. If Finn understood any two qualities in another person, stubbornness and contrariness came at the top of the list.

"Are you nervous?" she asked as the coach rolled to a stop.

"I'd rather pay a call at Newgate," Finn said, "but I ceased being nervous before I reached the age of eighteen. You?" He expected a peevish look for his impertinence.

"The same, more or less. If you can avoid leaving me alone with Her Grace, I'd appreciate it."

Not quite a request for aid, but certainly a request for solidarity. Finn emerged from the coach and assisted Mrs. Cathcart to step down. Her grip on his hand was light—a mercy, in the cold—and she took his arm without a fuss.

A lady who chose her battles.

They were received by a butler who might well have served in the Conqueror's army. He showed them into a parlor that enshrined the fashions of an earlier age. A rare set of Wedgwood chimneypieces graced enormous matching hearths and anchored a blue, cream, and pink decorating scheme. Despite the pastels and the roaring fires, the room had a sterile quality, as if the clock on the mantel ticked toward eternity rather than the next winding.

"Her Grace will join you shortly," the butler said, bowing and retreating.

"How do butlers do that?" Finn asked. "Never make the floorboards creak, never provoke doors to squeaking?" Pritchard had the same ability.

Mrs. Cathcart positioned herself near one of the fireplaces. "They are paid to know how. We cannot sit until our hostess joins us."

Finn scanned the furniture. All handsomely upholstered, all precisely placed. "Which is her favorite chair?"

"Don't you dare. I will be guilty of disrespect by association, and you promised not to throw the first punch."

Well, damn. "Isn't it disrespectful to make us wait? We were punctual." To the minute.

"Perhaps she's goading you."

Finn refused to be goaded. He'd come to a conclusion somewhere in the middle of the night about this whole duke business. As long as he could continue to work, as long as his step-aunt left him in peace, he'd do the pretty at court and make a pass or two through Parliament.

Whatever the required rigamarole was, he'd trudge through it and get back to his studio. Mama and Papa would understand that much compromise with the dictates of Providence.

Finn occupied himself studying the nearest chimneypiece, which boasted Wedgewood's signature blue and cream jasperware scheme. Ivy leaves with a few sprigs of laurel adorned the tablets, vases held pride of place in the corners. A white Carrara marble mantel topped the whole. Wedgwood hadn't produced many chimneypieces, and in this room, the work was set off to excellent advantage.

By some instinct, Finn sensed when the door opened behind him. A skinnyish, white-haired woman of dignified bearing and average height entered, a footman rolling a tea cart behind her. The lady wore an outmoded dress of dark brown velvet and a shawl of lighter brown wool.

Nothing on the cart rattled or even tinkled.

"Flaxman's work?" Finn asked, gesturing to the hearth. "Before his Roman period, I take it?"

Mrs. Cathcart's expression was carefully blank, suggesting Finn should have opened the conversation with some groveling. Too rubbishing bad.

"Your uncle commissioned those chimneypieces. I find them a trifle restrained, myself, but they've aged well." She inclined her head, which was probably her version of a curtsey. "Your Grace, good day." *Thank you for accepting my invitation* hung in the air *quite* unspoken.

"Your Grace." Finn bowed properly, but only just. "Good day."

A pause ensued, during which the duchess fussed at the footman and an elderly spaniel shuffled into the room. The dog's muzzle was white, and he moved without the bounce and verve of a younger canine. The duchess's dress matched the spaniel's coat nicely, an observation Finn kept to himself. An artist was doomed to notice colors, style, details, and so forth.

"Shall we be seated?" Her Grace settled into a plush armchair near a hearth. "How do you take your tea, Huntleigh? Wilhelmina, I wasn't expecting you. You can make yourself useful and pour out."

No small talk, no pleasantries about the weather, and—Finn noted this with particular impatience—not so much as a greeting for Mrs. Cathcart before the duchess was giving her orders.

He was abruptly exhausted, and he didn't want any damned tea from this nasty old woman.

"That fellow in the family livery can pour out," Finn said, "if Your Grace isn't up to the task. Mrs. Cathcart kindly accompanied me at my request. I labor under the impression that trustworthy third parties are Society's preferred means for introducing strangers to one another. Am I mistaken?"

He posed that question not to cause trouble, but to spare all and sundry needless skirmishing. Rudeness toward Mrs. Cathcart was unacceptable.

Wilhelmina looked to be on the verge of pouring oil on troubled waters, and that was unacceptable too.

"Am I mistaken, Duchess?" he asked again, quietly.

"We are not strangers," Her Grace replied. "I met you when you were eight years old. Perhaps the occasion has slipped your mind?"

That day was scored into Finn's memory like an epitaph carved into granite. "You *saw* me when I was eight years old," he replied. "You neither spoke to me nor offered me any sort of hospitality, though my mother and I were nearly starving. I recall the occasion quite well."

Wilhelmina scooted another half inch forward on her seat, and she'd already been at the edge of the cushion, but Finn wasn't about to let the duchess start with the upper hand.

The clock ticked, the fires roared, and a passing gust rattled the windows. Finn was prepared to leave if necessary to make his point. He would like to leave, in fact. Would love to leave and never come back.

He'd felt the same way about England itself for years.

"Very well," the duchess said. "Roberts, see to the tea. You will have to ask His Grace how he prefers his China black."

"Plain," Finn said, "but of course, the ladies should be served first."

The dog whined softly, and the duchess stroked his head. Roberts busied himself with the tea service.

"Plain will do for me as well," Wilhelmina said. "And some biscuits wouldn't go amiss either. Tell me, Your Grace, how is Charles managing the cold weather?"

The dog looked up at the mention of his name, and to Finn's surprise, the duchess launched into a discourse about the proper care and feeding of aging spaniels, to include daily exercise, stewed meat, and the occasional ham bone or old slipper to ward off boredom.

By the time the riveting topic of geriatric canine digestion had been exhausted, the minute hand on the mantel clock had advanced exactly one-quarter hour. Wilhelmina finished her cup of tea, and Finn took that as his cue to assist her to her feet.

The leave-taking was as abrupt and awkward as the greeting had been, with the duchess apparently unwilling to brave the chilly corridors. Roberts was charged with seeing Finn and Wilhelmina out, and Finn had the impression that old Charles would have liked some fresh air too.

"You will meet with the solicitors," Her Grace called as Roberts was bowing Wilhelmina through the parlor door. "They await your summons, Your Grace."

And how was Finn to know which solicitors to summon, and why would any sane man who could spend the day arguing with a block of marble instead inflict upon himself the blight known as solicitors?

"I'll explain," Wilhelmina murmured, brushing past Finn.

"I will see to the lawyers," Finn said, though he didn't say *when* he'd see to them.

The duchess nodded and remained standing, Charles at her side, until Roberts closed the parlor door, and the longest and most inane quarter hour of Finn's life came to an end.

He held his peace until he and Wilhelmina were in the coach. "What the hell was all that in aid of?"

Wilhelmina, again looking splendidly dignified on the forward-facing seat, pulled the shades. "I'm not sure, but I suspect that business about summoning the solicitors might have been the point. If Swime and Meebles run true to form, they've been using the old duke's death to do absolutely nothing for as long as possible, while charging as much as possible as they stand around looking concerned and trustworthy."

Finn felt the beginnings of a headache at the base of his neck. Ten years ago, even five, he could have missed a night of sleep and not noticed. Now...

"I understand that a title comes with responsibilities—the bit with the knee breeches at court, more ridiculousness for the House of Lords. St. Didier never mentioned solicitors, though, and I'm to *summon* them as if they are my own personal horde of demons?"

"They might well be. May I ask you to change seats? I'm unused to conversing with somebody on the backward-facing bench."

A gentleman always took the backward-facing bench, but then, Finn and Wilhelmina Cathcart were not strangers, and Finn hated traveling with his back to the horses.

He switched seats. He meant to inquire of Wilhelmina what the demon horde would expect of him, but the interior of the coach was dim, the bricks in the floor were toasty, and Finn's eyes soon grew heavy. He fell asleep and dreamed of dragons and bears and old spaniel dogs, all sitting down to tea together.

His Grace switched benches, and Wilhelmina waited for the questions to start, or the complaints. Edwardia had seemed for once at a loss, and that puzzled Mina as little else about the duchess ever had.

Edwardia was, to use William's term, a penance of a relative.

William's calls on his auntie had always presaged a good hour's worth of muttering and foul humor, though William had never once bestirred himself to deflect the duchess's criticisms of Wilhelmina—which had been legion.

"You need not have spoken up on my behalf," Mina said quietly, when the duke remained silent beside her. He was larger than William, more substantial, and far less fidgety. "The duchess took it upon herself to train me as her replacement. She has no excuse to lecture me anymore, but old habits die hard."

Edwardia had been obnoxious, offering Mina a rebuke where a greeting should have been. Finn Cathcart, whatever else might be true about him, had refused to ignore Her Grace's poor manners.

Or perhaps, the duchess had been displaying her version of nerves?

Wilhelmina had been too surprised—and touched—at His Grace's defense of her to intervene. Edwardia would have her revenge on some future occasion, of course, but for today that fellow *in the family livery* had poured out.

"You were naughty," Wilhelmina said, "to scold the duchess that way, but I thank you."

His Grace sighed. His weight beside Mina had acquired the inert quality of a man at his slumbers. He settled closer, his cheek resting against her hair, and muttered something in French about the bedamned stone.

A voice in Mina's head sounding very much like her old finishing governess told her to sit up straight, wake the duke, and have done with the foolishness. Another voice suggested that the man needed his rest, and where was the harm in allowing him a short nap, even if that nap had a passing resemblance to something like a cuddle?

She debated the proper course for the duration of two slow streets, with *I barely know him* losing ground to *he defended me* and *he's tired.* When the coach turned into the mews behind Mina's house, just as she was admitting to herself *I have missed simple human warmth,* His Grace stirred.

"Blast it to perdition. I fell asleep, didn't I? You are a curiously obliging pillow, Mrs. Cathcart, but I apologize for my lapse anyway. Present company is not to blame."

"You've been going short of sleep?"

He gathered up his walking stick, gloves, and hat from the opposite bench. "I work best after dark. No assistants or apprentices underfoot, no callers, no Pritchard scoffing at my French. Last night, I made a start on Lord Westhaven's statuary."

The statuary His Grace ought not to create, not for coin, anyway. "Why don't you come in for a bit? You are doubtless overdue for a second or third luncheon, and we can discuss the solicitors. They were the bane of William's existence, though he learned to retaliate once he reached his majority."

"I am peckish, and thus I will accept your kind invitation." He adjusted his purple scarf and climbed out, making the coach rock, and then handed Mina down. "We will pay a call on the nursery, too, if that's convenient."

Mina did not want Emily growing attached to His Grace. The child had been attached to her great-uncle and her papa and was all too capable of becoming overly fond of the duke. But then, His Grace wasn't likely to expire of old age any time soon, and he wasn't likely to risk his life on some bet involving a steeplechase by moonlight on a half-broken colt.

"A short visit," Mina said. "Norwich is a great believer in the sanctity of a regular schedule in the schoolroom, and yesterday's ice already has me in her bad books."

The duke signaled the coachman to take the team home and opened the garden gate. "Are you in everybody's bad books? The duchess feels at liberty to scold you on sight. Your mama-in-law, after raising exactly one drunken wastrel, thinks it allowable to criticize your parenting of Emily, who is a paragon, and the governess begrudges you an enjoyable outing with your daughter."

To say nothing of Travers's constant, subtle deprecations. "When you characterize my situation thus, I want to object. I am so very, very lucky, compared to many."

"But there are days," His Grace said, ambling up the walkway, "when you long to toss the lot of them into the Thames. I feel the same way about most of my patrons. I used to call them customers, but Pritchard broke me of the habit. Turning the conversation to the dog was inspired. Edwardia dotes on the old beast, doesn't she?"

"Charles was a gift from the late duke on a wedding anniversary. You will find more spaniels at the family seat, but Charles is her personal favorite."

The duke stopped and looked about the winter-dead, snow-encrusted garden. "I want to hate her—I'm entitled to hate her—but how can I hate a woman who dotes on her aging dog? She did not know what to do with me. She issued her writ of summons, I arrived, and it's as if she wasn't prepared for me to obey, though everybody obeys her." His Grace settled onto the bench by the sundial, making that venerable seat creak. "If you aren't cold, I'd appreciate a moment in the fresh air. Helps me wake up."

"A sound nap would help you stay awake." Mina took the place beside him. "William had no patience with Her Grace either."

"Tell me about William. It's his fault the dukedom has been foisted upon me. If that doesn't put a blight on a fellow's memory, nothing will."

"He wasn't a drunken wastrel," Mina said, though that was hardly a glowing encomium for a departed spouse. "We were friends."

The duke took off his hat and set it on the bench, closed his eyes, and turned his face up to the sun. "You miss him."

"I do. We'd known each other forever." A pair of robins settled on the holly bush near the gate and began systematically picking away at the berries.

"But then, one day, you realized your friendship had deepened." The duke's tone was humorous, even mocking. "You glanced at your darling and admitted you were in love?"

"One day, our parents decided we should be betrothed. I was seven, William was eleven. I played betrothal games with my dolls for the next three months. William took his wooden sword and went off to fight Americans or Vikings or the French. I take it you don't have much patience with romance?"

The robins paused in their snacking. The male flitted to a different branch, and the female resumed eating.

"I have a great deal of patience with romance," the duke said, opening his eyes and studying the birds, "provided one maintains perspective. All too often, when affection and desire combine, one falls in love with life itself. The air is sweeter, et cetera and so forth. Inevitably, passion runs its course, and each time its course is a little shorter and more predictable. If one is lucky, the path leads to lingering fondness, but it can also lead to sheer disaster. I can't support the notion that passing fancies should be glorified into a myth of lifelong devotion. Much misery lies that way, and what was once lovely becomes mutual torment."

William would have agreed with him. He'd delighted in explaining to his friends that he and Mina were very fond of each other, but for passion a man needed outlets other than his spouse, be she *ever so dear*.

"You won't mind the duchess finding you a wife, then?"

His Grace sat up. "I *beg* your pardon?"

His indignation was a balm to Mina's spirits. "If Your Grace is a proponent of the pragmatic union, then Edwardia will be happy to line up prospective duchesses for you to escort starting Tuesday next. She's likely doing that regardless of your views on marriage. Speaking as somebody who had no choice of husband, I can tell you that my daughter will decide marital matters for herself."

The female bird joined her spouse, while another robin watched from the garden wall.

"And if your darling Emily chooses a disowned Catholic Scotsman?"

"Then she'd better choose one who loves her for herself." Mina was growing upset, and her usual ability to set aside angry sentiments was nowhere to be found, but then, humoring Edwardia would tax anybody's store of manners. "You must marry, Your Grace, and the solicitors will doubtless harangue you about draft settlements and jointures until your ears ring. You are no longer young, and the dukedom is hanging by a thread."

"The dukedom can go to blazes as long as you and Emily are well fixed. What else will the solicitors want with me?"

His Grace was trying to change the subject, but Mina's mood refused to change with it. What was so foolish about expecting a confluence of affection and desire to grow rather than wither? William had dismissed the notion with gentle derision, and that was one aspect of marriage to him Mina did not miss at all.

Had he expected Emily to settle for such a tepid union? "The solicitors will expect Your Grace to make a will."

"I have a will."

"You will need a new one, providing for your retainers, making charitable donations, distributing the unentailed assets. Mr. Rohrer specializes in the drafting of wills, and he has a particular aversion to codicils."

His Grace rose and extended a hand. "I have a particular aversion to solicitors. We should get along splendidly. I offended you, didn't I, with my views on romance and marriage?"

Mina rose and did not withdraw her hand. "You did, a bit, and now I have offended you with my honesty."

He patted her knuckles. "Just the opposite. You give me the truth, and I appreciate it. My opinions were formed by too many experiences of life pushing me onward, and some female trying to keep my feet planted. One hates to disappoint a lady, but one needs to eat as well. When I left Belgium for Rome..."

He dropped her hand.

"Unpleasantness?"

"Loud, protracted unpleasantness, and accusations and recriminations, though nobody had made any declarations, much less signed agreements. I have never been so pleased to bid a lady farewell. I meant no harm, but harm was done. I didn't care for the experience *at all*, and I regret my part in it."

The young lady probably regretted her part in it more. "Be as forthcoming with your prospective duchess as you have been with me, and all should go well." Mina started walking toward the house, wondering if she could retract her offer of sustenance. Finn Cathcart had demanded good manners of the duchess, but that hardly made him a prince among men.

"And if I'm not interested in a duchess, prospective or otherwise?" he asked, ambling at her side. "If I have no interest in settlements and jointures and trusts?"

He might hold out for a time, or plead the new peer's preoccupation with a change of station, but inevitably, Edwardia would see him appropriately wed. The sooner the better, as far as Mina was concerned.

"If you want to foil the solicitors, then you make a will, and every time the lawyers circle closer, you pen a handwritten codicil. William became a genius at codicils, and the solicitors learned to leave him in peace."

"You are hoping I'll just wander off home now, aren't you? I have vexed you with my opinions and wasted half your day on a diplomatic errand that was none of your responsibility. I am sorry. I do appreciate your efforts with the duchess on my behalf, but by now, Emily has spied us from the nursery, and I would not want her to think I've forgotten my bears and their favorite dragon."

Mina regarded him in the weak winter light. "Do you want to wander off home?"

He smiled, looking unaccountably bashful. "Whether it's lack of sleep or the duchess's hospitality, I seem to be starting on a headache. That nap you mentioned is acquiring some belated appeal."

"Very well, a short call on the nursery, and then I'll send you on your way, but heed me on one other point, Finlay Cathcart."

"Madam?"

"Your parents' marriage was not a disaster. They would agree with me that any union that resulted in *you*—creator of dragons and bane of impossible duchesses—was successful in at least one material regard."

Mina reached the house first and held the door for her guest. He had nothing to say, all through the house and all the way up to the nursery. He spent a quarter hour sketching robins for Emily—the detail as amazing as the speed with which he worked—and talking art with Norwich, then Mina showed him out the front door.

She wished he'd stayed for lunch, now that he was gone, and she wished life hadn't made him so wretchedly practical about what should be matters of the heart.

CHAPTER SIX

"You have our permission to proceed," the Earl of Westhaven said. "If the finished subjects are as lovely as the sketches, my garden will be the envy of the peerage."

Finn rolled up the drawings, uneasy with Westhaven's praise. "You are happy to put all twelve statues in a circle? I tried various arrangements, some of them requiring alterations to your garden, but the three Graces and the nine Muses seem to want a circle in your case."

"I like the circular design," the Countess of Westhaven said. "Gives the garden a central focus, surrounded by beauty, art, and laughter. You will set a fashion, Your Grace. All over rural England, the ancient philosophers and statesmen will cede the field to the arts and graces. If you gentlemen will excuse me, I am expected for tea elsewhere. I trust you will manage the rest of the discussion without me."

Finn rose and offered her ladyship a bow.

Westhaven was on his feet in the next instant and escorting his wife to the door. Some low conversation ensued, which might also have involved the near occasion of nuzzling the countess's ear. As

Finn pretended to study the parlor's appointments—gracious, elegant, unremarkable save for the fragrant red roses on the sideboard —Westhaven kissed his wife's cheek, and she slipped out the door.

"My countess has abandoned us for better company in the nursery. How I envy her." Westhaven smiled, and all his aristocratic reserve disappeared. "Parenthood followed closely upon speaking our vows—I'm told it sometimes works that way—and I barely recall who I was before. My father is vastly amused, and my mother would be gloating, except that Mama is too kind to gloat."

Westhaven was not quite the pattern card peer. His hair was chestnut rather than blond. He'd never served in uniform, though both of his older brothers had, one paying with his life for that honor. He was bookish, mannerly, and practical, and yet... he'd ordered the Muses *and* the Graces, and the project had to have his countess's imprimatur at every step along the way.

Wilhelmina would approve of such a union. Finn wasn't quite sure what to make of it, but then, he'd been vaguely out of sorts since taking his leave of Mrs. Cathcart yesterday. Since meeting her, in fact.

Which was of no moment whatsoever. "Will you withdraw the commission now?" Finn asked, rather than listen to more lovestruck maundering from an otherwise dignified man.

"Why would I do that? Brandy?"

"A fresh pot, if you don't mind. I am at risk for getting my days and nights reversed, and I haven't that luxury at present. Spirits can have a soporific effect." Finn had napped the previous afternoon for three hours, which had inspired Pritchard to making tut-tut faces without mercy.

Westhaven tugged a bell-pull twice. "If you will excuse an impertinent question from a sympathetic observer, how are you bearing up?"

Finn could dodge the interrogation, but Westhaven was no gossip, and he was—*rara avis*—a ducal heir who had expected the quiet life of an extra spare.

"I hardly know," Finn said. "I'm to make some sort of obeisance before Prinny, but I'd rather have commissions from him. I was told to expect that every commission I do have will disappear, and three of them have." Polite notes, assuring Finn that the financial details were of no moment, but in light of the extraordinary circumstances... "My aunt, the duchess, had me to tea and talked about nothing save her dog. A return to Rome has acquired significant appeal."

"Edwardia is keeping her powder dry," Westhaven said, going to the door again, though nobody had knocked. He admitted a footman bearing a tray with all the trimmings, suggesting the kitchen always had one in readiness.

The footman set his burden on the sideboard, bowed, and left, all without making a sound.

"How did you know he was out there?" Finn asked.

"New papas have extraordinary hearing." Westhaven took the tray to the reading table by the window. "The duchess is likely waiting until you've attended a royal levee and done the writ of summons bit in the Lords before she presents you with prospective duchesses. You must, however, stand firm in the face of all this distraction."

"A ducal title is a distraction?" Finn certainly saw it thus.

"Most assuredly. The hostesses will swarm you like locusts, the hooligans in the Lords will be even worse. Supper at the club or a hand of cards—they will graciously insist—when they are after one of two things: your tiara perched upon the head of their daughter or niece or granddaughter, or your support for their pet bills. A man can hardly review his ledgers without interruption if he permits such nonsense to flourish."

Westhaven motioned Finn into a seat at the reading table and took a chair at a right angle to Finn's.

"And yet, my lord, your marriage is said to have been a love match, and the evidence of my own eyes supports the theory."

"You disapprove?" Westhaven poured out and added a dash of honey to Finn's cup.

"It's not my place to approve or disapprove, but I am puzzled. If a dynastic match is required, why did you choose on an impractical basis?" Finn was haunted by Wilhelmina Cathcart's pronouncement about his parents' marriage being successful. She'd looked so still and alone in that cold, dead garden, but her words had been infused with subtle fire.

Emily's mama possessed a well-guarded store of ferocity, also some peculiar notions. How could a union that had ended in three premature deaths be considered in any regard successful?

Westhaven sipped his tea, a fine gunpowder laced with the fragrance of jasmine. "Do you know how impractical it is to bind yourself for life to somebody you hardly know? How impractical it is to attempt procreation with same?" He shuddered. "Ridiculous notion. In fairness, the duchess will probably give you until spring to find your feet. All the best brides have left Town for the winter, so you have a few months to start on my commission."

Westhaven's smile bore hints of the wolf.

"You aren't withdrawing from our agreement?"

"Why the devil should I? Society doubtless expects you to drop the project, and I will make no complaint if you do, but I've seen your work, Huntleigh. My countess wants those statues in our garden, and thus I will not rescind my contract with you. If you must negotiate, then take on the three Graces, and we'll haggle over the Muses later."

Huntleigh. Who on earth was this Huntleigh person? Yesterday, when making her outlandish argument, Wilhelmina had used Finn's name. *Heed me on one other point, Finlay Cathcart.*

"If I continue to sculpt, won't that cause a great scandal?"

"You will cause talk with this project—we will—and you probably should not accept money for future work, but you are a duke now. Whether the old duchess likes it or not, talk will follow you based on your horse acting up in the park, your housekeeper scolding a foot-man, or your tailor turning away a viscount's custom. The viscount might have been slow to pay, of course, but your elevated status might also have figured into the calculation. All part of the distraction. Have a biscuit."

Westhaven helped himself to two.

Finn took one to be polite. Lemon was not his favorite. The jasmine tea was pleasantly reminiscent of Wilhelmina Cathcart, though. One had to be close to her to detect the fragrance she wore, and Finn had been appallingly close. God help him, he might even have commenced snoring on her shoulder.

She'd taken his lapse in stride, while Finn... "I never wanted to be a duke." Too much bewilderment showed in those words, not enough confident, manly disdain.

"I certainly dread the day I trade my courtesy title for member-ship in the peerage," Westhaven replied. "I hope my dear, meddling papa lives forever, just as he likely hoped my grandpapa would. The current Duke of Moreland was an extra spare, gone for a soldier. I was the bookish younger son, and I am still nearly as bookish as I'd like to be, and yet, I have become the heir."

This conversation came as a surprise and a relief. "You love books?"

"I love books, I love my morning hacks on old Pericles, I love my family past all bounds, and I admonish you to establish here and now that this title business will not part you from what you love. Mind you, I would not have spoken thus before my countess sorted me out."

"You were a dull boy?" Westhaven presented himself as tending to stodginess, until he chose a dozen statues of scantily draped young ladies to adorn his rural garden. Until he nuzzled his countess's ear, until he went prosing on about loving his aging horse.

"I was at risk to become the dullest boy in captivity," the earl said, "and I do mean captivity. I found my courage and my countess, and you see before you an exceedingly happy man. More tea?"

"No, thank you. My art makes me happy."

"Then keep creating your art." Westhaven topped up his own cup. "And don't fret about the protocol. Moreland will happily be your senior peer before the Lord Chancellor, and we'll recruit

Anselm for the junior role. Only dukes will do, you numbering among same. The levee will be the longest three hours of your life, so be sure you're wearing comfortable shoes. We'll round up Hard-castle and Sedgemere to accompany you for that ordeal. Needs must, and those two have enough stamina and wit for the job. Their bickering alone will keep you amused. Do you have your Writ of Summons?"

"It arrived yesterday." While Finn had been sleeping the sleep of the dead.

"The timing of the next part is up to you. Get the robes refur-bished—the old duke was shorter than you and not as muscular through the shoulders—and don't forget the black tricorn hat."

Westhaven spoke casually of matters that would never cross the minds of most Englishmen, and yet, Finn had the sense this discus-sion had been on his lordship's agenda.

Confirm garden commissions.

Flirt with countess.

Lecture Huntleigh.

Demolish plate of biscuits. Dispatch Huntleigh to the tailor's.

Sneak up to the nursery, there to adore offspring and resume flir-tations.

Not how Finn anticipated a prospective duke filling his after-noon, and all rather impressive, for being mostly enjoyable.

"I can have your three Graces done before Easter," Finn said, though his hands would curse him for that much haste. "The Muses could take several years, if we get that far."

Westhaven scooped up the last two biscuits, wrapped one in a handkerchief, and slipped it into his pocket. "Genius cannot be rushed." He gestured oratorically with his remaining biscuit and then bit it in half. "I tell my countess that all the time. I especially like your three Graces. They bear a sisterly resemblance to one another, and yet, they are each distinctly lovely. Why the kitchen must be so parsi-monious with sweets, I do not know. Shall I ring for more?"

The three Graces, as Finn had sketched them last evening, all

bore a resemblance to Wilhelmina Cathcart, though Finn had yet to
see the woman truly smile.

"You must, of course, ring for more biscuits if you please, though I
can't stay but another few minutes if I'm to stop by the tailor's on my
way home."

Westhaven rose. "Don't let me keep you. My regards to your aunt
when next you see her. She dislikes me only a little, though I fear she
disapproves of my father wholeheartedly. He's a terrible flirt, a trait
I've thankfully been spared."

Oh right. Unless the Countess of Westhaven was in the same
room. "My thanks for your hospitality, and I will enjoy completing
your commission."

"One suspected you would. I'll see you out." Westhaven bounded
off for the parlor door, but paused before opening it. "You'll need a
hostess, Huntleigh. Society will want to look you over starting last
week, and the colder months are a fine excuse to test the waters informally. An open house, a musicale, a card party... You could begin
with any of those—Lady Helmsby is keen on card parties—but you'll
need a hostess."

Finn had never needed a hostess in his long and storied life. "I
need peace and quiet and a great deal of solitude."

"Mrs. Cathcart might oblige," Westhaven said, as if the notion
had only just occurred to him. "Lady Helmsby is a bit long in the
tooth, though holding up well, and the duchess is still—based on her
attire—in mourning for her duke. She's also too daunting by half."

"I haven't even met Lady Helmsby."

"Then you'd best be about it. She doted on that idiot William,
and you will have to hear her lament his untimely demise. You will be
a busy duke, sir, and sooner begun is sooner done."

Pritchard's maxim. "I would rather be a busy sculptor than a busy
duke." More bewilderment where manly disdain should have been.
Confident manly disdain.

"Good luck with that, and whatever you do, don't give up your
morning hack."

Westhaven himself held Finn's greatcoat for him, and a butler passed over Finn's hat, gloves, and walking stick. When Finn was suitably decked out, the butler surrendered Finn's purple scarf and withdrew.

Finn wrapped the soft wool about his neck. "Thank you, Westhaven, for your commission and your kindness."

"When I become a duke—may the day be put off forever—I will expect you to accompany me before the woolsack. I'm simply exercising a prudent interest in a future peer's situation. Go make pretty statues for my countess."

Finn turned to leave—the day was frigid, and the walk home would be most refreshing—but offered Westhaven a final question.

"William Cathcart was an idiot?"

Westhaven's countenance underwent a subtle transformation. He was still the cordial, articulate, self-possessed exponent of wealth, learning, and privilege, but his demeanor cooled about the eyes and mouth.

"I should not speak ill of the dead, much less of your own cousin, but the man was an idiot of the first water. His wife had her hands full, and the work was slow, thankless going. Are you free for lunch at my club on Tuesday? I hide from her ladyship's at homes in the usual masculine display of discretion, and the next invasion is scheduled for Tuesday."

"Lunch will suit nicely."

"Until Tuesday."

Finn jaunted on his way, and when he should have been pondering Euphrosyne, Aglaia, and Thalia, he was instead preoccupied with Westhaven's assertion that William Cathcart had been an idiot.

An idiot of the first water.

"I know, Mina dear, that you had no choice but to accompany His Grace," Lady Helmsby said. "I'm sure Edwardia made the occasion unpleasant for you, but you did your duty. Another half cup, if you wouldn't mind."

Wilhelmina did mind. She'd minded everything since watching Finn Cathcart—His Rubbishing Grace of Benighted Huntleigh— stride through her back garden into yesterday's chilly winter afternoon. He'd appreciated her honesty while pronouncing her notions of love and marriage ridiculous, but in all fairness, he'd seen a love match from a much closer perspective than Mina had.

A close and tragic perspective, and thus Mina's annoyance was tinged with guilt.

She poured Mama-in-Law's tea and cast about for more small talk, while the longcase clock ticked and a parlor that should have been cozy felt stuffy.

Mina marshaled her patience and soldiered on. "His Grace struck me as being somewhat at sixes and sevens, my lady. He will adjust, I'm sure, though he might remain unconventional in some ways."

Mama-in-Law sipped her tea. "Dukes are permitted a few harmless eccentricities. If we find him the right duchess, she will take him in hand soon enough. Have you any ideas in that regard? You've met the man, while I, alas, have yet to have the privilege."

Mina took her time selecting from among the dozen pieces of shortbread arranged on a plate. Two problems had just been dumped into her lap.

First, Mama-in-Law intended to matchmake for the new duke, when matchmaking was absolutely and unequivocally the duchess's demesne. Mama-in-Law's great joy was twitting Edwardia, and had been since the ducal family had chosen Mama-in-Law for Lord Helmsby Cathcart.

Second, Wilhelmina was to serve as an accomplice in Mama-in-Law's foolishness.

A third, lesser problem had also been presented: Finn had

slighted the previous heir's mother by calling upon first Mina and then Edwardia. True, he'd met the duchess only yesterday, but Mama-in-Law never wasted time when manufacturing a grievance.

And in the insult category, as opposed to problems, Mina noted the reference to having done her duty. As a wife, Mina had failed her duty spectacularly by not presenting William with a son or two. Lady Helmsby's references to duty, duty, and duty always managed to remind Mina of that point.

"His Grace will call upon you soon, I'm sure," Mina said. "He has a thriving business to wind down, a household to close, legal affairs to tend to."

"I don't suppose he has any bastards?"

Mina barely managed to swallow her tea. "Whyever... I beg your pardon?"

"Bastards, poor relations, scandals... When a man acquires great wealth and standing, every crossing sweeper and his streetwalking sister come around with their hands out. The old duke gave generously to any number of charitable causes, and heaven knows the present titleholder has a colorful past. I foresee many opportunities for gossip, and worse, where the Cathcart name is concerned."

Lady Helmsby was never overtly malicious, but she harbored a penchant for subtle spite, one that frequently lurked behind *isn't it a shame that...* or *let us be grateful that...*

Let us be grateful that we at least *have Emily to remember William by.*

Isn't it a shame the Pletcher girl's great good looks are marred by that horrid laugh?

Isn't it a shame that Edwardia was never able to present her duke with sons?

"Finn Cathcart is a successful and talented sculptor," Mina said. "He's studied on the Continent, is fluent in several languages, and commands all the gentlemanly graces. But for him, the title would have gone into escheat, so whatever his shortcomings, he is the duke we have."

"Are your menses upon you, Wilhelmina? I vow you've grown preachy in widowhood, and the tone is not at all becoming. Finlay is the duke we have; you are quite correct. I nevertheless wish St. Didier had turned up other possibilities, men who haven't been gadding about the fleshpots of Europe in the name of art, for example. I'll have some more of that shortbread, though it's a bit dry."

Mama-in-Law took three more pieces of shortbread, while Mina held out the plate and willed herself not to look at the clock. She'd received Mama-in-Law in the informal parlor because the fire was kept lit, but the disapproving looks—at the carpet, the curtains, the unread pile of letters on the mantel—had started as soon as Mama-in-Law had taken a seat.

"Before I take my leave," Lady Helmsby said, "I must look in on dear Emily. The winter months can be so hard on those with delicate constitutions."

"Emily is in good health," Mina said before she could check herself.

Mama-in-Law sent her a pitying look. "If you'd been a mother longer than a few years, you'd know that a child's good health and her good spirits are different concerns. I'm sure Emily seems well enough to you, but we both know she's grown subdued and melancholic. I fear for her, though I have no idea where she gets her mournful tendencies. William was always such a cheerful boy."

In the normal course, this fault-finding and blaming were merely what passed for conversation with Mama-in-Law, and Lady Helmsby was always careful to include an element of truth in her criticisms.

Emily *was* mournful—she was entitled to be mournful, for pity's sake—but she was improving. She was also healthy, intelligent, and well mannered.

And William might have been the most cheerful boy ever to throw his porridge across the nursery—which he had done, countless times, by his own recollection—but he'd been a man capable of petulance and thoughtlessness.

"Norwich believes that undisturbed routine is helping Emily find her way," Mina said, though an outing to Gunter's—and a few fanciful carvings—had helped Emily find some joy. "Perhaps we should forgo a visit to the nursery today."

"You mustn't let the governess tyrannize you, Mina. I promise you, if only William were here, that woman would not put on such airs. The last thing, the very last thing, I will do is yield a few moments with my only grandchild for the convenience of a jumped-up nurserymaid. Put the fear of unemployment in Norwich, or you will soon regret it. Boys go off to Eton at age six, and some very good schools accept girls that young too. Excellent schools."

If William were here, he'd jolly his mama past such ridiculous talk, but Mina's jollying skills had deserted their post as of yesterday afternoon.

"Those schools cost a great deal of money," Mina said. "Norwich's wages are modest, and she is devoted to her charge."

"A widow must always be mindful of her means—of all people, I understand that—but *Emily* can afford the very best education. Wiliam made sure of that much."

No, he had not. Mina's settlements, negotiated by her family's solicitors, had made sure her offspring were provided for. Lindstrom family funds that might have been shared between a half-dozen sisters were instead held in trust for one small girl. Those quarterly bank statements were one article of correspondence Mina enjoyed reviewing.

"William was in every way a loving and affectionate papa," Mina said. "I suspect that's why Emily treasures his memory so dearly."

Mama-in-Law dusted her hands over her cup and saucer. "Undoubtedly, my dear. Undoubtedly, but life goes on. The sooner Emily learns that fact, the sooner she will cease pining. Let's see how she's faring, shall we?"

The temptation to fling the shortbread at Mama-in-Law's head was as overwhelming as it was sudden. Mina rose and stepped away from the tea tray.

"You're sure I can't see you out? Darkness falls so early this time of year."

"You shall see me to the nursery." Lady Helmsby stood, gave the parlor one last deprecating glance, and tugged the bell-pull.

Mama-in-Law had never reconciled herself to the notion that Mina was the hostess in her own household. Summoning a footman to clear the tray, insulting the governess, and dropping by unpredictably were symptoms of a general malaise that began with *if only William...* and never ended.

"I do hope we have an early spring this year," Mina said, leading the way to the stairs. "Winter has barely begun, and I'm already missing sunny days and early sunrises."

"An early spring inevitably means more flies," Lady Helmsby said, rounding the landing. "William hated bugs. Loathed them. Squashed every one he saw as a lad."

How charming. "I'm particularly fond of honeybees," Mina observed, which was bad of her. "Silkworms have a place in my heart as well."

"You are trying to vex me." Lady Helmsby moved ahead as they approached the schoolroom. "Perhaps Emily's low spirits originate from her mama's sour mood, Mina. A widow must be at all times poised and gracious. I know of what I speak."

When Mina would have tapped on the schoolroom door as a basic courtesy, Mama-in-Law sailed straight in and earned identical scowls from Emily and her governess. Norwich's expression shifted in an instant to bland deference. She was a pretty blonde, with lovely blue eyes, a memory elephants would envy, and a good sense of humor.

Though that sense of humor was nowhere in evidence at the moment.

"Good afternoon," Mina said, holding out a hand to her daughter. "We've interrupted your drawing lesson, and I apologize for that, but your grandmama did so want to see you."

Emily stood, bobbed a curtsey, mouthed the words, "Good day, Grandmama," and returned to her seat.

"A drawing lesson?" Lady Helmsby said, peering at the day's subject. "What is this peculiar creature? Is this supposed to be a dragon of some sort?"

"This is Draco," Mina said, picking up the little carving before Mama-in-Law could touch it. "A recent gift to Emily from His Grace. He made Draco just for Emily. The detail is amazing."

"His Grace is a very talented artist," Norwich said. "Yesterday, he spent nearly half an hour explaining that sketch on the mantel to Miss Emily. She watched him create the drawing, and he even signed it." Norwich was complimenting the new duke, so her observations could hardly be called impertinent, but Mina wished the duke's previous visit had gone undisclosed.

The sketch was wonderful—the two robins among the holly leaves, a few berries yet remaining. The feathers were fluffed exactly so against the chill, the male's head angled as if he was listening to his lady. The whole magnificently vivid composition conveyed a bright moment in a chilly day.

"The duke has been introduced to Emily?" Mama-in-Law asked as she studied the sketch. "How on earth did that come about?"

Norwich bent over her own rendering of Draco and appeared to study the dragon's wings.

"He called upon me," Mina said, "as Emily and I were departing for Gunter's, and he offered to escort us. I wasn't about to refuse him, nor did I think Emily should have to give up her outing."

Lady Helmsby left off perusing the robins and took up Emily's sketch of the dragon. Mama-in-Law was an excellent amateur artist, but if she insulted the child's efforts, Mina would...

Do what? *Finn Cathcart's words came back to her: The duchess feels at liberty to scold you on sight. Your mama-in-law, after raising exactly one drunken wastrel, thinks it allowable to criticize your parenting of Emily, who is a paragon, and the governess begrudges you an enjoyable outing with your daughter.*

He wasn't wrong, drat him. He wasn't even close to wrong, and now Lady Helmsby had barged into the nursery, intent on her usual isn't-it-a-shame and if-only-William mischief.

The dragon in Mina's hand wanted very much to go flying. Instead, Mina put him back on Emily's desk and plucked the drawing from Lady Helmsby's hand.

"This is quite good, Emily," Mina said, which was the simple truth given the artist's tender years. "You have the wings exactly as Draco holds them. Please remember to sign Draco's portrait, and I would love to have the finished version for my sitting room. Grandmama must wait her turn if she wants a sample of your art."

Emily's gaze sharpened in the manner of a child picking up an interesting adult undercurrent. "Yes, Mama. I can draw the Ursulas for Grandmama."

Mina stroked Emily's bent head and gave the child back her creation. "The Ursulas would enjoy that, I'm sure."

"The feet need work," Lady Helmsby said, "but I agree with your mother. A very good first effort. Perhaps you get your artistic abilities from me. If only William were here to enjoy the results. Mina, you may show me out now."

With unseemly relief, Mina did as she'd been ordered. All the way down the steps, along the corridor, and into the foyer, she expected Lady Helmsby to launch into a lecture, about dukes being inappropriate in the nursery, Norwich speaking out of turn, or dragons being an unfit subject for a child's art lesson.

Mama-in-Law held her peace, until Mina was bidding her farewell.

"I realize seeing Finlay Cathcart stepping into the shoes intended for William must be hard for you, Mina. A sculptor, of all things. A gadabout bon vivant who likely hasn't a decent club to his name. The whole business is wrong, but allowing the crown to get its hands on William's legacy would be even more wrong, so we cope as best we can. If Norwich begrudges Emily an ice or a visit from the duke, then Norwich is in want of sense. You may tell her I said so. William would understand."

On that unprecedented note of encouragement, Lady Helmsby took her leave.

Mina, ignoring her correspondence for the third straight day, grabbed her cloak and made her way to the back garden. She took the bench she'd shared with His Grace the previous afternoon and mentally sorted what had just happened.

For the first time in ages, Mina had asserted a bit of maternal authority in the nursery. Mama-in-Law had offered something constructive in parting. While icicles dripped and Mina's backside grew cold, she tried to identify what exactly she was feeling about another tiresome visit from Lady Helmsby.

Relieved that it was over, of course, and annoyed—Mina had meant to catch up on her correspondence rather than waste nearly two hours speculating about the duke's past—but beneath the relief and the usual annoyance lay something else.

That exchange in the nursery had left Mina just the smallest bit proud of herself, and that felt *wonderful*.

CHAPTER SEVEN

"And you will need a specific style of hat," Pritchard said, his list in his hand. "A plain—"

"Black tricorn." Finn took up another handful of cold, wet clay and added it to the mass taking shape around the wire armature. "Ordered it yesterday. Old Peterson could not stop congratulating me. I've been buying my hats from him for years, but you'd think he'd been given the royal warrant. Please stop pacing."

"I think better when I pace."

"You lecture better, and you also block the light momentarily every time you pass by a window." The studio was the reason Finn had bought the house—a wealth of windows in what resembled a huge cupola. Because the room was the remains of a previous owner's attempt at an observatory, the light was abundant in all seasons, or as abundant as light in London could be.

Pritchard tucked his list into a pocket. "Why are you doing this? Building the armature is apprentice work and hard on your hands. Antonio in particular has an eye for structure, and Matteo is more than competent with an armature when Luciano leaves off insulting him."

"Today is their half day, and the quiet is simply too precious to waste. Also, Westhaven and his countess have approved the first phase of the project, and I want to get the Graces completed before Easter."

Pritchard's features acquired a ruthlessly composed quality that presaged more lecturing. "You should have given the earl your regrets rather than accept a commission that will take years to complete."

What remained unsaid was that Finn's hands might not have those years, especially if he insisted on doing work better left to younger, unschooled talents.

"Sooner begun is sooner done," Finn said, feeling pleased with himself for tossing that verbal dart. "Besides, the studio is typically the warmest room in the house, and more snow is on the way." The studio was also Finn's favored haunt because a privy staircase led straight down to the garden, which meant coming and going at all hours was easily and discreetly done. Antonio, the oldest of the apprentices, had been making frequent use of that staircase at odd hours.

"Your hands can predict the weather now?" Pritchard asked.

Finn's left hip was his best weather predictor, but his left knuckles were growing more reliable by the week.

"I can see the sky," Finn said, "when you aren't blocking my light. Those clouds are full of snow." He slapped another handful of clay onto what would be Euphrosyne's right breast. The apprentices never got breasts right, though not for want of trying. They insisted that a life model would aid their education enormously, the naughty blighters.

But then, their antecedents had been distinguished for criminal enterprise rather than refinement. Antonio hailed from a family of distinguished forgers. Matteo's people were confidence tricksters, and Luciano was the scion of a clan known for extortion and blackmail. All three young fellows were managing Town's temptations as best they could.

Finn was shaping the underside of the breast when some fool

rapped on the studio door. Pritchard was across the room in an instant.

The rule of the house was that nobody disturbed Finn at work save Pritchard. Apprentices were always permitted to watch him if their own duties were complete, and questions from them were always welcome.

Trivial interruptions were *unwelcome.*

"Apologies," Duncan said, blushing as only redheads could blush. "Mrs. Cathcart would not be deterred."

The lady herself stepped around Duncan and came to a stop just inside the door. Whatever she'd expected to see, it wasn't Finn, naked from the waist up, his hands covered in clay, and two plump breasts taking shape on an otherwise genderless form.

"I'll send up some tea," Pritchard said, all but shoving Duncan from the doorway.

"And sandwiches," Mrs. Cathcart called, turning a gimlet eye on Finn. "Real sustenance, not watercress affectations with the crusts cut off."

In Finn's mind, two questions wrestled with his manners: *Madam, what the hell are you doing here?* and *Will you please model for me?* Fortunately, he was too astonished at Mrs. Cathcart's presence to voice either inanity.

"So lovely to feel warm for a change," Mrs. Cathcart said, taking Finn's shirt from a hook on the back of the door and holding it out for him.

"I need to wash my hands first, or I'll get clay all over..."

"Of course."

As he wrapped the armature's freshly applied clay in wet cloth, he realized that Mrs. Cathcart wasn't embarrassed by his dishabille. Wasn't unnerved in the least. She was a widow, after all, while Finn was at risk for making a complete ass of himself. When he'd finished with the wet cloths, he used the basin of water always kept warming on the hearth and dried his hands. He took the shirt from Mrs. Cathcart, got it over his head, and pulled it down over his middle.

"You are too skinny," she said in anything but admiring tones. "I hazard you work too hard as well."

"I love my work." Next should come the buttons, but Finn's fingers were not up to buttons. His *mind* wasn't up to buttons. *What was she doing here?* "I can recall going for days without food, and thus I tend to appreciate any opportunity for gainful employment. Westhaven and his countess have approved a large project, and I want to make a start on the first part."

Mrs. Cathcart stepped nearer and started on the several buttons of Finn's shirt. "You still have clay under your fingernails. I assume you have a penknife on hand to remedy that situation. Westhaven, as in Earl of?"

"The very same. Moreland's heir. He tried to convey that vanity compels him to demand that I honor the commission, but I suspect he's motivated by pity."

She smoothed her hand over Finn's sternum, the gesture putting him in mind of his thumb, gently coaxing clay into the shape of human features.

"Have you a neckcloth, sir?"

A neckcloth, yes; the sense to keep his mouth shut, apparently not. Finn handed her the requisite article, and she trussed him up in a loose mathematical. His waistcoat came next, which she also buttoned, and Finn's mortification was complete.

"How is Westhaven's commission an act of pity," she asked, "when your knuckles are already swollen from overuse, Your Grace?"

"Please don't Your Grace me. Not here, not now. My knuckles will be fine by tomorrow." His knuckles would never again be fine.

"Not if you continue to abuse them."

"Now you turn up fierce? With the duchess, you were deference itself. Emily's governess—who has some artistic talent, by the way—reigns supreme in the nursery, and your mother-in-law treats you like some clueless schoolgirl, but with me, you breathe fire?"

"With you, I state the obvious."

"For a woman merely stating the obvious, you seem very sure of yourself."

She smiled, and in that moment, Finn realized why William had chosen Wilhelmina over the entire throng of heiresses and diamonds who'd vied for his attention. Not because of some family-approved betrothal, not because of her settlements, which had doubtless been generous, and not because she radiated the robust good health necessary to hatch a brood of little lords and ladies.

That smile promised joy, laughter, and endless good fun to all in its ambit. Her expression wasn't even flirtatious, and yet, mischievous glee shone forth, along with a hint of challenge.

"I am sure of myself," she said, "and pleased to have caught you in your lair. You really are a sculptor."

"And once upon a time, I really did go for days without eating. Divine Providence and some skilled teachers have given me an ability to earn a living, and I will not ignore that gift."

She paced along the walls, where Finn had pinned Westhaven's sketches. She gave no sign that she saw any resemblance between her own good looks and the Graces.

"I suspect you cannot ignore your gifts." She repinned Aglaia's sketch slightly lower, to hang parallel with Thalia and Euphrosyne. "At the same time, you try valiantly to ignore the pain you're suffering. You eat a lot of sandwiches, don't you?"

"If I'm working." Cutlery was the very devil when a man's fingers throbbed. "Westhaven, abetted by his lovely countess, has seen to it that I will have work for years, if I need it. He cares nothing for the money spent or the bragging rights won, but he felt very strongly that I should have an excuse to continue sculpting."

Mrs. Cathcart picked up a stylus and passed it to Finn. "For cleaning your nails. You don't want those sandwiches to taste of clay." She settled on the divan that faced the fireplace, and there being nowhere else to sit comfortably—the desk was a mess—Finn took the place beside her.

"Did you sleep last night?" she asked.

"Not well. A new commission will do that, but my schedule is also off." He dealt with the clay beneath his nails and tried to ignore the note of jasmine blending with the peat smoke and mud that fragranced his place of work. "I suppose you enjoy the uninterrupted slumber of those with an easy conscience?"

He was hungry—very hungry—and hadn't realized it. Another symptom of a new commission, or perhaps of a new title.

"I do better in winter," Wilhelmina said. "A full night's rest when the sky is light until ten o'clock often eludes me. Books are my salvation in warmer weather."

A soft knock on the door had her on her feet and retrieving a tray. She closed the door with her hip, a charming, domestic movement, and set the tray on an upended crate before the divan.

"Eat, Your Grace."

"Call me Finn, please. If you call me Cathcart, that will put you in mind of your late spouse and put me in mind of him. You eat too, Wilhelmina." Finn was a duke, which should mean he was allowed to bend a few stupid rules when it came to forms of address.

"My familiars call me Mina."

She poured two mugs of tea—Mugs. What was the kitchen *thinking?*—and added a dash of honey to both.

"I prefer Willie for you," Finn said. "Has more substance."

She put two sandwiches on a plate and held it out to him. "You need more substance. You have good bones, but on close inspection, they are a bit too prominent. I will have a word with your cook and with Mr. Pritchard."

"Best of luck with that. Pritchard would make a better duke than I will, so great is his self-possession."

Mrs. Cath—Willie—bit into a sandwich. "Your majordomo is supposed to have self-possession, but he also has your best interests at heart. You vex him sorely with your self-neglect. This is good ham."

Good ham, good cheddar, fresh butter, and fresh bread, the lot gently toasted with a subtle dash of smooth mustard. "Ambrosia."

By the time Finn had started on his third sandwich, he was

feeling more the thing, and a light snow had begun to fall. His spirits were more settled, and somewhere in the house, Pritchard was scowling at the weather.

A cheering thought.

"You are probably wondering why I've intruded," Wilhelmina said, selecting a French chocolate from the offerings on the tray. "I haven't had one of these since last Christmas."

"Pritchard likes them. I suspect his mama was French. When he speaks French, his accent is pure Parisian salon. Have all you want."

Finn considered raising Pritchard's wages, because Wilhelmina in contemplation of a French chocolate was the embodiment of joy. Euphrosyne to the life, with a dash of Ate's penchant for mischief and reckless impulses.

"One," she said. "I will have one. You must have one as well." She held out the sweet, and rather than take it in his sore, clumsy fingers, Finn nipped it from her grasp.

He should have been appalled at his own forwardness. The lady was William's widow, the closest thing Finn had to an ally in the Cathcart family, and a decent woman.

And yet, he was not appalled. He took a second sweet from the tray and held it out to her. A dare, a passing foolishness, an impulse. Pritchard would despair of him for such nonsense, but Wilhelmina looked intrigued.

"They're scrumptious," he said. "Divine. You must not deny yourself."

"You are a bad influence." She nonetheless delicately took the treat between her teeth and, if such a thing could be done primly, savored her chocolate primly.

Then she grinned, helped herself to another chocolate, and Finn knew, beyond all reason and past any possible doubt, that he beheld a woman who could knock him top hat over teakettle and make him enjoy the indignity.

The chocolates were fresh, which told Mina that Finn Cathcart's household was well run. The merchants respected his custom enough to provide him prompt service and high-quality goods. He bought the chocolates for his butler, which further confirmed that the new duke could be generous with his means.

To Emily, he'd been generous with his time and talent, and with the duchess—whom he had every reason to revile—he'd been, if not gracious, at least civil.

Mina savored her chocolate and looked anywhere but at the present Duke of Huntleigh. In a thousand years of conjecturing, she'd never have anticipated finding him half naked, hands and forearms streaked with clay, every muscle and sinew rippling as he moved.

Some talented artisan should be sculpting *him*. He had the warrior's lean fitness on a grand scale, and yet, those hands suggested he'd fought too many battles with cold, wet clay, exhaustion, and demanding patrons.

"I'm here to bother you," Mina said, mentally admonishing herself that two chocolates were quite, quite enough, to say nothing of any foolishness involving same. Though, to be fair, His Grace had started the foolishness. "You have yet to call on Mama-in-Law, and she has remarked your oversight."

"You couldn't simply send a nagging note?"

He was doing justice to a third sandwich, and Mina was pleased to note that his manners were as delicate as the fare allowed. His lips were delicate, too, when taking a sweet from her hand.

Foolishness on top of nonsense wrapped up in imprudence, but also... winsome. Sweet rather than shocking.

"You would have ignored a note. I know all about ignoring correspondence. A note would have required a reply, and holding a pen after a day in the studio is likely beyond you. You would glance at my words, conclude the matter wasn't urgent, and elude the problem indefinitely."

"Holding a pen at the end of the day isn't beyond me, but neither does it have much appeal. Pritchard relieves me of as much of the clerical burden as he can, though he wouldn't touch my personal correspondence. Tell me about your mother-in-law."

Gone was the fellow with the mischievous forget-me-not eyes, and in his place was a tired man gathering information on yet another ordeal to be endured.

"Lady Helmsby is not awful," Mina said. "I much prefer her to the duchess. Her Grace is aloof, while Mama-in-Law is only occasionally catty and often simply talkative. She loved William to distraction, and he was very fond of her. Through William, she was to have the final triumph over Edwardia, who was merely a second duchess. Lady Helmsby foresaw becoming the mother of the next duke, you see, and grandmother of the one after that."

Finn cradled the mug of tea in his hands, likely enjoying the warmth. "Disappointed women give me the collywobbles. I disappointed a countess once. She destroyed a month's worth of my work without breaking a sweat. She compensated me when her temper had cooled, but the wound never quite healed."

"Mama-in-Law is not given to overt drama. She is patience itself when pursuing her ends, and her star rises or falls with your own, so she will charm you to the best of her ability. She's likely hoping to become your hostess."

Mina's observation provoked a scowl. "I have no intention of entertaining Mayfair's fops and fashionables at great expense to me when I've work to do. The Season is months away. Let them wait until spring to inspect me."

Well, then. His Grace meant to hide away in his studio, perhaps for the rest of his life. While great art would result, so would sore hands, missed meals, and—Mina had to mentally cast about for the word—loneliness.

"All work and no play makes Jack a dull boy," she said, resolutely ignoring the remaining six chocolates.

Finn snitched a chocolate, tossed it into the air, and caught it in his mouth. "All play and no work makes Jack a mere toy, to say nothing of turning Jill into an insufferable twit. Have another chocolate."

"They are better for being savored."

He finished his tea. "Three is hardly an orgy, Wilhelmina." His tone was gentle, perhaps pitying, and pity was the one sentiment Mina never wanted to endure from anybody.

She was not the perennially bereaved widow, pining for the lost glory of her marriage and never had been.

"William was a toy," she said, gaze on the roses decorating the porcelain teapot. "Lady Helmsby disparages you for being a gadabout artisan, but Willliam was the prince of gadflies. He was easily bored, restless, always buying a new hunter or a new hat simply for the pleasure of acquisition without respect to practicalities." Mina willed herself to cease speaking—cease complaining. "An excess of chocolate apparently turns me up loquacious. I do apologize."

Finn topped up her mug and poured more for himself. "I knew William in passing. He struck me as harmless, without malice. Also without more than garden-variety honor, which suffices in most instances, though he chafed under the otiose existence of the heir."

"Otiose?"

"Fribbling, useless, having no practical purpose, fruitless. I suspect as an extra spare, my father felt the same way about his life in polite society. I picked up the word from a theological author. Earned me a raised eyebrow from Pritchard the first time I trotted it out. I live to raise Pritchard's eyebrows."

"You live to make your art too."

Finn patted her hand, a callused palm stroking over her knuckles. "Exactly. Don't be too hard on old William. He was always cordial when our paths crossed, and once he even asked if I was managing adequately. He might have steered one or two commissions my way."

"I didn't know that." But the knowledge helped, and that Finn Cathcart would pass it along helped too. "I do miss him, sometimes."

"I miss the difficult countess, sometimes. I owe most of my knowledge of Italian painting to her."

"Did she toy with your affections?" And would it have been a bad thing if she had?

"She was seventy if she was a day. Toying with my affections didn't come into it, but with my pride, my self-confidence, my artistic abilities, my arrogance... She put me through my paces like a drill sergeant with a particularly green recruit. We parted friends, I think. Did William toy with your affections?"

The question was posed casually. Mina was tempted to offer a flippant response, but in all other company, she was limited to a widow's respectful platitudes. Finn expected honesty of her, and that was... a rare relief.

"Yes, in a sense, William toyed with my affections—or took them for granted. As if adoring him was both my duty and pleasure, though he didn't feel compelled to adore me in return. I wanted our marriage to be a union, a partnership in spirit, though I understood that our spheres would not overlap much. I had no interest in playing cards at all hours at the club—not that they would have admitted me—and William would have been a terrible shopping companion."

"But you wanted some common ground?"

"Common ground, common goals, common activities. Westhaven and his countess hack out together regularly. The old duke escorted Edwardia to Almack's and stood about in his knee breeches making small talk by the hour, because Almack's was her royal court, so to speak. The only goal in my marriage to William was to produce a son, and—though I am mortified to admit it—that pursuit became perfunctory and tedious. I should be blushing."

Or leaving, never to return. Those French chocolates must have contained some elixir of indiscretion, because the conversation had moved beyond honesty to confidences.

"You should be kicking William in memory," Finn said. "If there's one aspect of marriage to which a man is honor-bound to apply some imagination and consideration, it's intimate congress with his wife. A lady risks her life in childbed. She should at least have some pleasure in pursuit of conception. Now I should be blushing." He sipped his tea placidly and offered Mina a half-bashful, half-piratical smile.

Mina sampled her tea as well, the better to adjust to some extraordinary thoughts. The first idea to upend her mental landscape was the notion that *this* was what she'd wanted with William—an ability to discuss anything, at any time of day. To share a tray of sandwiches and honest conversation with him while the fire burned down and the next snowfall started up. To be at ease with him behind a closed door and to relish the time spent.

No intrusions, no distractions, no concern for the fellows at the club or the duchess's latest summons—just two people, expressing themselves and listening to each other on topics that mattered but were seldom aired.

More than that, though, Mina was aware that Finn Cathcart's version of *some imagination and consideration* would be the blazing opposite of perfunctory. Glorious, in fact.

Dangerously glorious, and he'd ruin her for anything less. Most shocking of all, a disappointed, determined part of Mina longed for that ruin to the exclusion of all else.

CHAPTER EIGHT

Finn was accustomed to appreciating the female form in all its guises. He knew from careful observation how a woman's breasts shifted when she raised her arms above her head, and he understood that women inhabited their bodies differently from men.

For some ladies, the body was a weapon wielded to stupefy the unwary. For others, the body was a testament to domestic wars fought and lives brought forth and nurtured. In the usual case, the male form wasn't half so full of *life*.

He noticed Wilhelmina Cathcart's appearance as any artist would—vivid coloring, statuesque proportions, feminine curves—all quite lovely, worthy of oils rather than watercolors, certainly—and that should have been an end to it. Instead, he'd gone on noticing— her concern for Emily, her stubborn refusal of her favorite ice, her kindness to the duchess, and now, her ferocious honesty where William was concerned.

He took her hand loosely, owing to his own limitations and because he wasn't entirely sure what the gesture was supposed to mean. He simply wanted her to have his hand to hold if she pleased to hold it.

"I'm sorry William bungled, and that is precisely what he did."

"Your Grace—Finn—I should not be burdening you with my unflattering recollections. Mama-in-Law has harangued me at length about my duty as a wife, and my shortcomings, and my inability to—"

"Do hush, please. I'm trying to think, and the task has become unaccountably difficult."

She rubbed her thumb across his palm. "You are befuddled?"

"If you keep that up, I will become incoherent. Willie... The last thing I want to do is offend or disappoint you, and the first thing I want to do, much to my own astonishment, is kiss you."

She glowered at their joined hands. "I'm not kissable?"

Truly, William had been an idiot. "*I* am not kissable. I'm not the kissing sort anyway. I focus on my work. I have learned to avoid entanglements and navigate around any temptation that could become complicated."

Wilhelmina withdrew her hand. "I haven't exactly been a merry widow, if that's what you're implying." She sat back with more dignity—and more dearness—than any mere duchess had ever commanded.

"I haven't been the itinerant rogue Lady Helmsby paints me either. I am at sea here, my dear. On the one hand, I want to kiss you and damn the consequences. On the other hand, if my overtures fall short or offend, I will feel like the greatest fool ever to drop an ancient Greek vase of incalculable beauty. This is new terrain for me."

What had he just admitted? He, who believed that romance was an illusion and a trap and that fondness was the wiser course for any couple? Perhaps he'd admitted nothing more than that he'd had too much of work, and Wilhelmina had had too much of dullness.

"I am at sea too," Wilhelmina said, curling herself along his side and repossessing herself of his hand. "I am sensible. Sensible girl, sensible wife, sensible widow. No frolics allowed. Perhaps, if we are both uncertain, then we can agree that rushing in any direction won't serve us."

He looped an arm around her shoulders and considered her

suggestion. "I don't want to rush away." Another surprise.

"Though some part of you, and a very loud part of me, advises that very course, but let's not rush forward in any sort of panic either." She drew her knees up so she was positively cuddled against his side. "This is nice."

Finn would have used a few other words—unexpected, a bit awkward—but nice too. Not passion, not folly, but something steadier than either, something that rewarded patience and courage—Westhaven's word—and built a foundation for more than simple passion.

He didn't quite fall asleep on the comfy sofa with a warm bundle of Wilhelmina tucked against him, but he came to a state of utter relaxation and peace and hoped she did as well. Her breathing slowed, her head became a weight against his shoulder, and *nice* became a moment of such sweetness that Finn simply marveled.

Mama-in-Law was in good form, welcoming Mina and the duke with a smile of such dazzling graciousness even Mina was impressed. The tea was hot, and the if-onlys were mostly kept at bay until the requisite two cups had been consumed.

"If only William had settled sooner to marriage," Mama-in-Law said, gaze upon the wall that held various portraits of the deceased. Sketches of William as a boy surrounded a formal portrait done on his twenty-first birthday. Over the mantel, a pair of portraits in oil—William at five-and-twenty next to his late, distinguished sire at the same age—held pride of place.

"Had William lived," her ladyship went on, "Your Grace would not have been forced to abandon the work that has gained you such acclaim, and poor Mina and I would not be prostrate with grief."

That was doing it rather brown. Mina had been surprised by William's death, shocked even and deeply saddened. At the same time, the manner of his dying had not surprised her at all—a foolish lark gone tragically awry. Mourning for William had come and gone.

Mourning for the old duke had as well, and Mina wasn't prostrate with anything save boredom.

Mama-in-Law offered the duke the plate of tea cakes, though Mina had found them a bit stale.

"No more for me," His Grace said. "What does settling to marriage have to do with a young man falling from a fractious horse?"

Mama-in-Law was the picture of patience as she helped herself to a cake. "Marriage assists a man to step into his responsibilities. We had so hoped that Mina would be a steadying influence on William, and she doubtless would have been, eventually. William doted on Emily—excessively, some might say—but a son would have been the making of him. A man needs sons, you know."

His Grace—notably manly in all details—looked puzzled. "As I understand it, William was approaching thirty when he went to his reward. You're telling me he had yet to comport himself as an adult?"

Lady Helmsby studied her half-nibbled cake. "An heir's lot is difficult. He cannot assume the titular duties, and he cannot turn his hand to the professions. I'm sure Mina tried to guide William gently into calmer waters, but a young wife must be, above all things, patient in her duties. Had William not been so reckless, so full of youthful zest... Ah, well."

That balderdash was accompanied by more fond, wistful gazes at William's personal portrait gallery.

Mina mentally counted to twenty in French while holding the gaze of Mama-in-Law's obese white cat. William hadn't cared for Hector at all, and Mina suspected the sentiment was mutual. The cat occupied a hassock near the hearth, one reserved for him, if the abundance of feline hair thereon was any indication.

The old duke had been after his nephew constantly to take the solicitors in hand rather than hide away in the clubs, fencing salons, and gaming hells. William could have applied himself to managing the ducal properties, reading law, pursuing a seat in the Commons... Many doors had been open to him, but the only doors he'd sought to darken were in St. James's and its surrounds.

"I don't recall my mother being very patient with my father," Finn said, finishing his tea. "And he adored her."

Lady Helmsby's tea cup clattered to its saucer. "I do beg your pardon, Your Grace, but it must be said that your mother ruined Lord Thornton. You weren't born yet, so you couldn't possibly appreciate the scandal she caused, tempting him from all propriety. The times weren't as tolerant as they are now, and she was a Papist, Scottish, from the merchant class... A perfect *horror* of a choice for his lordship. A discreet arrangement would have been acceptable, perhaps, if—"

Finn rose. "My mother was a good, decent, godly woman who suffered much for the privilege of becoming Lady Thornton. If you continue to malign her, my dealings with you are at an end."

The duke had expressed himself civilly, but such was his height and his ability to speak with gravity rather than volume, that he might have been hurling thunderbolts from Olympus.

Mina grasped that he was truly angry, his honor offended. He did not mean that he'd take his leave, he meant that Lady Helmsby would be cast into the social darkness reserved for those whom His Grace disdained to acknowledge. Mina had seen William pitch any number of tantrums—throwing his boots at the wardrobe, dashing a glass of brandy against the hearth, ranting—but this quiet warning was evidence of real outrage.

"I..." Lady Helmsby's expression became guarded, then calculating as she gazed up at her guest. "I meant no offense, Your Grace. I do apologize."

For Lady Helmsby to apologize without appending a *but*, *nevertheless*, or *however* was surely deserving of a notice in the *Times*.

Well done, Your Grace of Huntleigh. Mina sipped her tea—weak, for all it had been served hot—and thought of rich, French chocolates and the brush of Finn's lips against the back of her hand. Two days ago, they had stayed on the couch in his cozy aerie for nearly an hour, sometimes talking, sometimes falling silent.

Finn's hand caressing her hair had been a revelation of tenderness.

They had not kissed, had not even fully embraced, and yet, everything Mina thought she knew about desire and closeness had been turned on its head. Desire was more than the urge to rut, or it could be. Desire could encompass the mind as well as the body. Desire could inspire endless patience and passionate curiosity, rather than mere lust.

Mina had been pondering the puzzle of what she felt for Finn since he'd bowed over her hand in parting and brushed his lips across her knuckles. Whatever was emerging between them, it was neither the giddy foolishness of infatuation, nor the passing annoyance of animal spirits.

Finn resumed his seat. "Apology accepted. What can you tell me about the family seat, my lady?"

He was gracious in victory and let Mama-in-Law prattle on about the Elizabethan wing and the neglected gardens—"Edwardia dotes on those wretched dogs, but hasn't a care for maintaining the grounds"—and the aging stewards. By the time she'd concluded her recitation, Mama-in-Law was back on her mettle.

"If you ask me—not that you have, Your Grace—old Gooch needs to be put out to pasture. He can barely hear on a good day, and the tenants feel no compunction to heed his direction. The land will suffer, mark my words, if Gooch continues in the post of steward. William always had such great feeling for the land, you know. He was considering having the Riddle boy raised to the post of under-steward."

That was news to Mina. William had dreaded his annual sojourn to the ancestral pile, and his feeling for the land had been limited to assessing whether the terrain lent itself to a good gallop. Mina wondered, not for the first time, how William had turned out as good-natured as he'd been, what with his mother's endless fantasies weighing down his spirit.

"Before I make any changes," Finn said, "I will have a long and detailed discussion with the solicitors and the senior retainers."

Mama-in-Law's eyes took on a particular gleam. "You will not consult the duchess?"

"She will have her say in matters that directly affect her."

Lady Helmsby sat up very straight. "Please know that what I am about to impart is meant with only the sincerest regard for your welfare, Your Grace."

As surely as sparks flew heavenward, to paraphrase an appropriate verse, Mama-in-Law was about to slander somebody with faint praise and neverthelesses.

"Do go on, my lady."

"Her Grace has only the best intentions as well—we must state that at the outset. Nevertheless, you surely grasp that—as outlandish as the notion is—she regards finding you a duchess as both her right and duty."

Finn put his empty cup and saucer back on the tray. "Surely, Lady Helmsby, a woman of your discernment and perspicacity can convey to Edwardia that her meddling will not be tolerated. I am of age and in possession of my wits. Should the day ever come when I seek to marry, I will—*like my father and my mother*—make my choice unencumbered by any Cathcart family schemes."

Mama-in-Law was rendered at a loss for words, however briefly. She recovered, bowing her head with an uncharacteristic display of humility.

"Of course, Your Grace," she said. "Of course, I shall attempt to reason with Her Grace, though you will find that Edwardia is not one to heed sensible guidance. I will try my best, but she *is* the duchess. Mina will confirm that Her Grace can be very fixed in her opinions."

"Very fixed," Mina said. Rather like Lady Helmsby, William, the late duke, the solicitors, and even old Charles.

Finn smiled, showing a lot of white teeth. "I am accustomed to fashioning my art from solid stone. Her Grace will either accommodate my wishes or make the very close acquaintance of whatever passes for the Huntleigh dower house."

That was sufficient to inspire Mama-in-Law to cooing and beaming, though after five minutes of her raptures, His Grace was on his feet again. He handed Mina up into his gargantuan Town coach shortly thereafter and took the place beside her.

"God and all his angels, Willie. My sympathy for William, and for you as his appointed supervisor, knows no bounds, and I swear I have eaten my last stale tea cake. That woman is a terror."

Willie. So much friendlier than Wilhelmina. "You handled her well. Firmly, but without malice. I wish I'd realized earlier that she responds to that approach."

The coach pulled away at a sedate walk.

"She positively glowed at the notion of banishing the duchess to the dower property. I'm doubtless expected to inspect that and all the other real estate held by the dukedom."

"You needn't sound so put upon. The land is all in the Home Counties, most of it in Kent and Surrey, with a hunting box out in Berkshire. The dower house is lovely if somewhat outdated in its appointments. I would be very comfortable there."

"No, you would not." He tossed his hat and gloves onto the opposite bench. "You would go utterly to waste, entertaining the vicar and his wife the first Sunday of every month, admiring new babies, and dutifully keeping up your correspondence."

"As long as I have Emily and enough books, I will manage, and when it comes to correspondence, I'm not nearly dutiful enough."

He slanted a look at her. "How is it you still have Emily? She must be something of an heiress, and having met Her Grace, I can't see Edwardia content to leave the girl in your hands."

"William's will, which he changed monthly when put out with the solicitors, was very clear that I am to have the raising of Emily. Her funds are safely in trust until such time as marriage settlements must be negotiated, or she attains her majority, whichever shall first occur."

"Are your funds adequate?"

Mina liked that he would ask her rather than the solicitors. "I'm comfortably fixed. My family made certain it would be so."

Finn rapped a gloved fist on the roof, and the horses swung into a trot. "Lady Helmsby is either given to cheeseparing or she's an incompetent manager."

Mina attributed many faults to Mama-in-Law, but she *excelled* at managing. As for the cheeseparing... "Lady Helmsby patronizes Madame Bernadette, and that is not the behavior of a woman given to economies."

"The tea was weak, the wallpaper curling at the side of the hearth. The tea cakes were stale. Nobody has brushed that obese cat since it strutted off the Ark, which suggests staff indulging in the sort of rebellion that smacks of wages paid late. The pillows did not match the sofa, though they were close. Borrowed from a room that gets less sunlight, I'd guess. Her ladyship makes me uneasy."

How had Mina missed those blatant lapses in the home of a woman who criticized others so freely? "You made her more than uneasy."

"Suppose I did. Shall we go for an ice to reward ourselves for having done our duty?"

For about one revolution of the coach wheels, Mina considered demurring. "My correspondence can wait. An ice would be lovely."

Finn rapped three times on the coach roof, suggesting he'd anticipated an outing to Gunter's before he'd even arrived at Lady Helmsby's door.

"You will indulge in a vanilla treat this time, won't you?" Finn asked. "I certainly intend to."

French chocolates, vanilla ices. What next? "Yes."

"Excellent. Then that only leaves me to wonder when, darling Willie, you will indulge me with a kiss."

Finn's challenge met with a silence that filled the entire coach, the same sort of silence that arose when he'd misread a client, and the client was looking at sketches that were all wrong for what they'd had in mind.

An awkward, fraught, *bungled* silence. "I'm teasing, Willie. You needn't take offense."

"I am not offended." She wasn't delighted, either. "But I had hoped..."

While the carriage rolled on its stately way, Finn pondered what could be worse than having offended Wilhelmina? Having disappointed her, that's what. Amusing her with his overtures would be worse still, which was some consolation. Wilhelmina wasn't laughing at him. Yet.

"You had hoped?" Finn had certainly hoped. That little interlude in his studio had filled him with all sorts of unnamable longings, and a few that he could label all too easily.

"I was... forward the other day, when I interrupted your work," Wilhelmina said. "I intruded, and I might have displeased you."

"Pritchard displeases me. You... I don't know when I've enjoyed an intrusion more."

"But you might have ordered me from the premises, and I would have had no choice but to decamp with my tail between my legs."

Finn, whose tail had spent plenty of time between his legs, made a leap. "You had to make all the overtures with William?"

She pulled off her gloves, finger by finger. "If I had to characterize my marriage to your cousin with one word, that word would be 'exhausting.' William hadn't a mean bone in his body, but he had an ample store of lazy bones. I had to rewrite his correspondence because his spelling and penmanship were terrible. His valet bothered me constantly because William never made a decision if he could avoid the effort. He loved Emily, but other than when he was showing her off in the carriage parade, he couldn't bestir himself to learn to *know* her."

Finn's hands were bare, and that seemed to him to be a fine coincidence when Wilhelmina's were too. He slipped his fingers through hers.

"And the ducal succession hovered over your marriage like a foul miasma. William expected you to take the initiative there too?"

That question earned him one short, unhappy nod, while Wilhelmina gazed at the window shade, which had been pulled down.

"I was to *inspire* him. That was his word. Inspire his passion. According to William, a man is not a stud colt who merely has to catch sight of the breeding shed to rise to the moment. I knew that, but one grew weary and *bored* with the challenge. I am revealing my rural upbringing and my forthright nature. Not well done of me."

Poor William. He had *bored* his wife, intimately and otherwise, and that had to be worse than provoking her disappointment *and* her ridicule simultaneously.

"Sometimes, I'd go for days without seeing my husband," Wilhelmina went on more softly, "but he was always underfoot in the darkness, night after night, unless the week of the month had arrived that allowed me the privacy of my bed. I sometimes think he kept a mistress strictly for appearances. She never conceived. I made it a point to inquire after the funeral."

Finn was comforted to know William had bungled—bungled too —and also relieved, because the way forward was clear and within his abilities—*quite* within his abilities.

He wrapped Wilhelmina's hand in both of his. "So you might find me interesting, but you are hoping your turn has come to be on the receiving end of inspiration?"

The shade was receiving steady scrutiny. "You are very interesting. Nonetheless, I am sure that if the inspiring cannot be at least mutual, most of the time, then a vanilla ice will be the extent of the pleasures we share."

"You've thought this through." Cause for delight, as far as Finn was concerned.

"I'm not the sort who can treat intimacies lightly, and you bring to mind intimacies, Finn Cathcart."

"So do you, darling Willie." He looped an arm around her shoulders, and she settled against him and tucked her hand into his. The coach stopped—London traffic frequently stopped—and Finn wished Wilhelmina wasn't wearing a bonnet.

She had the softest hair and a will of granite. A lovely combination.

"I once went at a lovely piece of white Carrara too fast," he said as outside the coach, shouting arose. "My commissions were beginning to stack up, and I was worried that they would unstack if I couldn't produce results quickly."

"You knew better."

"I knew better, but you have no idea how the ghost of poverty can haunt a young man. In any case, I whacked when I should have tapped, and the marble obliged my efforts. I'd been disrespectful of my medium, and a sizable chunk of stone went crashing to the floor when I'd intended only a minute reduction. I was shaping a shoulder, and abruptly, my subject went from a graceful goddess to... an expensive mess."

Wilhelmina snuggled closer. "What did you do?"

"The only thing I could do. I reduced that statue in all of her dimensions. The odd thing is, my goddess was a better creation for being smaller and more delicate. Instead of looming in her alcove, she imbued her surrounds with serene grace. Maybe we should take our inspiration from her."

The coach lurched forward.

"Reduce our expectations?"

"You do not have to inspire me, Wilhelmina, and I am no god, to rouse passion and devotion past all bounds. I'm a man with sore hands, some talent, and a good eye for detail. We are interested in each other, and that's for us to savor and explore as we please. Ducal successions, family expectations, and meddling relatives don't come into it unless we say they do."

"Your aunt's spies will leave us little privacy."

"There are no spies in this coach. Might I remove your bonnet?"

"Yes." Her reply was immediate.

Finn's fingers were up to the challenge of easing the bow undone and lifting Wilhelmina's millinery from her head. His heart was up to the challenge of posing the next question.

"And might I kiss you?"

"I was hoping you would."

Finn's marble goddess—and a thousand other blocks of stone—had taught him the utter necessity of patience, of paying attention, and of noticing what others missed.

He noticed, for example, that Wilhelmina's breathing was slow and even. She wasn't nervous, and that was good. He noticed that when sitting, the difference in their heights was less evident, but he nonetheless left the bench and knelt, facing Wilhelmina on the carpeted coach floor.

He slipped his hands along Wilhelmina's waist, and she leaned near enough to rest her forehead on his shoulder. They stayed like that for a moment, his arms around her, her weight resting against him, then Finn marshaled his fortitude and kissed her cheek.

She went still, and he did it again, aiming closer to her mouth. By degrees, she turned her head to meet him, until soft lips met softer, and everything in Finn rejoiced. So sweet, so... feminine and luscious and lovely.

The coach horses plodded along while Finn's heart soared. He remained in the position of a happy supplicant until the coach again came to a halt, and even then...

"You'd best get up," Wilhelmina said, trailing her fingers along his jaw. "If we aren't at Berkeley Square, we will be soon."

"Then John Coachman should set a course for Bristol."

Wilhelmina ruffled his hair and smirked at him. A ladylike, impish smirk, but a smirk all the same. "You'd kiss me all the way to Bristol?"

Finn resumed the place beside her. "We'd kiss each other." He stated a simple fact rather than a boast. They *had* kissed each other, and caressed each other, and breathed together, and smiled together when the coach had swayed around a corner and Wilhelmina had clutched at his shoulders.

"I like kissing in your coach, sir."

Finn applied his mind to that announcement, when he wanted to trace the shape of Wilhelmina's lips while she spoke.

"Because we were kissing simply to kiss," he said, "without eighteen generations of peers lurking in the mental shadows, tapping their booted feet until the Huntleigh nursery is overrun with little boys?"

"Precisely. A kiss for kissing's sake. I hope you enjoyed it." Wilhelmina busied herself restoring her bonnet, but Finn heard the question she'd nimbly dodged.

"If I enjoyed it any more, the coach would have burst into flames of celebration. All of my goddesses will be smiling if I think of that kiss while I sketch them."

Wilhelmina was smiling, too, and that... that was better than all the vanilla ices and exquisite marble in the world.

"I like this," Wilhelmina said, patting Finn's knee. "This honesty and affection and plain speaking. I like it a lot."

"That's not the best part," Finn said, taking her hand lest she pat him right out of his wits.

"What's the best part?"

"I am an excellent speller in four languages."

When Duncan let down the steps some moments later, Wilhelmina had composed herself. To appearances, she was the proper widow on a short outing in the company of the new title-holder. Nothing remarkable about that, and nothing remarkable about vanilla ices, even if the day was chilly.

To Finn, Wilhelmina was the most remarkable exponent of creation ever to walk the earth, and—wonders abounding—she apparently rather liked him too.

CHAPTER NINE

"What has you in a taking now?" Finn asked, adding a dollop of wet clay to the underside of Euphrosyne's left breast.

Pritchard prowled the room, straightening sketches that hung perfectly plumb, turning the same potted fern he'd turned yesterday.

"One might better ask, Your Grace, what had you whistling the *Catalogue Aria* when you came in from tea with Lady Helmsby?"

Pritchard knew opera, and for reasons grasped by only the Almighty, Mozart's *Don Giovanni* was one of his favorites.

"The tune is lighthearted and written for my range. Hand me that butter knife."

Pritchard inspected the requisite article before passing it over. "When did Greek nymphs acquire such generous endowments?"

"This is a Grace, not a nymph." Finn began humming the aria in hopes of driving Pritchard back to whatever ledgers and pantries he'd abandoned. "This Grace is named for merriment, mirth, joy... She's entitled to her endowments."

The memory of Wilhelmina's endowments danced in Finn's mind as he used the butter knife to define the crease between the underside of the breast and the chest wall. Darling Willie had snuggled close enough to his side that nature's generosity had been evident, and now...

"Why not use a palette knife like a normal sculptor?" Pritchard asked.

"Because I prefer the butter knife. Palette knives are for smearing and scraping paint. Clay is not paint, and I am not a painter. Why are you perpetually blocking my light?"

"If tea with Lady Helmsby hadn't taken up half your afternoon, you'd have more light to work with." Having fired off that flaming arrow, Pritchard repaired to the desk.

"If you organize my desk, I will call you out." Finn came around to regard Euphrosyne from the front. Not quite symmetrical, which was exactly as God had made most women, but Euphrosyne was a Grace, not a mere mortal.

"She's perfect," Pritchard said. "Don't turn her into one of your English dairymaids."

Even for Pritchard, this was a testy mood. "What do you have against dairymaids?" Finn asked as he used the warm water on the hearth to wash his hands.

"I have nothing against dairymaids, Your Grace, and Wilhelmina Cathcart is not a dairymaid in any case."

Pritchard had no need of pistols and swords when he could expertly pluck Finn's last nerve from across the room. "Get Antonio in here to wrap this for me, would you? I'm done for the day."

"Antonio has gone out."

"And yet," Finn said, "you are spoiling to scold *me* rather than taking the truant apprentice to task. Today is not half day." More to the point, Antonio, who came from a long line of respected Neapolitan forgers and copyists, could not be trusted to stay out of trouble.

Pritchard began sorting stacks of correspondence—by date, of course, while Finn preferred to sort by urgency. "I fear our Antonio is smitten."

"Again. Well, it has been two weeks, and Antonio cannot deny the force of true love. Ever. For even fifteen minutes."

"He's seventeen, and his articles will be completed next year. He's probably afraid you'll send him back to Italy. If he marries an Englishwoman, you will be more inclined to keep him on. The lad is merely human, and Italy holds hard memories for him."

Hence the boy's attempt to branch out from the family business. "He's human and has talent, but he lacks discipline and vision. He could manage without one or the other, but the boy gets by on charm." And guile. Antonio had heaps of guile, which was probably how he'd survived in Naples as long as he had.

"Have you been charming Mrs. Cathcart, Your Grace?"

Finn put a basin full of wet cloths on the blotter. "I will now put right all the chaos you have caused with my letters. You will wrap the day's work, please. You can lecture me while you make yourself useful."

Pritchard complied—he was nothing if not compliant—and Finn took the seat at the desk. Wilhelmina procrastinated dealing with her correspondence. Knowing that about her made facing Finn's stacks of missives, invoices, and contracts easier.

"What are your intentions where Mrs. Cathcart is concerned?" Pritchard asked.

En garde to you too. "She's a widow and a very astute woman. She doesn't need you to interrogate me as if I were some beamish young suitor."

Pritchard paused long enough to send Finn a critical glance. "You are a duke now. She is your cousin's widow. Every matchmaker in Europe will be placing bets as to who bags your tiara, and Mrs. Cathcart does not deserve to be your passing fancy."

"What makes you think your sermonizing has justification in reality, Pritchard?"

"Don Giovanni. *Non si picca — se sia ricca, se sia brutta, se sia bella; purché porti la gonnella, voi sapete quel che fa.* You haven't whistled since you received St. Didier's first epistle more than a year ago."

It doesn't matter to him if she's rich, ugly, or beautiful; as long as she wears a skirt, you know *what he does...* Finn hadn't been thinking of the lyrics when he'd whistled the tune.

"That was not St. Didier's first epistle. He contacted me when we were in Rome. I wanted no parts of his damned dukedom, and thus we removed to Naples."

"Proving that your nature is streaked with a few less than forthright tendencies."

"Personal discretion is not a bird dropping, Pritchard. I had work to do, and England has plenty enough dukes and whatnot without my adding to the throng. I like Mrs. Cathcart, and she apparently enjoys my company as well."

Pritchard finished with the wet cloths. "How did you reach that conclusion?"

Luscious kisses had something to do with Finn's logic, but they were not the deciding factor. "Last night, Cook served some sort of bourguignon for supper."

"I enjoyed it. Not too heavy on the burgundy, and the beef was tender."

"This morning, where my ham and eggs should have been, I found a savory omelet."

"With cheese, ham, chives, and I'm not sure what else. Very tasty. What has this to do with trifling with Mrs. Cathcart's affections?"

"After she stormed my citadel the other day, the lady had a word with Cook. When my hands are sore, even cutting into a steak defeats me. Mrs. Cathcart reasoned that if holding a pen hurts, then so must many other activities."

Pritchard became inordinately absorbed with scrubbing his fingernails at the wash basin. "Your hands are worse in winter."

"I'm worse whenever I overwork, and in winter, there isn't much else to do, and the light is limited, so I apply myself with fewer pauses. Mrs. Cathcart made me pause, and then she made a few suggestions to Cook, and she's patient with dogs and old ladies."

Pritchard dried his hands. "You are neither a dog nor a dowager."

"Good of you to notice. I never said anything to her about my hands. She saw them and realized... She saw *me*. Not the art I could make for her, not the title that's dangling around my neck like a stained cravat, not my supposedly scandalous family past. She saw *me*."

Pritchard settled on the divan. "What do you see when you look at her? And if you say she'd make a good duchess, is already trained for that harness, and is a proven breeder, I will smash Euphrosyne to bits."

Finn considered the question and Pritchard's threat. "I see the obvious parts, of course, but also... common sense, kindness, fortitude. A lot of fortitude, and more humor than you might suspect. William didn't appreciate his good fortune, and I doubt either the duchess or Lady Helmsby appreciates Wilhelmina's stalwart virtues either."

To say nothing of her affectionate nature, that dash of mischief, a treasure house of maternal devotion, and an instinctive ability to manage the family besoms.

Pritchard rose and stretched in an uncharacteristic display of informality. "I had a whole exegesis prepared on the subject of how you must comport yourself with the ladies now that you are a peer, but I will save my breath."

"I'm not toying with Wilhelmina's affections, Pritchard."

Pritchard crossed the room and stopped with his back half turned to Finn. "Then please recall that she might be toying with yours. She has no need to remarry. I gather that she hadn't much choice in the matter with William, and they rubbed along adequately, but she has her freedom now. Allowing you to court her would simply land her right back where she was, and this time the gossips will whisper that she hasn't much time to present you with the requisite heir and spare."

Pritchard meant this warning kindly, of course. The soul of

compassion, that was Pritchard. "Find our lovelorn Antonio and tell him I won't send him back to Italy when his articles are completed unless he wants to go. The boy would be better served as your apprentice than mine, though. Teach him how to run an Englishman's household. He'll scurry back to Italy and become the most sought after majordomo among Rome's ex-patriots."

"Not just an Englishman's household, a *ducal* household. I take it we aren't moving again any time soon?"

The question was far from casual. "We are not. Lady Helmsby would love to see the duchess banished to the dower property, and for that reason alone, I can't do it. Besides, Wilhelmina assures me the dower property is lovely, and banishment works only if the outcast dwells in misery. The duchess stays where she is, and we stay here. Mind you, she will try to infiltrate the house with her spies."

"I will warn the apprentices. Watch your step with Mrs. Cathcart, please. The hardest marble can shatter if the blow is well placed."

Pritchard withdrew on that telling observation.

Finn tried to go back to his correspondence, with very indifferent success.

"His Grace has made the difference," Norwich said. "He has given me a place to start with Emily. I thought she was too young for drawing lessons, but I was in error."

In Mina's experience, Emily's governess was very seldom wrong, and even less frequently did she smile when admitting her missteps.

"Lady Helmsby is quite the amateur artist," Mina said. "She has volumes of sketches of William, and many of them are very good." All of them flattered the subject, and the best of the lot graced the walls of Mama-in-Law's sitting room. "She suggested Emily gets her interest in art from her grandmama."

Norwich went to the parlor window and watched as, out in the garden, her charge, supervised by a nurserymaid, sketched the holly bush.

"I can't say that Emily is a prodigy, ma'am. It's more the case that because somebody has taken an interest in her, and that somebody has artistic skill, Emily has bestirred herself to some scholarship. Regardless of her specific motivation, she and I now read about the art left behind by the ancient Greeks, and that leads to discussions of history and philosophy. An outing to the British Museum on the next fine day would appeal to Emily because of the sculpture we'll find there. I can build vocabulary lessons around architecture and so forth. I have a place to start, and I have the duke to thank for that."

"Emily is six years old, Norwich. Are musty philosophers really necessary at this point?" And why did even a six-year-old grasp the benefits of managing her abilities to better gain the duke's notice?

"A love of learning is necessary," Norwich said. "An ability to use the imagination for constructive purposes is necessary. Emily asked me this morning how to say 'my friend is a duke' in French. She invited *les deux ours et le dragon* to share her *petit-déjeuner*. She has decided that His Grace is family, and His Grace seems to appreciate the honor."

Mina joined her at the window in time to see Finn taking the place beside Emily on the garden bench, hoisting the child into his lap, and bending his head to examine her sketch. Emily's initial reaction was to perch gingerly on the ducal knees, but as Finn began speaking and adding lines to the page, Emily's shyness thawed. By the time His Grace rose and presented his back for Emily to scramble onto, the child was beaming.

"I rest my case," Norwich said. "I'd best return to the schoolroom, where I will be peppered with questions about holly bushes, robins, and how to say everything in French. A governess delights in such challenges."

Norwich truly did, which vindicated Mina's decision to keep her on rather than capitulate to Lady Helmsby's endless criticisms.

"Stay," Mina said. "His Grace doesn't stand on ceremony, and if you brag to him a bit on your pupil's progress, Emily's efforts will double." Did suggesting that strategy betray Emily by reinforcing the notion that male approval should be sought above all things?

Perhaps, a little, but Finn's affection for Emily was genuine. Dismissing his regard merely because he was the duke and the family patriarch—a notion at which he'd scoff—was neither fair nor rational.

Out in the garden, Emily fisted her hands in Finn's hair—his hat remained on the bench—and trotted him around the garden. When the duke pretended to buck, Emily went off into whoops and threatened to send her dragon to dispatch her unruly mount.

"They're playing," Mina said, somewhat puzzled. Why was Finn eligible for playmate honors when a doting mama was not? Perhaps the doting Mama was too much of an authority figure, or perhaps that mama hadn't much skill at play herself?

"Emily will be less prone to the fidgets for having had some diversion," Norwich observed.

Horse and rider soon presented themselves in Mina's parlor. Emily's cheeks were ruddy with cold and exertion, and Finn appeared entirely at home with a small girl clinging to his back.

"Child," Finn said, "you must dismount. I cannot remove my horse blanket while you remain in the saddle."

"He means his greatcoat," Emily said, budging not one inch. "I like where I am."

"Shall I buck you off?" Finn made a few admonitory gestures that sent Emily into giggles.

"You shall not," Norwich said. "I'm told hot chocolate is to be served in the nursery, but only for children who mind their elders and are kind to their ponies. Emily has been applying herself to her lessons with particular diligence lately, Your Grace, especially her art lessons, and I do hope the trend continues."

"Finn is a horse, not a pony, Norry," Emily said. "May I have whipped cream on my chocolate? Finn, do you like whipped cream?"

Finn backed up to the reading chair. Emily scrambled down and seized his hand immediately upon finding her feet.

"I like whipped cream in moderation," he said, bowing over her hand. "Thank you for a fine time, Miss Emily, and I insist on seeing your sketch when you and Norwich say it's ready for an exhibition. Your mama is doubtless proud of you for your diligent scholarship."

"An exhibition is a public showing," Mina said. "Like the Royal Society annual exhibition, and, Emily, I am proud of you for many reasons."

"Come along, my girl." Norwich held out a hand before Emily could launch a barrage of dilatory questions. "I will tell you all about the Royal Society and how, once upon a time, they even admitted a pair of ladies as members, though of course, those ladies had no voting privileges."

When Norwich and her charge departed, Finn bowed over Mina's hand. "Shall we make good our escape?"

He held her hand as he spoke, not quite a rapturous greeting. Then Mina noticed the nursemaid retrieving Finn's top hat from the garden bench.

The nursemaid who could see very clearly through the windows into the parlor.

Mina curtseyed. "I don't know as an appointment with the solicitors qualifies as an escape. More like another version of captivity. You should have ordered them to attend you at your residence at the time and day of your choosing."

"The duchess indicated as much."

The nursemaid appeared with his hat and was subjected to a dazzling smile and a profession of ducal gratitude. The poor girl looked ready to burst with equal measures of mortification and delight.

"Are you disobeying the duchess on principle," Mina asked as Finn escorted her to the foyer, "or have you some other reason for trekking across Town in the middle of winter?"

"I have many reasons," he said, helping Mina into a dark green merino wool cloak.

Subdued enough for a call on the lawyers, but not from Mina's mourning wardrobe. She had finally stashed those garments away in cedar chests, perhaps never to be worn again.

"I am not disobeying Edwardia," Finn said. "One cannot disobey a woman who holds no position of authority over one." He brushed his palms gently along Mina's shoulders. "My aunt made a suggestion. I am complying with the spirit if not the letter. To be honest..."

He passed Mina her bonnet, and she settled it on her head. When she would have positioned herself before the mirror over the sideboard the better to tie the ribbons, Finn put a hand on her arm.

"Allow me." He did up the trailing ends in a tidy, off-center bow, as impersonally as the job could be done.

And yet, his proximity, standing so close without touching her, had its effect. He was a good cuddler and a better kisser. Mina had speculated at length on where that progression led.

"You have the loveliest eyes," he muttered. "Let's be off before I make a cake of myself, shall we?"

A cake of himself, served with whipped cream, would do very nicely.

Finn handed her into his carriage, and Mina felt an inordinate sense of relief. *There are no spies in this coach.* When he settled beside her on the forward-facing bench and pulled down the shades, the relief became pleasure, and when he took Mina's hand, the pleasure became joy.

"I've missed you," he said as the horses walked on. "I know it's been only two days—two and a half—but there I am, working on Euphrosyne's chin—a bit stubborn, because even a good-humored daughter of Zeus will have a mind of her own, methinks—and I'll want to ask your opinion, but I have only rubbishing Pritchard or prattling Antonio to consult, and I must forge ahead blindly... Tell me to be quiet."

He'd missed her, and he *admitted* that he'd missed her. The day, despite the looming ordeal with the solicitors, brightened.

"Do lawyers make you nervous? Is that why you didn't want them calling on you?"

"Lawyers and I get along well enough, provided they see their role as preventing trouble rather than profiting from it. I wanted to inspect their quarters. Their surrounds will tell me a lot. Are they obsessed with appearances, starving their clerks, overrun with clerks? Then too..."

Half the fun for William in drafting his endless codicils had been summoning the solicitors, forcing them to cross Town, attend him at his whim and pleasure, and await his permission to depart. To inspect their premises would never have occurred to him.

"Then too?" Mina asked.

"I like my house," Finn said. "I looked carefully before I chose it, and I chose it precisely because it barely qualifies as a Mayfair address. It's much too small for fancy entertaining, and the top floor is an ideal studio. I didn't want the place where I work and dwell contaminated with lawyering, much less ducal lawyering."

Not a rational sentiment—lawyers were not an influenza—but Mina understood it. "Your home should be your refuge." Hers was not, not with Travers and his minions listening at keyholes and lurking in doorways.

"Precisely, and I look at that mausoleum where the duchess dwells... I don't ever want to live there, Willie. The place is a monument to the past—her past, which is doubtless a glorious tale in her own eyes—and life should move forward."

"Perhaps you can sell it." Which would be a shame. The ducal residence was a grand edifice, and Finn Cathcart was up to its weight in presence.

"The lawyers will hate the notion."

"Too bad for the lawyers. You will pay them generously to see it happen, and they won't hate that at all."

"Willie?"

"Finn?"

"I know how to deal with patrons—be flattering, but not obsequious, firm but not stubborn. I know how to deal with apprentices, which is much the same sort of challenge. These legal fellows... They know the family history. If they think as Lady Helmsby does, that my mother was a strumpet and my father a wastrel, I will do them an injury they won't soon forget. I vow, I will delight in every blow I land."

Mina thought of her own family—two sisters who were loyal correspondents, a mama who had minced no words when it came to the settlements her daughters were to have, and a papa, now gone to his reward, who had cherished his womenfolk. Even the earl—an uncle on papa's side—had taken a benevolent interest in Mina's betrothal contract.

"That you are loyal to the family members who deserve your respect speaks well of you, Finn. Land all the blows you like, provided they are retaliatory and verbal. To strike first would be to abuse your authority, and to allow disrespect to pass unremarked would be to allow the lawyer to abuse you. You can bet this coach that the duchess doesn't put up with any nonsense from them."

That observation apparently gave Finn something to think about and Mina something to think about too. Her own funds were handled by her family's firm, while Emily's trust was in the hands of the Cathcart solicitors. Not ideal, but conventional. Perhaps once Finn had the lawyers in hand...

The coach slowed and took a corner.

"I miss Italy," Finn said, which Mina took for a general lament on the burden of ducal responsibilities when a fellow would rather be in his studio making beauty out of cold clay.

Mina smacked his arm. "When you were in Italy, you missed London. You are the duke. Dukes never fret." She kissed his cheek, for courage, to steady him, to remind him that he had allies, or at least one ally. Maybe that's what Emily sensed, that here at last was a friend who could be trusted and relied upon.

"Right, I am the duke. For better or for worse, and nobody forced me to return to London. My mother would tell me to be grateful for the many blessings I enjoy and stop whining. My father would tell me to stand up straight and look every man in the eye."

He kissed Mina a smacker on the mouth, and she tasted resolve, courage, and the confidence of a man who'd earned his own way in an unwelcoming world.

These kisses—for luck, as much as anything—were new to her. A different kind of pleasure, a different way to hold hands. As Finn assisted Mina down from the coach and politely offered his arm, she realized how limited her wifely vocabulary of kisses had been.

How limited her wifely *everything* had been, or how limited her *husband* had been. The thought was more liberating than disloyal. William would never have begrudged Mina happiness, and that was a good thing.

When she was with Finn, she was happy. She was also sometimes vexed, puzzled, amused, impatient, or worried, but mostly she was wonderfully, even dangerously, happy.

Leopold St. Didier looked up from his ale to find no less personage than Lucien Philomel Pritchard standing beside his table. This humble tavern was not exactly Pritchard's milieu, and yet, in uncharacteristically worn attire and wearing a bowler rather than a high-crowned beaver, he blended seamlessly with the surroundings.

"Pritchard, greetings. Have a seat."

Huntleigh's butler slid onto the bench beside St. Didier, which, of course, faced the common and had a clear view of the door.

"St. Didier. What the hell are you doing here?"

"Enjoying passable potation." He caught the eye of a serving maid and gestured with his chin at his unexpected guest. "What brings you to the Fractious Mare?"

Pritchard took off his hat, ran his hand through his dark hair, and managed to both smooth out the hat creases and leave his normally orderly locks in slight disarray.

"I was thirsty. You?"

"Oh, parched, of course. How did His Grace's meeting with the solicitors go?"

Pritchard was too naturally self-contained to show any reaction to the question. "He left them less than an hour ago. How should I know?"

His Grace had left with Mrs. Cathcart by his side. That she'd come along to provide introductions and add a bit of family presence to the legal tedium made sense—up to a point.

"*They* left the lawyers an hour ago," St. Didier said. "I assume Mrs. Cathcart was monitoring the meeting, the better to guard young Emily's interests."

Pritchard's ale arrived, along with a plate of toast dripping with melted cheese. Clearly, this was not Pritchard's first foray to the Fractious Mare. He slipped a coin into the tavern maid's hand and graced her with a rogue's smile.

"To the lady's health," he said, blowing the foam to the floorboards, as any regular patron would before drinking.

St. Didier joined in the toast, which he suspected was meant to give Pritchard time to assess strategy.

"I don't know anything about Miss Emily's interests," Pritchard said. "My role is to guard His Grace's flank, and I am here on his orders."

Here being the closest watering hole to the law offices of Swime and Meebles, solicitors to His Grace of Huntleigh, among other notables.

"He's spying on his solicitors?"

"Monitoring. The man is not a fool, which you should know by now."

The present Duke of Huntleigh had led St. Didier a dance worthy of sixteen vexatious Boston barons and their ladies. From Berlin to Prague to Paris and down to Munich, only to end up in Rome, at a pensione full of black-clad old ladies who'd coyly and convincingly lied through their remaining teeth.

"I know the man evaded pursuit with a skill I've seen previously only in pickpockets."

"His Grace was giving the Cathcart ladies time to deal with their grief." Pritchard took another sip of his ale. "Or perhaps he was dealing with his own grief."

"I fail to understand why inheriting a dukedom is cause for bereavement." The duchess had alluded to strained relations with Finn Cathcart's parents, and the old scandal had been easy enough to research, but wealth and admission to the peerage were not to be sneered at.

Finn Cathcart hadn't exactly sneered, but he'd certainly put on a convincing show of indifference. Thank heavens for the child Emily, or the duke might once again be enjoying the salubrious breezes on the Bay of Naples.

"A loss of independence," Pritchard said, "the loss of a flourishing career, of respect as an artist, all deserve proper mourning, as does a loss of privacy, particularly when the beneficiaries of Cathcart's sacrifice are a family previously indifferent to his straitened existence."

St. Didier was not in the mood to extend condolences. "Her Grace was determined that he be found. She is a far from indifferent aunt."

Pritchard considered his ale. "Aunt by marriage only, and escheat would have put her on the street."

The crown was seldom as avaricious as all that. Overtly. "Edwardia has her own means. She would have managed." Lady Helmsby's circumstances were less secure, but Mrs. Wilhelmina Cathcart was fixed quite well.

"The duchess would nonetheless have been without her place in Society."

Not quite. Edwardia was shrewd. She'd done enough favors—introduced enough younger sons to pretty heiresses, seen vouchers to Almack's end up in the hands of enough lesser luminaries—that she wielded power in her own right.

"If Cathcart is so embittered toward Her Grace," St. Didier

asked, "why not consign her to the winds of fate? Why leave Italy at all?"

Pritchard took out a pocket watch, the case winking brightly in the otherwise dim common. Gold—durable, resistant to tarnish, valuable as an heirloom, and pretty. Not a typical possession for a butler.

He snapped the watch closed and put it back into its pocket. "His Grace came back to England because he was homesick, and if you ever tell him I said that, I will find myself without a post the same day."

"I have reason to know that England is worth being homesick for. His Grace doubtless has some good memories here. His family is buried here. He could have come home for a visit, but he's purchased that exquisite residence on Galloway Lane. Why?"

Pritchard smiled again. This time, the charm was muted, but no less powerful. "*I* was homesick. I also explained to my employer that to reject a title and its wealth without having first had a look at the prize was pigheaded in the extreme. *Almost* as pigheaded as disowning a younger son for making a love match. He was taking your word for the situation instead of acquiring his own assessment of the facts. He's sensible enough to have seen the logic in my reasoning, and then you lit on the tactic of pleading the case of the innocent womenfolk."

"So here we are, and here—unless I mistake the matter—comes the fellow we were both intent on treating to a drink."

A blond, ruddy young man in the law clerk's typical dark garb sauntered into the common, raised his hat to the serving maid, and nodded to the bartender. His insouciant air faltered when he saw St. Didier sitting side by side with Pritchard.

Pritchard waved him over, and once the clerk collected his drink, he joined them.

"Morse, I believe you know Mr. St. Didier," Pritchard said, rising slightly and resuming his seat. "You were kept overlong at your desk."

"As usual." Morse gulped half his ale, produced a limp handkerchief, and patted his lips. "So which of you two fine gents is buying my drinks?"

"We both are," Pritchard said, which was the same answer St. Didier would have given, because Morse was asking only tangentially about money. "Both Mr. St. Didier and I are here to ensure His Grace's best interests are well guarded."

Morse glanced around the room and lowered his voice. "I thought St. Diddy-ay worked for the duchess."

"No longer," St. Didier said. "I simply like to ensure that a new peer gets off on the right foot." The truth, whether or not Pritchard believed it.

Morse looked skeptical and directed his next question to Pritchard. "You'll be sure the duke knows I'm his eyes and ears at the law office?"

Pritchard looked amused. "I will not. You spy for coin, while you arguably betray your employers. That they've inspired so little loyalty in an articled clerk speaks ill of them, but that your loyalty can be purchased doesn't exactly speak well of you—or so the duke might see it."

Morse aimed an aggrieved glower into the depths of his pint. "You try being one of eleven and your pa a mere vicar. I'm a good clerk, and old Meebles wouldn't know one file from another without me."

"Doubtless true," Pritchard said. "I can sympathize more than you might think. Tell us how the meeting went."

"Went very quietly. His Grace said something to the effect that he didn't want to be the duke, and anybody who made the road harder for him would wish His Grace weren't the duke too. Meebles got all agreeable and smarmy, and Swime bowed so many times he's likely seasick. The duke said nothing was to be sent to Her Grace without he sees it first, and I think Swime and Meebles will toe that mark. Old Rohrer tried to get in his sermon about wills, and the duke cut him off. Said he had personal attorneys for that work."

Prudent of him. Not every titled lord kept private and peerage dealings separate.

"What of the last duke's will?" Pritchard asked. "Have you copied that yet?"

"Almost done. Don't ask for Wiliam's will, though. Wretched thing is pages and pages. To my horse, I leave my amber snuffbox, and to my dog, I leave my horse... Except the blighter had three horses, four amber snuffboxes, and no dog. He also couldn't spell for shite and had wretched penmanship. Was good entertainment for the junior clerks watching old Rohrer's apoplexies, though. Chancery would be an age wading through that mess if anybody contested the particulars."

So much for not speaking ill of the dead.

"I won't ask for William's will," Pritchard said. "Please do keep a sharp ear out for anything your employers might say regarding their impressions of the duke."

"I always keep a sharp ear out." Morse finished his ale and signaled for another. "I don't suppose His Grace needs a new senior clerk?"

Ten siblings was a lot, and the vicarage was often a family's last stop on the road to penury.

"His Grace employs no clerks," Pritchard said gently. He pushed a folded banknote across the table. "A donation to the vicarage's maintenance fund."

Morse stared at the note, sighed, and stuffed it into a pocket. "Thank you. I know I shouldn't be telling tales out of school, but my sisters are turning into old maids, and when Papa dies... We won't inherit any dukedom."

"Consider yourself lucky in that regard." Pritchard put some coins on the table, rose, and donned his hat. "St. Didier, I leave you to further discussions with Mr. Morse. Morse, my thanks for your insights."

Pritchard sidled out the door, the picture of a hardworking man who'd enjoyed his pint and was on the way to his 'umble lodgings for a well-deserved night's sleep.

"That fellow doesn't add up," Morse said. "He's part clerk, part solicitor, part lord, if you know what I mean. Like an actor, but sober. Too sober. He didn't finish his drink nor touch his toast."

St. Didier would bet his walking stick that Pritchard had ordered the toast with a hungry clerk's finances in mind. Kind or shrewd of him, probably both.

"Mustn't let good food go to waste," St. Didier said, pushing the plate across the table. "Now that we have some privacy, I have a few questions for you regarding Mrs. Cathcart."

CHAPTER TEN

Wilhelmina would never again think of spring as the time of renewal and fresh starts. A hibernation of sorts was ending for her in the depths of winter, one hack in the park, one vanilla ice, one sketching session in the schoolroom at a time.

She was a merely passable artist, but she loved eavesdropping on Finn's discussions with Emily. The duke and his small cousin had spent half the morning sketching the Ursulas while Wilhelmina had lurked in the window seat, pretending to read her correspondence.

"You made Minor's nose too big, Finn," Emily observed, crowding against his forearm. "She's not a rhinoceros."

"What do you know about rhinoceri, Emily Cathcart, and how do you know it?"

Emily returned to her seat, a reading chair positioned, like Finn's, near the hearth. "Norwich told me. She knows everything."

"Then I bow before manifest omniscience. You shall fix the nose, if you please." He passed over his sketchbook, and thus did Emily learn the challenges of drawing a nose to scale on a portrait of a wooden bear.

"What are om-nish-unts?"

"The word looks like omni-science when you write it—I had to ask Pritchard to say it for me—and it means knowing everything. Your mama is omniscient when it comes to your favorite treats. Norwich is omniscient about literature."

Norwich, who occupied the third reading chair by the hearth, looked up from a book to roll her eyes.

"Grandmama is om-nish-unt about *everything*. She is a *real* lady. She forgets to knock, though, and doesn't say good morning or good afternoon like you're supposed to when you greet somebody."

Finn sent Mina a look that spoke volumes about rude, presuming grandmamas. "What of the duchess? Does she know everything?"

"She knows about dogs. She lets me brush Charles and gives me mints when Mama isn't looking, but I have to promise not to share the mints with Charles. He has a delicate tummy."

Finn left his seat, perched a hip on the arm of Emily's chair, and frowned at her work in progress. "Now Minor's nose is too small. She won't dare go out in Society with that minuscule snout."

"Minny-scule?"

And thus it went, until Minor's nose was just right, Emily had learned four fancy words, Norwich was sending the clock repeated glances, and Mina couldn't pretend to read her correspondence for one more moment.

"Enough noses for now," the duke said, rising. "I must abandon you, Miss Emily, so that you and Norwich can discuss the proboscis of a rhinoceros. Might be a poem in that, or a limerick, at least."

"Nose," Mina said, springing from the window seat. "P-r-o-b-o-s-c-i-s, which is not to be confused with a horn. Norwich, thank you for your patience. Your Grace, I'll see you out."

"Bye, Finn!"

He bowed over Emily's hand. "Farewell, sweet cousin Emily. Next time, we'll sketch your mama, if you think she can sit still long enough."

Emily regarded Mina skeptically. "Mama doesn't like to sit still. She's always having tea with Grandmama, or writing letters, or doing the menus, or the ledgers, or finishing a bonnet for me when I don't even like bonnets."

"And yet," Finn said, "your mother lurked over there without saying a word the whole time we were sketching, just to keep us company."

Emily looked from Norwich to Finn to Wilhelmina. "Will you come again to keep us company, Mama? Norry says I'm getting better at my schoolwork."

Mina bent to hug her daughter. "I will come again. I love keeping you company. The schoolroom is always so cozy, and I will be delighted to learn all about the rhinoceros when next I visit."

Emily wiggled away and repositioned the Ursulas and Draco on her desk. "Promise?"

The hope in the child's question—and the doubt—broke Mina's heart. "I promise, Emily."

"Now I'm jealous," Finn said. "I will be surrounded by experts on the rhinoceros. Next, you'll be explaining hyenas and ocelots to me."

Emily was in close conversation with Norwich when Mina escorted His Grace from the nursery.

"Stop that," Finn said as they descended toward the foyer.

"Stop what?"

"You are wondering if you are a bad mother, which is ridiculous. Children wheedle. That Emily is trying to pluck at your heartstrings is an encouraging sign. You stop by the nursery every morning, do you not?'

"Without fail. I have a cup of tea while Emily is having her porridge."

Finn paused at the foot of the steps. "You look in on lessons daily."

Mina stopped one step up. "Briefly. Norwich prefers to minimize interruptions." Mina was at eye level with Finn, a novel and disconcerting posture. His gaze was serious, and he was trying to reassure Mina about her maternal qualifications, but she was distracted by the notion of kissing him when he hadn't such an advantage of height.

"You read her a story at bedtime," Finn went on.

"Or we chat about the day, and I hear her prayers." Why did he have to have such a lovely speaking voice, all rumbly and warm? Such knowing blue eyes?

"You try to get her out of the house on fine days, if her grandmother doesn't pop by to eat all your tea cakes, or Norwich hasn't raised the drawbridge, or the duchess hasn't summoned you to a gratuitous scolding."

"I have tea with the duchess most Tuesdays." Mina abandoned her step, lest Dalton or Travers catch her making a fool of herself. She and Finn were discreet, always proper in public. Their most passionate moments had taken place in his coach with the shades down.

She delighted in those moments, but they also frustrated her. What were Finn's intentions? What were *her own* intentions? The duchess would waste no time come spring deluging Finn with prospective brides.

While Mina...

"Now you frown at me," Finn said, "when only a moment ago, the look in your eye was so much more encouraging. Are you hungry?"

The wrong question. "Peckish."

"Then let's pop around to Gunter's and have a winter picnic."

Travers chose then to emerge from the stairs that led to the kitchen. "Will Madam be going out? Your Grace, good day."

"Madam is making up her mind," Finn said, "and I will happily help her into her cloak. Away with you, Travers. You might have a word with the footmen about beating the hall runners. The coal dust gets into everything this time of year."

Travers's brows rose, then descended precipitously, stopping somewhere between consternation and affront. "Very good, Your Grace." He retreated on a bow.

"You should sack him," Finn said, taking Mina's cloak down from its peg.

"He'll hear you," Mina muttered as Finn did up her frogs. She liked that he was attentive in ways William never had been, but the brush of his fingers against her chin threatened her composure.

"Let him hear me—a proper reward for eavesdropping. Travers takes his post for granted and is giving less than dedicated service. Your gloves."

Finn busied himself with his greatcoat rather than tie Mina's ribbons. Perhaps his own composure was growing imperiled.

"You did not bring the coach today," Mina said, passing him his top hat.

"I needed the walk to clear my head, and bothering the stable for a distance that I can cover in a quarter hour on foot is ridiculous."

Mina grinned as she shoved his walking stick at him. "You are finding much to be ridiculous today."

By the slightest flare in his gaze, he betrayed his own frustration. "Am I ever. Let's be off."

They strolled along, arm in arm, though an arctic breeze tickled the ends of Finn's purple scarf, and Mina was soon longing for the comfort—and privacy—of Finn's coach.

"If you are not averse to a change of plans," Finn said, "I'd like to show you something."

"Something not very much farther? My toes are about to freeze." And how Mina longed to walk with him hand in hand.

"Two streets that way," Finn said, nodding to the north. "Something I hope you will enjoy."

"Lead on."

He glanced around, took off his scarf, and wrapped it about Mina's neck. "Go ahead. Tell me I am being forward and brazen and overstepping and so forth."

His scarf was warm and soft and bore the scent of balsam fir. "Keep walking," Mina said, taking a firm hold of his arm. "I will scold you at length when I am before a roaring fire with a spicy toddy."

The neighborhood changed, from stately town houses on geometrically straight streets, to smaller dwellings, some detached, on lanes that curved and wound to accommodate the occasional grand maple or oak.

"We have arrived," Finn said at the gate of one of the modest detached houses. This one was only two stories above a half basement. Peat smoke curled from the highest chimney, and the curtains were of such intricate lace that even on a sunny day, the occupants would have privacy. "What do you think?"

Mina didn't think—she *knew* she was disappointed past all bearing. She hadn't rebuffed Finn's overtures—she had returned them in full measure—but neither had she foreseen this development. Not so soon, not... with such an overt lack of sentiment.

"You are eager to show me the inside?"

"Also eager to get you out of the cold. It's modest, but I like that." He opened the gate and held it for her with an air of happy expectation, like a footman new to his livery.

What Mina had to say should not be conveyed on the street. She followed Finn through the gate, onto the porch, and into a foyer notable for warmth and the scents of beeswax and lemon. Finn had apparently already hired a housekeeper.

Lovely.

Mina felt tears gathering, and that would not do.

"I won't be staying," she said. "While I'm sure you meant this... this gesture as a thoughtful display in a progression toward... toward..." What? Clandestine groping on Mondays and Thursdays, while Finn bided his time in anticipation of the spring crop of brides? "As a thoughtful display, I cannot—I will not—be trysting with you here."

"Trysting with me *here*?" He took off his top hat, ran his hand through his hair, and gave Mina the same frown he likely aimed at disobliging blocks of stone. "*Trysting* with me here."

The tears were making Mina's throat ache, and yet, she held on to her dignity. "Is that notion so outlandish? Given the way we conduct ourselves in your coach, at every opportunity, and the ices and the hacking out, and the... what? You bring me to a snug little hideaway in the middle of the day, no staff to greet us. What am I supposed to think?"

And the absolutely hellish part was, she wanted to go upstairs with him. Wanted to indulge in the most intimate of pleasures with Finn Cathcart, *but not like this.* Not in the context of some tidy, adult, expedient arrangement that would be abandoned with a fond kiss when he went duchess-shopping in earnest.

"Willie, don't cry."

"I'm not crying, you oaf." Would he expect her to introduce his new duchess around Town? To rejoice for her when she conceived the heir Mina had failed to produce?

Finn brandished a monogrammed handkerchief, and Mina snatched it because she'd soon be sniffling. Finn's duchess would never sniffle, of course. She'd give birth to robust male triplets within a year of marriage too.

Finn untied Mina's bonnet and set it on the sideboard. "Wilhelmina, listen to me. Please. This was my parents' first home. They lived here for the first year of their marriage. I was born in this house. I have no memories of it, but I know my parents were happy here. I bought it because—"

Mina ceased dabbing at her eyes. "Your parents' first home?"

"They couldn't afford the address for long," Finn said, looking anywhere but at Mina. "Mama and I would walk past this place, and she'd regale me with tales of that year. She started a patch of bluebells in the backyard and grew roses in pots by the door."

Mina launched herself at Finn and wrapped her arms around him. "Your parents' first home."

His arms looped around her shoulders, and his chin rested on her crown. "Living on love has limitations, but I believe that even the sight of this house gave Mama joy. For a year, she and Papa proved the whole world wrong. The previous owner was willing to sell, and I wanted... I wanted a woman's eye on the appointments. I've kitted it out as best I can, but the place wants... Please don't cry."

Mina was back to dabbing at her eyes. Finn had not intended any disrespect, just the opposite. He'd wanted her assistance. He'd sought her advice. He'd done something of which he wasn't quite certain, and Mina's opinion on the matter would carry weight.

She stepped back and stuffed the handkerchief in a pocket of her cloak. "I have made a complete cake of myself."

Finn smiled his most piratical smile. "If your foolishness results in a close embrace, feel free to indulge whenever I'm near."

She set about unbuttoning his greatcoat. "Finlay, we need to talk. I don't know what I'm doing with you, and now I am overset, and..." She leaned in and rested her forehead on his chest. "I am all at sixes and sevens, and I don't care for it one bit."

Finn wrapped her in a hug, which was lovely.

"I took the liberty," he said, "of asking the housekeeper to make us a lunch before she decamped on her half day. I'll give you the whole tour, but let's eat first, and if you insist, we will have this talk you are so set upon."

He took her hand and began discoursing knowledgeably about the egg-and-dart molding, though Mina barely caught a word of his lecture. If Finn had not intended that they embark on an affair, then just possibly, he had another objective in mind, one that involved a short ceremony at St. George's Hanover Square.

While he waxed eloquent about the genius involved in the design of the inglenook, Mina held his hand and strove to organize a riot of emotions.

Pritchard had been wrong.

Finn stirred a pot of cider steaming over the coals in the kitchen hearth and contemplated the extent to which Pritchard the Perfect had erred.

Make no presumptions, Pritchard had said. *Go slowly. No declarations, no expectations. Test the waters, watch and wait...*

And the whole time Finn had been following Pritchard's advice, Wilhelmina had been leaping to erroneous conclusions.

Finn tossed another dash of cinnamon into the warming cider and half a dash of cloves, then adjusted the pot swing so the mixture sat closer to the flames. Heaven help the lady Pritchard chose to court. She'd be an elderly spinster with an expert command of chess before her swain stated his intentions.

Though Pritchard's ideal mate probably already had an expert command of chess.

When the cider began to bubble. Finn swung it free of the fire and wrapped a towel around the pot handle. The scent was heavenly —rich, spicy, and sweet. He poured two mugs as Wilhelmina emerged from the pantry with a supply of cutlery.

"Luncheon is served," Finn said, gesturing to the plank table. "And I, for one, am famished."

Mina passed him half the silverware. "I get the impression that feeding you is a nigh constant challenge."

"I'm nowhere near the bottomless pit I was as a younger man. I could put away more tucker at one sitting than you'd manage in a day and be hungry an hour after leaving the table. I could not seem to stop growing, and wrangling stone is hungry work. I slept better then too."

She surveyed the table, which held a platter of sandwiches, a dish of batter-fried pickles still hot from the Dutch oven, and a basket of cinnamon biscuits.

"About what I said earlier," Wilhelmina began. "I was hasty, and I was wrong, and..."

"And I am hungry. Might we eat before embarking on any fraught conversations?"

Finn held a chair for her, and she sat, but he wasn't fooled. Wilhelmina would have her say, and he was increasingly certain that say would include a farewell. Kissing in coaches was a pleasant diversion, and sketching in the nursery fit in well enough with her plans,

but becoming the next Duchess of Huntleigh had ceased to appeal—
if it ever had.

Pritchard hadn't been *all* wrong, damn the luck.

"I haven't had fried pickles in ages," Wilhelmina said, forking
several onto her plate. "I had forgotten how much I like them."

"Leave a few for me, please. I requested them because I'm fond of
them too." *Fond of*—stupid choice of words. Finn shoved a pickle into
his mouth and nearly got a scalded tongue for his efforts.

"Delicious," Wilhelmina murmured. "An excellent complement
to ham sandwiches and perfect for a chilly day. How is Westhaven's
commission coming along?"

He let her lead the conversation onto safe paths, and the whole time
they chatted—about Aglaia's hips, the spices in the cider, or Emily's
fascination with wild animals—Finn wrestled with his conscience.

If Willie was done with him, he'd retreat, tail once again between
his legs, and go back to arguing with blocks of marble for hours
on end.

"Finn, has your plate offended you?" Wilhelmina dunked a
biscuit into her cider and took a bite. "You are glowering at the
crumbs of an excellent meal."

"I nearly offended you. That bothers me."

She held out the dripping half a biscuit, and Finn took a nibble.

"I was mistaken, Finlay. Your views of relations between the
sexes are more pragmatic than mine, and I assumed you were taking
things in a practical direction."

A tawdry direction. He recalled making some asinine pronounce-
ments about dramas at parting and the demands of his art.

"When I'm kissing you, Willie, I don't feel very pragmatic at all. I
feel…"

She dunked another biscuit. "Yes?"

"The Italians have a word—*morbidezza*—and it can refer to the
delicacy of a piece of music, or to the luminous quality a skilled
painter gives skin tones. Sculpture aspires to the same glowing,

natural beauty when depicting living subjects. The fiction that stone can be soft, warm, and alive... Canova excels at it."

"Finn," she said, looking both concerned and puzzled, "what are you going on about?"

"When I'm with you, I feel that... a vitality and sweetness that's out of the ordinary for me. Desire is part of it—a substantial part—but so is joy and curiosity and... hope. I no longer feel like myself, Willie, and it scares the hell out of me, but I like it too."

She frowned at him over her biscuit and cider, and Finn ceased prattling by force of will.

"I am in something of the same boat," she said. "Not myself, and not sure whether that's good, bad, or both at once. What are we *doing*, Finlay? Though you weren't intent on embarking on a liaison with me, I was tempted. I have given you reason to believe I might be... tryst-able."

Finn resigned himself to the demands of honor. "I am not tryst-able. I have been in the past, and yes, Willie, for money or the near equivalent. A comfortable place to bide for a time, intimate companionship, square meals and plenty of them... I have never misrepresented myself, but I'm not proud of my behavior either."

He finished his cider and sat back. "I am courting you. You ask what we are doing, and I can only answer for myself: I am courting you. I realize that becoming the next Duchess of Huntleigh is not on your list of aspirations. You've seen the view from that prospect and you were unfavorably impressed. As I am not particularly concerned with being the Duke of Huntleigh, I thought you might consider my suit."

"Courting me." Wilhelmina reached for another biscuit. "Oh, Finn..."

"What sort of 'oh, Finn' is that? Because if it's oh-Finn-you-do-me-great-honor, that's a very different matter from oh-Finn-I-would-love-to-be-your-duchess."

"I never wanted to be a duchess."

Didn't every little girl want to be at least a duchess if not a queen? But then, Wilhelmina hadn't been a little girl for some time.

"I understand your reluctance. I never wanted to be a duke. I still don't, but I care for you very much, and I can't help the duchess part. Please, either laugh at my presumption or allow me to hope. I hate being hopeful, Willie. Hope looks disappointment in the eye and pretends not to notice. I do a miserable job of ignoring looming failure, but here I am..." Bleating on like the passionate shepherd boy to his love.

"And you have been courting me."

"Not very effectively, given the present discussion." The present babbling.

Wilhelmina rose, and Finn's hopes—stupid, brave, mortifying hopes—sank. She moved away from the table, retrieved the last of the cider simmering by the coals, and brought the pot to the table.

"I have not been courted before," she said, pouring them equal measures of fragrant, steaming potation. "I did not know the signs. I suspected, I hoped—and I know exactly what you mean about hope being ill-fitting finery—and I doubted. Tell me more about courtship, Finlay, as you envision it."

She took the place on the bench beside him and set her mug before her.

"Courtship is the part where we let the whole world know we're looking each other over with a view toward marriage," Finn said, "but I don't need to look you over, and I don't give a cracked brick what the world thinks. I know my own heart. You have full possession of same."

Pritchard had been very clear on many points, but the ostinato beneath all of his exhortations had been the clearest: *Do not, for pity's sake, tell her you love her. Show her your feelings in your actions, spare her the words that often mean so little.*

For a man devoted to chess and ledgers, Pritchard had spoken with great authority on that point.

"Marriage," Wilhelmina said, peering into her mug. "Well. The duchess won't like it."

Her again. Of all people... "I am not asking leave to court you because that will annoy the duchess, Willie."

"I believe you. You want to hate her, but the campaign isn't going in your favor. She dotes on her dog and sneaks mints to her great-niece."

"Bother Edwardia. May I court you?"

"Yes."

Finn waited for the *but,* the *however,* the humor at his expense. "Yes?"

"Yes. I have never been courted, so my part of the dance might lack finesse. William and I were betrothed, and that was that. We'd run into each other socially, we stood up together for an occasional waltz once I'd been presented, and when I'd been permitted my Season, we were wed. The wedding night was a friendly, awkward, somewhat disappointing affair, but I'd been warned to expect the disappointment and awkwardness, so I made do with the friendliness. Courtship not included. I didn't realize..."

"You didn't realize what William had denied you."

She sipped her cider. "A harbinger of things to come. William was a lazy husband. Not mean, not in any way difficult, but lazy and self-absorbed. One courted mistresses and doted thereupon. One appreciated one's wife, when one recalled he had one."

"I'm sorry," Finn said. "You deserved much better." *I'm here to see that you get it.*

"Do not smile at me like that, Your Grace. I haven't said I'll marry you."

Finn tried to stop smiling and failed miserably. "Of course you haven't. You have given me leave to try to earn your esteem, nothing more. I have years of doting and kissing and fond gazes and vanilla ices ahead of me. You will ambush me in my studio and demand to be taken shopping for bonnets. I will send you little notes full of inane rhymes and naughty innuendo. Why would I have any occasion to smile?"

One corner of Wilhelmina's lips twitched up. "Will you doodle my name?"

"I am an artist," Finn said as lightness and relief bubbled through him. "I sketch, I do not doodle." He took out the pencil and paper ever present in his pocket and did a quick drawing. "My darling Willie, my three hundredth or so attempt at a likeness." And that was a conservative estimate.

Wilhelmina considered the sketch. "You will court me, then, but, Finn?"

"I dislike like this 'but, Finn,' business. But nothing. I am courting you. You have given me permission, and I am determined to make a proper job of it."

"I'm sure you will dazzle me with your gentlemanly virtues, but you will please dazzle me discreetly? The duchess expects you to at least look over the spring crop of beauties, and Society in general—"

Finn seized Wilhelmina's hand. "To blazes with the duchess, Society, your rubbishing nosy butler, and William's meddlesome mama. I want the whole world to know that the place at your feet has been spoken for."

Wilhelmina laced her fingers through his. "So do I, but not yet. We might find we do not suit. Emily is already growing attached to you, and I don't want her getting premature ideas about your role in her life. She will be devastated if she thinks we are to marry, and then we don't. I'm asking for discretion, Finlay, not that we worship each other from afar."

Finn sampled his cider and considered this request. The duchess's expectations were of no moment to him, and he didn't think they meant all that much to Wilhelmina either. Emily's situation was deserving of consideration, of course, but Finn would remain part of her life regardless of how matters developed with her mother.

Finn seized upon the notion that Wilhelmina needed a quiet courtship *for herself*. She did not—could not—trust that Finn's regard was durable, when he himself had disdained the possibility of an abiding romance. She wanted to try on the idea of marriage to Finn in private without all of Society goggling over her shoulder.

As they had with her first engagement.

"We shall have the most discreet, delightful courtship in the history of besottedness," Finn said. "I promise you that. Any other conditions?"

Wilhelmina did her version of a glower, which was adorable. "You mean that? You will not post a notice in the *Times*, and you will continue to dismiss Travers, and sketch with Emily, and lick your ices?"

"Lick my ices, Wilhelmina?"

"Forget I said that."

"It's forgotten," Finn said, helping himself to one of the last cinnamon biscuits. "What did you say your name was?"

Her glower melted into a smile of such glowing joy that Finn knew he'd never capture it, not in stone, not on paper, not anywhere but in his heart.

"My name is Wilhelmina, but when we are private, you may call me Willie."

"I am honored. Shall I show you the rest of the house, Willie?"

"I'd like that."

When Finn would have trotted up the steps and launched into a lecture on the venerable provenance of post-and-lintel construction, Wilhelmina stopped him. She wrapped her arms around his waist and rested her cheek against his chest.

Finn reciprocated and silently thanked her. Willie was right. The moment deserved savoring. If he was very lucky, and fate was kind, they'd share many such moments throughout a long and happy marriage.

The words *I love you* begged to be spoken, but then Wilhelmina pulled away and aimed a smile at Finn that would have dazzled the sun.

"I want to see every closet and chest of drawers, sir. Let's start with the bedrooms."

CHAPTER ELEVEN

"Your nephew is impossibly stubborn," Edwardia murmured, saluting the late duke's portrait with her tea cup. "I know precisely where he gets that quality, Your Grace."

Finlay also got his bachelor-button blue eyes from the Cathcart side of the family, and those hands... Michaelangelo's *David* would envy those hands. Masculine, elegant, talented... The hands were all Cathcart too.

"He'll come around," Edwardia said, sipping her tea. "The lad is sensible. Must get that from his mama." But would he come around in time? "He's met with the solicitors once, and I'm told he brought home a satchel of documents. That bodes well."

Charles, who was accustomed to these one-sided conversations, put his doggy chin on Edwardia's knee.

"Naughty boy," she said, smoothing a hand over his head. "Winters are hard on the old guard, aren't they?"

Winters were lonely, without the social whirl to distract a lady from her grief. Edwardia had disdained the company of other widows earlier in mourning. If Vanessa, Lady Helmsby, was any indication, the lot of them were gossipy, meddlesome, and more inclined to chatter about doing good works than to actually take up the practice of same.

Wilhelmina, by contrast, was sensible, kind, and devoted to her child. She dutifully appeared every Tuesday with the latest cheerful gleanings from her correspondence, but clearly, she humored Edwardia out of pity.

"Pity is the worst," Edwardia muttered. "God spare me from pity. Disgust would be preferable." Though Finlay clearly held her in some sort of polite disgust, and that had become a trial.

A tap on the door interrupted what should have been a pleasant afternoon spent over an embroidery hoop.

"Come in."

Balcomb stepped into the parlor. "A caller, Your Grace, Lady Helms—"

"Don't be so uppish, Balcomb." Her ladyship plowed past the butler. "Announcing family is the worst sort of affectation. Edwardia, send him for the tea, please. I vow this cold will give me an ague."

Would that it did. In Edwardia's head, the voice muttering that wish had been her husband's. He'd stood up with Vanessa three times as a young man, and ever since, Vanessa had hinted that his true affections had lain with her, but she'd chosen Helmsby instead—a love match. His Grace had settled on a consolation duchess, the first of two.

An accurate chronology of events contradicted that fantasy, but Vanessa clung vociferously to her version of history.

Edwardia tugged the bell-pull twice as Charles whined softly and sat beside her chair. "The kitchen will send up a tray directly. Balcomb, thank you for escorting her ladyship."

The butler and the dog exchanged a look that suggested a pact to never dignify rudeness with a reaction, then Balcomb withdrew.

"You really should pension him, Edwardia." Unbidden, Vanessa took the opposite wing chair. "He positively creaks when he walks."

At least his knees don't pop like certain unexpected callers I could name. "I'll thank you to leave the running of my household to me,

Vanessa. To what do I owe the honor of this intrusion?" The duchess's at homes were the second and fourth Thursdays of the month, as Vanessa well knew.

"So churlish, Edwardia, when I always try to be gracious to you. You must let ancient grievances remain in the past, my dear. Had you produced a few sons, even one, you wouldn't be this discontent in your final years. I am still far from my threescore and ten, but my memories of William are such a comfort—and of dear Helmsby, too, of course."

Charles whined again.

"Does he have to tee-tee?" Vanessa gave Charles the same look she'd aim at a stain on the carpet. "Why does he make that disagreeable sound?"

Charles doubtless wanted to go out. He was a discerning fellow, and present company fell far short of his standards.

"He's bored by idle chatter and futile attempts to provoke me. What brings you here, Vanessa? If you are short of funds, apply to the solicitors."

"I'm always short of funds. You know that, and you don't seem to care a bit that I have become the pathetic widow, saving string and hoarding coal."

"Reduce your staff." Edwardia had certainly reduced hers immediately upon becoming bereaved. "Stop patronizing Madame Bernadette. She'd lower her prices to lure you back rather than let you go to a competitor."

Vanessa left off taking visual inventory of the parlor's appointments. No figurines had been pawned, no antique side tables discreetly sent to Christie's—yet.

"The idea has some merit," Vanessa replied. "You might actually have lit upon a useful notion, Edwardia. How interesting."

Further effusions were interrupted by the arrival of the tea cart. The staff had decided that standards were to be maintained, especially before the enemy. When Lady Helmsby came around, no matter how impromptu or short her call, a near feast was always presented for her delectation—or envy.

"Your kitchen still knows how to prepare a tray," Vanessa said, helping herself to three cheese tarts and two profiteroles. "Though the tea could be hotter, couldn't it?"

That remark was intended to insult Edwardia for using porcelain rather than silver service. "Mine is perfect, thank you. Too hot and one cannot drink the stuff."

Rather than once again prompt Vanessa to disclose her objective, Edwardia enjoyed her tea. Finn hadn't complained about being served gunpowder, though she wished he had. That boy had learned too early and well not to complain about anything, more's the pity.

Vanessa took a sip and grimaced. "I suppose old age does affect the palate."

"Your barbs used to at least aspire to wit, Vanessa. Something has rattled your usually iron nerves. Has Travers threatened to go to the penny press about your debts?"

"Why would Wilhelmina's butler have any notion of my finances?"

Vanessa was nowhere near as adept at bluffing as she believed herself to be, which was why some of the debts had resulted from card parties.

"Domestic service requires that he be observant. Perhaps you've been indiscreet with Wilhelmina's towheaded footman. You wouldn't be the first widow to impose on a younger man."

That was nasty, but then, Vanessa was nasty. Edwardia tried to make allowances—losing a son and a husband would sour any woman's nature—but Vanessa had been a scheming baggage long before the Huntleigh tiara had caught her eye.

"Go ahead and insult me," Vanessa said, adding another tart to her plate. "I am a widow without substantial means or powerful allies, but I have eyes, too, and I am here to warn you, Edwardia. Wilhelmina and His Grace are becoming quite close."

"Good. Wilhelmina is sensible, and His Grace needs allies."

Wilhelmina also more or less controlled Emily's funds, which were the last bastion of real wealth in the family. The money was tied up in the usual trusts, but the Lindstrom family solicitors had ensured that Mina, as Emily's physical custodian, would have the final say over the accounts during Emily's minority.

The arrangement was unusual, but no less person than Edward, Duke of Kent, had established royal precedent for it. William hadn't quibbled, for once, lest he appear petty before the lawyers.

"Edwardia, you must listen to me. Forget all that has gone between us, forget the money and the sniping. By 'close,' I mean the two of them are *enamored*. His Grace spends half the morning in the schoolroom, ostensibly teaching Emily how to draw, and Mina is there for every moment of it. They go for ices at least twice a week—who goes for ices in winter?—and they hack out on what passes for fine mornings at this dreary time of year. Mark my words, Edwardia. No good can come of this."

No good for Lady Helmsby. "Because you have decided that His Grace must marry money?"

"Of course he must marry money. That's what dukes do." Lady Helmsby rose and paced before the fire. "What was the point of engaging the services of that odious St. Didier fellow if not to find us a duke who would do his duty?"

St. Didier was mannerly, determined, and honorable. Only Vanessa would find that combination odious.

"I'll tell you what the point was, though I doubt you will grasp its significance. I promised my husband on his deathbed that I would see justice done where Finlay Cathcart was concerned. This family did that boy and his parents a grievous wrong, and my husband went to his grave regretting it. I promised His Grace his nephew would be welcomed with full honors, and that means no one, not you, not Fat George, or the interfering biddies at Almack's will trespass one inch on Finlay Cathcart's happiness."

Finlay himself would find that stirring declaration laughable, if not insulting, and heaven knew he had reasons for his ire. Rome hadn't been toppled in a day, and Edwardia expected that demolishing Finlay's resentments would take a nearly comparable effort. He had come to tea, though. He'd astonished her nearly witless with that bit of civility. Next time, she'd be more gracious—and there had to be a next time.

Vanessa ceased pacing. "His Grace will be overjoyed to visit us in Marshalsea debtors' prison."

"If you practice economies, it won't come to that." The solicitors had assured Edwardia of as much repeatedly, but they were ducal solicitors. What they knew about real poverty would probably half fill a demitasse.

"You preach to me about economies while you feed that mongrel steak."

"You begrudge a loyal hound his table scraps, when you should be figuring out how to stop your own spies from blackmailing you. Our present duke does not suffer fools, my lady, and you are being very foolish."

William had been foolish, too, but the boy hadn't been mean. Vanessa, by contrast...

"Finlay hates you," Lady Helmsby said, resuming her seat and wrapping her remaining treats in a handkerchief. "The present duke would love to see you ruined."

And that prospect pleased Vanessa immensely.

"This family has been heading for ruin for years," Edwardia said. "I expect we will reach our destination ere long, regardless of how Finlay marries." The situation wasn't hopeless, but nearly so.

"You blame me, because William wasn't keen to break any entails."

"To have freed up the remaining entailed properties would have been a great boon. Without an adult heir to consent to breaking the entails, that solution has been taken from us." Very likely because Vanessa had advised William to dig in his heels. Such a pity, that.

"Mock me at your peril, Edwardia. I am not a doddering dowager to go gently into penurious obscurity. If William had lived..."

"But William is dead." The foolish boy had fallen to a foolish death and without leaving a son behind, which, of course, was blamed upon dear Mina.

"He went to a very untimely reward," Lady Helmsby said, gathering up her reticule and standing. "I have tried to make you see reason, but you refuse my overtures. This business with Mina and His Grace is all wrong and must be stopped. If you cannot aid me in that endeavor... I will simply have to take matters into my own hands, as I always have."

Oh, right. As she'd taken Lord Helmsby into her bed without benefit of a proposal and so cleverly had her own mama discover the cavorting couple before any real mischief could be done.

"Vanessa, please attempt to apply reason. If I told Finlay that his interest in Wilhelmina could go nowhere, he'd be proposing to her in the next quarter hour. He hates me, as you have so graciously noted. Mina would be tempted to accept him. The Cathcart men have charm, lest you forget. Emily could not do better than a duke for a step-father, and Mina would consider that too. The best you can hope for, Vanessa, is that this tempest of attraction blows itself out as quickly as it has arisen."

Though it wouldn't. Edwardia wasn't so doddering that she was blind to budding romance.

"You could still forbid the match. Wilhelmina would abide by your wishes."

"That might have been true when she was a girl of seventeen, but she's quite grown up now, Vanessa. I believe marriage to William taught Mina the perils of allowing others to do her thinking for her. Shall I have Balcomb show you out?"

"No need. He'd be until spring getting up here from the kitchen. Good day." She marched from the parlor, dignity in full sail, purloined treats in her hand. The door closed with an audible thump.

Edwardia took a profiterole and dunked it into her tea. "Do I warn Finlay, or trust him to deal with her?"

Charles eyed the cheese tarts longingly.

"Finlay won't listen to me," Edwardia went on, tossing the dog a treat, which he consumed in a single bite. "I wasn't exaggerating about that. The Cathcart male has a will of granite, witness Lord Thornton's nonsense, and Finlay's prejudices have a basis in fact."

Edwardia finished her tea and two more profiteroles before deciding that Charles really did need some fresh air. Finlay and Wilhelmina were adults, and they'd suit. Whatever nonsense Vanessa was plotting would come to nothing, as all her nonsense came to nothing, as her son had come to nothing.

And the family finances were simply an unavoidable fact of life.

Edwardia aimed a final observation at the portrait above the mantel. "We can still afford to feed the pups, my love, and that won't change. We'll manage. Come, Charles. Old bones want regular movement, or they soon want for a shroud."

"You are playing house with a respectable widow," Pritchard said, passing Finn the purple scarf. "If Antonio knows what you're up to, then half of Mayfair cannot be far behind."

In the two weeks since Finn had shown Wilhelmina his parents' former abode, he and she had enjoyed its privacy on a half-dozen damned-near-platonic occasions.

"The dwelling has acquired airs and graces since my parents lived there," Finn said, arranging his scarf. "The ground floor is unchanged, but upstairs, walls have been knocked out, the ceiling raised, two balconies added. Mrs. Cathcart has sound ideas for the appointments, and I value her opinions."

"If you value her reputation, you will cease these *rendezvous*." Pritchard shoved Finn's hat at him. And, of course, Pritchard was delivering this sermon in the very foyer, within earshot of the steps leading above and below.

"Mrs. Cathcart is a widow in excellent standing," Finn retorted. "I am nominally the head of her extended family. I think better about the ducal nonsense when I'm there with her." Finn tapped his hat onto his head and took up the satchel he'd been trying to avoid—with limited success—since he'd been harangued by the solicitors.

"Pretending to tote around sketchbooks won't fool anybody, Your Grace."

"My Rubbishing Grace can sack you, Pritchard. You insult a woman whom I esteem greatly." *Whom I love.*

That threat, which Finn hadn't made for at least a year, provoked Pritchard to removing Finn's hat and settling it at a more rakish angle.

"If you aren't disporting like minks, then what do you and she *do* on these cozy afternoons?"

"None of your business." Finn plucked his walking stick from its hook near the umbrella stand and would have decamped on that note, except that Pritchard looked worried.

Pritchard excelled at conveying vexation, amusement, annoyance, long-suffering, impatience, and a host of other superior attitudes, but he never allowed anxiety to show in his features. Finn well knew where and at what cost a fellow learned that skill.

"Mrs. Cathcart was supposed to become the next duchess," Finn said. "She thus knows the properties, the pensioners, and the tenants. Which steward is new, which is the fifth of his line to serve in that capacity. She knows what the solicitors would never think is important—which neighbors have five daughters to launch and not a feather to fly with. We *talk*, Pritchard. The lady and I talk, and she tells me the stories that the ledgers cannot reveal on their own."

Wilhelmina also touched Finn with maddening and delightful frequency, but never as Finn increasingly longed to touch her and be touched by her.

Pritchard passed over Finn's gloves, the ones lined with rabbit fur. "She's making a duke of you."

Wilhelmina was also, one smile, one soft embrace, one pot of tea at a time, driving Finn daft. "I'm not about to ask Edwardia for this information." Had honestly not known such intelligence was necessary to managing the estates, but it absolutely was.

"Of course you won't, and may Her Grace perish amid horrid scandal and be consigned to eternal flames," Pritchard said, making a circling motion with his hand.

"I have been nothing but civil to that old woman." Finn tucked his walking stick beneath his arm and pulled on his gloves. "Willie would scold me within an inch of my life if I showed Edwardia any overt disrespect."

The slight crease in Pritchard's brow disappeared. "*Willie?* You refer to this lady whom you esteem as *Willie*, and you vow to me that your private assignations with her are glorified business meetings. I fear the cold has affected your wits."

They *were* glorified business meetings. Friendly, even affectionate business meetings, God help a poor, besotted duke. "I will sack you without a character."

"Well, in that case, I apologize for my thoughtless words and beg Your Grace's pardon. I don't want to be sacked just yet, you see. This woman whom you esteem *and call Willie* has also inspired you to pace yourself in the studio, to enjoy regular rest by dark of night, and to deal more patiently with your apprentices. Whatever your designs on her might be, she is a good influence on you, and those, I point out in all delicacy, have been in lamentably short supply."

Pritchard retreated down the steps to the lower reaches, humming the tune to Mozart's lovely aria "Voi Che Sapete."

Tell me what love is, what can it be
What is this yearning burning me?
Can I survive it, will I endure?
This is my sickness, is there a cure?

"You are sacked!" Finn yelled. "Turned off without notice or a character. Your wages withheld for improper conduct."

Laughter floated up from below—Pritchard audibly laughing—and thus, when Finn left the house, he was whistling. He was still whistling when he joined Wilhelmina before the blazing hearth where his own parents might well have spent some pleasant afternoons.

"Finlay, welcome." Wilhelmina rose and hugged him, and just like that, Finn's world came right. Aching hands, a meddling major-domo, lovestruck apprentices, and boring ledgers all faded like snowflakes landing in a spring freshet.

Finn wrapped his arms around her and breathed in sweetness and warmth. "You beat me here."

She tucked closer. "I wanted to get out of the house."

"How is Emily?" He always asked that question first, because Wilhelmina was powerless to resist the subject. She could be aloof regarding Mayfair gossip, reserved when it came to discussing her disloyal staff, and detached about the family properties, but when it came to Emily, Wilhelmina was simply a mother who adored her child.

"My daughter is writing stories." Wilhelmina took a reading chair by the fire. "They are all set in dark, exotic forests or steaming jungles. I do not know where the child gets her imagination."

"A mystery, truly. Remind me who staged an entire coronation procession for her dolls when she was but six years old?"

"Hush, and stop looming. You loom so well, and I am unaccustomed to being loomed over. You brought the ledgers again, and your smile isn't quite as bright as I prefer. I demand an explanation."

Wilhelmina had demanded the occasional kiss as well, and to Finn's fierce satisfaction, she had also taken to wearing boots with one-inch heels. He settled in the second chair and laid the satchel of doom at his feet.

"I've been thinking about all these properties," he said. "My ruminations are gloomy, Willie."

She tossed him a pillow, which he wedged behind his back. "Tell me these dreary thoughts."

"The lawyers danced all around the truth, didn't they? On paper, the dukedom has vast wealth, but I own some quarries in Italy. I understand the difference between assets and solvency."

"You own quarries, plural?"

"I won the first one in a card game, and it wasn't nearly as played out as the previous owner thought. I've been lucky and made some good investments, and yes... I own three quarries, and they all yield excellent-quality stone. They also mean I can offer lower prices for my wares, and I get the best choice of specimens to start with."

"You *trade* in marble?"

"Marble and alabaster, primarily. Pritchard invests in art. We're trying to coax Antonio into the cent-per-cents as a place to start, but coaxing a lovesick adolescent who holds a dim view of legal commerce requires patience."

Wilhelmina toed off her slippers and tucked up her feet. "Fortunately for Antonio, you have patience, vast quantities, if your lessons with Emily are any indication."

Lately, Finn's patience had been in short supply. Too many dreams of Wilhelmina taking off more than her slippers.

"Emily is an apt pupil. In any case, I grasp how wealth on paper can reflect poverty in reality, and the ducal ledgers savor of precisely such a scheme."

"Scheme?" Wilhelmina's expression became severe. "Finlay, are you saying the solicitors are crooked? Those same fellows manage Emily's funds, and if you think—"

Finn held up a hand. "So fierce. I believe the solicitors have done everything possible to avert the present situation, but even they could not have foreseen how disastrous peace would be for the British economy." Well, a century of mostly war, with the expenses attendant thereto, followed by peace.

"Bread has become very dear," Wilhelmina said, "but I thought that was because of the Corn Laws."

"The Corn Laws allow the landed classes to starve the poor, but even the squires are struggling. The problem for the Huntleigh dukedom is that we cannot sell many assets. We own tens of thousands of acres, true, but the value of land has fallen precipitously. Much of that land is mortgaged, and thus the property isn't worth enough to eliminate the debt by selling the acres."

"We are in difficulties?"

Such a polite term for a mare's nest of trouble. "Heading for difficulties. I haven't worked out the full extent of the problem. The old duke broke the entail on some smaller properties, but as I understand it, I cannot break any entails until I have an adult heir willing to consent to breaking them."

"Correct, as far as I comprehend such arrangements. William was adamant that the entails remain in place 'for the sake of our sons,' and Lady Helmsby was nigh rabid on the topic. Entails protect future generations, according to their thinking, even though Lord Helmsby—when he was the heir presumptive—agreed three of the properties could be freed from legal restraints. Helmsby died, and the old duke hoped that William would eventually see reason, but here we are."

"Here the dukedom is, sliding into ruin. This is why the old girl tracked me down, isn't it?"

Wilhelmina shifted on her cushions. "Edwardia sent St. Didier to find you because you are the duke."

Finn moved to sit at her feet and take her hand. "You are too pure of heart to see mischief in others. The duchess does not care that I am the rightful heir—she was happy to see me starve as a child—but she cares very much that nobody knows the title is insolvent. Had the crown taken possession, the situation would have become fodder for gossip overnight."

Wilhelmina stroked his fingers. "You have a very dim view of Her Grace, though I doubt scandal figured in her thinking. Lady Helmsby saw breaking entails as admitting to financial strain, but Edwardia is above all pragmatic."

Finn rested his temple against Wilhelmina's thigh. "I detest ledgers. I deal with them out of necessity, but I see entire volumes filled with numbers and I want to get drunk."

"William did get drunk." She caressed Finn's hair. "Frequently, and over less provocation than ledgers. Will you meet with the solicitors again?"

"I must. I will bring Pritchard, to whom figures are the Creator's most delightful handiwork. The man sees an abacus and nearly starts purring."

Wilhelmina bent down and kissed Finn's cheek, lingering near enough to whisper in his ear. "I see you and I want to start purring. I'm sorry about the ledgers."

When she kissed him like that, when her breath whispered across his cheek, Finn did not care one feeble *arrivederci* about the ledgers.

He got to his feet, aiming for languid grace and doubtless potting awkward haste smack on the nose. "The ledgers are a nuisance, but I'll manage. My grasp of the workings of mammon would probably horrify the duchess. What is Emily reading these days?"

Wilhelmina stood as well and pursued Finn over to the sideboard. "You are rattled. This business with the money bothers you, doesn't it? You are the duke, Finn, and the finances have apparently been suffering for years. You cannot blame either circumstance on Edwardia."

"The money is irksome, but from what I can tell, the old duke did not inflate the value of his properties in an attempt to qualify for bigger loans. He was prudent, within the limits of his situation."

Wilhelmina smoothed a hand over Finn's sternum and brushed his hair back. These little touches were becoming frequent, and Finn adored them, truly he did.

But adoration wasn't his only response to being stroked, patted, caressed, and whispered to by the woman he esteemed.

He took Wilhelmina's hand lest she grow more affectionate. "I am courting you."

"*We* are courting, discreetly."

"Wilhelmina, I am also human, male, and in full possession of my faculties. I should be above the tyranny of my animal spirits, and I am, but if we continue to enjoy..." He fell silent and tried to reorganize his thoughts into something delicate and diplomatic.

Something *dignified*, for the love of winged cherubs.

"Willie, if you keep looking at me like that, I will have to go for a long walk in the elements without my greatcoat, gloves, or scarf. Or hat."

She used her free hand to pat his lapel. "How do I look at you?"

"Like I am a vanilla ice much in need of... licking."

She studied him with a solemnity that steadied Finn's wits —slightly.

"Let's sit," she said, leading him by the hand back to the hearth. "I need to explain something."

Something brief, God willing. "Separate chairs would be best if you expect me to make coherent replies."

"I do," Wilhelmina said, taking a seat and tucking her feet up again. "And I don't."

Finn took the second chair and prepared to rely on his supposedly vast stores of patience. He could wrestle flying angels from solid stone. Listening to Wilhelmina lecture him was certainly within his abilities.

He hoped.

CHAPTER TWELVE

How was it possible that Mina had known Finn only a handful of weeks, and yet, she felt closer to him than she ever had to William? And she and Finn weren't even lovers—yet.

There Finn sat, looking earnest and slightly worried, but willing to listen to whatever nonsense Mina spouted. He'd take her words seriously, take her feelings seriously, and even were he a homely specimen with little address, Mina would still be drawn to him for that quality alone.

But he was not a homely specimen with little address, and thus...

"I've insulted my late spouse by referring to him as a toy," Mina said, though that wasn't where she'd planned to start.

"All play and no work," Finn murmured, rearranging the pillow at his back. "Was that an insult or a simple statement of the truth?"

Heaven help her, she liked even the sound of his voice. "Some of both, perhaps, but William was what he'd been raised to be. His father was the spare and something of a fribble—Lady Helmsby was able to all but entrap his lordship into marriage, if I can believe the gossip—and William was not by nature studious."

Finn's right eyebrow lifted a quarter inch, and such was Mina's sense of this man, she even understood the language of his eyebrows.

Out with it, my dear.

"I honestly found William handsome," she said. "Tall, blond, genial... His attitude toward me was that we were thrown together by fate and might as well muddle on as good-naturedly as possible."

"He wasn't cruel," Finn said gently, "but he hurt you."

Accurate. "I prefer to think that he disappointed me, tried my patience, perturbed my peace... but yes. He'd kiss my forehead and flit off to see his mistress, then stumble home after midnight, much in need of a bath, and expect me to offer him a cheery welcome."

"Which you did."

Mina considered equivocating, but for this discussion, only the truth would serve. "I told myself he'd been at the clubs playing cards or off to a gaming hell. I don't think he ever actually... not on the same night, but I can tell you his mistress wore Séduction by the House of Honoré. Every time I smell that fragrance, which is quite dear, I want to hurl a boot through a window."

Finn wrinkled his nose. "Not a subtle perfume. Cloying. Almost vulgar in its lack of subtlety. Honeysuckle deserves a light touch."

Mina took courage from that observation. "I deserve a husband who will not send his mistress to the same modiste my mother-in-law patronizes." Though again, that wasn't quite what she'd wanted to say.

"An exclusive establishment?"

"I was still sewing my own nightgowns, and... yes, exclusive. Madame Bernadette is no more French than I am, but she has the accent down and a good eye for how to flatter whoever needs flattering, with both her words and with her needle."

"You are angry at William," Finn said slowly. "I am furious with my parents—still, to this day. I love them, too, of course, and appreciate the many sacrifices they made for me. But in here,"—he tapped his chest—"there is still a small boy who rages at his parents for abandoning him. Doesn't make any sense, but I look at Emily, and I know the rage is still there."

And when he looked at Emily, he saw a dear, small child wrestling with big challenges. He did not see her as proof of anybody's virility, much less care—God in heaven—that she *wasn't a boy*.

"I am angry at William," Mina said slowly. "Not for dying, and that is bad of me, but for how he expected me to live as his wife. How they *all* expected me to live as his wife. Meek, biddable, gracious, sweet, *fertile*... I was to placidly accept all the disrespect and polite fictions, to understand that a prospective duchess who does not have sons also lacks bargaining power in any sense. I was a charity case, and I was to be perpetually grateful for *everything*."

Finn was quiet for a moment, and that was helpful, because Mina hadn't put her thoughts into words previously, and stating the truth was painful.

Also a relief.

"You should try your hand at sculpting," Finn said. "When you can turn a block of marble into the object of your choosing—a dove, an angel, a philosopher—you regain some sense of your worth. Patience and skill have the power to transform stone, and that is a fine consolation for a fellow who cannot change one iota of his past."

"You have regrets." He'd said as much, but Mina understood now that one could be driven and defined by regrets.

"I have tons' worth of regrets. If I ever become one of yours, I don't know how I'll live with myself."

"That's... good." The wind soughed down the chimney, and the fire flared. Peat, because Finn preferred the scent and milder heat to coal and the price to wood. "Finn, if we marry—I'm not saying we will—promise me there won't be any mistresses. I'm not asking for perfect fidelity, a man grows restless, I know, and a duke has many options, but I'm asking not to be regularly subjected to another woman's perfume."

Perhaps Mina was asking too much, but better to know that now.

Desire was no excuse for abandoning all dignity.

Or not a good enough excuse.

"Why not ask for fidelity?" Finn replied, crossing his legs at the knee, Continental fashion. "Why not demand it? William expected that much of you."

"That's different. He was responsible for the succession, as was I."

Finn propped his chin on his right fist and gave Mina the sort of perusal he likely turned on a truant apprentice. In that posture, his left index finger tapping slowly on the arm of the chair, he put Mina in mind of Draco—testy, elegant, his powerful wings half folded, claws curled for the nonce.

"I was rattling about somewhere on the Continent," Finn said, "so the succession wasn't destitute for heirs. William could have given you a few years of devotion. He could have tried to hold up his end of the bargain."

A thousand demurrals clamored for voice. William had been young. He'd been an exponent of the values he was raised with. He'd never promised Mina fidelity, and...

And *nothing*. Mina had been William's junior by four years. Honor was a value any child ought to be raised with, and Wiliam had spoken public vows of fidelity and caring.

"Very well, then," Mina said, feeling a bit like a dragon herself. "No mistresses, no affairs. If we marry, we agree to rub along for better or for worse, or we won't marry at all."

Finn sat up. "I'm still courting you, you besom. That you felt you had to establish my bona fides on the matter of exclusivity nearly offends me, but you have your reasons."

"Lord Helmsby had mistresses," Mina retorted. "The old duke was a rake during his first marriage. William's friends would have taunted him without mercy for falling in love with his own wife. You haven't been about in Society much, Finlay. The typical Mayfair match is a political, social, and financial alliance. Finer feelings aren't supposed to come into it."

"How fortunate for me that you hail from sensible Wiltshire stock and are above such venery. Are you quite finished counting my teeth, Wilhelmina?"

"Yes, and fine teeth they are too." Wilhelmina took her courage in both hands, rose, and deposited herself in Finn's lap. "Now I want to try your paces."

She'd taken a risk, and for one instant, she feared her gamble would result in laughter, mortification, or a courtship abruptly gone sour. Then Finn's arms closed around her, and his cheek rested against her temple.

"Darling Willie, I feared you would never ask."

Finn cradled Wilhelmina in his lap—the proceedings had moved to a wing chair point by mutual agreement—and reminded himself of two abiding realities. First, he was *courting* the lady. They were not engaged, and how he comported himself in the next hour could well decide whether they ever became betrothed.

Much less married.

Second, he would withdraw. No matter the temptation, no matter the inspiration, he would not risk a conception that took away the freedom both parties had to choose from the heart.

To be chosen from the heart.

"Kiss me," Wilhelmina said. "Please."

Finn obliged, trying to keep the undertaking light and pleasant, but Willie had other ideas.

"Kiss me like you mean it, Finn."

"If I kiss you like that, I will mean it, and parading through the house in a state of blatant—"

Wilhelmina got him by the nape and kissed the daylights out of him. Lips, tongue, soft murmurs of pleasure, sighs...

I am doomed.

"This is the housekeeper's half day," she said, wiggling diabolically on Finn's lap, "and I asked her to lay a fire in the main bedroom before she went to call on her sister."

"Whyever... Willie, please *sit still*."

The infernal minx grinned. "Sorry. I sometimes nap after you leave, or I bide upstairs and read while the light lasts. I have privacy here—true privacy—and that is a rare treat."

Finn considered romping on the parlor floor before the fire, which arrangement had the advantage of being three feet away, but no. Wilhelmina had created the option of a bedroom, and putting his best foot forward did not entail carpet burns on the lady's backside.

Think, man. The only thought he could claim was Pritchard's maxim. *Sooner begun is sooner done,* though in this case, that also implied that sooner begun was sooner done again and again.

"To the bedroom with us," Finn said, "where you can kiss me witless, and I can return the favor—for starts." He rose, Wilhelmina in his arms, and made for the door. She was a delightful burden, and by the time he reached the bedroom door, his back and arms were protesting. A helpful distraction from other bodily clamorings.

Wilhelmina lifted the door latch, and then they were at last alone, together, in a toasty bedroom. Finn deposited Willie on the bed and stood back lest she topple him onto the covers.

"Wilhelmina Cathcart, I am not a vanilla ice."

"Heaven be thanked for small mercies." She lifted her skirts to the knee and began fussing with her garters.

"No," Finn said, the sight of silk-clad ankles robbing him of eloquence. "Please, stop, rather. I'd like to do that."

Wilhelmina let her skirts fall. "You want to be my lady's maid?" The notion seemed to intrigue her.

"I want to be your lover, and I pray I have the fortitude to survive that honor. Assisting you to undress would be my greatest joy." Well, one of his greatest joys. He knelt before her, and she tentatively pointed a toe in his direction.

This part, Finn could manage. He slid a hand under her hems and caressed smooth muscle until he encountered a satin garter. By

degrees, he raised Wilhelmina's skirts until the garter was winking at
him from among a froth of lace and velvet.

"The darker greens become you," he said, untying the ribbon and
rolling her stocking down. "You are among few women who'd also
look good in garnet or violet." He kissed her knee, both to gratify a
roaring need to touch her anywhere and to shut his fool mouth.

"I love green," she said. "Wiltshire is endless green. I miss it."

"We'll go there on our honey month." He moved to the other
knee, which Wilhelmina was keeping quite close to its twin. Finn
lingered in the neighborhood as long as his imagination would allow,
then sat back. Truly, William Cathcart hadn't acquitted himself well
at all, poor sod.

"Hooks next," Finn said, rising and offering Wilhelmina his hand.
She took it—encouraging sign—and gave him her back.

More kisses, to her nape and neck, while Finn unfastened four-
thousand-eight-hundred-and-forty-three hooks, all the while resisting
the temptation to slip his arms around Wilhelmina's waist and press
himself against her intimately.

When he'd emerged victorious from the war of the hooks and
acquitted himself successfully through the siege of the corset strings,
Wilhelmina turned in his arms.

"You are driving me mad," she muttered. "I can't think. Your
hands are warm and—" She fastened her mouth to his, and all the
kissing that had gone on previously was so much exhibition jousting
compared to the pitched battle she embarked on now.

By the time Wilhelmina allowed Finn to take a breath, he was at
full salute, and he'd tactilely explored the perfection that was her hips
and bum.

"Out of the dress, Willie. Please."

"Clothes off, Finn. Now."

They separated like a pair of prizefighters at the end of a glorious
round and stood panting and grinning at each other. Wilhelmina's
dress hung loosely from her shoulders, and Finn had lost his coat and
cravat.

"You know what you're about," Wilhelmina said. "You don't treat me like I'm made of glass."

Finn started on the buttons of his waistcoat. "You don't act like glass, all cool, smooth, and fragile." The last button went sailing to the carpet, and Finn stuck his hand out in Wilhelmina's direction. "Some assistance would be appreciated."

She extracted his sleeve buttons and dropped them on the vanity. Finn pulled his shirt over his head and let the lady gawk.

"I'm a brute," he said. "Comes of carrying hod and hauling stone from an early age."

Wilhelmina strolled around behind him. "You are a work of art. God above, Finlay. No wonder you were sought after as a life model."

She traced a finger down his spine, then wrapped her arms about his waist and hugged him from behind. Her contours were pressed to his, and some unnamed anxiety lost its grip on Finn's heart.

"I have never been a work of art before."

"Yes, you have. When you went off to Belgium with barely a penny to your name, when you sought your fortune in Rome, when you disdained St. Didier's importuning, when you kept Westhaven's commission... You *are* a work of art."

She came around and stood before him. "Some assistance would be appreciated." She'd managed to mimic his tone—imperious, impatient—and her smile was pure devilment.

Finn eased the dress over her head, undid the petticoat tapes, and freed her from her stays. The lot of it went onto the nearest available chair.

She stood before him in bare feet and a wrinkled chemise. "You first, sir."

Finn's lover wasn't referring to who should be first to climb into bed. He sat on the only free chair and pulled off his boots and stockings. "I am not a work of art, Wilhelmina. In some regards, I am truly a brute."

He stood and peeled out of his breeches, adding them to the

heap. He was thoroughly aroused—no disguising the obvious—and prepared for awkwardness.

He was not prepared for Wilhelmina to push him back onto the bed and climb upon him like a woman finally granted a full serving of her very most favorite flavor of treat.

The whole canoodling business was both familiar to Wilhelmina and entirely new terrain. William hadn't been a prude, but he'd expected modesty from his wife. His attentions had been restrained, sometimes pleasant, always affectionate, and often... boring.

Wilhelmina had come to consider marital duties under the same heading as concocting menus—which she occasionally did as William exerted himself to sire an heir—and attending the duchess's at homes. Not drudgery, but shading very close to dull.

With Finn... She knelt over him on the bed and beheld the expanse of his chest, a landscape of muscle, flesh, and bone.

"You are always warm," she said, tracing a rib with her index finger. "Even in winter, everywhere, you are warm."

"The longer you touch me, the warmer I shall become, until you find yourself playing with fire."

She dismounted and crawled to the head of the bed. "Idle promises. You'll have to do—*oof.*"

Finn had caught her about the middle and flipped her to her back, then appropriated the superior position.

"Turnabout is the least you deserve, madam."

He remained on all fours above her, his hair coming loose from its queue. They hadn't lit any candles, so the only illumination, other than the dreary winter overcast, was the fire in the hearth. The flames sent shadows dancing across Finn's features and picked out garnet highlights in his dark hair.

"Finn..." Wilhelmina wrapped a hand around his nape and twined a leg around his flank.

"The time for philosophical discourse is behind us, Willie. You can give me orders in small words spoken very clearly, but don't expect brilliant conversation from me for the next hour. Not with words."

Give him *orders?* A suggestion worth testing. "Get. Under. The. Covers."

He sat back, pushed his hair off his brow, and was soon situated beside Wilhelmina beneath the quilts. He truly did throw off a scrumptious amount of heat.

"I meant what I said, Willie." He threaded an arm beneath her neck and pulled her close. "You must be very honest and forthright. I haven't disported since well before returning to England, and my finesse might desert me."

Had William ever once worried about his *finesse?* "I haven't any finesse. I know every place where cobwebs start in the corners of my bedroom ceiling. I know how to breathe with fourteen stone of exhausted male atop me. I can compose correspondence in prose that reflects the rhythm of straining bed ropes." She sniffed the warm skin of Finn's shoulder—faintly scented of balsam—and wanted to both laugh and cry.

Finn kissed her nose and began working at the pins securing the braid of her coronet. "You don't fool me. A woman who can compose menus in the midst of a passionate interlude is simply keeping her powder dry. When you decide I've earned your regard, your finesse will topple me flat, and I will be the most pleased and happy of fallen lovers."

Wilhelmina liked the idea that she'd simply lacked proper inspiration. Liked it a lot. The notion that Finn had to *earn* her passion was wonderfully encouraging.

"Will I be exhausted too, Finlay?"

"Ecstatically so. Kiss me. I'll show you."

Wilhelmina kissed him, half rising on an elbow, and by the time she was again flat on her back, Finn had demonstrated that kisses could be tender, humorous, and devastating by turns. Her braid came undone, and the first time Finn cupped her breasts in his fiendishly talented hands, her wits unraveled as well.

"When you do that..."

"This?" His caress was both cherishing and maddening.

"Like that, I want to tear off my own chemise."

"Willie,"—he nuzzled her throat—"is that a request?"

What was he...? "Up." She shoved at his chest, and he heaved back onto his haunches. The Finn staring down at her was a far cry from the Finn who'd joined her in the cozy sitting room. His hair was wild, he was as naked as the Apollo Belvedere, and his endowments—which said Apollo would envy—were unashamedly anticipating copulation.

Wilhelmina frankly stared.

"Your chemise," Finn said, running a finger around the inside of her decolletage. "You sought to remove it."

She tried to hike herself onto her elbows, but that left no hands free to wrestle yards of linen.

"Here." Finn put a palm between her shoulder blades, half cradled her against his chest, gathered up her chemise, then lifted it free. "Much better." He tossed the garment aside and kissed Wilhelmina onto her back. "Much, *much* better."

Wilhelmina regarded her chemise, now adorning the privacy screen at a jaunty angle. "This is your finesse in action?"

"Heavens, no. If you'd like to get to the finessing part, I can oblige."

"Oblige me, please."

His version of finesse involved leisurely caresses to every part of Wilhelmina's body—shoulders, calves, hips, even her ankles did not escape his explorations. He touched her as if his hands were learning more than the turn of her elbow or the curve of her knee. Wherever those hands went, Wilhelmina's awareness went too, and thus she learned along with him.

Her palms were sensitive to the brush of Finn's callused thumb. The back of her knee was ticklish. The sensations evoked by soft circles at her nape turned her boneless, until he resumed kissing her, and then a restlessness took over.

A solution to the restlessness popped into her mind all of a piece: *turnabout*. This fiend, sculpting passion one sweet touch at a time, was deserving of all the turnabout Wilhelmina could conjure.

Finn's nipples were sensitive—a delightful discovery—and he liked to have his hands touched, too, if a soft, manly sigh was any indication. Gently, of course, and it occurred to Wilhelmina that Finn Cathcart had known too little of gentleness. That insight infused her lovemaking with a dangerous tenderness.

When her caresses wandered to the splendid evidence of Finn's arousal, she was careful. William had humored her curiosity, but never more than that, almost as if his desire was a fragile thing that would wilt at too much handling.

"You don't mind?" she asked, tracing Finn's contours.

He lifted his head from the pillows and regarded her in the gloom. "*Dio aiutami*. How could I mind a dream come true?"

Tears threatened again, for no reason whatsoever. Wilhelmina pressed her cheek to Finn's shoulder and wished... What? What was the regret that gilded this lovely, extraordinary moment?

"I have never been anybody's dream come true before."

Finn's arm became more snug around her shoulders, and his hand cupped the back of her head. "A lack of imagination in others was no reflection on you, Willie. You have filled my dreams and my heart in equally wondrous measures."

His earlier warning, about the time for brilliant discourse having passed, made sense to her then. She had no words to describe the sort of loneliness she'd endured from the moment she'd grasped what an arranged betrothal was, to the moment Finn Cathcart had taken her in his arms. No words for an exhausted spirit that was finally, finally regaining some vigor.

No words for a passion that refused to wait one more moment.

Finn sensed a change in Wilhelmina, or a series of changes. She went from cautious to interested to determined, and then... some shift in sentiment had imbued her curious touches with lyricism, with a reverence that left Finn humbled and determined.

Very, very determined.

"Cry if it pleases you to cry, Wilhelmina." He gathered her close so they lay on their sides, her nose tucked against his chest.

"I have cried enough, and so, I hazard, have you, though in your case tears were seldom permitted. Today, we rejoice." She hiked a leg over his hip and urged him closer.

Finn yielded, though he refused to retreat from emotion into mindless passion. He wasn't ashamed of tender feelings—though they unnerved him considerably—and he ached for the younger Wilhelmina, who'd never been cherished as she deserved to be.

He kept his kisses unhurried, even as he trailed his hand lower and asked delicately for more of Wilhelmina's trust. She shifted, parting her knees... enough.

She muttered something against his neck. *Gracious*, perhaps, so he dared a bit more, and while she didn't exactly fall into a wanton sprawl, she didn't resist the pleasure either.

Finezza. He schooled himself to restraint, to delicacy, to focusing on Wilhelmina's every breath, on the way her fingers bit into his shoulder.

"I cannot... Finlay, enough." She let go of his shoulder and manacled his wrist when Finn would have nudged her over the edge. "I want you." She glowered at him. "I want *you*."

Small words spoken very clearly that went straight to his heart. "I am yours."

He eased over her. She welcomed him with a fierce embrace, and then the moment was upon him to exercise every iota of his *finezza* along with his entire store of *pazienza*. He hadn't even set up a proper rhythm before Wilhelmina lunged at him with her hips and made a sound between a laugh and a groan.

"Drat you, Finlay. Drat you, and don't you dare stop."

He did not stop, and neither did she for a good, long moment—in fact, she went galloping after her pleasure—until she subsided to the pillows on a sigh.

"Shall you go again?" Finn asked, settling onto his elbows.

"I could not possibly."

He gave her a few minutes to marvel at her good fortune while he marveled at his—the lady was a bonfire waiting to happen—and then she did, possibly and even definitely, go again, and again.

"You will be sore," Finn said, easing himself free of her. "I will be too." He brought himself off in a few strokes, retrieved his handkerchief from the nightstand, and dealt with the mess.

He tossed the handkerchief in the direction of the privacy screen and rolled to Wilhelmina's side. She bundled close and hiked a leg across his middle.

"I can nap atop you if you'd rather," he said. "Or you can nap atop me. I might like that."

To his surprise, Wilhelmina straddled him, then cuddled down to his chest. "Hold me, please."

He embraced her gently and realized that now came the true test of finesse. He hesitated to declare his feelings, but some words were needed. Some special words.

"Hold me, too, Willie, please." He brought the covers over her shoulders and stroked her back with a lazy hand. "I came here today grumbling about ledgers and now... All is right with my world. Unnerves a fellow to have his brooding upended with so little notice."

"I love it when you touch me like that." She kissed him, then closed her eyes and gave every evidence of having retired to the land of Morpheus.

Finn breathed with her and decided that her words were special, and the day was special, and all was, indeed, right with his world.

At last.

CHAPTER THIRTEEN

"Lady Helmsby." Leopold St. Didier bowed, though not too low. This particular ducal heir's widow was not a duchess, though she expected that degree of deference. "This is a surprise. Would you care for some tea?"

"Tea would be lovely. A stout China black on this dreary day." She began a circuit of St. Didier's public parlor, which was carefully appointed to show good taste, a proud lineage, and merely respectable wealth. The furniture, while elegant and well uphol-stered, did not qualify as antique. The carpet was good British Axminster rather than some Continental affectation, and the curtains were stolid burgundy velvet rather than Belgian lace.

The parlor was intended to reflect reduced rather than humble circumstances.

"You do resemble your father and grandfather," Lady Helmsby said, pausing before a portrait of both men done shortly after St. Didi-er's birth. "That has to be a bit inconvenient at times."

An exploratory and rude reference to the loss of the title, couched as a sympathetic murmur.

"They were both accounted good-looking devils, in their days,"

St. Didier said, tugging the bell-pull twice. "I am pleased to think I continue the tradition. Dear me, that sky looks like snow."

Bad of him, to borrow His Grace of Huntleigh's tactic.

Her ladyship glanced at the window, which by design faced the walled back garden rather than the street. "We are in the depths of winter. Snow is to be expected, and railing against the inevitable is unbecoming."

"Was I railing? I do beg your pardon."

Her ladyship took up examining a slender porcelain vase holding dried sea lavender St. Didier had brought back from Italy. Though the flowers were quite dead, their imperial purple hue was the most vivid splash of color in the room.

"His Grace made this vase, didn't he?" she asked, tracing the delicately fluted column. "You have on display as a sort of prize of war."

Another clumsy thrust, for which she likely thought herself arch and sophisticated.

St. Didier's instinct had been to avoid Lady Helmsby—Edwardia avoided her, and Mrs. Wilhelmina Cathcart was certainly not clinging to her mama-in-law's company either. Lady Helmsby had known nothing relevant to finding the present duke, and St. Didier wouldn't have trusted her to aid him in that objective anyway.

Prize of war indeed. "I own that vase because it's lovely, and the shape and color complement the preserved flora well."

The tea tray arrived, and St. Didier did not ask his guest to pour out. Giving her control of even the tea service seemed ill-advised.

"The shortbread is fresh," she said after several moments spent lamenting the state of society generally. "I cannot abide stale shortbread."

"Am I to be flattered that you approve of my shortbread?"

She smiled at him. "You are trying to rile me into revealing the purpose for my call. I approve of the tactic and use it myself frequently. Be a trifle outrageous, and people grow more careful in your company. I learned that by watching dear Lord Helmsby, to whom the strategy came naturally. William was shrewd enough to adopt it, too, though William was a kind soul at heart. If only that wretched horse hadn't proven so unsound."

St. Didier had observed William on many occasions. He'd been too lazy to engage in true social combat and too wellborn to have any real enemies.

"My lady, what brings you here today?" A widow could call on whomever she pleased, and not even Edwardia cast aspersions on Lady Helmsby's reputation. On her character, yes, but to disparage the lady's reputation would tarnish the family escutcheon.

"I have questions for you, Mr. St. Didier. I am sorry to trouble you—more sorry than you can possibly know—but I have nowhere else to turn."

He let that show of gentle humility pass unapplauded. "Ask your questions."

"How certain are you that Finlay Cathcart is the *legitimate* holder of the Huntleigh title?"

The duke had made his bow before the sovereign barely a week past and was preparing to endure the rigamarole in Parliament in the next fortnight.

"Very certain. Outside of a few venerable fellows at the College of Arms, I am likely the reigning expert on the proper documentation of a titular succession. Finlay's parents were married, that marriage was valid, and Finlay was born to them during the marriage. The late duke had no surviving sons, and Lord Helmsby's only legitimate male issue has tragically expired, as you know only too well. Unless Lord Thornton was somehow not a legitimate scion of the house, despite being the third son of the union, Finlay holds the title and is at present without heirs."

She took another piece of shortbread. "Lord Thornton was legitimate. Born to the duchess with the same pomp and celebration as his older brothers, more's the pity. What about the marriage? How can a Catholic wife produce the heir to an English ducal succession?"

"She converted. Became Church of England prior to the marriage. Finlay is Church of England and apparently always has been, which is the more relevant inquiry. I've seen his baptismal lines." St. Didier might have asked what all this curiosity was in aid of, except that he knew.

Lady Helmsby was looking for material with which to blackmail the present duke, and she wasn't even being subtle about it. She could have hired her own inquiry agents, made the rounds of the aging roues who'd known Lord Thornton back in the day, combed through old family correspondence, peered at a few parish registries, but she'd disdained to exert the effort.

Or perhaps time was of the essence.

"What about Finlay himself?" She gestured with a piece of short-bread. "How do we know this largish fellow with the overly long hair is truly Lord Thornton's get?"

Her ladyship came very close to insulting St. Didier and this time, when the aspersion mattered, she didn't seem to realize it.

"We know, my lady, because I can produce a host of witnesses, from the former curate of His Grace's late parents' parish, to men who apprenticed with him fifteen years ago, to servants, teachers, and acquaintances in a half-dozen nations. They will all attest to the identity of the fellow now holding the title." In fact, they all had, in writing, with proper, sober witnesses who knew the affiant personally. "Finlay Cathcart never used an assumed name and never denied his patrimony, despite the scandal."

A greedier man would have cut ties with his disgraced parents' memory. Finlay Cathcart was careful with money, but no miser, and he'd loved his parents.

"This is dreadful," her ladyship said, rising. "His Grace, if he is His Grace, is still *taking commissions*. All of Society will think we are rolled up, and when that happens, one quickly *becomes* rolled up."

Manners had St. Didier on his feet as well.

Her ladyship was right. When a noble family's finances were called into question, credit—upon which the aristocracy depended—evaporated. Debts were called in or accelerated. Goods were provided in exchange for cash only, invitations ceased, and servants of long standing tended to find other posts without giving notice.

St. Didier knew the litany all too well. "His Grace has kept one commission, my lady, some garden statues for the Earl of Westhaven, and that was at Westhaven's insistence. The first three should be done by spring, and that will probably be an end to it."

"One cannot offend a Windham," Lady Helmsby muttered. "Nevertheless, the situation is not as one would hope."

She had doubtless *hoped* that William would become the duke. "The Cathcart family is not rolled up, my lady. I had occasion to inquire of the solicitors in great detail on that topic. His Grace demanded the information before leaving Italy."

"Then he's come to bleed us dry, mark my words."

Not for the first time, St. Didier sympathized with the frequent lament of the lower orders, to which he, working for a living, now arguably belonged: *Oh, the Quality.*

"His Grace cannot bleed the title dry with so many of the estates still entailed. He's also powerless to touch Miss Emily's settlements, if that is your concern. Have I answered your questions, my lady?"

She stared at the burgundy curtains, which were draped and pleated in exactly symmetrical folds. "Emily is my first priority, of course. No father or great-uncle to look out for her. This cousin-come-lately duke having no notion of a child's needs, and Wilhelmina ingratiating herself shamelessly with him for all the world to see. A widow losing her dignity is a very sad business, Mr. St. Didier."

More bait, tossed upon the waters to see what gossip would surface.

"Mrs. Cathcart has assisted the duke to acquaint himself with his new and very unusual situation. As far as I know, Society grasps her role and commends her for it. Shall I see you out?"

"Mrs. Cathcart should pay more attention to my granddaughter and less to a duke who never should have inherited. The whole business is dreadful, St. Didier. You may show me out, and you have been no earthly assistance."

A small consolation. "I do apologize for disappointing you, but whatever fears you harbor regarding the family's future, I can assure that escheat would have been more dreadful still."

She sniffed and harrumphed and nevertheless all the way to the foyer and was still grumbling when St. Didier handed her up into Wilhelmina Cathcart's Town coach. When he returned to the foyer, his butler was on hand, his expression suggesting an unpleasant odor had befouled the air.

"She wasn't hiring me," St. Didier said. "You need not lecture me about standards and decorum, Comfrey."

"Of course not, sir."

Comfrey was young to be a butler, but he'd come highly recommended and didn't mind working for a plain mister. He was also extremely valuable in St. Didier's investigations.

"What has you sniffing and scowling, Comfrey?"

"She bribes Mrs. Wilhelmina Cathcart's servants. That sort of mischief never ends well for the one doing the bribing."

Interesting. The coach pulled away in a clatter of hooves. Good riddance. "You think Lady Helmsby is being blackmailed? She's a widow who has no claim on the title, is adequately set up, and in good health. Why would she take the risk of hiring spies who will learn her every secret and regret?"

Why was she looking for a means of blackmailing the duke, unless she was motivated by plain old spite directed at William's replacement?

"She hates the old duchess," Comfrey said, opening the door and removing the knocker. "She isn't any too fond of her daughter-in-law either." He hung the knocker—a lion's head—on the hook on the back of the door fashioned for the purpose.

A discontented woman. "Why did you take the knocker down? Proper calling hours are only beginning." Not that many people called on St. Didier in a social capacity. Falling from the peerage had yielded at least that singular advantage.

"I suspect you will be going out, sir. Lady Helmsby did not hire you, and thus her call merits no confidentiality."

"I am going out, but not to look in on the duchess. Has she paid us yet?"

"Regrettably no, sir. I will inform you the instant that situation changes." He took down St. Didier's greatcoat and held it open. "You will send word if we're to hold dinner?"

"Dinner at the club tonight. I have inquiries to make." Hat, gloves, and walking stick followed. "Why don't I wear scarves, Comfrey? The weather is bitter, and a scarf keeps the face warm."

"I will remedy the oversight with a sortie to Bond Street this afternoon, sir. Gray, brown, or black?"

"Scarlet merino wool, please. I wear enough sober colors. Here in London, on my own turf, I needn't blend in. Everybody knows who I am anyway."

Comfrey studied the knocker hanging on the back of the door. "Scarlet, sir? Not burgundy or a stately aubergine?"

What a dear fellow he was. "Not scarlet, then, but some variety of red. Carmine, burgundy, or blood red. Blood red would do nicely. Different, but not garish."

"Now you trifle with my composure. I will need two cups of tea before I recover. Good hunting, sir."

St. Didier jaunted down the steps and charted a course to Finlay Cathcart's front door.

"You're having suppers at the club now?" St. Didier asked, looking profoundly bored to find himself in the dining room of Finn's least-unfavorite club.

Finn gestured to the seat opposite. "Pritchard is very strict with me since I've been acquired by a title. I am to dine out two days a week lest I be thought reclusive. He doesn't seem to grasp how limited my options are and how sparse the available company. Westhaven sponsored my membership here. Anselm is seeing me dragooned into Brooks's. I don't think I could stomach White's, but Moreland offered."

His Grace of Moreland had passed along some advice too: *Find a good woman to sort you out—a woman who brings out the best in you—and by God, cleave to her with everything you have. The rest doesn't signify until you get that part right.*

"Their Graces are closing ranks in support of you." St. Didier took the proffered seat. "You likely have the ladies to thank for that. A youngish bachelor duke is not to be treated ill."

A waiter not-quite-hovered ten feet away until Finn gestured him over. "St. Didier will be dining with me. St. Didier, what will you have?"

"Whatever you're having."

"Very good, sir." The waiter produced a second place setting like some sort of conjurer and bustled off to the kitchen on silent feet. Such was the quality of the establishment, or perhaps such was the nature of St. Didier's standing with the staff, that no sniffy airs were displayed at any point.

St. Didier glanced around the dining room, which at this early hour was sparsely populated. "I called upon you this afternoon. The estimable Pritchard gave me to understand that at the sight of my handsome phiz, you'd decamp for the Antipodes, never to return."

"I was working. Prinny could come around for tea, and Pritchard would wave him off if I were working." Pritchard had strict orders to admit Mrs. Wilhelmina Cathcart at any hour. "You look about this venerable establishment as if you expect the gendarmerie to toss you out on your ear."

"They have to let me in," St. Didier said. "Loss of a title isn't grounds for loss of membership. Or it wasn't, and they couldn't apply such a rule retroactively without looking like snobs."

"I'm sorry," Finn replied. "One wants to be accepted on one's merits, not on a technicality. How long has it been since your fall from the peerage?"

"Twelve years, and I don't consider it a fall."

"You did at the time."

St. Didier swished his glass of claret gently. "I was at university. A few of the other students cut a wider berth around me, but the whole situation had been brewing for years. My mother had seen the writing on the wall and planned accordingly."

Finn was learning the path a new peer must travel—solicitors, royal levees, parliamentary mummery in ermine and velvet (mustn't forget the black tricorn), more solicitors—but he'd not considered what awaited a man moving in the opposite direction.

"How did you become the aristocracy's preferred heir-hunter?"

"I'd been expected to salvage the family's situation practically from infancy, and thus I was educated in all the protocol and arcana that goes with preserving a succession. The fellows at the College of Arms were sympathetic to my situation, so they imparted yet more wisdom regarding where to find documents, the reading of law Latin, or when rules might have exceptions based on exigent precedents set in previous centuries."

"All to no avail?"

"All to no avail, but then, I did not truly expect a reprieve. The crown was determined—the family seat was quite profitable and commodious—and my family of no great political standing, but ancient history is not the reason I'm sharing this meal with you."

And St. Didier, poor sod, likely always had reasons for his actions. No unplanned afternoon lovemaking for him. No morning spent sketching in the nursery for the simple pleasure of watching a child develop some proficiency with her art. No mad gallops first thing on a frigid morning just for the pleasure of putting roses in Wilhelmina Cathcart's cheeks.

"Then to what do I owe the honor, St. Didier? Have you prepared a lecture for me about the folly of returning to Italy?"

St. Didier studied Finn, wineglass in hand. The heir-hound

would be a good-looking devil if he'd ever abandon his signature severe expression. Finn began a mental sketch, starting with the line of that aquiline nose.

"Your Grace doesn't care for the wine?" St. Didier asked.

They were to discuss vintages? "This offering is too polite for my tastes. The humbler Italian reds have more to recommend them than the fussy French nonsense passing for genteel 'claret.'" Finn did not add, *And you are prevaricating*. St. Didier would get around to airing his agenda soon enough, though perhaps the fellow wanted to enjoy a decent steak in acceptable company first.

"Your Grace lacks that prisoner-in-the-dock look you had when I tracked you down in Naples."

"I let you track me down. You may thank Pritchard for my attack of..."

St. Didier finished his wine and set the glass on the table. "Conscience?"

"Stupidity. I was gaining renown, which for an English sculptor isn't so easy. My fortunes were on the rise, and there was Pritchard, muttering about he who turns his back on ladies who have no champion, he who ignores his birthright, he who eschews the opportunity to turn his own good fortune into good fortune for others more deserving. He's quite the angel of guilt, is Pritchard."

"You were successful in Italy, but were you happy?"

Had St. Didier asked that odd question a fortnight ago, even a week ago, Finn would have answered in the emphatic and put-upon affirmative. He'd been awash in contentment, commissions coming to him from the best families, all his ambitions approaching fruition.

But ambitions were not dreams, and neither ambitions nor dreams had prepared Finn for the reality of sharing a bed with Wilhelmina. She'd allowed him not simply a romp, but true intimacy. A connection of the heart that made all the rest unfathomably sweeter.

And she'd parted with a smidgeon of her trust, which was a headier potation than any wine ever created by human hands.

"I was content at the time," Finn said. "Pritchard was homesick, though, and when Pritchard is miserable, heaven weeps, along with the maids, footmen, apprentices, and cook."

St. Didier topped up their wineglasses, which was either presuming of him, an attempt to cozen Finn into believing the conversation was friendly, or... a compliment.

"How are you getting on with old Moreland?"

The food arrived, and as the meal passed, St. Didier regaled Finn with some of the peerage's wrinkled—not quite soiled—linen. Moreland had been a younger son gone for a soldier when his prospective duchess—a plain miss with no title and fewer prospects—had got her mitts on him. They were a love match, at a time such undertakings had been beyond unfashionable. Two illegitimate offspring had been raised with the ducal horde, both antedating the wedding vows by several years.

As the pudding was brought out, St. Didier segued into the *dramma comico* known as Devonshire House and then on to some of Prinny's lesser-known peccadilloes.

"But his interest in art is sincere and well informed," St. Didier said. "Don't mistake our Regent for a fool. He is foolish at times—frequently, in fact—but well aware of his milieu and shrewd when it suits him to be so."

"Is he your enemy? You've kept him from plundering dozens of estates." What would that require of a man, to count a future king among his enemies?

"A plain mister cannot afford the luxury of enemies. Prinny's objectives and mine diverge, is all. He's too much of a gentleman to regard me as anything other than a particularly wily rook in service to his troublesome nobles."

"You and Pritchard would get on famously. Challenge him to a few games of chess."

St. Didier took three bites of his dessert, a concoction that put Finn in mind of the Scottish sticky toffee pudding, and set the dish aside.

"Pritchard would not trust me to be after a mere game of chess, and his caution would be justified. Would Your Grace care to take a short constitutional with me after so fine a meal?"

The dining room had filled up as the meal had progressed, and Finn well knew a bid for discretion when one was proffered. St. Didier had bad news to pass along, apparently, but in Finn's present mood, in the mood that had followed him home from the little house on Ballater Court and wrapped around his heart ever since, anything pertaining to the ducal situation could not qualify as truly bad news.

Bothersome news, annoying news, inconvenient news, but nothing short of harm to Willie or Emily could qualify as bad news.

"Speak your piece, St. Didier," Finn said when they'd gained the quiet of a dark and frigid street. "You should wear a scarf, you know. Vanity won't keep the ague from laying you low in weather like this. Your ears will thank you too. Choose the color yourself, don't leave it to the dubious fashion sense of your valet."

"Lest I be decked out like Father Christmas?"

"Green would not suit you. Claret, perhaps. Nothing too subdued. Give the world a bit of warning of your approach. Fair play and all that."

Finn set a brisk pace, given the temperature, and St. Didier kept up easily.

"In the name of fair play," St. Didier said, "you should know that Lady Helmsby called on me today."

As annoying news went, her ladyship qualified, though merely annoying. "My condolences. How many times did she lament William the Paragon's death, and did she leave you any shortbread?"

"Several, and no, but she also questioned me with a view toward putting your legitimacy and the validity of your parents' marriage in doubt."

What would Wilhelmina think of this rear-guard action? "Bit late for that, isn't it?"

"Much too late, and I could not get a proper sense of what motivated her, until I recalled that you are unmarried."

Not for long. Finn hadn't yet chosen a ring, and his speech wanted some polishing. The ring would be old garnets, for protection, commitment, love, and trust.

Then too, wooing Wilhelmina had become a delightful undertaking—more delightful—and Finn sought to luxuriate for a few weeks in the pleasures of courting. Wilhelmina deserved that, and Finn needed it too. Marry in haste, and Society would jabber endlessly.

There had been enough jabbering in Finn's parents' day. "My marital status concerns nobody but me," Finn said.

"You know better. Every matchmaker in Mayfair will be watching you like a hawk watches her winter fields. Come spring, the betting books will be filled with your prospects, and if you don't know how to waltz, you'd best learn."

Finn stopped on a street corner as a passing dray heaped with steaming manure lumbered by. "The waltz is a Continental dance. We English were late to that party, but I'm too tall to partner most ladies comfortably." Not too tall to partner Willie. Lovely thought.

"Clearly, Lady Helmsby seeks to guide your choice of bride. I can think of no other reason why she's looking for ways to blackmail you."

"And you judged the threat was serious enough that you have warned me. Is this more of her ladyship's rivalry with the duchess?"

"Perhaps, though I think that rivalry is mostly in Lady Helmsby's head. Take care not to find yourself locked in any linen closets with the wealthy and vapid goddaughter of Lady Helmsby's choosing."

"That's how it's done? I won't fit in the average linen closet."

"Perhaps you don't fit comfortably standing up."

"And here, you look as if you have no imagination whatsoever," Finn mused, crossing the street. "I will inform Pritchard of this nonsense, but I can't be too troubled by it. Her ladyship is welcome to dig into my wicked past and display before all of Society the means by which I kept body and soul together when the Cathcart family had no use for me."

Wilhelmina knew the worst of it, and her opinion was the only one that counted—well, hers and Pritchard's, and Pritchard was no prude. "Besides," Finn went on, "I never wanted to be a duke, if you'll recall. I went to great lengths to avoid the whole business. If Lady Helmsby sends me back to the sculptor's livelihood, I'll manage."

"My path takes me that direction," St. Didier said, nodding to the east. "Lady Helmsby likely cannot fathom that you'd toss the title back to the crown without a qualm."

St. Didier was clearly puzzled by the notion too.

"The solicitors have assured me that the ladies, and Emily in particular, have adequate means. Whether or not the rubbishing title is preserved in my blameless and innocent person, the Cathcart womenfolk will be comfortable enough."

"I see."

No, he did not, but Finn wasn't about to announce that since he'd secured Wilhelmina's permission to come courting, the rest of the world—with few exceptions—had ceased to matter. Old Moreland was clearly on to something. Some fine day, perhaps St. Didier would find himself the happy recipient of a similar shift in perspective.

"I'll be careful," Finn said, because St. Didier apparently needed to hear the reassurance. "My thanks for your company at dinner. I feel like a hyena in that place, taking my meal while the public gawks. I don't suppose you're free next Wednesday?"

St. Didier looked—for him—flustered, which amounted to a slight lift of his right eyebrow. "I would be honored. Shall we say nine of the clock?"

"Eight. I need my rest."

"Eight, then. Good night, Your Grace."

"*Buona notte.*" Only as Finn was strolling slowly up the alley behind Wilhelmina's house—purely for his own pleasure—did it occur to him that St. Didier's company at dinner might have been offered by way of a kindness to a new duke with few friends.

Tomorrow afternoon at two of the clock, Finn would consult Wilhelmina on that question, after he'd asked after Emily, of course.

"Mrs. Cathcart has been out shopping more than usual, my lady," Travers said, as if this were some great revelation.

Lady Helmsby gathered the fraying ends of her patience, while Hector, enthroned on his hairy hassock, switched his tail. Travers was simply doing as he'd been paid to do—report, rather than think—and besides, more than middling intelligence in a domestic would have been a troublesome characteristic.

"Of course she's shopping more," Lady Helmsby said, jabbing her embroidery needle into a corner of the fabric. "Spring approaches, and one doesn't have new dresses made up overnight." Then too, Wilhelmina could *afford* to shop. "I'm sure Mrs. Cathcart is anxious to rejoin the social whirl. Mourning is a lonely time, and she's young yet." Young for a widow, too old to give the matchmakers any anxiety. "Is that all you have to report, that Mrs. Cathcart has been haunting the shops?"

Travers, hands folded behind his back, went to the window. "She has resumed her morning hacks on fine days."

Wiltshire born and bred. Not much to be done about that. "Do you imply that my daughter-in-law is trolling for flirts among the equestrian bachelors, Travers?"

He stood very straight, not quite turning his back on his hostess. "I would never be so disrespectful, my lady, and besides, His Grace escorts her, and few bachelors would have the temerity to approach her in such company."

Not with flirtation in mind. "Mrs. Cathcart is introducing His Grace about informally. Shrewd of her. The old guard leaves Town in winter, but the young bucks like their London pleasures. She's starting him with the lower ranks—the heirs and spares. By spring, he'll be ready for Almack's."

Though one could, of course, put another and altogether more alarming construction on the facts. If only Edwardia had listened, a futile hope, but one was honor-bound to try.

"I'm certain my lady knows what's afoot."

Travers's tone was deferential, mockingly so. Such rudeness suggested that the alternative explanation for Mina's attentiveness to the duke—and the duke's to her—had been discussed belowstairs.

"My lady should also know that Mrs. Cathcart is assisting His Grace with the redecoration of a small dwelling on Ballater Court. They've met there several times, though I can present you no evidence that the trades have begun the refurbishing."

An uneasy current in Lady Helmsby's vitals became laced with dread. "Several times?"

"In the middle of the day, usually when the housekeeper is out."

Did Travers take particular satisfaction in passing this news along? "Well, of course. Her ladyship is doubtless teaching His Grace to waltz—not an easy challenge for one of his ungainly height—and how to step through the quadrille, which fork to use, and so forth. He has much to learn if he's to impress the hostesses and matchmakers in a few short weeks. What a sculptor knows of etiquette would likely fit into a teaspoon."

Travers maintained a silence that conveyed unseemly skepticism.

"Might you add some coal to the fire?" Lady Helmsby asked. The parlor was somewhere between cozy and stifling, small rooms being easier to heat. "Half a scoop should do."

A butler did not tend the hearth. That dirty job was for footmen and maids. Travers nevertheless did as he'd been told.

"Will there be anything else, my lady? I do like to visit my sister on my half days, and we have so little light this time of year."

Butler, lord, or duke, men could not abide taking orders from women. "You will please inform Dalton that I no longer require his services. He has little to report and can't be bothered to attend to business when there's a pretty girl to goggle at."

Travers regarded her with impertinent directness. "My lady, I would not advise such a course. A butler cannot lurk at the perimeter of Hyde Park, watching who comes and goes with whom for a dawn hack. A butler cannot trot 'round the shops as a footman can. A butler has no direct access to the schoolroom, while the footman has many excuses to intrude. Dalton is a valuable informant, and he works hard to give good service to all who provide him remuneration."

In other words, Travers would have much less to report but for Dalton's aid. "Then put him on notice that I am skeptical of his contribution."

"Very well, my lady. If you will excuse me, I have a considerable distance to walk if I'm to see my sister and be home before dark."

His sister likely ran a gin palace—or worse. "On your way, then. I would like to see both you and Dalton on Friday. I will call upon Mrs. Cathcart to express my appreciation for all she's doing to smooth His Grace's path. His success with the peerage is the family's success. One would do well to remember that."

Travers bowed and let himself out.

Lady Helmsby took up her embroidery hoop and tried to resume the butterfly border she'd been sewing on a linen handkerchief, but for once, her needle brought no peace of mind. William had appreciated the little touches she could add to his gentlemanly attire, but William was gone and not coming back.

Lady Helmsby's warning to the duchess was proving prophetic. Mina was setting her cap for the duke. Foolish, foolish woman.

"Nevertheless, one cannot blame her," her ladyship murmured, which earned her a scowl from Hector. "He's a brute, but he has that Continental flair, and Mina has grieved William properly." Or so Society would view it. "Huntleigh is doubtless trifling with her, or perhaps she's trifling with him. Still..." Her ladyship put aside her embroidery and scooped Hector into her lap.

"His Grace must marry money. I know it, Edwardia knows it, Wilhelmina knows it. The Cathcart family fortunes rise and fall with his prospects."

This was not strictly true. Wilhelmina and Emily were well fixed, and the duchess would likely be extended credit until she was gathered to her eternal reward. The plain fact was that Lady Helmsby's fortunes rested with the duke's ability to bring cash into the family coffers.

"And there sits Emily, playing with her dolls and sketching robins, while I must rely on dim-witted butlers and lovesick footmen."

Hector began to purr and to knead her ladyship's leg, such that even through layers of petticoats and skirts, she felt the sting of his claws.

"Bad kitty!" She shoved him off her lap and onto the floor. "Naughty puss. I treat you like a king, and you repay me with cruelty."

Hector, tail up, returned to his hassock and squinted imperially at the hearth.

Hector was a spoiled, arrogant creature, and yet, he wanted for nothing. Emily wasn't spoiled yet, but she surely had more funds than any child needed. Lady Helmsby sat in her toasty parlor with her spoiled cat and considered possibilities and probabilities.

The issue was money, and if the duke was to marry profitably, then Wilhelmina must not be distracting him with her favors. Accidents, in the form of children arriving to the wrong people at the wrong time, happened all too frequently.

Wilhelmina was part of the problem, too, and she wasn't about to decamp for Wiltshire when a bachelor duke needed help choosing wallpaper.

Wilhelmina and money, money and Wilhelmina. What to do? What to do?

The answer came to her ladyship from, of all places, something that odious St. Didier had said. Even the duke was powerless to touch dear Emily's funds. William's wishes in that regard had been clearly documented.

The solution to the whole situation lay in the person of one small child, and for once, Lady Helmsby was glad that William's only legitimate issue was female.

CHAPTER FOURTEEN

"Emily really does show some ability," Norwich said, holding out her hands, a long hank of yarn looped between them. "His Grace's interest in her art helps, of course, but she has an accurate eye."

"He's a good teacher," Wilhelmina said, winding the yarn gently into a ball. She'd invaded Norwich's private sitting room in a nominal bid for assistance. "He will be a splendid duke." He was also a splendid lover, a splendid *person*.

"Speaking of His Grace..." Norwich glanced at the closed door. "You should know there's gossip belowstairs."

"Gossip belowstairs? What has the world come to? Tell me, Norwich, where in all of London isn't there gossip? We gossip in the churchyard, the park, the marketplace, the public houses, the drawing rooms, and most especially the ballrooms. That servants enjoy the national pastime is no surprise. If they will gossip to Her Grace for pay, why not tattle a bit amongst themselves?"

"You honestly don't mind?"

The yarn was a rich, imperial purple, a shade brighter than Finn's preferred scarf, but close enough. The wool was lovely to the touch, much like Finn himself.

"Why should I mind? Her Grace has little left except gossip. I understand better now why widows are permitted, and need, some latitude."

Norwich watched Wilhelmina winding the skein into a ball. "This tolerance on your part has to do with His Grace?"

"And with me. In His Grace's example, I see how a gentleman acts on his best behavior. William never had to offer me that, and I wasn't smitten enough or smart enough to make him try. We both muddled along, unsatisfied in some regards, but complacent. If we'd tried harder, we would have had more of a marriage to show for it."

And that insight left Wilhelmina sad, for herself and for William, but also at peace. They had done the best they could and perhaps in later years might have done better. The whole business was that simple and that deserving of sorrow, but she'd never have put the past to rest had Finn Cathcart not come whittling and whistling into her life.

Norwich laid her hands in her lap, yarn and all. "That is unfair to you, madam. William wasn't an ogre, but he was a spoiled nincompoop. You were good to him, and even he had sense enough to know that."

But not sense enough to give up his mistress, his carousing, his stupid wagers, his dissolute friends...

Wilhelmina wound the last few yards of wool into the ball. "William is my past, may he rest in peace. Castigating his memory serves no point. I am looking forward to spring, Norry. I can't recall the last time I looked forward to spring."

Norwich took the ball and dropped it into Wilhelmina's workbasket. "You will have more than Her Grace's at homes on your calendar for a change. Do you plan to entertain?"

"I must brace the duke on that very topic," Wilhelmina said, rising. "He would hide in his studio until Emily made had her coming out ball, left to his own devices." But on that occasion, he'd do the pretty. Wilhelmina would have bet her mare on that.

"Pritchard would not allow His Grace to hibernate that long," Norwich said, getting to her feet.

Neither will I. "What do you know of Mr. Pritchard?"

Norwich began tidying up Wilhelmina's workbasket, which was a monument to organization to begin with.

"Mr. Pritchard thought it expedient to introduce himself to the staff here. To gain, as he put it, a sense of the expectations the household might have for His Grace."

"Spying?"

Norwich paused with Wilhelmina's embroidery hoop in her hand. "No. Reconnaissance, perhaps, and certainly nodding to diplomacy between households, but not spying. He struck me as trustworthy and devoted to the duke. Where are you off to this afternoon?"

Ballater Court. A distance Wilhelmina could travel in twenty-seven minutes on foot. "I am off to harangue a certain duke about his social obligations. Wish me luck."

"Haranguing is not your strongest suit, madam, meaning no insult."

"Then I'd best use other means of persuasion."

She'd surprised Norwich with that one. Feeling pleased with herself, Wilhelmina peeked into the schoolroom and found Emily raptly involved in some adventure tale.

"I'll see you at bedtime, dearest."

"Yes, Mama." Emily's words were preoccupied and dismissive, rather than offered with whispered diffidence, and how wonderful was that?

Exceedingly wonderful. Wilhelmina arrived at Ballater Court less than thirty minutes later and was delighted to find Finn waiting for her. His smile when he rose to greet her was shy and sweet, and that pleased her too.

Not buccaneering, smug, or leering. Bashful. Wilhelmina went into his arms with the same blend of glee and shyness.

"I've missed you," she said, though that wasn't on her list of planned admissions.

"It's been only two days, darling Willie."

How she loved the feel of his voice when they were close like this. "Two eternities. I have given up embroidering for the nonce after stabbing my fingers half a dozen times. I stare at my correspondence when I ought to be penning some pleasant reply. You are driving me daft."

He kissed her on the mouth. "Daft was never so fetching. My work is going well. My work never goes well. Every piece is a battle, but lately... my hands are happy to take up the tools."

Wilhelmina stepped back enough to examine his hands. No swelling, no redness, just power, calluses, and masculine grace.

"I love your hands." She loved his touch, too, and his voice, and how well and naturally he cuddled after lovemaking, and...

The realization came over her like the solution to a vexing riddle: She loved *him*.

"How is Emily?" Finn asked, looping an arm around Wilhelmina's shoulders and settling with her on the sofa. "This dreary weather has to be making her restless."

Wilhelmina loved that he asked and loved that he listened to the answer, every time. "She has become a fiend for stories. I think my days as the best reader of bedtime tales are numbered. She's no longer content with Aesop. I shall be forced to graduate to the Lambs' *Tales from Shakespeare*."

"Don't you dare. For Miss Emily Cathcart, only the originals will do." He poured Wilhelmina a piping-hot mug of fragrant mulled cider, put two pieces of shortbread on a plate, and passed them over.

She loved that he served her and wasn't fussy about it. "Original Shakespeare in the schoolroom, by order of His Grace of Huntleigh?"

"By recommendation of a fellow who was starved for good reading material in his misspent youth. Emily has brains aplenty—she gets that from you—and she thrives on a challenge. She might go off and ponder strategy for a time, but she doesn't shrink from interesting work."

And Wilhelmina loved that Finn knew her daughter well enough to offer this accurate description. "Was your youth misspent?"

He sipped his cider, steam curling up from his mug. "My youth was too cold, hungry, exhausted, and anxious, but I learned a lot and had plenty of good fortune. What of yours?"

"Governesses, finishing schools, deportment instructors, fittings... I was lucky to be given an hour a day to spend with my mare. I was permitted that much liberty only because a prospective duchess must be a competent equestrienne. William bought me a new horse on our first anniversary, and I wanted to smack him."

"Because you loved your trusty mare, and she had plenty of spirit left," Finn said, choosing some shortbread for himself. "What did you do with her?"

"I sent my dear Morgana to the duchess's stable to enjoy semi-retirement as a guest horse, and I thanked William sincerely for his thoughtfulness. I found out later he won the birthday mare in a card game. She was nearly green, poor thing."

"Have you brought Morgana home?"

"I should." Why hadn't this occurred to Wilhelmina previously? "She'll be twenty in the spring. Venerable, not ancient."

"Would she enjoy trotting Emily around the park?"

Wilhelmina considered the notion. "Very much. I should have thought of this." She snuggled closer to Finn's side, turning the idea over in her mind. "Desdemona is an old hand now, but I still miss Morgana."

"I am available to escort you ladies should you decide to attempt a morning hack. In fact, it would be my pleasure. I'd advise a few outings with Emily up before me first, to give her the feel of the saddle and some practice with the reins."

Wilhelmina took his cider from his hand, set aside their plates, and arranged herself in his lap. "You are so dear."

"Why, Mrs. Cathcart, how friendly you've become." Finn's arms settled around her. "I've missed you too. I have far more sympathy for young Antonio these days, and for Pritchard."

Wilhelmina nuzzled Finn's jaw. "Why?"

"Antonio is in love—albeit calf-love—but his sentiments are once again unrequited, and his suffering is real. Pritchard needs somebody to love, but won't even admit the problem. St. Didier is similarly afflicted and pretends otherwise. While I... I have somebody to love, and she admits to missing me when we're apart. I am the most fortunate of men."

That laugh-and-cry sensation threatened again. "You should not say such things. I will get an inflated idea of my consequence."

"Wilhelmina, I love you. I realize that dukes oughtn't to dabble in maudlin sentiment, but I'm only recently afflicted with the title, and what I feel for you is far too fine and substantial to qualify as maudlin sentiment."

Wilhelmina could not see Finn's face as he made this declaration, but she was held securely and gently in his arms, and she could hear the sincerity in his voice.

"I came here determined to lecture you about your social obligations," she said. "You need to start entertaining. Invite some fellows to dine with you in the clubs, host a card party—Lady Helmsby adores card parties—or show up at a few of the duchess's at homes."

He kissed her brow. "I declare my love for you, and you reciprocate by threatening me with Edwardia's at homes. Have mercy, Willie." He sounded amused rather than affronted.

"On my way here, *Your Grace,* I inventoried dates, venues, possible guest lists for your socializing debut," Wilhelmina replied, "but then I see you, and I can't think. I can only be glad in my heart, and relieved, and overwhelmed." The word fit. So did the term *in love.*

"Ah. Overwhelmed."

Wilhelmina patted his chest. "Now you sound smug."

"Relieved. Pleased. Not smug. Never that."

Wilhelmina understood that admission too. "Would you also be pleased to take me upstairs, Finlay?"

He rose with her in his arms, a presumption she could get used to.

"I would be overjoyed to take you upstairs, and then perhaps you can explain this overwhelmed business. Is it a good thing, when a fellow's wooing leaves his intended overwhelmed?" He climbed the stairs as if hauling a lady about bodily was all part of a Finn Cathcart courtship.

His intended. *Well.* "Turnabout is the least you deserve for that remark, sir."

Outside the bedroom door, Finn kissed her cheek. "I live in hope, my love. I live in hope."

Finn made his living with his hands, and he also experienced much of his world through physical sensation. Was the clay the right consistency as he began shaping it? Was the chisel sharp enough when tested against the pad of his thumb? Was the studio warm enough?

With Wilhelmina, the word *overwhelmed* applied to his bodily awareness of her. She was substantial, strong, and curved abundantly in all the right places. Sculpting goddesses would be simpler for having carried Wilhelmina up to the bedroom. The crinkled-silk pattern of freshly unbraided hair would be easier to achieve in marble, and the luscious curve of a muscular feminine hip would come infinitesimally closer to life.

He'd worked with models on numerous occasions, but they were, by profession, life-size dolls serving as visual inspiration. Not houris who haunted his dreams by night and gilded his days with joy.

"I want to both toss you on the bed and keep you in my arms," he said, setting her on her feet beside the bed. "I also want you out of that dress. Might I oblige?"

He'd undone her hooks the first time they'd made love, and his present sense of treasure to be revealed was more intense for being coupled with anticipation.

Wilhelmina gave him her back and swept the tendrils at her nape up with one hand. "To make love in daylight feels decadent."

"Your definition of decadent needs work, but we have time for that, and I do relish a challenge. I'd say, making love with you at any hour feels splendiferous." He yielded to the impulse to draw her close, her back to his chest. "I truly did miss you."

That bothered him. He'd firmly believed that women might be fondly remembered, but they were not to preoccupy him day and night, sleeping and waking. They were not to play havoc with his focus while inspiring his work to greater excellence.

What would Wilhelmina think of allowing Antonio to take a wife?

Wilhelmina would not be content with that shoulder, old boy.

Did Wilhelmina love watching snow fall as Matteo did?

She turned in his arms and kissed him. "I count the hours, then chide myself for foolishness, but I am the lady who argued passionately for romance and sentiment when I'd had so little of both. If this is romance, it's considerably more disconcerting than I'd anticipated."

Finn kissed her in return, not that he was keeping score, and draped his arms over her shoulders. "My word was 'unnerving.' I take your meaning." But Wilhelmina didn't seem panicked by this new, disconcerting, intensity of emotion on her life, and neither was Finn, exactly.

"I refuse to be the only person wafting about this bedroom in dishabille," Wilhelmina said. "I'll have that coat, Finlay."

"You have a flair for giving orders." He stepped back and shrugged out of his morning coat, then unbuttoned his waistcoat.

"Small words, spoken clearly and slowly," she replied, hanging both garments on the bedpost. "Boots, Finlay."

Finn sat and tugged off his boots and stockings, though even the way Wilhelmina used his name required an adjustment on his part.

"Nobody else calls me Finlay. I'm Finn to a very few, or Cathcart,

English, Your Grace. Some of the less reserved among the senior peers at the clubs will refer to me as Huntleigh. You alone use my given name."

She started on his right sleeve button. "Nobody else calls me Willie, much less darling Willie. Other one."

Finn gave her his left hand. "Do you mind?"

She jostled his sleeve buttons loosely in one hand, like dice, and peered down at him. "I not only don't mind, I like it, and that..."

He tugged on her wrist, an invitation, and she once again bundled into his lap. "Go on, lovely Willie."

"Pet names," she said, laying her head on his shoulder, "lovemaking by day, galloping in the park and not caring who's watching... I have longed for these boons, and now that I have them, I'm afraid I'll lose them."

She was brave enough to put her feelings into words. Finn cast around for what he could say, what he could admit.

"I am afraid I will lose myself," he said. "I will become an indolent fool who stares off into space for half the day, who hangs his mallet on the peg intended for his smock, who composes mawkish poetry and thinks himself brilliant."

"Antonio?" she asked, biting Finn's earlobe gently.

"His poetry is at least in Italian. I catch myself whistling and wonder if poetry will be next. I am Finn Cathcart. I don't suffer fools, my work is in demand, and I give good artistic value for substantial coin. I am a sculptor, not a schoolboy."

"Finlay, in case you haven't noticed, I am not a schoolgirl." Wilhelmina rustled around in his lap until she was straddling him, and the conversation arrived to a general pause. Kissing and undressing and laughing came next, until Wilhelmina was panting and Finn was thoroughly aroused and even more thoroughly enchanted.

"Do we add the chair to our erotic repertoire?" he asked, "or muster the resolve to get ourselves into bed?"

Wilhelmina drew her finger down his nose. "I want your

breeches off, and for that, you must stand, so we might as well make use of the bed. We'll save the chair for another day, when you don't get me so riled..."

He traced her lips with his thumb. "So riled?"

"So flummoxed that I forget that lovemaking goes more smoothly with fewer clothes."

"Or no clothes at all."

She climbed off his lap and wiggled out of her dress, petticoats, and stays, then raised her chemise over her head and pitched it at his belly.

I am so in love. Finn sniffed her chemise—jasmine, his new favorite fragrance—rubbed the soft linen against his chest, and rose. He treated himself to a circumnavigation of his lover, whose unclad form was female magnificence personified. As he glossed a hand over her backside and leaned in for a few kisses to her nape, she undid his falls.

"Are you in a hurry, Willie?"

She made a production out of getting his arousal free of his clothing. "Are you?"

"Yes." He scooped her up before her boldness cost him his composure. "And no. I am in a hurry to get under the covers—can't have you taking a chill—and I am in no hurry whatsoever to leave the bed once I join you there."

"You might simply ask, you know. All this being wrestled about, while it has a novel charm, isn't strictly necessary."

Finn set her gently on the bed and peeled out of his breeches. "I like wrestling you about. It's my humble version of small words, spoken clearly and slowly."

She scooted back under the covers and patted the quilt. "Don't try it at Almack's. A simple 'Wilhelmina, shall we dance?' will suffice."

Finn climbed in beside her, spooned himself around her, and mentally tested the notion of waltzing at Almack's with Wilhelmina.

What should have been a ridiculous social burden loomed as... enjoyable.

Let them gawk. We're courting, you know... And then he'd hold Wilhelmina a smidgeon closer on the turns.

"Wilhelmina, shall we make love? We can do it like this, you know." He nudged intimately at her from behind, and she sent him a curious look over her shoulder.

"Like this?"

"Like this. It's... relaxed. Less kissing, more caressing." Finn slipped a hand around to her breasts to demonstrate. More sighing, too, apparently.

Wilhelmina put him through his paces, changing positions three times and having her pleasure of him twice. By the time she was sprawled beneath him, rosy and warm, Finn was edging close to the limit of his self-restraint.

"One more," he said, starting a lazy rhythm. "Let me do the work."

She brushed his hair back from his brow. "No heroic measures, Finlay. Go easy."

That, he could manage, but only just. Once Wilhelmina was again a boneless heap of female satisfaction, he withdrew. Despite every particle of his body and soul screaming at him to drive home, he spent on Wilhelmina's belly. He hung over her, panting and dizzy, despite being on all fours in a solidly built bed.

Wilhelmina reached for the handkerchief. "I wish you didn't do that."

"If you are asking me not to spend, I can try, but I can't guarantee the results." Madness would number among them, surely. Crossed eyes and gibbering might come into it.

She levered up to hug him. "I mean, I miss you when you leave me."

Finn fished about in the morass of satisfaction and fatigue that had replaced his mind. "When I withdraw?"

She nodded against his shoulder, and Finn lowered her to the bed, himself barnacled around her. "I must withdraw, and even withdrawing is far from foolproof. Children are all too often held accountable for the sins of their parents—I have reason to know this—and any gossiping Mayfair beldame can use a calendar."

Wilhelmina was quiet for a moment, her hands wandering in soothing patterns on Finn's back. "You mean we'd cause a scandal if I conceived when we weren't wed?"

Maybe she was having trouble thinking too. "We aren't even *betrothed*, my dear. When and if we reach that milestone, I'll be much less wary of conception. Anticipating vows is not only forgiven, it's nearly expected."

He crouched over her—never let it be said she'd had to learn how to breathe with *fifteen* stone of exhausted male atop her—and waited.

"Then I suppose," Wilhelmina said sleepily, "between snubbing Her Grace, escorting Emily and me on our maiden equestrian outing to the park, and fashioning marble goddesses, you'd best find some time to propose to me."

Everything in Finn turned to light and wonderment. He nuzzled Wilhelmina's temple when he wanted to open the window and shout his rejoicing to the heavens.

"I'll ask Pritchard to find me a free afternoon," he said. "A proposal will want some thought and a bit of rehearsing. Maybe a lot of rehearsing. Which poem to quote, what time of day, location... This invitation to propose demands lengthy consideration."

Wilhelmina smacked his bum. "Small words, spoken slowly and clearly. They've served us well thus far."

"Yes, beloved." Finn considered proposing right that very instant. Whispering in her ear while they were both still glowing with shared satisfaction, but no. Wilhelmina deserved a proper proposal, complete with heartfelt declarations and a sparkly ring.

Finn shifted to lie beside her, pulled her into his arms, and fell asleep designing the perfect ring for the perfect woman. His last thought before surrendering to slumber was that Wilhelmina was the one woman he could not think of leaving.

Not for any commission or opportunity, not to avoid scandal, not for *any* reason, could he see allowing his path to diverge from hers. The notion provided long overdue insight into his parents' situation— all that hardship, the bitterness, the family rift, the loss of social standing.

Finn understood the why and the how, much better for having fallen in love with Wilhelmina. For better or for worse and, most especially, for always.

Edwardia was restless, and an aging duchess had few means of quelling agitation other than sheer self-discipline. Self-discipline was making little headway against the fractious mood she'd fallen into.

"Come, Charles," she said, rising from her escritoire. "If I spend another quarter hour listening to that infernal clock tick, I will confuse which godchild has the benefit of my correspondence today. Not that anybody needs fourteen godchildren." Fourteen silver spoons with matching porringers, fourteen books at Yuletide every year. Fourteen deposits in accounts at Wentworth's bank on each child's natal day, to be disbursed upon that child's majority, regardless of gender or marital status.

"And half of their own children now," she muttered as she waited for Charles to heave to his paws, indulge in a tail-high stretch, and then a shake.

When she and Charles had been in the back garden for less than five minutes, a footman bustled out of the house, the collar of his great coat turned up to his ears. Roberts was as loyal to Charles as he was to his employer.

"Shall I throw the ball for Charles, Your Grace?"

The poor lad was shivering. Should have worn a scarf, but young fellows were vain. "We'll manage without tossing the ball today. If you'd have the kitchen put together a tray, I'd appreciate it. Not tea. Such a chilly day wants chocolate."

Charles went snuffling along the stubbled remains of the lavender border, and Roberts offered a quick bow and retreated. London lads weren't up to real weather. The air was merely cold, not even approaching bitter.

The duchess walked along the swept paths, while Charles ventured into flowerbeds buried beneath crusty snow. He lifted his leg on one or two favorite corners—the maple sapling endured a baptism, as did the holly bush—while Edwardia completed her first circuit of the garden.

Three was the daily quota in winter. Six in more temperate seasons.

Lately, though, she'd had to rest between laps, and that... that was not to be lamented. Ashes to ashes, and all that. Charles came over to the bench where Edwardia took her first intermission.

"You have inspected to your heart's content?" she asked, smoothing a gloved hand over his glossy head. "Or aren't you as curious as you used to be?"

Charles put his chin on her knee.

"You are being a bad influence, my boy. Three circuits before we go into the house. Let's be about it." She got to her feet, then had to pause to catch her breath while she waited out a twinge in the center of her chest.

The wretched twinges came and went, and lately they were coming more frequently. Edwardia set off down the path again, her pace more measured.

"Cease whining, Charles. I am fine. Age takes a toll, and that is the natural order ordained from on high. We have no cause to fret."

Charles hung his head and padded meekly at her side, not the sign of a dog chastised, but rather, of a dog too polite to argue.

"Oh, very well. I am worried about His Grace. He's being stubborn, and nobody can be as stubborn as a Cathcart male. With Lord Thornton for Finlay's paternal example, and that mother of his... The Scots excel at stubbornness. Worse than the Irish, and that's saying something."

She fell silent out of necessity until her second respite on the bench. "Cold air is supposed to be invigorating," she all but panted.

Charles whined again, and he wore that worried expression that spaniels did so convincingly.

"Stop that. I ought to do an extra lap to fortify me against importunate puppies." Though Charles had a point. Worry made for bad sleep, twinges of the heart made for bad sleep, and bad sleep made for fretfulness, and so the cycle went. Round and round, night after day.

Shuffling about in the frigid air was supposed to aid sleep and hold the fretting at bay, but today the standard remedy offered no benefit.

"We'll take our time," the duchess said, easing to her feet. "I refuse to dodder about on the arm of a fawning footman like every dowager ever to leave crumbs on her bodice. Next thing you know, Wilhelmina will buy me an ear trumpet and make me wear it 'round my neck."

Wilhelmina would buy a very pretty ear trumpet, of course. Engraved brass with copper trim. A cowbell for all of Society to admire. Even Vanessa's carping and sighing hadn't daunted Mina's basic generosity of spirit. Vanessa's spoiled son hadn't either, though in that case, Edwardia had taken a hand.

William had been warned to treat his bride respectfully, lest Edwardia speak to the solicitors about a reduction in William's quarterly allowance. William had complied with firm guidance, as usual. Perhaps if he'd had more time to grow into his birthright...

Roberts had come back outside and was standing by the terrace door, hands behind his back.

"*Once more unto the breach, dear friends, once more,*" Her Grace muttered, moving forward with a full complement of dignity. "Charles, come along."

Charles padded beside her, whining softly. Roberts stood like a frowning governess by the door, and Edwardia nearly turned in his direction.

But no. Even a Cathcart by marriage was entitled to stubbornness. She made a slow progress around the garden, her final turn putting her in the way of a sudden, cutting headwind.

"One must persist and be patient," she murmured into her scarf. His late Grace had often invoked that maxim, for which Edwardia had wanted to cosh him. The memory made her smile.

Finlay was refusing to be hurried, and that was all to the good—a duke should be above haste—except that the creditors wouldn't wait indefinitely, and nobody lived forever. Then too, Vanessa was working up to one of her tantrums, and those always resulted in drama, bills from the modiste, and much whimpering into handkerchiefs adorned with the family crest.

Vanessa, too, claimed a surfeit of determination.

By the time Edwardia reached the steps at the foot of the terrace, Charles was whining again, softly, insistently.

"Oh, very well. No victory lap. I can be set in my ways, but unlike her ladyship, I draw the line at blatant pigheadedness." She climbed the steps, earning herself a stout twinge, and stood as if surveying the view when she'd reached the terrace.

"Shall I take Charles, Your Grace?" Roberts asked when nobody had indicated that he need leave his post by the door.

"Please. He doesn't like to wear his coat, but he's no puppy to be frolicking in the snow as he once did."

"Oh, course not, Your Grace. Into the house with us, Charles." Roberts did not offer the duchess his arm—she'd have raised his wages for that display of discretion, had she been able—but he did set a glacial pace for the house.

"The air is so very disobliging today," Her Grace said when she was once again in the relative warmth of the back hallway. "Too much coalsmoke. Please convey to Cook my request that she keep a pot of toddy going in the kitchen. I cannot have my staff coming down with agues and lung fevers for want of a bit of fortification. Spring is still weeks away, and I suspect more snow is on the way. Afternoon tea should have some substance to it today as well."

"Of course, Your Grace, and we have a ham bone in the kitchen that Charles might enjoy."

"Roberts, you spoil that dog, and I thank you for it. I'll be in my personal sitting room, if you'd send along my chocolate."

Charles trotted down the kitchen steps with considerably more bounce in his stride than he'd shown after five minutes in the garden, the wretch.

Edwardia made her way more deliberately to her personal sitting room, which was blessedly, sumptuously warm. When her tray came up from the kitchen, she took a seat at the escritoire and considered penning another invitation to His Grace of Stubbornness.

"Finlay obliged me the first time only because Mina put him on his best behavior," she informed her late husband's portrait. "I could not bear for him to snub me outright. Not after all these years."

Though bear it she would, if she had to. Mina was keeping an eye on the new duke, and she was nobody's fool. That Mina and Finlay were growing close was driving Vanessa daft, which suited Edwardia enormously. Served her ladyship right, after all the meddling and carping she'd done over the years.

Edwardia put her pen back in the standish and decided to leave coaxing Finlay into another call up to Mina. When Mina next brought Emily around for tea, Edwardia would drop a few hints in the child's hearing, and the case would be argued on Edwardia's behalf by an expert.

One's stamina decreased later in life. One's capacity for strategy and patience grew ever more abundant.

CHAPTER FIFTEEN

"The damned title is bankrupt," Finn said, rubbing his eyes. The library was harder to heat than the studio, but Finn refused to pollute his working space with the ducal ledgers. He wasn't due to visit Ballater Court for another twenty-two hours, but how he longed for those cozier confines—and the better company.

Across the reading table, Pritchard's nose came out of its book like a hound catching the scent of fresh quarry. "Bankrupt? Truly insolvent?"

"Bankrupt in the sense of unable to pay debts in the ordinary course, despite owning substantial acreage." The inevitability of the conclusion was matched only by Finn's resentment of it. He did not want to spend his afternoon poring over accounts. He wanted to be wrapped in Wilhelmina's arms, her warmth, her laughter. "The old duke refused to skimp on property maintenance, which is why he left no reserves and also a possible ray of hope if we must sell the smaller estates."

All that money for drainage, marling, and new thatching, and not a bent farthing for family in need.

Pritchard laid a silk handkerchief across the page he'd been reading and closed the book. Mrs. Radcliffe, of all the peculiarities.

"If you sell the estates, then word goes out that the Huntleigh coffers are empty. You will get very little return on the land, and the collateral you can borrow against is further compromised."

Finn rose and stretched, bracing his hands on his lower back. "You sound like a solicitor." A competent solicitor, drat the luck.

"I did read law. Rather enjoyed it. Like a very large chessboard with dozens of different kinds of pieces."

An image to terrify the mind of a mere mortal. "I look at those ledgers and ask myself why Lady Helmsby manages so poorly on a generous widow's portion."

Pritchard pulled the relevant ledger across the table. "I see Madame Bernadette among the creditors. She's exorbitant. Hoby has his fingers in the pie. The premier milliners, glovemakers, parfumiers... You'd think her ladyship was the family duchess. How does the true duchess compare?"

Finn turned his back to the hearth, the warmth a blessing to the body. "Her Grace is curiously thrifty."

Pritchard turned a page. "And you begrudge her that thriftiness."

"Yes. No. Edwardia is thrifty, but my mother was far thriftier of necessity."

Perhaps because he valued his post, Pritchard let the issue drop. "How fares Mrs. Cathcart's exchequer?"

"Mrs. Cathcart, who maintains a coach and pair as well as a riding horse and cart pony, to say nothing of a nursery staff and the expenses of the child herself, is a model of fiscal responsibility. She manages a larger household on about half of what Lady Helmsby spends."

Pritchard wrinkled his nose. "You do notice the details. Perhaps her ladyship is maintaining a *cavalier servente*. She's not ancient, and she strikes me as disinclined to resume the yoke of wifehood."

"Your imagination is rearing its head again. English ladies don't go in for paid gallants."

Pritchard gave him a pitying look. "Suit yourself, Your Grace. Her ladyship's problems might include gambling debts, blackmail, staff bilking a careless employer... Or she might simply be a spendthrift. Shall I look into the matter?"

Finn turned, facing the fire. What was Wilhelmina doing on this day grown blustery and gray? Was she counting the hours until their next encounter on Ballater Court? Was she neglecting her correspondence and dreaming of the moment when Finn proposed?

"*Your Grace?* Shall I have a look into Lady Helmsby's situation?"

"You needn't shout. For a majordomo found larking about the coast of Italy, you seem to know a great deal about the perils that can befall a lady's Mayfair household."

"The same ills can plague a lady's household in Rome. I'll make some preliminary inquiries, shall I?"

Pritchard seemed keen on the notion, and he was less of a martinet when he could tilt at windmills. "Very well. Be discreet. Invoke the title as a last resort."

"Right." Pritchard rose and went to the sideboard. "Waste time, beat about the bush, leave innuendo in the air as thick as evening fog rather than take a direct, entirely appropriate route. You are the duke, the head of the family. If Lady Helmsby requires frequent infusions of cash from your coffers, that is absolutely your business, because— contractual niceties aside—*you* will be expected to cover her defaults."

I never wanted to be a duke. Finn batted that lament aside, because becoming the duke was how he'd met Wilhelmina, and no complaint had a patch on that miracle.

Pritchard brought him a serving of brandy. "Will you dine out this evening?"

"Don't make me drink alone," Finn said, nosing his drink. "I will remain at home, and I don't care if that means I miss my quota of lurking at the club this week. The temperature dropped today, in case you didn't notice, and the wind picked up. This weather is enough to make a man miss Naples."

Perhaps a wedding journey to sunnier climes would appeal to Wilhelmina. If Norwich was game, they could bring Emily along too.

"About the debts," Pritchard said. "What will you do? Interest charges being the nuisance they are, the longer you put off selling some land, the deeper the hole you dig."

When Finn hadn't been contemplating the curve of Wilhelmina's jaw, or the memory of her laughter, he'd been applying his mind to the financial problem. A real duke would not accept the solution he'd decided upon.

"If we can't sell the entailed properties—and I'd rather not in any case—we can rent them out to wealthy cits. The denizens of the City aren't shy about commercial transactions. Five-year leases, first and last year payable upon signing, plus a deposit to be held in security. Rental terms applying to only the dwelling, the home farm, and the stables. We keep the tenant income and the responsibility for repairs, though there shouldn't be many of those in the first few years."

Pritchard poured himself a drink. "You've thought about this."

"Ever since Mrs. Cathcart dragged me to the solicitors' office. If you wouldn't mind another assignment, find out how Emily's settlements are faring. Better to know now if she'll be the first ducal grandchild dowered with an Italian quarry."

Pritchard held his drink without nosing it. "You'd *do* that?"

"I'll keep the best of the three, but yes, I'd do that."

This earned Finn a thorough perusal. "What you ought to do, if Your Grace is open to suggestions, is lease out the quarry and make a personal loan to the ducal estate. Reducing your personal wealth to stop the bleeding on the ducal holdings won't end well."

"And how is the patient to recover unless the wound is treated? You'd have me turn my children into my debtors. Call me backward and common, but that notion is repugnant." More to the point, Wilhelmina would never approve, and that decided the matter.

Pritchard sipped his brandy. "You know the crown will get the whole business if you fail to have a legitimate son."

"One grasps that fundamental, and I have a plan for addressing the need. Shall you join me in an informal meal, or will you begin your investigation of Lady Helmsby's profligate spending?"

Pritchard's brows drew down.

"Forget I asked," Finn said. "Beat me at one game of chess and then take yourself off to lurk and reconnoiter and whatever else it is you do."

Pritchard got down the chessboard and brought the decanter to the reading table. Finn lost to him all three times, but made him work for every victory.

"I don't like it." Norwich passed Wilhelmina her cloak. "Her ladyship is not an early riser."

Wilhelmina did not know what to make of Lady Helmsby's invitation. "A late breakfast doesn't require rising early." Though why had the invitation arrived only last evening?

"She has learned that you and His Grace are growing close, and she realizes she must curry your favor."

Wilhelmina dealt with frogs and buttons. "I hope we've been discreet."

"You are too trusting. Whenever you leave the house, Dalton finds it necessary to sally forth in search of some ingredient Cook neglected to pick up at market, though he always returns empty-handed."

"You are telling me this only now?" And in the foyer where any passing butler might overhear it?

"I didn't think Her Grace's spies in the household were any secret, and the schoolroom has an excellent view of all the exits. One notices who is coming and going. One also assumes that what the duchess's minions learn eventually finds its way to her ladyship's staff as well." Norwich held out a pair of black wool gloves. "Once you are the duchess, you can sack the lot of them."

"I don't like to think about being the duchess." Wilhelmina

pulled on her gloves. "We have a duchess, and she excels at her duties, including her duty to watch my every step, blast it all. I'll wear a scarf today."

Norwich knelt to rummage in a drawer of the sideboard. "You never wear scarves."

"And my chin freezes accordingly. If I arrive to Mama-in-Law's with red cheeks, I will hear about how a lady is never careless of her complexion, and why didn't I take the coach, and what sort of example am I setting for her ladyship's *only* grandchild."

Norwich rose with a forest green merino scarf in her hands. "It's Emily's, but fit for the purpose."

"I love that shade."

"You have the right coloring for it. Have you told His Grace that Edwardia keeps a close eye on you?"

"Yes, but I don't like to give him any more reasons to resent his aunt. His arguments against her are valid, though decades old, and she can be difficult. She genuinely dotes on Emily, though."

Wilhelmina wrapped the scarf around her neck, covering her ears and cheeks. The wool held the scent of lavender, a brisk fragrance for a brisk walk.

"You could take the coach," Norwich said, adjusting the end of the scarf over Wilhelmina's shoulder. "Those flurries could turn into something."

"Mama-in-Law envies me the coach, though she's not about to take on the expense of maintaining a team when she can instead borrow mine whenever she pleases. The topic is sensitive, and one avoids giving her ladyship offense."

Norwich's expression turned governess-mulish. "If you were less concerned about offending these old besoms, your life would be considerably easier. They take advantage of your good nature, madam."

Finn was of much the same opinion, and so, increasingly, was Wilhelmina. "I have accepted Mama-in-Law's invitation to breakfast, and I will be an agreeable guest. It's entirely possible Mama-in-Law will approach me about a small loan."

Norwich glanced in the direction of the steps that led down to the kitchen. "Don't oblige her. Her ladyship wears a new dress to divine services nearly every week and never puts tuppence into the poor box. Her portion is generous, and she hasn't been entertaining to speak of this winter."

Wilhelmina wanted the hour to magically advance to two of the clock, wanted to be sitting before the fire on Ballater Court, beholding Finn, ruddy cheeked and smiling, as he held out his arms to embrace her.

"Nobody entertains much in winter." Wilhelmina gathered up her reticule. "William often made loans to his mother. She hasn't asked me for money yet, and I am not inclined to become another one of her creditors."

"She will never pay you back."

The flurries beyond the foyer window were turning into a light snow shower. "I don't care about a modest sum unrepaid here or there. If I open my purse to her, I tacitly acknowledge that she's entitled to my assistance. Emily knows enough to set aside some of her allowance every week, a penny for the poor, another few pennies for a future expense. Mama-in-Law, who will toil ceaselessly to gain an invitation to this Venetian breakfast or that grand ball, has far more self-discipline than she's choosing to apply to her finances."

"And if she simply cannot manage her funds, why should you subsidize that failing? Edwardia would tell you to send her ladyship to the solicitors."

A fortifying thought. "Edwardia has doubtless told her that very thing, and so shall I. I should be home well before noon."

"Offer to lend her Dalton. Let him spy on her for a change."

Wilhelmina paused with a hand on the door latch. "You really don't like him?"

"I like him well enough. He's canny, and he executes his duties conscientiously, but I don't trust him. His loyalties are divided, and that is not how a post in service works."

Wilhelmina departed on that observation and, on the walk to Lady Helmsby's front door, debated whether to sack Dalton and Travers. She wanted to. She paid good wages, wasn't unduly demanding, and deserved some loyalty from her staff.

Though ignoring Edwardia's orders would challenge anybody.

When I accept Finn's proposal, the whole household will change. Another fortifying thought, because Wilhelmina most assuredly would accept his proposal. Becoming the next Duchess of Huntleigh appealed not at all. She had been cozened with that prospect in girlhood, and she well knew the tiara itself was no prize.

Edwardia, whatever might be said about her, had not had an easy lot in life.

Becoming Finn Cathcart's wife, though... Wilhelmina wanted to twirl about in the falling snow and laugh out loud, the idea gave her such joy. She instead quickened her pace and prepared to be a well-mannered, attentive guest who cleaned her plate with polite dispatch.

"Mama and Grandmama are having breakfast together," Emily said, nose pressed to the schoolroom window. "I'm glad I didn't have to go too."

Norwich tugged her scholar's braid. "Because it's cold outside?" Mrs. Cathcart made rapid progress down the walkway, her figure turning to a dark blur against the falling snow.

"I like a snowy day," Emily said, skipping away from the window. "I don't want to have breakfast with Grandmama. She talks a lot, and she wouldn't let me put butter and honey on my porridge."

"You do like your porridge just so." With a dash of cinnamon, which was fortunate, because Norwich liked hers the same way.

"Grandmama wants me to get married. I don't want to *be*

married. I want to live with Mama and you and the Ursulas and Draco. And Cook." Emily slid onto the seat behind her desk and took out her sketchbook. "Finn could live with us too."

From the mouths of babes, though Emily was no longer a toddler. She was a girl, and blessed with her parents' height. Though how dare Lady Helmsby speak to the child about betrothals and marriage?

"You would not have a butler to greet your guests, or a footman to haul the tea trays about?"

Emily made a face. "I like the duchess's butler and footmen. I don't like Travers. He sniffs a lot." She opened her sketchbook to a blank page and fished about in a drawer before producing a pencil. His Grace had a whole learned discourse on which pencils to use and how, and Emily had lapped up every word.

"It's winter," Norwich said, tossing another log onto the fire. "People get sniffles." His Grace advised a wood fire in the nursery—a great extravagance—and Mrs. Cathcart had agreed. The result was better air and less dust.

"Not that kind of sniff. Sniffs like, 'I am better than you.'" Emily demonstrated. "The duchess can sniff like that, too, and so does Draco. I heard Travers and Dalton arguing."

The automatic response—*that is none of our business*—was nudged aside by a more pressing concern. "When was this?"

"You and Mama were having tea and winding yarn. I went down to the kitchen for some bread and butter. Travers was in the butler's pantry, and he was *loud*."

This was a patent fabrication. Mrs. Cathcart believed children should enjoy some liberty within their own domiciles. A nursery suite, according to Madam, should not be a jail. She emphasized that edict with the firmness of one who had felt imprisoned in her own childhood.

"Your mother and I had tea shortly after luncheon yesterday, my dear. You were not in search of a snack. You were snooping about."

Emily stared at her blank page. "Travers and Dalton snoop. They were arguing about it."

What on earth to say to that? "They upset you?"

Emily nodded. "Travers said her ladyship isn't paying Dalton to flirt with the maids, and if Dalton expects Lady Helmsby to part with good coin—is there such a thing as bad coin, Norry?—then Dalton had better be more dil-i-gent. Dalton said her ladyship could do her own spying, and a few damned coins isn't worth a man's post. 'Damned' is a bad word, unless Vicar says it, like 'the prayers of the damned.' It means you go to the bad place when you die."

Norwich braced herself for the next logical query: *Is my papa in the bad place?* Emily began her sketch instead, a small, curved line that became a fleshy nose.

"You're sure they mentioned your grandmama by name?"

"Yes. Grandmama never gives *me* any pennies. The duchess does, sometimes. For sweets. Will Dalton be sacked for saying a bad word?"

"No, not for one bad word when he was upset and thought he had some privacy. Who else overheard this disagreement?"

Emily added a chin to her subject, who would bear an uncanny, caricatured resemblance to Travers. "Nobody. Cook and the house-keeper were having tea in the housekeeper's parlor with the door closed. I heard them laughing. Molly was out at market. Tim went with her."

A budding, if doomed, romance, given their respective stations, though Mrs. Cathcart might abet the course of true love. She was growing increasingly independent-minded in the domestic sphere, and thank heavens for that.

"Emily, snooping is not honorable. Not when Dalton and Travers do it, not when you do it, but I'm glad you told me what you heard. If Lady Helmsby is intruding on the privacy of your mama's household, then Lady Helmsby is being naughty. I will let your mother know what you heard, and I think it's time you learned to whistle."

Emily's pencil went still. "Grandmama says ladies don't whistle. It makes their cheeks fat."

More of Lady Helmsby's mischief. "Then we need to teach you

some songs so that when you lark about the house, using the servants' stairs and appearing in unlikely locations, you give notice of your approach."

Emily grinned. "Like birds sing, and we know what tree they're in because we hear them."

"Precisely. Spying is bad manners, and now that you know it, you can refrain from overhearing what isn't meant for your ears."

Emily drew a line that began a thin top lip. "Grandmama oughtn't to be spying, Dalton and Travers oughtn't to take her money to do it, but you are scolding *me* when I wasn't even trying to over-listen. They were nearly yelling, Norry."

And that, more than anything else, would bother Emily. She'd been raised in a calm, orderly household, thanks to her mother, and yet, her short life had been full of upheaval and loss.

"Bad manners again, but they don't expect family to lurk below-stairs, just as you don't expect Dalton to hang about outside the schoolroom door."

"He brings the coal one bucket at a time, though. He could bring two buckets, but he doesn't."

Children noticed *everything*. A governess forgot that at her peril. "We're burning wood now, and it's Tim's job to bring it up in the evening, when your studies are done. Tell me, will that homely fellow have some hair, or will you make him bald?"

"Balding, like Travers, and I might give him horns, like that fellow from the bad place."

"Your art is making you fierce," Norwich said, tossing on a second log, because the day would be chilly.

"Is that bad? Draco is fierce, and Finn said he made him that way for me."

Norwich rose and swung the kettle over the flames. "Fierce is very good, child, and never let anybody tell you otherwise."

Though somebody would have to explain to Madam that Travers and Dalton were either in the pay of two meddling beldames, or that

Lady Helmsby alone had overstepped all bounds. Not a cheering development. Not cheering at all.

But then, Madam had as much as admitted that she and the present duke were courting, and that was a very, very cheering notion indeed.

CHAPTER SIXTEEN

When Wilhelmina arrived, Lady Helmsby was in the breakfast parlor, sitting at the head of the table, one extra place setting to her left. The room was warm to the point of stifling, and a footman stood at attention by the sideboard.

"Mina, darling, there you are." Her ladyship swanned down the room and bussed Wilhelmina's cheek. "Dortmund, a fresh pot, please. China black. Nothing is too good for my late son's widow."

All the misgivings Wilhelmina had felt earlier came rushing back. A pot of China black was hardly an extravagance on a winter morning.

What is she up to? "You are in good spirits, Mama-in-Law. It's always a pleasure to start the day with cheerful company."

Lady Helmsby led Wilhelmina to the sideboard. "Isn't it just? Help yourself to as much as you please. Cook has a very light hand with an omelet, and I can vouch for the ham myself. Not too smoky, not too salty."

Wilhelmina put modest portions on her plate. She was hungry, but she was also determined that the meal be quick. Lady Helmsby came behind and filled her own plate generously.

"Do have a seat, dear. You must be wondering why I've invited you here at such an hour."

Help yourself to as much as you like. Do have a seat. Such abundant—and pointless—graciousness. Lady Helmsby must need funds urgently.

Wilhelmina took the indicated chair and waited for her hostess to enthrone herself at the head of the table.

"Dortmund, at last," Lady Helmsby said, as if her footman had returned from an arctic expedition. "I'll pour, and you may close the door behind you when you leave."

The footman set the pot at her ladyship's elbow, bowed, and withdrew.

"I love a stout cup of tea early in the day." Her ladyship poured Wilhelmina's cup too full to admit of even a dash of milk. "How is my darling Emily on this dreary morning?"

"She's enthralled with mythology these days. The Greeks in particular, though the Norse tales interest her too. She has become an excellent reader."

"She gets that from her father, may he rest in peace. What of sums? A lady must be able to manage sums if she's to manage her household."

William had never, to Wilhelmina's knowledge, completed a single book. Even the newspapers merited only a passing glance, though he could pore over racing forms at length. He claimed he'd been booked to death at public school and university.

"Emily is quite competent with sums," Wilhelmina said. "She enjoys them, in fact. A problem that admits of only one correct answer appeals to her."

"William, God rest his soul, was the same way. Had the sort of mind that naturally gravitated to order and logic. The eggs are best when consumed hot, dear."

William had been capable of logic, but he'd been much more a creature of instinct and impulse. "The omelet is quite good." Finn's cook had a better recipe.

Wilhelmina tried to picture Finlay at this table. The whole fussy, overly warm breakfast parlor, her ladyship's too cheerful greetings... Finn would not lend her ladyship a groat. He'd tell her to sell her curiosities and the books she kept about for show. To cease patronizing Madame Bernadette, whose fashions were too frilly and pale for a mature woman.

"William's father favored omelets. Lord Helmsby preferred meat in his, but I daresay that's the masculine palate. Not inclined to refinement when basic sustenance is at issue. Have some tea, dear."

Wilhelmina brought her cup ever so carefully to her lips, keeping the saucer under it lest she spill. "Very strong," she said. "Have we cream or milk on the table?"

"Cream is too rich. A lady must be careful of her figure, and besides, we need the cream for butter."

If Lady Helmsby's cook churned her own butter, she'd be among few Mayfair households to do so. Wilhelmina sipped her tea and prayed for patience.

"Toast, my dear?" Her ladyship asked when the weather, the lack of social entertainments, and fashions likely to become popular in spring had been exhausted.

The toast was dry, not a smidgeon of butter to be seen. "No, thank you," Wilhelmina said. "I enjoyed the eggs and ham."

"Excellent. One must start the day properly nourished. I often said as much to William and his lordship." Mama-in-Law demolished the food remaining on her plate and poured herself more tea. "You've had quite enough? These frigid temperatures demand that we fortify ourselves against the cold."

"I find the winter weather refreshing, for the most part." The coal smoke was less than enchanting.

"You are so hardy," Lady Helmsby said, setting aside her tea cup. "One cannot take that away from you, despite your lack of fecundity. Your Wiltshire upbringing laid a foundation for lifelong good health, and you must be grateful for that much."

Anytime her ladyship referred to Wilhelmina's rural childhood, an insult was threaded through the comment somewhere.

"Your health is also remarkably sound, my lady."

"So it is, though outliving both a spouse and a child is more tribulation than blessing. One bears up, and now, I am delighted to inform you that a great consolation has befallen me."

Wilhelmina's patience, which had been stretched several tollgates past its usual limit, acquired an edge of unease. Did Mama-in-Law refer to a supposed investment opportunity?

Please, no. "Good fortune is to be celebrated," Wilhelmina said, crossing her knife and fork at the top of her plate.

"This is better than good fortune, my dear. This is the answer to many prayers, and even you will admit it's a blessing all around. I found another codicil to dear William's will. A very interesting codicil."

The eggs and ham in Wilhelmina's belly threatened to rebel. "Oh?"

"My dear girl, you have been so brave all these months, these *years*, since William left us, soldiering on, raising Emily to the best of your ability. I'm sure you've made the best job of it you could, but this latest codicil removes from you the burden of Emily's upbringing."

No. No, it did not. William would not, at his pettiest and most disagreeable, have put Emily into his mother's keeping.

"May I see the document?"

"Of course." Lady Helmsby bustled over to the sideboard and extracted a single page of vellum. "Signed, witnessed, written in William's own hand."

Wilhelmina rose and took the document to the window, not so much for better light as for cooler air and some distance from her ladyship. The penmanship was William's scrawl, decipherable to Wilhelmina only because she'd seen so much of it.

The terms were simple: Physical custody of Emily, management of her funds, and day-to-day supervision of her particulars were to be given to Lady Helmsby, William's own mother, who had raised a child to adulthood with results William modestly referred to as impressive. Like several other of his codicils Wilhelmina had seen, this one was witnessed by Dalton and Travers.

"That is his signature," Lady Helmsby said, returning to the table. "I must say I find the whole business a surprise. I was searching for something to read on a deadly dull evening, and that fell out of the pages of *Emma*. Dreadful book about a dreadful young woman, though I haven't read it myself."

Wilhelmina stood by the window, breathing the cooler air as calmly as she could. A war raged within her, a battle between the instinct to object—William had *never* hidden his codicils, much less in books, much less in his mother's household, and *Emma* was not a dreadful book—and the habit of capitulating.

To the dictates of manners.

To the Lindstrom family's idea of a splendid match.

To William's faithless version of matrimony.

To Edwardia's spying...

Except the spies had never been Edwardia's, had they? *Of course not.*

"Say something, dear. I realize this is a shock, but it makes all the sense in the world when you think about it. You are young for a widow, though you have a few good years left. You can lure some baronet or even a viscount into parson's mousetrap if you don't come to the altar with a child to raise. William was always so considerate of you, and I'm sure he wrote this codicil with your best interests in mind as well as Emily's."

A considerate husband at least washed off his mistress's perfume before rejoining his wife. A considerate father learned to *listen* to his daughter.

"I am surprised," Wilhelmina said, remaining by the window. "William and I discussed arrangements for Emily, and he was adamant that she be raised in our home." *By me.*

"That won't be any problem." Lady Helmsby slathered jam on a piece of toast.

"You will leave her with me?" Wilhelmina's voice was calm, but to put that question into words filled her with equal parts dread and rage.

"Oh, no, dear. William's wishes are very clear. Emily can remain in familiar surrounds, and I will bide with her."

A glimmer of hope winked at Wilhelmina from the depths of frigid dread. "You'll move in with us?"

Her ladyship put down the jam knife and motioned for Wilhelmina to resume her seat. Wilhelmina complied, not because she was feeling obedient, but rather, because her knees might soon give way.

"The best idea might be to switch houses," Lady Helmsby said. "I've been up half the night considering the possibilities. You will be happier in a smaller establishment. Emily will be happier in the only home she's known. For me to change abodes will be an imposition—I have been so content here, you know, and I have so many fond memories of this place—but it's a sacrifice I am willing to make to honor dear William's wishes."

A sacrifice. To move to the larger, better address, the coach and team handy... William would never have done this.

And yet, he had disappointed Wilhelmina just as bitterly on previous occasions. He'd forgotten their anniversary every year, without fail. He'd left a rental invoice for a small residence on a quiet, elegant street among the household bills. During Wilhelmina's long and difficult labor, he'd gone to the club and become thunderingly drunk while losing a small fortune at cards. By that point, her expectations of marriage to him had landed in the bottom of the jakes.

He'd surprised her, again, with this rubbishing codicil. Ambushed her.

"You need not worry about Emily," Lady Helmsby said, taking a bite of toast. "I will sack that wretched excuse for a governess that you've tolerated for so long, and Emily will learn some real discipline."

"She's six years old."

"Better late than never. For example, memorization improves the mind, though I do prefer the New Testament to the Old Testament. *Proverbs* isn't that difficult, though, what with all those useful aphorisms. Spare the rod and so forth."

Emily would go mad memorizing King James hour after hour. "That passage refers to sons and to providing them guidance, not beating them." Wilhelmina would go mad. Emily had only recently started back on the path to the normal good spirits of a lively child.

Finn had done that, or played a significant role in her progress. Finn, Norry, time, and love.

Lady Helmsby leveled a stare at Willemina over her toast. "Mina, please accept the good fortune that William and the hand of fate have sent your way. I am a noted hostess, I am a *lady* by title, I am an experienced parent, and I love Emily as if she were my own. I offer her advantages you cannot, and heaven knows, leaving her funds in the cent-per-cents is a hopeless tactic. This is for the best."

Is not, is not, is not. "I trust you will not keep my daughter from me?" Another excruciating question.

"Of course not, dear. After a period of transition, to allow Emily to accustom herself to her improved situation, you will be permitted to visit from time to time. I am not cruel, and the child is attached to you. That presuming governess, however, had best start packing."

Wilhelmina knew two things as she watched Lady Helmsby munch her toast. First, this new codicil was a disaster. The handwriting was William's, the complete lack of consistency or consideration was William's, and Lady Helmsby's glee at getting her hands on Emily, the funds, staff, household, coach, and better address was genuine too.

But a second and more significant truth settled around Wilhelmina's heart: The part of her that sought to keep peace, to accommodate others, and to quietly accept what could not be changed had just died, never to be revived.

"Mina, that is a very unbecoming expression. This is an opportunity for you, and some day you will thank me for honoring William's wishes."

Was Finn thanking St. Didier for thrusting the title into his hands? "I am in shock, Mama-in-Law. Simply... in shock." Wilhelmina aimed for a subdued, cowed tone and nearly achieved it. "William has been gone so long. Are you sure this codicil is still valid?"

Lady Helmsby finished her toast and dusted her hands over her plate. "Of course it's valid, and if some misguided instinct for maternal hysterics tempts you to make legal trouble, Mina, please recall that nobody—not the Regent himself and certainly not some duke-come-lately—can tell Chancery what to do. You will in time see that this is a happy development for all. I have more experience of the world than you do. You must trust my judgment. Shall I see you out?"

Such a courteous offer.

"No need. The corridor is a bit chilly. Spare yourself that. How soon will you be changing abodes?" *You wretched, selfish, conniving termagant.*

A gleam of satisfaction came into Lady Helmsby's eyes. "I must look your premises over first and decide which of the appointments can stay and so forth. You have a fortnight before I will expect you out of the house. You know, you might consider moving in with Edwardia. She could certainly use a companion, and I could rent this house out. I do think that might be a better arrangement than simply trading abodes, but I'll give you a few days to adjust to your good fortune before I make that decision."

"Thank you, Mama-in-Law. I have much to think about."

"I'm sure you do, dear. Run along now and expect me tomorrow afternoon for my first inspection tour."

"Until tomorrow, my lady."

Wilhelmina had never contemplated murder before, but she did on her walk home. How fortunate for William that he was beyond the reach of her ire. The same could not be said for Lady Helmsby.

Finn's question was not whether to propose, but rather, where and how to put the question to Wilhelmina. He readjusted his scarf and turned onto Ballater Court with a sense of elated anticipation. He must look a fool, carrying roses through falling snow, but he was the happiest of men and about to become the luckiest too.

He tried the door latch and found it locked. Odd. Perhaps the weather had slowed Wilhelmina's progress. She was usually early. The key was over the lintel, which both he and Wilhelmina could reach easily, especially now that she wore proper heels on all her footwear.

Finn hadn't teased her about that, but he'd *noticed*. She was wearing brighter colors, too, probably delving more deeply into her pre-mourning wardrobe, because the dresses were several years behind fashion. He'd delight in assisting her to refurbish her wardrobe, just as she'd assisted him to learn the particulars of his ducal holdings.

Marriage to Wilhelmina would be a joy too profound for words. Finn would have to sculpt her as Venus or Nike or maybe both. She was already immortalized as a Grace, but that wasn't nearly a sufficient tribute.

Finn let himself into the house, which was warm enough, and yet, something told him Wilhelmina had yet to arrive. No hint of jasmine floating on the air, no sensible cloak drying on a hook beneath a dampish bonnet, and no intangible sense of welcome about the house.

Rather than shout like an apprentice in love, Finn tried the parlor, the bedrooms, the study, and then the lower reaches.

No, Wilhelmina. She'd been delayed, then, by some upset in the nursery or squabble among the staff. Finn set the roses in a vase and left them on the kitchen table, then decided to trace the path from Ballater Court to Wilhelmina's doorstep—the slow, public, proper path rather than his usual shortcuts.

He expected to meet her around every street corner, but no.

Ah, well, he was overdue for a sketching session in the nursery, and he had a lifetime to bring Wilhelmina roses. The ring in his pocket would have to do.

Ten minutes later, Finn was no longer the happiest of men.

"What do you mean, she's gone?" He tried for civility and missed the mark, based on Travers's expression. "Mrs. Cathcart is the lady of the house, your employer, and of sufficient substance that she's hard to misplace. How long ago did they leave?"

Travers swallowed, glanced at the clock in the hallway, and all but announced that he was deciding exactly which lie to tell.

"She left more than an hour ago, Your Grace," the footman Dalton said, coming up the steps from the kitchen. "Told me if I followed her this time, she'd sack me without a character and notify the agencies that I wasn't to be in service in any proper household ever again."

"Keep your mouth shut," Travers snapped. "His Grace has no call to be interrogating anybody."

Finn was new to this duking business, but he was fairly certain his authority exceeded that of a scheming butler in the house of a Cathcart lady.

"His Grace," Finn growled, "will start interrogating incompetent and disloyal retainers with his fists if you think to prevaricate. Did Mrs. Cathcart give any indication where they were going?"

"None," Travers said. "None at all."

Finn counted to ten in Italian. "That is a proper London snow storm brewing out there, and two women and a girl struck out into that mess with no explanation and no escort. You took notice of that, but not of the direction they walked?"

"They went east," Dalton said, "but they won't get far in this weather, not carrying valises."

Valises. Plural. Sacking was too good for these conscienceless dimwits. The duchess's dwelling was to the north by a few streets.

Such was Finn's upset that he would have been grateful had they traveled in that direction.

Where could they have gone, and why?

"You," Finn said to Travers, "will send the sturdiest, most vigorous junior footman to me." If the man was at all canny, he could discreetly track the ladies' progress by querying shop owners, beggars, flower girls, pickpockets, anybody still out and about. At midafternoon, the streets wouldn't be deserted, but snow had a way of reducing traffic.

"Very good, Your Grace."

"Travers can't do that," Dalton said.

Travers glowered at Dalton. "I am the senior-most staff in this household, you jackanapes. If I tell you to set off for the Antipodes, then set off, you shall."

Ye cavorting putti, the man was overdue for sacking. "Why can't Travers dispatch a footman?" Finn asked.

"Because Your Grace said to send the youngest and fittest, and that would be Haines, but Missus directed him to take a note to the duchess just before she left. Note was sealed, not that Haines would peek. He's a proper sort, fresh from the country."

"And he's not back yet?" Even at a footman's leisurely dawdle and with snow coming down, even allowing for a cup of tea and a chinwag belowstairs, the lad should have done the job in an hour.

"Not a sign of him," Dalton said. "He's a Yorkshireman, and the weather won't bother him. Sizable, young, sensible." That last word was emphasized with a sneer aimed at Travers.

A soft triple tap on the parlor door saved Finn from descending into profanity in three languages. "Come in."

Pritchard stepped into the room, closed the door behind him, and bowed. "Your Grace, I received your message." He nodded to Travers and Dalton. "I understand from the housekeeper that a situation is brewing. How might I be of assistance?"

To have Pritchard on hand took the edge off Finn's temper, but not his worry. "Search Mrs. Cathcart's quarters, Miss Norwich's, and

Miss Emily's, in that order. You are looking for what isn't there. The ladies have decamped without notice, carrying their own luggage. I want to know if Mrs. Cathcart took her jewels or items of sentiment. Did Miss Norwich bundle up all of her worldly possessions or merely stash a few items in a bag? Did Emily leave behind favorite toys or gather those up for this journey?"

Pritchard stared at the hearth, where a fire had burned down to coals. "Anything else?"

"These two," Finn said, "are to be consigned to the servants' hall and remain there until further notice. Lock them in if you have to. You will search their quarters and keep an eye out for sums of money that suggest income in addition to their already generous wages."

"In my case," Dalton said, "you won't find a spare groat. I send it all home to my family. This one,"—he jerked his chin at Travers— "might be a different situation."

Travers glared daggers at his minion, but a bit of dishonor among snoops was much less than the butler was due.

"Downstairs with you two," Pritchard said, gesturing toward the door, "and know that there isn't a gin palace, doss house, hell, crib, or alley in London where I wouldn't find you."

Dalton marched for the door. Travers wasn't as smart.

"I always gave good service," he said, sniffing righteously. "This household has been managed to the best of my ability, and what a fellow does with his free time is his own business."

Finn smacked his right fist against his left palm—not even a twinge in either hand—and Travers scampered for the door.

Pritchard closed the door and went to the window. "What can you tell me?"

"Appallingly little. I was to meet Mrs. Cathcart at two of the clock on Ballater Court. She never showed. I came here in search of answers and found that she'd left on foot after the noon meal, Emily and Norwich with her. Carrying valises, for pity's sake."

"No note? No warning?"

"If no note arrived for me at home, then no. Nothing. She had a late breakfast at Lady Helmsby's and apparently came home preoccupied, but calm. Before she had her bonnet off, she gave orders that luncheon was to be a tray in the nursery and specified ham and cheese sandwiches as well as meat pasties, plenty of shortbread, and fruit tarts. A portable feast, in other words."

"They took some provisions with them. What about cash?"

"You will have to investigate those particulars. I'm more concerned about the jewels."

Pritchard continued to watch the falling snow, likely a courtesy directed at Finn's dignity. "Because," he said, "if she took the jewels, she intends to travel some distance and be gone for some time, and you have no idea why?"

"Precisely. I would have suggested you keep Travers and Dalton separated, but we haven't sufficient resources to manage that."

"We do," Pritchard said. "Your apprentices are on the way. Did you know Antonio carries a stiletto in his boot?"

"I gave it to him. Luciano has one, too, and so does Matteo." And they were exceptionally sturdy young fellows, who could do a convincing impersonation of bloodthirsty banditti when necessary. "Well done, Pritchard. Send two of the lads to make queries between here and various coaching inns to the east. Discreet inquiries."

"London has more than a hundred coaching inns."

"A fact I am well aware of. I will send word to you when I have further orders."

"And if Mrs. Cathcart should trundle up the walk a quarter hour after you hare off?"

"You know damned good and well where I'm headed," Finn said, praying the snow was lightening.

"You are off to speak with the duchess. She's the logical party to question next."

"If I was cast on the street again, coatless and groatless, I would not ask that old woman for a lump of coal." The issue in question was not mere bodily warmth, however, but the safety of three defenseless females. Pritchard was gracious enough not to point that out, nor did he need to.

He moved away from the window, tossed half a scoop of coal on the fire, and wiped his hands on a pristine handkerchief. "You intend to search for Mrs. Cathcart yourself?" The handkerchief, still spotless, was returned to its assigned pocket. "Does that mean questioning Lady Helmsby?"

"At some point, yes, but her ladyship will delight in any development that casts Wilhelmina's judgment in a poor light. If Lady Helmsby knows anything relevant, she'll also likely lie or twist the information to suit her ends."

Edwardia would not lie. Finn could admit that much, grudgingly. Prevaricate, equivocate, and omit, but not lie outright.

"Then where will you start?"

"I will seek the assistance of a man who excels at finding people who don't want to be found. St. Didier knows the family secrets, and if there are any he hasn't yet told me, I will make him rue the day. He might not know where Wilhelmina is at the moment, but he'll have some educated guesses as to why she fled and where she might be headed."

"Or so you hope."

Finn saluted and left Pritchard in the little parlor, then made haste, by every shortcut he knew, to St. Didier's front door.

CHAPTER SEVENTEEN

"Draco doesn't want to go on an adventure," Emily said, loudly enough for half the crowd in the inn's common to hear. "The Ursulas don't either."

This adventure was not at all the one Wilhelmina had planned to embark on. "Why not?" she asked pleasantly. "Do your friends need a nap to restore their energy?"

Emily scowled roundly at the bustling interior of the Swan With Two Necks. The din within and without was amazing, amplified by the old-fashioned stone courtyard, which was surrounded by three galleried stories of rooms.

The whole, complete with iron-shod hooves clattering by the dozen into and out of the courtyard's stone passageway, amounted to acoustics designed in hell.

"It's too noisy to nap here," Emily replied.

"Not for that wee baby," Norwich said, nodding at a young woman whose infant slept on her shoulder. "Poor thing is exhausted."

Wilhelmina was in that state in which exhaustion, despair, fear, anger, and other luxuries were subsumed into the overarching need to flee. Once she had Emily safely away from London and away from Lady Helmsby, she'd indulge in strong hysterics.

And not one moment sooner.

"This would be a good time to play patience," Norry said. "Fortunately for Draco and the bears, I brought a deck of cards."

Emily brightened, and Wilhelmina silently blessed Norry's foresight. There'd be no playing patience on the coach, but a great deal of patience would be required.

Emily was soon absorbed with explaining the game to her friends.

"You aren't wrong," Norry said softly. "Disappearing from Town is the right thing to do. Her ladyship was correct that the duke can't tell Chancery to ignore a valid codicil, and if Lady Helmsby was watching your every move, she might well be having His Grace followed as well."

The knowledge that Lady Helmsby—not the duchess—might have eyes and ears everywhere, that she'd known of Wilhelmina's visits to Ballater court and who she'd met there, infused Wilhelmina's panic with rage.

"Mama-in-Law's objective might not be to raise Emily," Wilhelmina said. "Her goal might be to force Finn to the altar with the bride of her choosing. He'd do it, too, to protect Emily, to see her remain with me. I thought the duchess was keeping an eye on me, and I resented that, but she became the head of the family until His Grace showed up. Taking her to task would have been pointless."

Blowing retreat without explaining matters to Finn was excruciating, but he could not be manipulated into a loveless marriage if Wilhelmina kept him out of the affray. Emily could not be subjected to Lady Helmsby's supervision if Wilhelmina's flight from Town was successful. That left much to sort out—Finn did not deserve to be abandoned by loved ones yet again—but Wilhelmina was capable of focusing on only one disaster at a time.

"Her Grace is uppish and difficult," Norwich said, "but not malign. Lady Helmsby, by contrast..."

"Her Grace's home is the first place Lady Helmsby will look for us, else I should have gone there," Wilhelmina replied. "Mama-in-Law has been merely uppish, difficult, and devoted to her own ends until now. This ruthlessness... I wasn't prepared for it." And Edwardia was socially formidable, but legally... she had no influence over Chancery. In theory, only the law itself held weight in that court.

Emily turned over two cards on Draco's behalf, a knave and a queen. Draco rose a few inches above the tabletop and flew a circuit above the cards, then settled down between the Ursulas.

"You can write to His Grace," Norry said, even more quietly. "Once we're away. Explain the situation."

The coach was supposed to arrive in a quarter hour, but the weather was throwing the schedules into disarray. Wilhelmina kept an eye on the door, half expecting Travers and Dalton to storm through and snatch Emily.

Why didn't I sack them when I could? "I can't write to His Grace," Wilhelmina said. "Not yet. For all I know, his household is riddled with spies, too. I warned him that could happen." Would Finn receive St. Didier if Wilhelmina tried to use him as her messenger?

"I can send a letter to my sister," Norwich said, "with your epistle enclosed. She can post it for you from York to the duke's household."

Ursula Minor picked two queens. Draco turned his back to the bears and fumed.

"I can't think that far ahead, Norry. All I know is, Chancery will honor that codicil, and there's nothing anybody can do to change that. The courts exist to limit the power of dukes and nabobs, at least in theory. All that aside, Mama-in-Law will take her case to the gossips. His Grace should not have to deal with scandal when he's trying to turn a bankrupt dukedom solvent."

"Nothing like a good family scandal," Norwich muttered. "You should still write to him. Not because he can do anything, but because he cares for you and Emily."

"Who?" Emily asked, Ursula Major in her hand. "Finn? I miss him. I wish he was coming on this adventure with us."

"He'd take up a lot of room in the coach," Wilhelmina said. "He might bump his head on the coach roof he's so tall."

"He could ride with John Coachman. May I ride with John Coachman, Mama?"

"You'd turn into an icicle in five minutes, my dear. Who's winning?"

Emily took that bait, but over the course of the journey, she would doubtless become more fretful. In good weather, with sound horses, the average stagecoach could cover a distance of one hundred twenty miles in less than fifteen hours. The weather was not good at all.

The minutes ticked on, and if anything, the common became noisier, while the scent of wet wool, unwashed humans, and cooking meat became thicker. Wilhelmina made a trip to the jakes with Emily —another adventure that didn't remotely qualify for the name—and offered her daughter a determinedly cheerful patter of distractions.

Yes, the horses were enormous and cobbles slippery. Yes, the day was getting chillier. No, dragons did not mind the cold at all. Way up in the sky where dragons flew, the air was always chilly, and they liked it that way.

Wilhelmina disliked the direction of her own thoughts. She resumed her place beside Norwich in the teeming common, interested Emily in another round of patience, and felt the start of a headache.

"I know I am doing what I must to protect present company," she said quietly, "but I am also trying to convince myself that I had no choice."

"What do you mean?" Norwich brushed Emily's damp braid back over the child's shoulder. Emily, once more absorbed in her game, didn't appear aware of the touch.

"I told myself I had no choice but to marry William. Such a wonderful match! Such a coup! A triumph! Even though I knew him to be self-indulgent and far from in love with me, I tried to believe I was making a splendid match. I had no choice but to make the best of it. I tolerated spies under my roof because I told myself I could not brangle with the duchess. I had no choice but to ignore her overreaching. Now I am telling myself that His Grace cannot keep Emily from Mama-in-Law, and asking him to try would be unfair. He'll end up marrying the heiress of Mama-in-Law's choice, and make the best of it. His Grace is practical, and he would give his life to keep Emily safe and happy."

Almost worse, he'd give up his freedom.

"He will never marry for money," Norwich said. "You know better."

"He thought he'd never be a duke, though, yes, I *should* know better. The habit of self-cozening is hard to shake."

"But not impossible. Witness, our present circumstances. And lest you forget, madam, that woman was already contemplating Emily's betrothal prospects."

The reminder fortified Wilhelmina's flagging confidence. Norwich spoke the plain, horrifying truth, and no measure was too extreme to protect Emily from such a fate.

"My daughter shall have the right to choose—whether and when to marry and upon whom to bestow her hand. Emily deserves to marry because she pleases to, not because marriage is presented as an escape from utter misery."

Emily deserved so much better than that. *I deserved better.*

When the coach arrived—only a quarter hour late—Wilhelmina climbed aboard and again told herself she was doing the right thing. Disappear to safety, beyond the reach of even the Chancery Courts. Sometimes retreat was a step in the direction of eventual victory.

With darkness falling, the coach clattered out of the yard and turned west on Lad Lane. Emily was soon asleep in Wilhelmina's lap, Norry snoring against Wilhelmina's shoulder. Then they were past the London tolls, through the first change, and still Wilhelmina could not find relief from a sadness that was becoming angrier by the mile.

She deserved better than to be sent fleeing in the middle of winter.

Emily deserved better than to be uprooted merely to avoid Lady Helmsby's scheme. Norwich's duties should not include accessory to a potential kidnapping.

And Finn would never understand yet another abandonment by a person who supposedly loved him. He of all people should not become a pawn sacrificed to a greedy woman's schemes.

The snow became mere flurries, the air bitter, and the coach horses cantered on into the darkness.

"I've looked for you at your home and in half the clubs in Town," His Grace of Huntleigh said. "Where the hell have you been?"

St. Didier was painfully familiar with peers throwing tantrums. Earls were generally the worst, though St. Didier had crossed swords with a widowed viscountess who could give any six earls a run for their strawberry leaves. Whatever had upset the duke, the result was a cold, measured calm that gave even St. Didier pause.

"I was *out,* Your Grace, and now I am once again home, so let's take whatever business you have to discuss with me behind a closed door, shall we?"

That earned St. Didier a terse nod. The duke did not stalk down the corridor, boots thumping, announcing a foul mood to the whole house, but rather, padded along in near silence. Such stealth was unnerving in so large a man, also impressive.

St. Didier took his guest to his study. "My choice of venue is informal," he said, "not because I intend any insult, but because the fire is always lit and the walls are thick. Brandy?"

"A tea tray, if your kitchen can oblige. I need a clear head."

St. Didier used the bell-pull and gestured to a pair of reading chairs by the fire. "The weather is beastly, and yet, here you are, ruining your boots, which suggests to me the matter is urgent. You weren't willing to wait ten minutes for the coach horses to be put to."

The duke settled into a chair. St. Didier did as well, rather than stand on ceremony.

"The horses can't cover the distance between your door and mine as quickly as I can on foot. Cast a child on his own wits, and he learns how to reckon Town by means other than street signs."

This again, though to be fair, St. Didier had known for years that his family's properties were likely to be snatched away upon the death of the old earl. Finlay Cathcart, at eight years old, would have had no grasp of what a penniless orphan could expect on London's streets.

"So here you are. What's amiss?"

The duke sat forward and held his hands out to the fire. "Mrs. Cathcart has disappeared, taking Emily and Miss Norwich with her. They carried valises, valuables, some food, and more than enough money to get to the coast. What I cannot fathom is why."

"Were you bothering the lady?" One could not call out a duke, but one could put the fear of dark alleys, royal disapproval, and bankruptcy in him.

"I was *courting* her, with her permission, and she received my overtures with apparent enthusiasm."

A tap on the door heralded the tea tray. The kitchen had performed to standards, including toasted cheese sandwiches, jam tarts, and hot cross buns among the offerings. The tea was hot and strong and the service silver.

"What do you know of the lady's departure?" St. Didier asked, pouring out. "Fix your tea however you like."

The duke drizzled honey into his cup. "Mrs. Cathcart had a late breakfast with Lady Helmsby, and immediately upon returning home, directed that a hearty luncheon be served in the nursery. Within an hour of that meal, she, Norwich, and Emily were trundling down the front steps, each of them carrying a smallish piece of luggage."

"The snow had started by early afternoon. I understand your concern." *Controlled panic* might be the better term. Barely controlled.

"Mrs. Cathcart was to meet me socially at two of the clock. She failed to show, left no word of her whereabouts or plans, and thus I went to her home. She took jewels with her, St. Didier. She means to stay gone and to travel far."

"And you expect me to find her?"

The duke finished his tea at one go and poured himself more. "I expect *myself* to find her, but tracking errant parties is your stock in trade. Any wisdom you have to share would be appreciated. All I know is she was last seen traveling east along Holborn Street."

"A good hike, especially for the child. If you know why she left, you might have a better sense of where to find her."

His Grace drizzled more honey into his tea cup. "She left because of something that meddling ninnyhammer, Lady Helmsby, said or did at breakfast. The order for a sumptuous lunch was given as soon as Mrs. Cathcart was under her own roof. She was planning her departure from that moment forward."

"Or she kept the breakfast appointment with her mother-in-law the better to prevent Lady Helmsby from suspecting travel was in the offing." St. Didier liked puzzles—who, how, why?—but he very much disliked the thought of the duke haring about London after dark, fearing for his lady and ready to break heads at the least provocation.

"The breakfast invitation came only last night. Pritchard is directing Mrs. Cathcart's household staff for the nonce—two of whom were in Lady Helmsby's pay, by the way—and the boot-boy recalled her ladyship's invitation arriving well after supper."

Pritchard was an interesting fellow. St. Didier was inclined to both like and respect him. Perhaps even to hire him, should he ever be in want of employment.

"Why aren't you pounding on Lady Helmsby's door, thumb-screws at the ready?"

His Grace leveled an attack on the sandwiches, his manners both dainty and determined. "The less Lady Helmsby knows of the whole affair, the better for all. She schemes, lies, and spies and that makes her an unreliable informant. Besides, the why of it doesn't matter half so much as finding the ladies. They could be in Portsmouth or Dover before midnight.

And sailing on the morning tide. A distressing thought. "The weather is on your side. The stage coaches aren't as passionate about keeping to their schedules as the post coaches are. Of course, the mail does travel on a lot of stage coaches, but so do human passengers, and heroics for the sake of gossipy correspondence doesn't sit well with John or Jane Bull."

"Mrs. Cathcart could have hired her own conveyance."

"You aren't convinced she did." Neither was St. Didier. "Why?"

"Because that's a conspicuous transaction, especially for a woman. On the face of it, a private coach is, well, private, but it's also outlandishly expensive, especially if a change of teams is needed every hour or so. The private coaches for hire also tend to be at least somewhat commodious. Both the expenditure of coin and the nature of the conveyance are noticeable."

Precisely. "A crowd is a fugitive's friend. That's why you sailed from Rome to Naples rather than travel overland. The docks were crowded and busy, while one carriage at a time travels down the road."

Two sandwiches remained. His Grace moved on to the jam tarts. "Sailing the Italian coast is preferable to jostling along what remains of the Appian Way with one's entire household in tow. For present purposes, I need to know where Wilhelmina has gone. The why can wait until I've found her."

"What if she doesn't want to be found?" St. Didier asked, sipping his tea.

"Then I will ensure she has safe passage to wherever she wants to go and wish her the best. I have to know, though, that she's not... not making a mistake. I'm well aware that a timely exit can feel like a solution when it's anything but. I stormed out of London as a young man and landed in a country where I didn't speak the language, knew none of the customs, had no friends... I didn't even understand the money, for pity's sake, and that was just the beginning."

A duke who admitted to errors and regrets was a rare sight, one that St. Didier should have enjoyed, but could not.

"You ought to consult with the duchess, Your Grace."

"If I were choosing my shroud, I would not ask that woman for her guidance on the selection of fabric." His Grace sounded more weary than affronted. Protesting for form's sake, perhaps.

Two jam tarts remained. The first hot cross bun had met its fate.

"Consider, Your Grace, that you are choosing the shroud in which you will bury your hopes for the future. If Mrs. Cathcart leaves England, you might never find her. Or you might get a letter five years from now, sent from someplace where she does not bide and will never pass through again. Five years after that, Emily might send you a note, or one of your legion of bloodsucking inquiry agents might claim to have spotted Miss Norwich on the streets of Dublin. Hard to tell for sure, after so much time..."

"You sketch a personal parlor in purgatory."

"Precisely. All because you wouldn't spend a quarter hour with Her Grace on a winter evening."

"Damn you. I need answers now, not sermons on ducal deportment."

What the duke needed was the sort of plain speech that slightly disreputable uncles and blunt godmothers could provide.

"The duchess might well have those answers," St. Didier said, "but your pride won't allow you to ask her for them." St. Didier topped up his tea, mostly to annoy his guest. "In the opinion of some, I was damned when I lost the title. In your opinion, a title is a form of damnation. Make up your mind. Not as the duke or the sculptor or the orphan, but as the man you are right now: Will you be able to live with yourself if snubbing the duchess costs you a future with your Wilhelmina?"

The duke rose, half a hot cross bun in his hand. He stood before the hearth, staring at the flames. "Her Grace is among those responsible for the fact that my only sibling never had a chance to thrive. That my mother died much too young. That my father's passing was far more painful than it should have been. I loved those people, St. Didier. They were all I had. I do not hate Her Grace, but neither do I like, trust, or respect her."

"Would Mrs. Cathcart ask the duchess to lie to you?"

His Grace took another bite of bun. "No. Willie wouldn't do that to me."

Willie. If nothing else, St. Didier's theory of the case was proved. "The duchess might well know where Mrs. Cathcart has gone. She might have a good idea of places to look. The ladies were not close, but Mrs. Cathcart seemed to prefer the duchess's hauteur to Lady Helmsby's endless chatter."

His Grace finished his bun and dusted his hands. "Wilhelmina sent Her Grace a note right before she left the house. The lad who delivered it never even saw the duchess. He dawdled belowstairs with her staff, getting all the news, putting off his return to the last minute."

"Then the duchess might know something of why Mrs. Cathcart left. I tend to agree with you that interrogating Lady Helmsby can wait."

"You agree with me?"

"Lady Helmsby will lie to you to suit her own convenience—you are utterly correct. Edwardia, however, probably hasn't told a lie since Mad George tried to flirt with her in his youth. Then too, she dotes on Emily, in her fashion."

Such a scowl! Not merely thunderous, *volcanic.* Almost as if His Grace agreed with St. Didier's observations.

And yet, St. Didier had tracked Finlay Cathcart all over half a Continent, spoken to women who'd recalled him fondly and fellow artists who'd resented him bitterly. St. Didier had watched the new duke from a distance and broken bread with him.

Not on St. Didier's most presumptuous day would he have

claimed that he and His Grace of Huntleigh were friends. St. Didier instead knew the duke on the instinctive level that fierce competitors know each other. Theirs was the familiarity of ancestral enemies more than friends, just as intimate, but in a different way.

And because of that familiarity, St. Didier saw in the duke's reaction to the mention of the duchess's fondness for Emily what should never have been made visible.

The duchess doted on Emily, while she'd left a very young Finlay to starve. She was capable of caring for a child, of affection, but she'd never exercised that talent in the direction of a small, lonely, bereaved boy. That flash of molten rage spoke plainly enough: *She never acknowledged my existence.*

"Think of Emily," St. Didier said gently. "She is small. She is just regaining her balance after dwelling in a house of mourning for much of her short life. Nobody will explain to her what's afoot. She will stop asking questions after a time, and she will not understand why the adults she loves and trusts are lying to her. The ladies will stay up late at night talking, believing the child is asleep, while she shivers on the far side of the keyhole, and—"

"Do be quiet." His Grace's expression had muted to a mere frown, but the firelight gave his features a diabolical cast. "Emily is why I have done the pretty by this stupid title."

"And was that the right decision?" St. Didier asked, pushing to his feet.

A flash of relenting, of humor, almost. "Yes. That was the right decision."

"Then go see the duchess now. She's an early-to-bed type, and as to that, you should know she doesn't enjoy the best of health. Her staff is concerned for her heart."

"That assumes she possesses one. I will see myself out, and thank you, St. Didier. You excel at speaking peace unto the heathen."

"Not a heathen, Your Grace. A man in love. Good night, and good hunting."

The duke left on a properly derisive snort, and St. Didier

returned to his chair. The toasted sandwiches were still warm, and he was hungry. He started on the first one and silently wished Her Grace the best of luck.

She'd need it. Whatever was true about Mrs. Cathcart's flight, the duke would not give Edwardia another chance to redeem herself, and a chance to redeem herself was likely much of what kept the old besom alive.

"We're making good time," Norry said. "We should take rooms for the night soon."

"Quite right," an older gentleman said from the backward-facing seat. "If miladies are bound for Bath or Bristol, ye'll find the road gets mighty hilly west of Newbury. That stretch is safer by daylight."

Wilhelmina held a sleeping Emily in her lap. "Where are we?" she asked.

"Coming into Theale, missus," the gentleman said. "We're a good forty-five miles from Town, and that wee child has slept for the past ten."

Emily would demand to use the jakes upon waking. For that matter, Wilhelmina was in rather urgent need herself. "The hills are bad?"

"With a sober hand at the reins, not so bad—I've seen worse—but they are many, and if John Coachman gets behind schedule and doesn't want to stop to affix the brake, the descents can be dicey."

All of life was looking dicey at the moment, and adding more risks to the list had no appeal whatsoever.

"We'll think more clearly when we're rested," Norry said, which Wilhelmina took for a plea.

The coachy called the stop, and the carriage careened around a corner to plunge to a halt before a two-story whitewashed building with a peaked, thatched roof. In the deep gloom of a winter night, the torchlit innyard looked cozy and the inn itself warm. The Olde Something.

"Off we go," Wilhelmina said, "assuming they have rooms."

Norry popped down first, and Wilhelmina passed Emily to her. The old gent directed the hostlers to toss the appropriate bags from the roof and into the arms of a waiting groom. A porter took charge from there, and—after a short excursion to Jericho—Wilhelmina was soon leading a half-awake Emily up to a largish room on the second floor.

"Stay awake long enough to eat something," Norry said, shedding her cloak as Wilhelmina got Emily out of her scarf and mittens. "You should let me do that."

"I'm her mother. You can inspect the sheets."

"Hungry," Emily murmured.

Wilhelmina produced the last of the strawberry tarts from lunch. "Nibble on that, and we'll have more substantial fare soon."

"Won't I spoil my supper, Mama?"

"Supper is late today. That will tide you over."

The sheets, thank the merciful powers, were clean and dry. The food was hot and hearty—beef barley stew with lots of fresh bread and butter. When Emily had been tucked into the trundle bed—"and bless Finn, and Charles, and Roberts, and Her Grace, and please tell Papa I am being good"—Wilhelmina divided the last of the tea between herself and Norry.

"I'm glad we stopped," Norry said, bending to unlace her boots. "I realize we could have been in Bath before noon tomorrow, or even Bristol, but Emily needs some semblance of routine, and that means sleeping in a bed at night."

Wilhelmina should unlace her own boots. "You are a great believer in routine."

"Sometimes a sensible routine is all we have."

A story lay behind that observation, but Wilhelmina was too exhausted to pursue particulars. "Thank you, Norry, for coming with us, and for everything."

Norwich set her boots on the far side of the chair, away from the fire's heat. "I haven't had an adventure in quite some time. No thanks are necessary. The offer to send a note to my sister in York is still open."

"I'm thinking about it." Though sooner or later, Norry would stop offering.

Long after Norry had commenced gently snoring, Wilhelmina sat up with her tepid tea. She contemplated matters of loyalty and love, and reached no easy conclusions.

She did admit that she missed Finn terribly and doubtless always would.

CHAPTER EIGHTEEN

Finn marched through the night, the cold unexpectedly welcome. The streets were nearly deserted, the occasional stray pedestrian moving quickly, head down, face swaddled against the frigid air. The alleys bore the deeper silence brought by a quantity of fresh snow, and thus Finn had peace and quiet in which to think.

He realized he'd made his decision only when he beheld the lamppost on Her Grace's walkway, its circle of light adding sparkle to the pristine snow.

St. Didier had been right: If a failure to interview Edwardia meant Wilhelmina disappeared for good, Finn would not forgive himself. Willie would never have fled like this unless she'd thought herself—or Emily—in immediate danger.

Finn could come up with no other explanation for her behavior, and he had no justification whatsoever for why she'd not confided her situation to him before leaving. Maybe a note explaining the urgency awaited him at home.

"I am putting off the inevitable," he muttered, mounting the front steps. He thumped on the door with his fist, the knocker being nowhere in evidence. He went on thumping until a footman of mature years appeared in the doorway.

"The hour is late, my good fellow, and the night—*Your Grace?*" The footman stepped back and bowed. "Good evening, Your Grace. Do come in."

The hour was not at all late by Mayfair standards. Formal suppers would just be getting started, the clubs only beginning to hum.

"Roberts, isn't it?" Finn asked, stepping into the relative warmth of the foyer. "You are the keeper of the spaniel, among other duties."

"I have that honor, Your Grace, though it's more the case that I am old Charles's friend, and the beast is very fond of Miss Emily so she associates me with the dog. Please allow me to take that cloak to the kitchen. We'll have it dry in no time."

While Finn's toes itched and tingled, he let the man fuss. Damp hat, damp scarf, damp gloves... the lot was consigned to the good offices of the kitchen hearth's drying pegs.

"I would like to see the duchess." Finn purposely avoided the more accurate statement: *I need to see the duchess.*

"I will ascertain whether Her Grace is in. Would a toddy be in order, Your Grace?"

"My business is urgent and not social."

Roberts's air of welcome faltered into bewilderment. "Very good, sir. This way."

Finn was escorted to a much smaller parlor than the grand chamber where he'd taken tea previously. These appointments also nodded graciously toward the last century, but the ceiling was a modest eight feet and the single hearth merely large.

The room was warm, suggesting somebody had recently occupied it.

"I'll be but a moment, Your Grace." Roberts bowed and withdrew, and Finn was left to confront a portrait of the duke and duchess as a younger couple. Not youthful—the previous duke had grieved his first duchess and then remarried—but not quite middle-aged either.

Edwardia, somewhat younger than her spouse, had never been a beauty, apparently, while her late husband had been considered handsome and charming.

"The resemblance between you and your uncle is remarkable," Edwardia said, swanning into the room, the old spaniel trotting at her side. "I've sent Roberts for a tray, because the kitchen will feel slighted if you don't partake of their offerings. Being a duke is work, in case you haven't figured that out. You must eat even when you aren't hungry."

She was in a pale blue night-robe, her hair braided into a silvery coronet. Despite her informal attire, she moved with queenly dignity, and her voice held the same imperious snap. The dog, by contrast, had settled immediately by the hearth, his grizzled chin resting on his paws.

Finn was relieved that she'd received him, and he resented that relief. "Being a sculptor is *hard* work. Good evening." When Edwardia continued to merely regard him, he made himself say the next part. "Thank you for joining me."

"Hah. You about choked on those words. You are such a Cathcart. Do sit down. I'll get a crick in my neck staring up at you, and one has enough cricks and creaks at my age."

Finn took a seat, and because the chair had been positioned near the hearth, the cushions were warm. The comfort was tantalizing, and the duchess likely knew that.

More resentment, which would aid Finn's present purpose not at all. He launched into his agenda rather than indulge in pointless sparring.

"I am concerned for Wilhelmina, Emily, and Miss Norwich," he said, the most unrude, accurate opening he could fashion. "They departed from London earlier today under irregular circumstances. I want—I need—to assure myself that the ladies are safe. I will not interfere if Wilhelmina orders me to keep my distance, but to leave without warning or preparation... She would behave thus only upon extreme provocation."

The duchess rose and, to Finn's shock, tossed a half scoop of coal on the hearth. When she resumed her seat, old Charles crept from the hearth rug to sit at her feet.

She stroked the dog's ear. "Wilhelmina sent me a note, the daft woman. 'Trouble afoot, but you must not worry. Details later. We are safe. Please receive Finn if he calls.' Finn... She refers to you as Finn. One shudders at the informality."

One did not appear to be shuddering in truth, but rather, quietly pleased. "Have you any idea where she's gone?" Finn asked.

"Where Vanessa won't find her—Lady Helmsby, to you. Her ladyship is pockets to let, or nearly so, and this business bears the stink of her brand of mischief."

"Is it too much to hope that you know particulars? Lady Helmsby apparently paid Wilhelmina's staff to spy for her ladyship, though Norwich was loyal to her mistress and her charge. Perhaps you have taken similar measures to limit Lady Helmsby's machinations?"

While Finn had been haring about London, the part of his mind that hadn't been focused on coaching routes and coastal departures had been considering motives. Was Wilhelmina caught in some sort of feud between the duchess and Lady Helmsby? Was she removing herself or Emily from a chessboard Finn had only dimly perceived?

Was she somehow trying to protect Finn?

The duchess ceased cosseting her spaniel. "You are asking if I paid Vanessa's domestics to spy on their employer, or paid Vanessa's myrmidons in Mina's house to serve two, no, three mistresses? My dear boy, I would never stoop to such measures in the first place, and I haven't the coin in the second. In the third, what sort of fool trusts a paid informant?"

"A desperate fool. Lady Helmsby's financial situation grows dire." Which suggested that Finn's earlier guess—that Emily, with her generous trust, was somehow at the root of the problem—bore more thought. "I can sort out the finances later. How do I find Wilhelmina? St. Didier suggested you might have some ideas."

The duchess gazed at a spot past Finn's shoulder, then turned a gimlet eye on him. "Has it occurred to you that Vanessa is having you followed, and if you find Wilhelmina, you will waste all the efforts she's made to elude notice?"

St. Didier hadn't quite raised that point. "Yes, it has occurred to me, and such is my familiarity with London's streets and alleys that I know I have not been followed thus far. That her ladyship might have my mews watched is also possible, but her two best snoops have been called to account, does she but know it."

"That would be Travers and the pretty fellow, Dalton. Mina had little use for either, but Vanessa foisted them on William when he and Mina were newly wed. What was a new bride to do?"

Finn cared nothing for ancient history. "Do you know where Wilhelmina has gone?"

"I do not. She did not tell me, which was smart of her."

"You'd have told me?" Finn didn't believe that for a moment.

"I might, or I might have made some attempt to intercede, and apparently secrecy is imperative." Her Grace stared off into the middle distance again, and Finn was reminded of St. Didier's warning: The duchess was growing frail, or so her staff claimed.

"If you have nothing more to say on the matter, I won't keep you any longer." Finn rose, ready to spend the rest of the night making inquiries at coaching inns and sending expresses to the compass points.

Though, of course, all of those activities would draw attention to Wilhelmina's departure.

"Sit down," the duchess said. "Please sit down."

Finn remained on his feet.

"Ye gods, boy. Must I beg? You can spare me another five minutes. Won't you please have a seat, Your Grace?"

Finn sank into the comfortable chair. Bullying an old woman, even this old woman, was beyond him. And this late in the day, Edwardia did look pale and not... not vigorous. Not sickly, but not on her mettle.

"Secrets can serve the greater good," she said, "but they can also overstay their welcome. I have something for you, but answer a question for me first. Do you intend to marry Wilhelmina?"

That is none of your business.

The dog turned his gaze on Finn, as if the damned beast could hear his thoughts. Charles's expression appeared gently reproachful. Disappointed, even.

I am losing my reason. Finn was also in no frame of mind to bicker. "I have a ring in my pocket, and Wilhelmina granted me leave to court her." The rest of it—that she might even now be carrying Finn's child, despite all precautions—would remain private.

"Very well, then. Give me a moment."

Edwardia crossed the room and opened a chest in the opposite corner. A whiff of cedar reached Finn's nose.

"I believe this belongs to you, sir." She passed Finn something made of soft fabric, the hue somewhere between blue and gray.

His body understood what he held in his hands before his mind grasped the reality. His vision dimmed at the edges, and the hair on his nape prickled. He resisted, barely, the urge to cradle the treasure to his chest.

"*Bo-Bo?* This is my Bo-Bo? Why on earth would you have my stuffed bear?"

The dog rose and put his chin on Finn's knee. Finn fell silent, lest childhood memories and an old dog entirely unman him.

Edwardia had seen men come home from the wars, and their gazes bore the same hint of bewilderment and never-forgotten pain Finlay's did when he held the remains of a stuffed toy. His touch on the worn velvet was reverent, and Charles—bless his canine soul—had taken up sentry duty at the duke's side.

"You left that here," Edwardia said, trying for a dispassionate tone, though a twinge was threatening to envelop her heart. "When last your mama called upon me, you forgot that... that creature."

"Mama said you'd likely given him to the rag-and-bone man or tossed him into the fire. I was devastated, but I knew we could not come back for him. For it."

Edwardia had never carried a child to term, but she'd conceived. Three times, she'd been given reason to hope, and three times, she'd grieved bitterly.

Finlay had been yet another grief, felt as deeply by the late duke as by his duchess, and for that reason—for the sake of her departed husband—Edwardia marshaled her tears and carried on.

"I promised your mother I would keep your friend safe, but I never could quite figure out what he was supposed to be."

Finlay's free hand moved over Charles's head. "A bear. Bo-Bo the Bear. Mama made nursery sachets to sell, sewing them in the shapes of animals and scenting them with lavender. She noticed how much I enjoyed playing with her inventory—I hadn't any real toys—and she made Bo-Bo out of the scraps. I chose a bear, and she did the best she could, though he has a prodigious number of seams."

The duke sniffed the velvet. "Camphor and cedar. You let Mama know you had him?"

Now came the hard part—the next hard part. "We communicated through the parish curate, a Scot who knew how to keep mum."

"Why?" A hint of ducal imperiousness infused the question.

The boy was quick to recover, another sign of a true Cathcart. "Why the curate? Because your dear father would have had six apoplexies and ten heart palpitations if he had known your mother and I were communicating."

"*My father?*"

Ah, the lad hadn't even suspected, then. Heaven help him. "Lord Thornton rebuffed every overture his brothers made, Finlay. He refused aid. He refused invitations. He knew his health was failing, and still, he would not be reconciled to his family. Fortunately, your mother was more practical."

Finlay's grip on the bear was quite snug. "*You turned her away. I* was there. I saw you dismiss her plea while the staff looked on and pretended not to see your cruelty."

"You saw what we needed you—and the staff—to see. Had I shown your mother any overt generosity, your father would have publicly flung the money right back in my face and likely removed his family to Dublin. The situation had grown dire, or Lady Thornton would never have approached me so openly."

Finlay was quiet for a time, his hand moving absently on Charles's head. "I don't understand. Why was Papa so stubborn? We had no food. No coal. I'm fairly certain I wore stolen boots that last winter."

"Not stolen. The curate gave them to you, but then he found a post up in Scotland. The vicar was given to talk and tippling. I am not ashamed to say that His Grace and I prayed for your father to be released from his earthly suffering. With your dear mama gone, we were ready to snatch you up, but you eluded our grasp, you awful child. His Grace was wild with worry, but of course, in the places you sought refuge, the last person anybody will speak to is a ducal inquiry agent."

"You needed a Pritchard, not a St. Didier."

"We needed a miracle, and eventually one came our way. After years of searching, we learned you were not dead—such rejoicing, my boy, you never imagined—and you were working your way through your articles as a mason. You had talent, we were told, and ambition. You were determined to make something of yourself, and—I fear the report was accurate—you had nothing but scorn for your ducal connections."

Did he still have nothing but scorn for those connections? Edwardia prayed not.

"Go on."

"There isn't much more to tell. You did make something—something impressive—of yourself, but then William expired of terminal foolishness, and you became the heir of last resort. I was content to leave you in peace until then, but I haven't that luxury now."

"Because the ducal coffers are scandalously empty?"

The lad had the Cathcart pride too. "They aren't that empty. Sell some of the properties, take a hand in the investments. The situation can still be brought 'round eventually. I haven't the luxury of leaving you in peace, because time is running out, Finlay. If you choose to turn your back on your birthright, the decision should be yours, based on facts rather than on your father's legacy of bitterness. He was the extra spare and never allowed to forget it. Some people only know how to go on if they have a grievance to rail against. Thornton became one of them, and rubbishing consumption didn't help."

Finlay made as if to rise. Charles whined, and the duke sat back down. "This is all... all very interesting, and I will consider what you've told me, but right now..."

"You have been hit by a runaway carriage you couldn't hear or see coming. I don't expect any great reconciliation, young man, but I promised my husband that if the moment was ever right, I'd at least give you another perspective on the past to consider."

"You have done your duty." The words were distracted. "One of your many duties."

"If you call sending out reams of letters, swilling tea by the hour, and dozing through divine services duties, yes, I still have a few." Edwardia told herself to get up, to end the interview when all parties were still capable of civility. Finlay would have questions, but he could ask them later, on some other day when he wasn't trying to locate his errant duchess-to-be.

Edwardia scooted to the edge of her cushion, braced her hands on the arms of the chair, and gave a stout push, only to be hit with a stouter twinge.

"Your Grace?" Finlay's voice was sharp, and Charles had left the duke's side to stand by Edwardia's chair.

"I'm tired," she muttered, mortified past all bearing, and angry as well. Was a woman to be allowed no dignity when dignity finally mattered?

"Come, then," Finlay said, getting to his feet. "We'll summon your familiars and get you up to bed. We shall talk more when I've located my ladies, so mind you don't go and expire on me. I've had quite enough of my elders expiring, I'll have you know. I have questions for you, and you are not to elude them by dying on me."

"Stop being dramatic."

He put a hand under her elbow, and Edwardia was on her feet in the next instant. She was not so surprised that she turned loose of Finlay's arm, though.

"Roberts!" the duke bellowed. "Get in here and assist Her Grace to her room."

The door opened immediately, and Roberts bustled in, bearing a tray. "Your Grace is ready to retire?"

"The duchess is awake past her bedtime," Finlay said. "Remedy the oversight, please, and keep Her Grace in good form until next I call."

"Finlay, I am old, but I am not deaf. Compose yourself." Edwardia allowed herself the smallest lean upon the duke before accepting Roberts's arm. The lad had said he'd call again. That was enough. That was so much more than she'd had from him for years.

Finlay stepped back and collected his bear. "To bed with you, madam. I am off to scour the length and breadth of the land, and you are keeping me from my appointed rounds."

"Mustn't have that." Edwardia began a stately progress toward the door, Roberts shuffling along with her, Charles at her side. "Send word when you find them, please."

"Of course, and if you need to contact me, my man Pritchard will know my whereabouts."

Edwardia kept moving, though she was well aware that Finlay had just taken a very long step in the direction of familial reconciliation. *If you need me...* By God, she had needed him. Needed him to be safe and whole and capable of happiness. Her duty was not complete, but the most important bits had been tended to.

Now it was back to napping in the front pew and correspondence with old friends too frail or sensible to come to London...

Edwardia paused at the door, a stray thought landing with the resonance of sound intuition. "Go through Mina's correspondence."

"I beg your pardon?" Finlay asked.

"Mina was conscientious about her correspondence, though when William died, the sycophants and toadies ceased pestering her. She was a loyal correspondent, and she remained cordial with the women who'd befriended her before her betrothal was widely known. If you sort through her letters, you might come across some of those friends—ladies who didn't take during their one London Season, ladies who've long since set up their provincial nurseries, but who remember Mina with sincere fondness."

"They would keep her confidences if she needed to rely on them?"

"Some would, and more to the point, Vanessa would have no idea who they were. I also think Mina would avoid Dover—too many fashionables depart for the Continent from there."

"Portsmouth, then?"

"Too close to Town. Look for old friends who've settled around Liverpool or some of the western ports, and do get some rest, Finlay. You're no good to anybody if you grow too tired to think clearly."

Edwardia departed on that note and made her way to bed. That night, her prayers were full of gratitude, and her dreams were sweet, though she was fairly certain neither boon would befall Finlay for some time yet.

CHAPTER NINETEEN

Perhaps every duke ought to come to his honors by back alleys and apprenticeships. Finn made his way through the night relying on the benefits of his irregular upbringing—stamina, determination, an ability to think ahead and sort possibilities for himself—as he approached Lady Helmsby's abode.

With her ladyship, Finn would rely on another skill learned in his travels as an artisan: the ability to flatter a potential client into believing she was liked and respected.

Light glowed from behind downstairs curtains, suggesting her ladyship kept Society hours. Her knocker was still up—was probably always up if she was on the premises—and Finn gave it two hard raps.

He was admitted by a housekeeper in mobcap and gray wool shawl.

"And 'oom shall I say is calling at such an hour, sir?"

Not the accent of London's premier domestics. "His Grace of Huntleigh." Finn passed over a calling card.

The housekeeper squinted at the card—had she never seen purple ink before?—and then at him. "A dook. Signs and wonders abounding. Let's have ye to the parlor, then. The fancy one a' course."

The fancy parlor, where Finn had taken tea on a previous occasion, was some sort of portrait gallery devoted to William and his late father. The sketches were competent but dull. Carefully composed, relentlessly flattering, not a bud vase or curl out of balance with the whole.

The artist responsible for these dutiful etudes was Lady Helmsby, whose image was nowhere to be found upon the walls. The oil portraits over the mantel had been done by one of Sir Joshua Reynolds's less inspired—and less costly—acolytes.

"Your Grace! What an unexpected pleasure to see you!" Lady Helmsby swanned into the room, hands outstretched as if Finn was supposed to offer both of his. "I trust nothing is amiss?"

He bowed. "Lady Helmsby, I come as a supplicant and apologize of the unorthodox hour of my call."

"Nonsense." She patted his arm. "Society will be up until dawn, and I am no early riser myself. Tea, or would brandy be appropriate?"

"Neither for me, though you must suit yourself. I am in somewhat of a hurry."

"Off to your club, no doubt." She tugged the bell-pull. "Do have a seat, Your Grace. Whatever service I can render to you, I will do so happily." Her smile was warm, reaching her eyes and adding to the air of gracious hostess.

She, too, had apparently learned to deceive others into thinking they were valued, though all around Finn were the vestiges of wealth. The carpet, albeit slightly faded, was an Aubusson, the curtains velvet. The cherry sideboard was inlaid with sufficient intricacy to impress Sorrento's master woodworkers, and every sketch had been expertly framed.

"My little tribute to my dear departed," Lady Helmsby said, gaze upon a drawing of William on horseback. "I would never claim to be an artist, but I was a devoted wife and mother. I am a devoted grandmama too." The smile had acquired a hint of sadness, and yet, the walls bore no likenesses of Emily, much less of her mother.

"You are talented," Finn said, and that was true. Lady Helmsby was talented as any engraver had to be talented—at copying precisely and repeatedly the images and designs devised by another. "You must miss your son terribly."

"Of course, Your Grace, of course. William was such a good man, so considerate of me and of others. That he didn't live to see Emily take her place in Society is my greatest sorrow. But let us not dwell on the past. What possible assistance can I offer you?"

The night was one for changing course, apparently. Finn had come here prepared to set a trap, to charm and cajole until Lady Helmsby let slip whatever developments at breakfast had sent Wilhelmina into flight—if any. With William and Lord Helmsby beaming down from the walls, Finn saw that life had sprung too many traps on Lady Helmsby.

She was neither the wife of a duke, nor the mother of a duke, nor the grandmother of another duke. She could not manage her finances and maintain appearances, and she had spies and gossips where friendships should have been.

"I will be honest," Finn said. "Mrs. Wilhelmina Cathcart has left London without notice and without any word as to her destination or the reasons for her departure. The time of year is not conducive to comfortable travel, and she took little luggage with her. I am concerned."

"Left London?" Lady Helmsby looked genuinely puzzled. "That wasn't necessary, but I do understand what she's about."

Finn waited, though he well knew Lady Helmsby was arranging facts and fiction to present to him in the manner most conducive to her personal agenda.

"Wilhelmina enjoyed breakfast with me just this morning," she went on. "I acquainted her with the fact that I'd found another codicil to William's will. He made a little game of codicils, a sort of revenge for all the misery the solicitors inflicted with their reports and budgets and whatnot. William had many strengths, but he was impatient with ledgers and letters."

"I'm sure he was a paragon, in his way." Which had not included even passing marks in the husband department.

"Exactly. He could charm the birds from the air, but I knew not to expect him to manage well on his allowance. That's what Wilhelmina was for. She has a good head for numbers, we must give her credit for that."

Lady Helmsby was not alarmed by Wilhelmina's departure. Was she pleased? *Relieved?*

"You discussed this codicil with Wilhelmina over breakfast?"

"I was duty-bound to acquaint her with its particulars. William was very clear in this document that I was to have the raising of Emily, to oversee her funds, and to smooth her entrance into Society. Upon reflection, that makes perfect sense to me, Your Grace. I am titled. Wilhelmina is not. I am a hostess of some renown. Wilhelmina is little better than Wiltshire gentry. Then too, if Wilhelmina is to remarry, she'll have better luck without Emily clinging to her skirts. It's for the best, Your Grace, I'm sure you'll agree."

No, he would not. Poverty could make people desperate—Finn knew that firsthand—but he hadn't understood before that poverty came in many forms. Perhaps a poverty of love or meaning was the worst, turning its victims up avaricious and depriving them of conscience.

While Wilhelmina's conscience had prohibited her from surrendering Emily into her ladyship's clutches. That realization brought a measure of relief—Willie was protecting her daughter—and also further puzzlement.

Did she think Finn would *support* Lady Helmsby's scheme—for it was a scheme, clearly. Fear he would?

"Might I see this codicil?" He posed the question as one of mere curiosity. "The solicitors will get their hands on it and attempt to explain William's words to me in terms so obfuscatory that the plain sense will be lost. They delight in their heretofores and notwithstandings."

"They absolutely do." Lady Helmsby rose and went to the sideboard. "I can assure you this document is written in William's distinctive hand, and now that I consider the matter, I'm not surprised that Mina has seized her freedom. I will take the best possible care of Emily—the child is merely in want of some discipline—and Mina is no longer in the first blush of youth. If she's to remarry, she'd best be about it, and some of the most eligible widowers are to be found in the spa towns. You must not blame her for being somewhat abrupt in her plans, Your Grace, though I know you and Mina were growing *friendly*."

Rather than react to that innuendo, Finn accepted the single handwritten page from his hostess. He rose and moved closer to the fire.

The language was doubtless correct and the terms legally binding, while the penmanship was execrable.

"Not complicated," Finn said. "William appears to have changed his mind about Emily's upbringing, as you suggest. Mrs. Cathcart was apparently not in agreement with him."

Lady Helmsby joined him at the hearth, a heavy floral scent wafting about her. "What mother thinks another woman can possibly do a better job of parenting her offspring than she can? Wilhelmina loves Emily, but she has no idea what the daughter of a ducal heir can expect later in life. Emily must make the best match, the best possible match, and I will call upon every iota of your influence to find that match for her."

"She's six years old. The matter of her betrothal is hardly urgent."

Her ladyship took the codicil from Finn's grasp. "You are an heir of last resort, Your Grace. If anything happens to you, the title reverts to the crown, and Emily's consequence reverts with it. She will have her funds, of course. I will see that those are invested more intelligently than in the cent-per-cents, but wealthy girls are thick on the ground of late. All this commerce, you see. What sets Emily apart is the title—*your* title—and the time to take advantage of that connection is now."

She tucked the codicil away and resumed her seat. "You must trust me on this, Your Grace. I am a veteran of the London ballrooms, while you have yet to stand up for your first waltz. Wilhelmina would disagree with me, so it's as well she has left the stage. And as to that, I have a list of possible duchesses for you to consider. My judgment in such matters is infallible, and you would do well to heed it."

Finn remained on his feet. On the one hand, he felt sorry for an aging widow with only the vestiges of her marital connections to give her any consequence. In her own eyes, she had failed the ducal succession by producing only the one short-lived son, but by heaven, she was determined to recover lost ground.

On the other hand, the woman was a horror, and Finn would bet his best chisel that the codicil was a forgery, done by no less talented hand than William's own mother.

"I notice that the codicil was witnessed by Travers and Dalton," Finn said. "They are in service to Mrs. Cathcart?"

"For now. I will assume management of that household, the better to ensure the least upset for Emily. I intend to make some changes to the staff, and those two will find themselves looking for new posts, along with that governess. I do hope Wilhelmina intends to stay gone for some time. That would be easiest for all concerned."

"And what will become of Mrs. Cathcart?"

"If she thinks to set her cap for you, Your Grace, you must in the name of kindness disabuse her of the notion. While Mina has some attractive qualities, her best years are nevertheless behind her, and it must be noted that a duke needs a youthful wife."

"You surprise me," Finn said. Appalled him, more like. Genteel qualifiers aside, Lady Helmsby was a sly, nasty creature.

"I try to be pragmatic, Your Grace, while keeping an eye on the appearances. Society is so quick to judge. The upheaval this codicil brings to my own life means nothing. I will respect William's wishes to the best of my ability and see that Emily has every advantage I can offer her."

This smile was both brave and humble. Quite a combination. "Very commendable, my lady, but your sacrifice might be premature. I forgot to mention that Mrs. Cathcart took Emily and Miss Norwich with her when she departed from Town."

"*She did what?*" All pretensions to graciousness fled, leaving only indignation in their wake.

"I have no idea where the ladies have gone or if they'll ever return. Remiss of me, not to state the obvious, but as the nominal head of the Cathcart family, I find the whole business unsettling."

"She took *Emily?*" Lady Helmsby sprang to her feet and paced before the hearth. "You must set the law on her, Your Grace. You must... William would be outraged at the very notion. She *took* Emily?"

"Apparently so. Hence the urgency of this late call. Have you any idea where she's headed?"

"None whatsoever. That foolish, foolish woman. If she goes to Dover, half of Society will see her. Mina speaks French—good French—and so does that governess." This skill was apparently a great failing and a cause for alarm. "Even Emily has a few tea words. This is... You must do something, Your Grace. The talk will be endless, and all of it bad. You'll never attach an heiress with this sort of rackety behavior fresh in the matchmakers' minds. They will think Mina fled because of *you*."

An impressive improvisation, which nearly concluded: *This is all Your Grace's fault.*

"Fled because of me? I've been in England for several months and cordially acquainted with the Cathcart ladies for weeks. Wilhelmina decamped within hours of you showing her that very upsetting codicil. I suspect the talk will be aimed more nearly in your direction, my lady."

"And Edwardia will support it. She has always been against me.

Envious of my looks and my son, I suppose. All the more reason why you must find Emily and bring her back."

"And what of Wilhelmina?"

Her ladyship put a hand to her throat and struck a martyred pose by the hearth. "Send her to the Continent, Your Grace. Put her on remittance, and we will all be much happier—one can live very frugally on the Continent, and widows have more freedom there— but bring Emily back to me. Were William alive, he'd implore you to bring Emily back to me."

Like hell he would. Finn bowed, and without making any promises or delivering any threats, wished her ladyship good night. As he made his way back to Wilhelmina's house, he was certain of three things. First, Lady Helmsby had no notion where Willie had got off to, and that was a very great boon.

Second, Willie had been right to disappear into the night.

Third, Finn had days, perhaps hours, to find her before her steps became untraceable, and find her, he would.

Wilhelmina had slept badly when she'd slept at all, and in the darkness of a winter morning, the only express she sent went west, to Bristol.

"I don't like this adventure," Emily said, pushing eggs around on her plate. "Draco and the Ursulas don't like it either. We want to go home."

"Today, we get to some of the fun part," Wilhelmina said, putting a piece of jam-laden toast on Emily's plate. Thank Providence, they had the ladies' parlor to themselves. The room was almost warm, and the scent of wet wool and mud was all but subdued by the coal smoke drifting up the flue. "Today come the hills."

Emily took a bite of toast. "Hills?"

"Small mountains, really, and the coach will gallop up one side and then gallop down the other."

Across the table, Norry went a bit green at that description. "Unless the coachy applies the brake, of course. Then we might merely canter down the hills."

"I don't like hills," Emily said, tearing off the crust of her toast and stuffing it into her mouth. "Draco flies over hills, and the Ursulas don't like hills at all."

Neither, as it happened, did Wilhelmina when the roads were slick with melting snow. "What about the sea?"

Emily munched on her toast. "I have never seen the sea."

"We should make Bristol tonight," Wilhelmina said, "and while Bristol isn't quite on the shore itself, enormous ships come and go from there on the river."

"Perhaps we shall see the sea later?" Norry asked, ever so innocently stirring her tea.

"Perhaps." Wilhelmina prayed not. Common sense said that Emily would remain at risk in Britain, that even Dublin offered some protection from Lady Helmsby's schemes, though Lisbon would be safer. Exhaustion and the certain knowledge that Finn deserved to comment on Wilhelmina's plans kept her from committing to an overseas destination.

Yet.

"I won't like the ocean either," Emily said, taking another bite of toast and chewing pugnaciously. "Draco says the sea is cold, and the Ursulas say it's too big and wet. The sea is *full* of monsters."

"Do the Ursulas always agree with each other?" Norry asked.

"Yes, and they agree with me, and *we miss Finn.*"

"So do I," Norry said.

"We can make it unanimous. Emily, eat up. The coach will stop briefly only for nooning and supper, and we'd best use the jakes while we can."

The predictable litany rose up, aimed at the jakes, coaches, hills, and even snow, with which Emily had been fascinated only yesterday, and through it all ran the ostinato of a child increasingly worried by her circumstances.

I miss Finn. I wish Finn were here. I want to go home to Finn.

"Mrs. Cathcart corresponded with half the Englishwomen under the age of thirty," Finn said, pouring himself more tea. Outside the breakfast parlor, dawn was struggling to subdue the darkness, such as dawn happened at all on a cloudy winter morning. "She also has friends in Scotland and Wales. I have never read so much drivel about trees leafing out, Her Grace's dog shedding, and the servants growing upset over trivialities."

Pritchard forked some ham onto a plate at the sideboard and took the place to Finn's right. "I doubt Mrs. Cathcart went north at this time of year, but then, that makes traveling north a good strategy."

"She went west." Finn knew this, just as he knew a certain block of marble was perfect for a particular project. Not quite instinct, less than logical argument, and more convincing than either. "Mrs. Cathcart has a friend from school who dwells in Bristol. The young lady married a prosperous merchant's darling son, and she has invited Mrs. Cathcart to visit any number of times."

Pritchard appropriated the teapot, poured out the remaining half cup, sent Finn a long-suffering look, and fetched the second pot from the sideboard.

"Why that friend? Why not the friend in Northumbria or York?"

"This friend—Mrs. Jonathan Aberworthy—has issued invitations, in the first place, and married wealth rather than a title in the second."

"A hard choice." Pritchard resumed his seat and topped up his tea cup. "Society would have urged the title on her." Spoken with both certainty and contempt.

"Wilhelmina thought she was marrying a title, but, in fact, ended up with neither a vast fortune nor a tiara." Did she miss either one? Was she missing Finn?

Pritchard stirred the merest drop of honey into his tea. "You are saying the two ladies were in sympathy?"

"Mrs. Aberworthy passed along details—the baby is teething again, Jonathan is fretful about the aldermen's supper, a cargo of Brazilian cherrywood is two weeks overdue—that go beyond platitudes. The rest of the correspondents were mostly concerned with being remembered to the duchess, and to dear Lady Helmsby, and 'please send along the most recent editions of all the fashion magazines.'"

"Ah. Toadies and mushrooms. You are off to Bristol?"

Finn debated another helping of eggs, then recalled the effect of coach travel on digestion. "I am. You've had a look at the codicil?"

Finn had dispatched Pritchard and the lawyers to retrieve the document from Lady Helmsby lest any harm—or alterations —befall it.

Pritchard considered his tea. "I have."

"And?"

"I asked Antonio to compare it to what samples I could find of William's handwriting. Antonio's expert opinion, albeit rendered with an aching head, is that the codicil could have been forged. Something about the angle at which the t's were crossed and the depth to which lowercase j's extend. All quite arcane."

Finn's future—Wilhelmina's and Emily's futures—needed more than a mere cup-shot could-have-been. "Please tell him to go over it with a jeweler's loupe, to imitate the hand himself, to consider every detail. I must know for a certainty one way or another. Find more samples of William's handwriting and give me a definite answer."

Pritchard buttered his toast with exquisite precision. "I have one of his old diaries. Pages and pages of scribbling."

Finn told himself to finish his tea and finish the discussion. A long, cold trip to Bristol awaited. Sooner begun and all that tripe. "And?"

"He loved her," Pritchard said. "Loved his wife madly, knew he wasn't worthy of her, begged heaven on his aching knees for a son—not for the sake of the succession, but for his wife's sake, because then Lady Helmsby might leave them in peace. I doubt William was sober when he made half the entries."

"I doubt he was sober much past the age of sixteen." Poor sod. Poor, stupid sod. "William was half right—he had by no means been worthy of his wife, though Lady Helmsby would never have left them alone. I received a list of potential duchesses by messenger last night, courtesy of her ladyship."

"Burn it."

"Already done. If William had enough courage to admit his failings, even to himself, I cannot see him writing that wretched codicil."

Pritchard made a sandwich of toast, ham, and eggs. "If that mother of his went to work on him when his head was pounding, his conscience was pounding, and his creditors were pounding at the door... He might have written the damned thing to silence her. He might have written another codicil the next morning and rescinded this one."

Pritchard apparently knew something of nagging mamas. Interesting. "The question," Finn said, "is not why did Wilhelmina flee yesterday, but rather, why didn't she elope with the nearest swineherd at the first opportunity?"

Pritchard considered his sandwich. "Because the finest flowers of English womanhood are stalwart creatures. Mrs. Cathcart spoke vows, and she meant them. I've packed a satchel for you, and if you're traveling by post-chaise, I can send a small trunk with you too."

A post-chaise. God help him. "How long to get to Bristol?"

"By post? Less than fourteen hours, assuming you survive the journey. Thirteen hours on good roads, and twelve isn't unheard of, though a passenger of your generous dimensions might slow progress. I've had Cook pack you a hamper and a few flasks. You will want at least one spare scarf and several spare handkerchiefs."

Pritchard knew something of traveling by post too.

"My will is in the safe." A precaution every sensible traveler undertook before a long journey.

"Of course. That other document you asked me to procure is also in the safe. I have reserved private post-chaises on most of the major routes out of Town this morning. You won't be traveling with the mail, Your Grace."

"Pritchard..."

Pritchard began on his sandwich. "I am the majordomo to a duke. The position has its advantages, few though they are. I was, *as ever*, discreet. You'd best be on your way, sir."

The day would be long, frigid, and bone-racking, but Wilhelmina could even at the moment be making arrangements to take ship. Part of Finn howled in protest at the notion, but another part of him... He was not his father, pitting his pride in a doomed battle against the fates. Wilhelmina had had too little of freedom and far too much of duty.

If she was leaving England—and Finn—he'd wish her a safe voyage and then he'd get drunker than Antonio had ever aspired to be. And then he'd commence a study of the Furies in marble so exquisitely wrathful that Canova himself would weep.

Finn rose. "I will send word once I'm in Bristol. Let Her Grace know what's afoot, keep Lady Helmsby in Stygian darkness, and ask Dalton what he recalls about the codicil."

"If he's smart, he'll have a serious case of amnesia."

"Precisely. Wish me luck."

Pritchard half rose and saluted with the remains of his sandwich. "Very best of luck. Wear a signet ring. You might need it."

"How on earth could you have occasion to know such a thing?"

"Away with you, Your Grace. Time is of the essence."

So was stealth. After taking various precautions over the next forty-five minutes to ensure his progress was unobserved, Finn squeezed himself into a private chaise, pulled down the window shades, and tried—in vain—to get some sleep. He was thwarted by the sure conviction that he must prove the codicil to be a forgery and do so thoroughly enough to convince both the courts and the gossips of its dubious provenance.

Even for a man who could coax winged cherubs from solid stone, that loomed as an impossible challenge.

CHAPTER TWENTY

"I simply need some air," Wilhelmina said. Yesterday had been spent in the close and chilly confines of a careening coach, as had much of the day previous to that. Today was for settling in and sorting out. "I also need to think. His Grace deserves to know what's afoot, but if he comes haring over the hills in hot pursuit, he might well put Lady Helmsby on our trail."

On the floor above Wilhelmina's sitting room, not-so-little feet thundered the length of a corridor.

"You can warn His Grace to be careful when you write to him," Norwich said. "He's a man of parts. He'll understand the danger." The herd thundered back the other direction. "Tell him his hearing might well be imperiled if he does join us."

Janessa Aberworthy had four children, starting with a pair of twin girls who were almost seven years old. A boy of five tried valiantly to keep up with his sisters, and a chubby two-year-old lad with prodigiously healthy lungs added to the din.

"Emily is in transports." And Wilhelmina was torn, between gratitude to a true friend, exhaustion, and missing Finn. Janessa had taken one look at her and enveloped her in the sort of hug only an old friend turned mother of four could offer. Secure, sweet, fortifying, and a bit too snug.

"The hooligans won't be speaking to each other by noon," Norwich said, drizzling honey over her porridge. "I will be called upon to referee displays of pugilism and to decide arguments that would impress the judges of the Old Bailey. I like the governess. Has a good sense of humor and a fine imagination."

Emily liked the Aberworthy's governess too. "Janessa found her in Bath languishing as a companion to some dowager. Said she was going completely to waste. Miss Harriman knows all about lapdogs, apparently."

"An expertise I hope never to acquire. Don't be gone too long, madam. Emily will fret."

"Long enough to stretch my legs and quiet my mind." Long enough to begin researching passenger departure options too. "Finish my breakfast if you're so inclined. The kitchen sent up enough rations to feed an army."

After the third child, Janessa and her husband had decided that breakfast was to be served on trays, enjoyed in the bedroom. The kitchen had less work that way, and busy parents had a quieter and more private beginning to their day.

"I like your friend too," Norry said. "Mrs. Aberworthy is sensible and gracious."

"And trustworthy," Wilhelmina said. "Above all, trustworthy. Lady Helmsby did her a particular unkindness when Janessa had her one and only London Season—a very public remark on the color of Janessa's dress. The sort of comment that can pass as humor, but is, in fact, cruel. I'd forgotten about it, but Janessa never will."

"Speaking of dresses, we should refurbish Emily's wardrobe while we're here. A few ready-made articles at least."

"This afternoon is soon enough for that. Right now, I need fresh air and relative quiet."

Wilhelmina was tempted to effect her escape through the garden, but chose the front door because that route was less easily viewed from the nursery. She hadn't taken ten steps along the brick walkway before a man approached her.

Big, dark, fit, his cloak flapping in the chilly, sea-scented breeze and a distinctive, purple-plaid scarf about his neck. In the next second, she knew him to be none other than Finlay Cathcart.

"Finlay! But how...?" His expression was serious, while Wilhelmina was so glad to see him she nearly hugged him on the street.

He stopped, touched a finger to his hat brim, and bowed. "Mrs. Cathcart. Good morning. A pleasure, though I'd hoped to have a few moments to stand about on yonder porch steadying my nerves and rehearsing my speech. You look tired."

"So do you." And dear. Very, very dear. "I have written to you. The missive will go out with the morning mail. Please don't trouble your nerves any further on my account."

Finn drew himself up very tall and fixed his gaze on the maze of masts, rigging, and docks at the bottom of the long, sloping street.

"Were you sending me a farewell letter, Willie?"

She faced a tired, dignified Finn, far from home and deserving of answers. Honesty was the only possible choice. "I considered attempting a farewell and will understand if you offer one to me. I've sent you an explanation instead, though the direction names Mr. Pritchard rather than your august self. Let's walk, shall we?"

Finn offered his arm and set a modest pace. When he started them down the declivity without further comment, Wilhelmina cast about for more honesty.

"I love your innate courtesy," she said. "Your manners are not merely for show, they are born of genuine consideration, a part of you rather than a garment you don for the flattering cut. Let's see the famous Floating Harbor, shall we? I cannot fathom tides that vary by nearly forty feet."

"I cannot fathom why anybody thought such a place would make a decent harbor, but Mr. Jessop has solved the problem of the tides for us. I have racked my brain for a way to solve the problem of Lady Helmsby and her ever-so-convenient new codicil."

"Gracious, you have been busy. The handwriting was William's, Finlay. I'd recognize it anywhere, and it's some of the worst penmanship you will ever barely be able to read."

"We can and shall discuss that issue at greater length later. How are you?" Finn asked as they strolled down the gentle grade into increasingly busy foot traffic.

"Tired, worried, glad to see you."

"That last part is an inordinate comfort and thoroughly reciprocated. Let's seize that bench, shall we? Assuming the seagulls haven't rendered it unfit for the purpose."

The bench was tidy enough, and sitting beside Finn, watching one of Britain's busiest seaports go about its business, was soothing. The urge to take his hand was nearly overpowering.

"How did you find me, Finlay?"

"The duchess suggested reviewing your correspondence for possible allies and urged me to consider the Midlands and other less populous locations, even if they weren't as handy to Town. She's not my enemy, by the way. Not yours either."

Wilhelmina shifted slightly so she sat hip to hip with Finn. Improper, but cozy. "You two have reconciled?"

"She was not to blame for my father's continuing estrangement from his family. That hubris must be laid squarely at Papa's feet, much to my shock and chagrin. When I considered pursuing you... I don't want to be like him, Willie. If you must flee Merry Olde for Emily's sake, I cannot and will not stop you—much as I'd like to try. I hope to give you other choices, but all I can do is offer."

There was more to that tale, much more, and Wilhelmina wanted to hear it when Finn wanted to tell it. For now, pressing matters required attention.

"Lady Helmsby terrifies me, Finn. She could have tossed that codicil into the fire—I'm a good mother, and Emily has been through enough upheaval—but no. She suggested I graduate to the post of companion to Edwardia while Mama-in-Law set Emily to memorizing Bible passages."

Finn rested an arm along the back of the bench. Not an embrace —they were in public—but a comfort nonetheless.

"She sent me a list of prospective duchesses to study and assured me that now was the time to see Emily betrothed. I could get hit by a runaway fish wagon tomorrow, you see. The problem with people like Lady Helmsby is that even their most outlandish declarations bear a passing connection to some sensible thought. I am mortal, that much is true. The rest of it... She doesn't care two hair ribbons for Emily as a child. She's purely after the girl's money."

"Ah. She did mention the investments. Mama-in-Law's station requires that certain appearances be maintained, you see."

"That codicil is a forgery, Willie. I know it, but short of a confession from Lady Helmsby, proving it will be difficult."

Wilhelmina watched a tall ship ease away from the dock by infinitesimal degrees, the sight at once majestic and wrenching. How far would that lone vessel journey across storms and tides before finding another safe haven?

"Finlay, I cannot and will not surrender my daughter to Lady Helmsby. You are right that I will leave England if I must."

"I know, and I commend you for your devotion to your daughter. Had my Mama not been so devoted to me... But she was, and Her Grace was. If you intend to sail without me, I can recommend Naples as a congenial, pretty, affordable place to bide, and I have many connections there who will welcome you."

He wasn't arguing with her, wasn't faulting her decisions. He was commending her for leaving London. "You'd come with us?"

"If you'll have me. I am a dab hand at toting luggage, and I can manage well enough in several dialects of the Italian language."

The ship glided out into the deeper water of the seventy-acre pool created by Mr. Jessop's engineering. He'd turned the harbor into the equivalent of a giant lock, sheltered from the river Avon's enormous tidal variations. The Floating Harbor was a flat expanse of calm water that kept Bristol in the running as one of England's busiest ports.

And Finn had pursued Wilhelmina across the length of England, ready to be sent back to London if that was her wish.

Though it wasn't her wish *at all*. "I will have you, Finlay, just as soon as you propose. I didn't put that part into my letter."

"The ring is in my pocket, my dear."

A cool, fizzy feeling welled up from Wilhelmina's middle. "Rings aren't made for hiding in pockets, Your Grace."

Finn rose, produced a little box from within his coat, tossed the box into the air, and caught it. "When I wasn't fretting over Lady Helmsby's mischief, I was rehearsing my proposal. I've decided that a few, short, sincere words will serve best in this as in other notable contexts." He went down on one knee, there in the middle of the walkway. "Darling Willie, I love you. I will always love you. Will you marry me?"

Passersby stopped, and even the seagulls seemed to pause to hear Wilhelmina's answer.

Though how was she to be coherent when a kneeling Finn was at her eye level, also at her lip level? "Will I still be your darling Willie when I'm gray and need spectacles and talk to my dog?"

"How can you doubt it? And I will be your Finlay."

A duke ought to hear his given name from somebody. "You'll sail away with us?"

"If necessary, of course. Yes or no, Willie?"

"You are proposing now? Beside a busy street, on this gray and worrisome day, you're proposing to me?"

He set the ring on the bench beside her. "If I wait until all is singing birds and blooming roses, the moment will never be right, and when I realized you'd fled, abandoned all that was familiar, fled from even *me*... Yes, I am proposing now. If you want me to seek Emily's approval of the match, I shall, but you can rest assured Edwardia approves."

"Good to know." Very good. Wilhelmina smoothed the purple

scarf over his shoulder, mostly to have an excuse to touch him. "You puzzled out the problem, you came after us hot foot, and you are willing to take ship with us. Yes, Finlay. Yes, I will marry you, and I can assure you, Emily approves as well."

He slipped his arms around her waist and hugged her while the crowd applauded with gloved hands, and out in the quiet harbor, the lovely ship began her journey onto the vast and distant seas.

Finn rose and raised his hat to the crowd gathered around the bench. "She says she'll have me!"

The cheering grew louder, and somebody yelled, "Havin's the easy part. Holdin's the challenge."

A woman's voice sang out. "Shut yer gob, Jemmie Kinross, or you'll be holding nobbut an empty tankard."

The mention of libation helped disperse the crowd, as did the plethora of drinking establishments lining the harbor. Finn resumed his place beside Wilhelmina on the bench and passed her the open ring box.

"Might not fit you just yet. I designed it to resemble my mother's ring, though I chose garnets for you, whereas hers was sapphires, as she described it. The thing had been pawned before I could walk." He could tell Wilhelmina that now without feeling the echoes of life-long rage. Bewilderment, yes—Papa's pride might never make sense to Finn—but the anger no longer clawed at him from within.

"It's gorgeous, Finlay, and I will wear it with shameless pride." She turned the open box this way and that so it caught the meager winter sun and turned it to fire.

"You will keep your gloves on for the nonce, if you please. That breeze is nippy."

Wilhelmina snapped the box closed, returned it to him, and possessed herself of his hand. "We are engaged to be married. I get to hold your hand."

"You will get to do a great deal more than that, madam. Are you sure?"

Wilhelmina treated him to a thoughtful pause, and that was good. Also nerve-racking as hell.

"You expect me to change my mind, Finlay?"

"I pray you do not, but you were dragooned into marriage once, given no meaningful choice in the matter, and wed to a man who probably felt he had even less choice. I've surprised you—ambushed you—when all about you is in turmoil. We will best Lady Helmsby one way or another, Willie. You need not marry me to see that situation put to rights. That is a promise."

She squeezed his hand. "I know. I will not change my mind, Finlay. We might have to marry by special license for the sake of discretion, and I will sleep with one eye open until Mama-in-Law is made to see reason, but I'm sure I will marry you."

"As it happens, I obtained a special license before leaving Town," Finn said. "I had Pritchard put the process in train some days ago. As for that codicil, I've sought the opinion of an expert. Antonio comes from a long line of skilled forgers, and he sees discrepancies between William's handwriting and the codicil."

Wilhelmina rose and tugged him to his feet. "You suspect that the issue is money, Finlay, and that theory seems sound to me. For a sum certain, Lady Helmsby might agree to forget the codicil."

Finn set a leisurely pace back up the hill. He was an engaged man now, a prospective husband. The change in his circumstances was larger than when St. Didier had foisted the title on him, more solemn and more joyous.

"What's to stop her ladyship from finding a new codicil every other year, Willie? Capitulating to blackmail sits ill with me."

"Sailing off to Italy doesn't sit ill with me, but I'd rather we save that pleasure for a wedding journey instead of putting ourselves on remittance. Emily will grow up. If we can hold out for a mere dozen years or so, her ladyship will lose the game by default."

Not good enough. Not good enough for Emily or for her mama. "How will you tell Emily that she's to acquire a step-papa?"

"We will tell her together."

Finn liked that idea just fine. "Will you bide here while I sort out Lady Helmsby?" An idea he did not like. Having acquired an intended, he didn't want to let her or Emily out of his sight.

They approached the Aberworthy domicile, a stately edifice that doubtless had a lovely view from the upper floors. Wilhelmina stopped on the porch steps.

"The matter seems to be one of trust. You trust me to bide here rather than take ship or marry a pirate prince, but Lady Helmsby could have had you followed from Town, Finlay."

Wilhelmina was so serious, so focused. How had she endured marriage to a fribbling lordling?

"In the first place, I took precautions. In the second, Pritchard took precautions, and he's surprisingly skilled at eluding notice when he wants to be discreet. In the third place, Lady Helmsby's means are increasingly limited, and she has neither Travers nor Dalton to order about. Following anybody who travels by post-chaise is an expensive undertaking. You should be safe here, but if you'd like, I can buy you passage to Dublin or Glasgow and send word to you when I have bested the enemy."

Wilhelmina's cheeks had grown pink with exertion and cold. Finn wrapped his scarf around her neck.

"But what of you, Finlay? Will you be safe in Town, taking on a woman who would slander the Regent for the sake of her next new bonnet?"

Though the breeze was brisk, and Finn's knee ached a bit, Wilhelmina's question filled him with warmth. "You would escort me to Town to *protect* me?"

Wilhelmina kissed his cheek. "I have waited years for you, and now that I've found you, I don't intend to let any harm come to you. Your days of taking on the world single-handedly are over, Finlay. Accommodate yourself to your improved circumstances."

She stood two steps above him, enough to give her an advantage of height, but her advantages only began there. Being a ducal heir had been of no use to Finn. Haring all over the Continent, earning the patronage of nobility, acquiring wealth... All very lovely, but not the sort of improvement in circumstances that Finn had been seeking.

In his heart, he'd been searching for a woman who scolded him with kisses, who took his safety seriously, and who would take on the world *with* him.

"Lady Helmsby would gain nothing by harming me," Finn said, ascending the steps. "She was very clear that my frail personage is all that stands between the Cathcart family and social disgrace. She won't fell me with a poisoned arrow, Willie."

Wilhelmina looked him up and down. "We will leave Emily here with Norry and with sufficient means to take ship for Dublin at the first whiff of trouble. Her ladyship thinks she has me cowed, but I am soon to be a duchess, and annoying me will cost Mama-in-Law her voucher to Almack's, for starts."

Wilhelmina enlarged on that theme after Finn had been introduced to their hostess. She embellished further on the idea of social retribution as Finn was led up to the nursery suite.

The riot momentarily quieted as the Aberworthy infantry and their pretty governess gazed up at Finn.

"The twins are almost seven," Emily informed him after she'd squeezed him witless and Draco had flown circles about him. "I am younger than they are, but older than Tommie or Jeremiah. I will *always* be older than the boys. Norry said, and so did Harry."

"Miss Harriman," Wilhelmina murmured. "Stalwart, good-humored, and much loved."

"I draw better than the twins," Emily went on, seizing Finn's hand. "I spell better than they do too. Papa was a terrible speller, but Norry says one can learn proper spelling. Norry is teaching me French, too, though all the twins know is *mare-see* and *bon jure*. I told the twins that you were an *excellent* artist, and you are teaching me to draw."

Wilhelmina kissed Finn's cheek again—she seemed to enjoy that little display nearly as much as he did.

"Go gracefully to your fate, sir. You are to impress the locals, flatter your princess, and reinforce the authority of the governesses, or it will go hard for you."

She patted his arm and swanned off, leaving Finn surrounded by five children, two governesses, an old hound, and two cats, all of whom apparently expected him to provide entertainment by way of a drawing demonstration.

"Very well," he said. "A portrait to commemorate the great occasion of my introduction to you lot, rendered in pencil. The results improve if the subjects *sit still*."

With the aid of the governesses and the complicity of the old canine—who excelled at remaining still in any reasonably warm location—Finn got a semblance of a group portrait under way. Not until he was adding the second tabby cat to the composition did he realize that Emily had given him the key to foiling Lady Helmsby and her endless schemes.

He added a smile to the cat's countenance, signed his sketch, and passed it over to Emily and her new friends for a critique.

CHAPTER TWENTY-ONE

The wedding day was all wrong for a new duke and his much-esteemed duchess, but perfect for Wilhelmina and her dear Finlay. Thomas and Janessa insisted on providing a wedding breakfast of sorts and would not hear of the happy couple repairing to even the elegant accommodations available in Bath, given that Wilhelmina and her new spouse needed to keep their situation private.

The wedding breakfast, a modest late-afternoon meal, resembled a melee more than a traditional celebration, particularly after young Tommie discerned that pitching his sisters' stuffed ponies to Papa was much more fun than simply flying them about the room while making horsey noises.

Jeremiah continued to make the horsey noises anyway, and bear noises, and dragon noises, while the young ladies—ably inspired by Norry—chased Jeremiah and Tommie hotfoot around the table.

When the host suggested the newlyweds enjoy a short constitutional by the harbor before the last of the light faded, Wilhelmina nearly tossed Finn out the nearest window and leaped after him.

"I'm glad I came here," she said as Finn wrapped his scarf about her neck. "Glad I brought Emily here."

"So am I, probably for different reasons. I know that children are supposed to be loud on occasion, but now Emily knows it too."

"I was loud as a young girl," Wilhelmina said, linking arms with her... her *husband*. Gracious. "Then that wretched betrothal ruined everything. I had to become quiet and demure—why are boys never expected to be demure?—and make botanical drawings of every weed in the garden."

"Tonight," Finn murmured near her ear, "you shall be as loud as you like."

Wilhelmina leaned on him for a moment in retaliation. If anybody was scandalized by a bride relying on her groom for support at the end of the wedding day, so be it.

"Naughty man. It's you who will be crying out for mercy."

"Promises, promises. Here is my morning gift to you, delivered prematurely in the spirit of the wedding formalities thus far: I know how to flush Lady Helmsby from her covert of righteous legal certainty."

Finn would not speak in mere possibilities, not about this. *He knew.* "Do tell."

As Wilhelmina and Finn wandered the twilight hour arm in arm and then hand in hand, they planned their return to London. Wilhelmina assigned herself the job of drafting a letter to the duchess. Finn would send an epistle alerting Pritchard—another epistle—followed by his own missive to Her Grace. When Wilhelmina suggested that St. Didier might be interested in the day's events, Finn went quiet.

"I like him," he said. "I respect him, in fact, and now that I am a duke, complete with duchess, daughter, and auntie, I'm not sure I could relinquish the title so easily. Thomas Aberworthy has some interesting ideas about how to import and market my marble for the British market, but would he have offered those ideas to plain Mr. Finn Cathcart?"

"Thomas would. He's not high in the instep, and that's precisely why Janessa chose him over the tulips and fribbles. You must find your balance with this ducal business, Finlay. When it became known that I was betrothed to William, Janessa was one of few who treated me no differently. We still exchanged bad puns, she still wrote faithfully when she wasn't in Town, and she refused to gossip about me and William with the tabbies."

They passed the bench where Finn had proposed. "Shall we sit for a bit?" he asked.

"Please. I am not quite ready for a return to the menagerie." The sun had set, the last of the light had left the sky, and Wilhelmina wanted a moment to savor what had become her wedding day. "Today was right, Finn. Right for us. Thomas, Janessa, Norry, and Harry standing up with us before the parson, the children fidgeting..."

"Draco and the Ursulas lending a touch of solemnity to the occasion in their unique fashion... I agree. St. George's and a carefully curated smattering of titles, an archbishop at the ready, would not have done. I wish Pritchard had been there, but he is a romantic at heart. He will understand."

Wilhelmina was feeling romantic, or sentimental. Weepy, for some reason. She would never again have to face Lady Helmsby alone. She would not have to surrender Emily to a purgatory of Bible verses and deportment instructors. She would not be compelled to abandon home and friends... She would not sleep alone unless she wished to.

"Finn, promise me something."

"Anything."

"If it ever gets to be too much—the Lords, the estates, the correspondence, the social nonsense—you will tell me. You will not soldier on in misery, lecturing yourself about gratitude and duty, or my wifely expectations, while you long for the feel of a chisel and mallet in your hands. You will tell me the truth, and I will tell you the truth, and we will manage, together."

He wrapped an arm around her shoulders, and that felt right too.

"I make you that promise, and you must promise me as well, that if it all gets to be too much, managing the households, managing me, dealing with Society, the staff, the correspondence, the charities, and social obligations—you will tell me. You will not lecture yourself about how fortunate you are and how His Grace's responsibilities must take priority. To blazes with His Grace. I am your husband first, or the rest doesn't matter."

A few tears spilled down Wilhelmina's cheek, hot and silent. *I am your husband first...* He wasn't, not quite. He was Finn Cathcart, a talented, honorable, shrewd, hardworking man who kissed like a fiend and loved with ferocious loyalty.

And he was also, by his own declaration, *hers.*

"I needed to hear that," Wilhelmina said, resting against him. "I might need to hear it again, more than you think."

Finn gave her a one-armed hug. "I love you. I do not love being a duke, or wrangling ledgers, or prancing around in ermine and silk. I love *you.* You must learn to accommodate yourself to your improved circumstances."

He kissed her cheek, and Wilhelmina kissed him back. A lamplighter went by, the moon rose, and still they remained on the bench, accommodating themselves to their vastly improved circumstances.

Until they wandered back up the hill, and Finn carried Wilhelmina over the threshold and off to bed, where their circumstances improved unimaginably yet still more.

Edwardia was resplendent in blue velvet that matched the azure hue of her eyes and complemented the blue of the Wedgwood chimneypieces. Charles had been brushed to a high shine. The tea service was silver, and Roberts was joined by a near twin in formal livery, one Riley by name.

Finn wanted witnesses to this occasion, and thus St. Didier was on hand, as was Pritchard, for once in morning attire rather than his more subdued majordomo's garb. Pritchard cleaned up astonishingly well, when he chose to.

The jewel in Edwardia's old-fashioned parlor was Wilhelmina, of course. She wore velvet of the same garnet hue as her wedding ring, which winked with subdued fire on her finger. A garnet brooch on a ruby velvet ribbon graced her throat, and Finn was having a parure made to match.

"Are you sure Lady Helmsby is coming?" St. Didier asked. He made an elegant picture near the hearth, a gentleman at ease among friends on a chilly winter afternoon.

"She will come," Wilhelmina said. "His Grace invited her to gather here to celebrate some unexpected good news. He also promised me he'd give her ladyship a chance to leave the field voluntarily."

Wilhelmina had extracted that promise when Finn hadn't quite had his wits about him, a frequent circumstance since speaking his vows. His only consolation lay in delighting his duchess with turn-about at every opportunity. Willie had also chosen to turn the unre-pentant Travers off without severance or a character, but to provide both boons to Dalton, as well as fare to York, from whence he hailed.

Dalton stoutly maintained that he'd never witnessed any codicil giving Lady Helmsby custody of Emily, and that he'd often heard William Cathcart state what a penance of a mother Lady Helmsby was, and how fortunate Emily was to have Wilhelmina for a mama.

"Her ladyship will come," Pritchard said. "If there is news, she cannot bear to be kept in ignorance of it. She apparently trades in news, though never for coin."

"Favors," St. Didier murmured. "Her ladyship trades in favors. Arrange for her to receive vouchers from Almack's, and she will keep silent about what she saw in the conservatory when she was lurking behind the potted lemons."

Sad, but some people could not appreciate the good fortune life dropped in their very laps.

Charles's ears perked up, and he looked at Edwardia.

"She's here," the duchess said. "Charles knows her tread on the stairs."

Edwardia's butler ushered Lady Helmsby into the parlor and withdrew, though two more footmen, of the young and muscular variety, would be stationed outside the door at Finn's request, now that her ladyship was on hand.

"Your Grace and Your Grace." Lady Helmsby curtseyed prettily to Edwardia and to Finn. She'd troubled over her appearance. Her coiffure was done up in ringlets better suited to a young lady in her first Season. The dress was appropriate for afternoon calls—lavender, a widow's color—but overly embellished with lace and embroidery.

Her ladyship's gloves hosted a small sea of seed pearls in the pattern of an open rose.

Lady Helmsby turned a tentative smile on Pritchard. "I don't believe I know you, sir. Perhaps the duke will make introductions, as I am here at his invitation."

She ignored St. Didier, though to be fair, he hadn't come forward to make his bow. She hadn't even looked at Wilhelmina.

Finn was about to point out the oversight when Wilhelmina spoke up.

"Your ladyship has one more curtsey to offer," Willie said. "Please felicitate His Grace and me on having spoken our nuptial vows."

Since making those vows less than a week earlier, Wilhelmina had ceased referring to Lady Helmsby as Mama-in-Law. Willie was also looking quite statuesque. Finn would have bet his second-favorite chisel that her heels of late were at least an inch and a half of sturdy wood.

"Vows." Lady Helmsby's features twitched. Brows, lips, and jaw all moved, though no particular expression formed. "Marital vows?"

"Exactly," Wilhelmina said, slipping her arm through Finn's. "A quiet ceremony, a few friends to stand as witnesses. You can be among the first to wish us well."

Her ladyship produced a pained smile. "I do, of course. I wish you both the best, and I shall do *my* best to present this development in the most positive light. A whirlwind courtship, a familial connection, a widow with many good years left. You may rely on me to do my utmost when the gossips start speculating, and speculate they will. Does one conclude hasty nuptials were necessary? Even among the best families, couples get carried away by an inconvenient momentary—"

"Vanessa, cease prattling." Edwardia's tone held as much amusement as vinegar. "They are in love. Society won't ignore the obvious."

"In love. Well. I see. Perhaps in light of the fact that two duchesses are on hand, I should offer to pour out? I am, I suppose, the most experienced hostess in the room after all. I have yet to be introduced to the gentleman in the burgundy morning coat."

Finn grudgingly admired Lady Helmsby's attempts to take over management of the gathering. She was insinuating herself into the role of hostess, giving tacit orders, and ignoring Edwardia's rebuke.

"Remiss of me to delay an introduction," Wilhelmina said. "I do apologize. Lady Helmsby, may I make known to you Mr. Lucien Pritchard, late of Rome and various Continental addresses. I believe his hobbies include collecting fine art. You'll find him spectacularly proficient at chess and well-read in the best gentlemanly tradition."

Finn had never seen Pritchard smile, but clearly, Wilhelmina had amused him. He bowed prettily over Lady Helmsby's hand. "At your service, my lady."

Lady Helmsby simpered. "A pleasure, sir. If you are present on this occasion, then I must conclude you are among His Grace's trusted familiars."

"I have that honor."

"Well, let's do all have a seat," Lady Helmsby went on. "I shall pour out, and I'd like to hear a few details regarding the wedding ceremony. I must also say, in all honesty, Wilhelmina, that I did not appreciate your disappearing with Emily. She is my responsibility now, and the sooner you send her along to me, the more easily my conscience will rest."

Wilhelmina sent Finn a glance he could accurately interpret despite his limited tenure as a husband: *You promised, Finlay. Give her one chance to maintain her dignity.*

"Oh, come now," Finn said, seating his duchess next to Edwardia. "You cannot possibly put any stock in yet another purported codicil to William's will. Would William want Emily raised in the ducal household, the very situation she was born to enjoy, or in the company of a widow no longer young?"

"He has a point, Vanessa," Edwardia muttered, gesturing to Roberts, who moved the tea tray to the dowager duchess's end of the low table. "Wilhelmina has been a devoted and conscientious mother. She married William intending that the roles of duchess and mother would be complementary, and William wrote codicils as often as he ordered new hats."

Lady Helmsby allowed Pritchard to seat her, and St. Didier found a place at the far end of the sofa. Finn sat across from Lady Helmsby, the better to keep his eye on her. The second footman, Riley, took up the post immediately behind her ladyship's chair, while Roberts stood at attention behind Edwardia's chair.

Charles, without any visible sign from the duchess, positioned himself at Pritchard's knee.

"My duty is not to be shirked," Lady Helmsby said, "and William's wishes were very clear. Emily and her affairs are to become my responsibility. I'd think, given the plethora of duties that befall a titled couple and the pressing responsibility to see to the succession, that allowing Emily to remain in my care would make perfect sense to all concerned."

"Emily has never been in your care," Wilhelmina said. "And William was consistently adamant that she never suffer that fate."

Finn's offer of a dignified retreat had been rejected, and Wilhelmina had joined battle accordingly. Charles put his chin on Pritchard's knee, and Pritchard stroked the dog's head.

"Mina," Lady Helmsby began, "legalities must be acknowledged. If you thought marrying the duke would sway me from what my conscience knows to be the only proper course, you were much mistaken. With all due respect, you will please send Emily along not later than tomorrow morning. She can bide with me until your former abode has been refurbished to my standards. You need not send that governess with her. Give the woman her severance and write characters for the rest of the staff. A new broom sweeps clean, and I will not have divided loyalties among the domestics."

She sat up very tall. "I am prepared to be very firm about this, and you should know that, in an abundance of caution, I have already ordered the legal clerks to make copies of that codicil."

This was intended to be by way of an ambush, of course. Alas, for her ladyship, the best-laid crimes...

"You will be interested to know," Finn said, "that you are not the only one to find yet another codicil, my lady. Roberts, if you would oblige?"

That good fellow retrieved two documents from a drawer in the sideboard and laid them on the low table between Finn and Lady Helmsby.

"On your right," Finn said, "you will see the codicil you claimed to have found. On the left, a codicil I found. You will note that mine, dated a week after yours, rescinds yours, claims it was the result of hectoring on your part and an excess of drink on William's, and renders your claim to supervision of Emily and her fortune null and void."

Lady Helmsby picked up the newer codicil. "This is not William's hand. It's close, but a trifle too neat. I know my late son's handwriting, and this is a forgery."

"On the contrary," Wilhelmina said, "that is William's penmanship, which I grew to know intimately as his secretary, wife, and amanuensis."

Finn waited, hoping Lady Helmsby would blow retreat.

"Your Graces think to bully a widow," she said, chin coming up.

"Badly done of you, considering that my William should have been the duke. Your disrespect of his memory disappoints me, as does the necessity—the pure, honorable necessity—of involving the courts in this matter. I have only the one granddaughter, and I intend to stand by her despite underhanded machinations by people all too willing to exploit their considerable privileges."

St. Didier was staring fixedly at nothing in particular. Pritchard was absorbed with spoiling the dog. Edwardia had poured tea for herself and Wilhelmina.

"My lady," Finn said gently, "you are more than welcome to involve the courts. They will note that on your codicil, the flourish on every terminal *y* exactly matches the flourish *you* append when you sign yourself as Lady Helmsby."

"So my son learned a bit of an artistic habit from me. No court will be persuaded by so small a detail."

"That detail never appears in any writing over William's signature, nor in his diaries, journals, or correspondence. Moreover, the ink on your codicil is fresh. Compare that to the entries in William's diaries of the same date, and the difference is marked."

"Then the ink on your codicil is fresh too," she retorted. "I will not sit here and be insulted. Send Emily to me, and I will forget this whole tawdry scene."

"My lady," Wilhelmina said, "William couldn't spell to save himself. Every piece of writing we have of his—every one—attests to his unwillingness to adopt any sort of standardized spelling. His friends will remember this when they can't recall anything else about him, and they will report that recollection under oath, as will the solicitors, who hold the originals of every other *thoroughly misspelled* codicil. The spelling in your codicil is flawless. The courts are unpredictable and tedious, but they can hardly ignore reams of evidence proving that you—a very competent artist—forged your son's hand."

Before her ladyship could damn herself with more lies, Finn added what he hoped was a final, convincing argument. "The solicitors will also attest that William warned them you'd try something to get your hands on Emily's money. Your son chose his daughter's welfare over your fripperies, and I heartily commend him for it."

To commend William for that much, to ensure his honorable wishes were respected, felt good. Not ducal, perhaps, but as the head of a family ought to behave.

Lady Helmsby took up the newer codicil and tore it to pieces. "You would see me ruined. See me reduced to living in a garret, turning my hems, burning tallow, when I should have been a duchess, the mother of the next duke, and the grandmother of the one after that. You ought to be ashamed."

Wilhelmina took a leisurely sip of her tea. "I'm not—ashamed, that is. I am proud of William because he for once stood up to you, and I am overjoyed to think Emily will have the most devoted of step-papas to help me keep her safe and happy."

Lady Helmsby sat fuming, while Edwardia sent a cup of tea around, which Finn set before her ladyship.

"Will you press charges?" St. Didier asked, a bit too casually. "Forgery is a hanging felony, and the evidence is quite strong."

Edwardia poured out for the gentlemen. "Wouldn't that be a delightful scandal, and I daresay, the only parties to lament her ladyship's fate will be the owners of the most fashionable shops."

Her ladyship pointedly ignored her tea. "They'd rather see me dying of some dread disease in debtors' prison, and you all wouldn't mind that either. I am Emily's grandmother, her dearest, devoted grandmother, and you threaten me in this most heinous fashion."

"Your sort of devotion," Wilhelmina said quietly, "nearly drove William barmy. And you threatened Emily, with Proverbs, with bread and water, with a legally binding betrothal before she's even reached the age of reason, all so you could wear the latest fashions and put your servants in embroidered livery."

"Appearances," Lady Helmsby snarled, "must be maintained."

No jury in England would be sympathetic to her situation, though Wilhelmina had insisted that mercy at least be offered. Finn held his peace, while Edwardia and Wilhelmina held some sort of silent council, the gentlemen sipped their tea, and Charles sighed a doggy sigh.

"My lady," Wilhelmina said, "heed me, because I will not repeat myself, and I will fully support charges against you should you force that option upon us. Emily cannot grow up haunted by your attempts to steal her happiness and her fortune. I know you. You will write new codicils. You will pour poison in the ears of the gossips.

"I will not allow it," Wilhelmina went on. "His Grace will not allow it. I can see your debts paid, your premises rented with proceeds remitted to you, your staff settled elsewhere, provided you leave Britain within the week and stay gone. Emily will write to you, if you and she wish to maintain a correspondence. You will be welcome to return to England upon her marriage or financial independence at age one-and-twenty, whichever shall first occur. You either accept those terms or await the justice of the criminal courts."

Pritchard, in a move Finn would never have predicted, patted her ladyship's hand. "One can live very cheaply on the Continent, and the culture and art are amazing. All of polite society is seeing the sights these days. Your departure ahead of the spring crowds would hardly be remarked."

Finn had heard that same cajoling, commiserating tone from Pritchard before, when Pritchard had been consoling Antonio for his fortnightly heartbreaks or jollying Cook past a fallen soufflé. That Pritchard had charm was no secret, but its appearance was a rare occurrence.

"What would a young man like you know about it?" Lady Helmsby snapped.

"More than you'd think," Pritchard replied. "I was at loose ends in Rome when His Grace and I crossed paths. A beautiful city in a gorgeous country."

"The Eternal City," St. Didier said, "so named by Tibullus, Ovid, Virgil, Livy... One could do worse."

"Vanessa," Edwardia muttered, "you'd be a fool not to take up a few years of traveling. Your income will go much further on the

Continent. Ask Her Grace of Richmond how that works, and she will tell you."

"His Grace of Devonshire is enamored of Italy as well," St. Didier said. "Something to consider."

Wilhelmina rose. "You will excuse us. Both Mr. Pritchard and Mr. St. Didier are familiar with the Italian peninsula, Paris, and points in between. Your ladyship should mine their expertise and plan accordingly. I have said all I have to say to you, Lady Helmsby, other than *bon voyage*."

"And I wish you the same," Edwardia added, getting to her feet with notable alacrity. "If you write to me, Vanessa, I will return the courtesy, but don't expect more than platitudes to wave about over your tea. Charles, you may bide here, though your intentions toward the shortbread do not become you."

"I am needed elsewhere," Finn said, rising and offering an arm to each duchess. "Lady Helmsby, you are being kept under surveillance, so turn your imagination to making a dignified exit rather than attempting any rearguard action. My fondest regards to Rome."

He escorted his ladies from the room, and the pair of them were laughing merrily before they reached the head of the steps.

Edwardia saw Finn and Wilhelmina to the front door, and a light snow was falling as they climbed into the conveyance Wilhelmina referred to as their kissing coach.

In subsequent years, the coach saw a good deal of kissing, also tired embraces, stolen naps, and dandling of babies. Through all of those years, the Duke and Duchess of Huntleigh held pride of place as Society's premier love match.

What Society had to say about Mr. Lucien Pritchard wasn't quite so uniformly adoring, but that, as they say, is a tale for another time!

Author's Note

I cannot claim to have come up with the quip, "All play and no work makes Jack a mere toy." The Irish playwright and author Maria Edgeworth gets credit for that *bon mot,* first published in the play *Harry and Lucy Concluded,* which dates from 1825. Because Finn and Willie's tale slightly predates the play, I could not attribute the quote in the story, but it was too clever to pass up entirely. Who says maintaining a healthy work/life balance is a modern concept?

Made in United States
North Haven, CT
19 April 2024

51489975R00173